wolf.e

Paisley Hope

Editor: Caroline Palmier—Love & Edits

Consulting Dev. Edits: Jordan Valeri

Proofreading, Book Design: Cathryn Carter—Format by CC

Cover Design: @whiskeygingergoods

ISBN: 978-1-7380294-8-8

a note from the author

This book is a standalone MC romance that houses darker elements. It is intended for people 18+

Please read the trigger warnings below before you continue your journey:

Violence expected with the life of an outlaw motorcycle club including but NOT limited to:

Torture, Gun violence, Murder, Discussions of sexual assault of a sixteen-year-old (nothing descriptive nothing on page-talk of past occurrence). Flashback of domestic abuse and death of a family member, mild alcohol and drug use.

Sexual Triggers are NOT fully listed to conceal plot points and pivotal moments but are of a darker nature. They include but are NOT limited to:

Blood, breath and knife play, anal sex, sex in a religious setting, sex that feels ritualistic, consensual non consent. Degradation, borderline captor/captive setting.

Discussions of life as a marine, traumatic moments.

To all my good girls who know falling in love with the king of an outlaw motorcycle club doesn't mean your mission in life is to change him. Instead, it is to embrace the wicked inside you and become his bad ass queen.

glossary of club lingo

MC: *Motorcycle Club*

Club business: *Illegal /non-illegal activity that benefits the club*

Cut: *Leather vest or jacket bearing the club insignia*

Sweetbutt: *A girl who hangs around the club, often offered for sex or help, hoping to become a member's ol' lady*

Ol' Lady: *Wife or serious girlfriend of a club member*

Patch over: *When one MC takes over another*

Sprite: *Good girl, fairy, princess*

Squid: *A poser rider the club looks down on, someone who lacks biker common sense*

Code: *The rules club members live by*

Chapel: *The room in which the club conducts their daily/weekly meetings*

Service: *The meeting to discuss club business*

President: *The highest level of power. The boss. The conductor of business*

VP: *Vice President*

Enforcer: *Upholds club laws, protects patch holders, defends club's reputation, assists in conflict resolution.*

Sgt at Arms: *Sergeant at Arms, protector of the president, his number one*

Prospect: *A club apprentice. Usually wears the prospect patch for one year to prove his loyalty through service, trust and a series of really shitty tasks no one else wants to do*

Rally: *A gathering of bikers, normally for fun but club business is generally conducted as well*

wolfe & brinley's playlist

1. God's Gonna Cut You Down by Johnny Cash
2. Hummingbird by Carly Pearce
3. Enter Sandman by Metallica
4. Hotel California by The Eagles
5. Killing In The Name of by Rage Against The Machine
6. Seven Nation Army by The White Stripes
7. Sweet Child O' Mine by Guns N Roses
8. Hard Row by The Black Keys
9. Are You Satisfied by Reignwolf
10. Ghetto Cowboy by Yelawolf
11. Desperado by Upchurch
12. Vincent Black Lightning 1952 by Logan Halstead
13. Power Over Me (Acoustic) by Dermot Kennedy
14. Simple Man by Lynyrd Skynyrd

PROLOGUE

Gabriel

THE ART OF A PRESIDENT'S WAR

In two generations, you will be completely forgotten.
The illusion that you won't be keeps you going.
The illusion that somehow you are different.
Illusions serve no one.
The illusions we have about ourselves make us feel
good about what we do every day.
Grow up, get married, work, have babies, raise them,
die.
For what? For most people, to simply return to the
earth and be forgotten.
In turn, none of it matters.

As I stand over the battered body of the middle aged man who raped one of my men's little sisters, I don't feel sorrow over his impending doom. I don't feel remorse.

Instead, I feel all the things they say that you shouldn't when taking a life.

Joy.

Satisfaction.

Gratification.

His bloodied, broken body gives me peace.

The illusion that killing him should torment me isn't real.

I've seen enough to know there's only here and now, there's no after. And whether I'm good or not has no bearing on my fate.

"I don't want to die... please, I didn't know she was sixteen," he whines. The drool and blood dripping from his mouth lands in a pool in front of him, where most of his teeth now sit on the tarp below.

"I'm sorry, it wasn't my call... I didn't have a choice."

"Nah... don't make excuses. You always have a choice. It's fucking weak to go out like that man," Mason, my treasurer and the older brother of the girl this sick fuck drugged, raped, and recorded to keep photographic evidence of his fucked up conquests spits out as he smacks the guy they call Gator in the back of the head. Should've known with a nickname like Gator the guy would be a sleazeball.

Mason nods to Kai, my enforcer. Kai doesn't say a word, he's a brick wall, showing zero hesitation. He moves forward and assumes his position behind Gator, bracing his forehead with one hand and holding his mouth open with the other.

Mason thinks for a minute, looking into Gator's mouth at what's left. The pickings are slim, but he chooses a back molar. He clamps down on it with his pliers and wrenches it free from Gator's mouth then drops the broken pieces to the ground amidst those peaceful garbled screams that sing to my soul.

My turn.

I fire up the butane torch again, time to take a little more ink off Gator's neck and left arm where he bears the *Disciples of Sin* insignia.

Their club has been our club's natural enemy for years, ever since my grandfather, Ira Wolfe, started our legacy, *The Hounds of Hell* in the sixties.

I grin as I see the horror on Gator's face while I stalk toward him, the blood—dark and syrupy— leaking from his mouth now heavier than the drool.

I run my first two fingers through the flame as I eye Gator up—or what's left of him. I don't even know how he keeps coming back to consciousness at this point.

All we want is a name, and he's holding out a lot longer than I thought he would.

"Time to take some more ink unless you're ready to talk," I tell him. In truth, we stop when the stench of burning flesh gets too strong in this small cabin.

"This is your last chance to do the right thing," I say, preying on the human instinct that salvation is real.

He hovers on the edge of consciousness as my flame meets his skin. That's when he jolts awake, his bloodshot eyes wide as he screams. It's a pathetic scream really, barely more than a whisper.

"Stop... please. It was Foxx. He said he wanted me to hit you guys where it hurts. I was just doing my job, man." he whimpers.

"Fucking finally," Kai says lighting a cigarette.

It's what we assumed but we needed the confirmation before we plot to kill their club president.

I assess Gator. Men tend to tell the truth in the last seconds of their lives so I'm sure he's being honest.

"And our clinics?" I ask. "Who ordered the theft of our product?"

"Foxx," he answers with the same soon-to-be dead president's name, looking up at me through one barely open eye, the other swollen shut.

"Please, Wolfe. I wanna die." His voice is a whine. "Please... kill me," Gator begs.

I stop my flames and set down the torch. Moving towards him again, I grab a handful of his hair in my gloved hand, lifting his pathetic face up to view the last soul he'll ever see.

"It's fucking pathetic that you beg me for death now," I bite out.

"I've heard enough," Mason says from the other side of the room.

I promised him. It was his sister, so it's his call.

Gator lets out a sigh, his fate settling with him.

"*Please,*" he whispers.

I draw my gun and take aim at his forehead. Just as I'm about to shoot, Kai says my name and nods toward the other side of the room in my periphery.

I follow his gaze to the cabin door, and I'm met with horror. The rawest form of fear lines every plane of her perfect face through the screen. Her long onyx hair blows in the ocean breeze around her moonlit shoulders.

I may be a killer but I'm not a savage. I would never want her to see this if I had a choice, but now she's made her own bed.

I have no idea how or why she's here but there's no turning back. My eyes hold hers as the innocence drains from those beautiful blue eyes, the same color as her dress. She's on her knees outside the cabin door.

Every single hope she had about me, about my club, shatters around her and falls to the earth.

I never lied about who I am. The hopes she had were her own.

I don't pretend.

I am the villain she sees now, but that's not all I am.

She will learn to understand. She has no choice but to.

I find her eyes again, mouthing to her the only escape I can give, then press my gun to the spot between my prisoner's eyes and pull the fucking trigger.

CHAPTER 1
Brinley

"Bankrupt?" I ask, sinking into the chair behind me. I generally try not to stay long enough in my boss's office to sit, but at this moment I have no choice.

The roll of thunder, the steady seep of rain against the glass this morning, and my sandal clad foot stepping right in a puddle as I crossed Briarwood Avenue on my way into the office should've been my first indications that today was going to suck.

"Yep. Chapter 11 came out of nowhere," my boss, Paul, grunts as he leans back in his chair, taking a break from packing up his office. It's the scene I walked into when he called me in here to break this news.

I cross one leg over the other, pulling my skirt down so he doesn't try to sneak a glance up it. I've had men look at me appreciatively since I was fourteen years old. It's why my mother cut my hair into a bob when I started middle school. She said its naturally black color and long length brought the wandering eyes of the wrong kind of man. I hated that haircut and always asked myself why *I* had to change to stop a man from looking at me. I've rarely cut it since, to her dismay. Even when I told her I wanted it long because I liked it that way, she didn't agree. My friend Layla said it wasn't my hair, but my body that made men look and I can't do much about that. My boss is always looking at something he enjoys about me. I catch him almost every day.

Three years I've put up with late nights, not really having a social life, early mornings, inappropriate looks and comments from this man, and a job that most of the time bores me to tears. All because the possibility of becoming design director at the end of the year when my supervisor was to retire was dangled like a carrot over my head. I've been waiting for that to feel settled, to show my boyfriend, Evan, and his family that this is a serious career, one I can go somewhere with.

"I don't know what to tell you, doll. The news came from corporate late last night. People just aren't buying home décor magazines anymore, not with everything available online and apps to design your space."

My eyes snap back to my greasy superior. His combover is extra mussy today and his polyester shirt—covered in cat hair—is more wrinkled than usual. I've always been taught not to judge someone on appearance, but his is accurate. He works like he dresses—messy and unorganized.

"Brinley," I say, reminding Paul that *doll* is not my name.

Keep quiet and be polite, would be what my mother would say. She'd tell me not to burn any bridges, but that doesn't really matter now. What difference does it make if I let him know how disgusting I think he is? I'm officially unemployed, effective today at noon.

"Right, sorry I forgot how touchy you are," he raises his hands in truce.

I'm not touchy, you prick. I just don't enjoy you looking at me like I'm dessert every damn day.

7

"You'll get a severance, six weeks' pay in full, from corporate, and the four weeks' vacation you haven't taken." He pushes his glasses up on his nose. "Look, I've always been fond of you, *Brinley.*"

I don't miss the way he emphasizes my name just to prove he thinks I'm touchy. My eyes meet his and I feel like I might vomit. A sixth sense tells me he thinks of me in very inappropriate ways.

"I'd be happy to write you a good reference. We could go for drinks and talk about what you'd like me to put in the letter?" He continues opening his remaining mail like the way he's speaking to me isn't highly unprofessional.

My position of assistant design director paid me peanuts. So, what I'm hearing is, if I play my cards right, and let this man openly stare at my breasts and split a dinner bill at some shitty diner, I'll get the reference I already deserve?

I smile sweetly and fold my hands in my lap, resisting the urge to stab him with his letter opener, and be courteous, the way I've always been taught.

"Oh, Paul, I'm not going out for anything with you, but I'll take the reference anyway because you owe me that after putting up with you leering at me for three years. I know Brenda wouldn't want to hear how often I catch you doing that." I mention his wife as I stand and hope he doesn't notice I'm shaking like a leaf.

"Thank you for the opportunity, can't say it's been enjoyable," I hold in my need to tell him what a disgusting pig he is. I cock my head and smile bigger, my mother Wendy Beaumont's type of smile that says he's less than. "I'll expect that reference letter before I leave, or my first stop tomorrow morning will be HR."

My former boss doesn't speak, only leans forward, like he's

trying to decide if I'm bluffing. The buttons on his shirt strain under the pressure of his beer gut.

"Good luck to you, Brinley. I'll have the letter to you by noon," he says meekly.

Wow, acting like my mother really works.

I nod and turn, feeling proud of myself for standing up to Paul as I round the corner to my tiny office down the hall. Normally, I wouldn't even correct my Starbucks order if it were wrong, I'd just smile and say thank you before dumping it in the trash. A side effect from years of being told that it's proper to be seen and not heard.

My phone buzzes in my pocket as I shut the door behind me.

EV

Stopping for a haircut after work, I'll meet you at home by six. Can't wait to share tonight with you, make sure you're ready babe, I have reservations.

Evan has had this night with me planned for a week and he's being so secretive about it. It leads me to believe he might *finally* be proposing. After two years together, I feel like it's the next step and I've been hinting at it for six months. I've tried not to push him but ever since my mother died, I have been feeling a little disjointed, like I just don't really belong anywhere or to anyone. Having a husband like Evan, maybe starting a family, exactly what my mother always wanted, will help me feel like maybe I'm on the right path, one she and my father would've been proud of.

Thing is, I know he's been struggling to get through his final year of law school and all he wants to do is get it done and please his own parents.

I sigh, wanting to be honest and tell him I just lost my job, but instead I make the instant decision to wait. After the day I'm having, I seriously need something good to come from today.

> I'll be ready. Are you going to tell me where we're going?

EV

> Nope. But be ready for a life changing night. 😊

I lean back against my office door and stare out my window at the brick wall of the building next door. Taking a deep breath, I try to stay calm.

This morning sucks, but it's only the morning.

Maybe tonight will make up for it.

CHAPTER 2
Brinley

Evan squeezes my hand in the back of the limo, the same familiar comfort he always offers washes over me.

"You look lovely," he says, taking in the way I have my long black hair sculpted into a high twist. I left some pieces out and curled them into loose waves just the way he likes and I'm wearing his favorite dress. It's not mine but he likes the structured, navy A-line that falls slightly off the shoulders and accentuates my pale skin. He says it's pretty but leaves something to the imagination.

I smile up at him, always wishing for more. More words, more touching, more passion. I squeeze his hand back, forcing myself to be positive. We need this night. For the last year he's been so busy with school, he's been more distant than normal. Do I wish he hugged me or kissed me when he came in the door tonight? Sure. Pinned me up against the wall and made love to me with some semblance of hunger or need before his shoes even came off? Absolutely. But that is not Evan's style. For as long as I can remember, I've had cravings for a man who wants me so much he finds it impossible to keep his hands to himself.

When my friends craved the good guy in the movies we watched growing up, I secretly always wanted the villain with his hand around the main character's throat. I want a man to look at me like he can't wait to touch me at any given time of the day.

When I was young, I was told that sex was a sin unless it was with the man I was married to, so I knew my desires would never be met, therefore there was no harm in fantasizing about a man like that.

Reality has shown me that men like that don't seem to exist in the real world anyway. At least not in my world.

Lovely is as close to a compliment as Evan ever gives me but I know he means it. After two years, the niceties come a little less, but Evan is always kind. I should be grateful to have someone like him in my life. He's always steady and reliable and we get along very well. We always have.

Just thinking about him wanting me at all has me clenching my thighs together. I try to remember how long it's been for us and I'm sad to say I think it was his birthday a couple months ago.

"You okay?" he asks when I sigh.

I look up at him in the dark. "Perfect," I lie before turning my glance back out to downtown Atlanta passing by my window.

When I get frustrated with the lack of time we spend together, he reminds me he's just trying to secure our future. I secretly hope an engagement is just what we need to rekindle a spark between us. Visions of a white dress and all our friends surrounding us fill my head, followed by visions of him burying his face under it.

God, I need to make sure we have sex tonight.

Evan and I may not have a ton of passion right now but we're going to create a nice life together and that should be all I want. I can see it all now—the white picket fence, him running a law practice and me maybe having my own shop or consulting with a design firm. Hopefully, we'll have two or three kids because I'm sure after Evan is over the stress of taking the Bar he'll change his mind on that too.

"You seem quiet," he says.

I glance at him. "Just curious to see what you have up your sleeve tonight." I grin but feel a little guilty for not telling him about losing my job. I quickly shoo it away and forgive myself. I want this night to be memorable. I don't want to make him worry or ruin the experience or stress him out causing him to change his mind.

I'll tell him tomorrow.

I have talked myself off the ledge all afternoon. I have three years' experience and a design degree under my belt now as well as a surprisingly glowing letter of reference from my slimy ex boss. I'm sure I can find something else in no time, even if it's outside my field.

I reach over in the dark and wonder how much longer of a drive we have. I slide my hand from Evans suit clad knee, up the inside of his strong thigh, maybe we can have a little limo fun—

"Babe," Evan grabs my hand before it reaches anywhere near his cock. "We're almost there."

He places my hand back in my lap and my heart sinks.

"Of course," I say. "I just miss you." I hate how pathetic that sounds.

"Aww, Brinley. I miss you too."

Not *I can't wait to get my hands on you,* or any kind of touch at all. *Be grateful,* I remind myself.

Sixteen minutes later—more than enough time to get some back-of-the-limo sex in, especially when it's been so long—we pull up to Evan's favorite restaurant. I should've known this is where we'd come. Evan was bred to throw money around and this place is expensive. His family has always been well-off, and he came into a substantial trust fund when he turned twenty-five last year. My favorite place, on the other hand, is a little bistro on Virginia Avenue, a lot more reasonably priced, quiet, and rustic. The food is authentic Italian and incredible.

"Come on, babe, I got us a special table." He smiles down at me with all his boyish charm, and I can't help but smile back. He bends down and kisses my cheek. I remind myself of all the effort he's gone to tonight—renting the limo, the flowers he brought me, the suit he's wearing.

We turn some heads as we enter. I'm often told Evan resembles a young Brad Pitt. He's the quintessential dream man every woman wants to end up with—rich, kind, handsome, going places.

We're seated at the nicest table at *Le Cadran Solaire*. With a three hundred and sixty-degree view of the Atlanta skyline from the top floor, the picture outside the floor-to-ceiling window is stunning, I'll admit that.

We chat casually as we drink wine and order appetizers. The meal is pleasant, but I can't help the sinking feeling that Evan doesn't seem appropriately nervous for someone who is about to propose. He talks about all the changes happening around his office, our friends, and random gossip. Again, it isn't exactly proposal worthy as the night wears on.

By the end of our dinner, Evan orders dessert with the sweetest smile on his face. Cheesecake—my favorite—and champagne.

"Brinley, you know how much I appreciate you," he starts as he grabs my hands across the table.

My heart rate accelerates. *This is it.* How will he do it? Glass with a diamond ring in it? Hell, I wouldn't care if he gave me a ring made of twine.

I'm about to get engaged to the kind of man my parents always wanted for me. I just wish they were here to see it.

"I'm sorry if I've been distant lately. I've been under so much pressure with the Bar coming up."

I place my hand on top of his and smile. "I know, and it's okay."

"No, it's not. I promise once I pass and this next chapter is closed, we'll have more time to spend together. I need to know if you want to move onto the next step with me, and if you do it's going to require us to be open and honest and willing to sacrifice a little."

I smile. "I mean, I've always envisioned moving forward with you," I trail off, slightly confused by his lead up.

"It won't be easy, but if you stick with me through this, we can talk about taking the next step after that. If by the time I'm all settled you've sorted out your career and got your promotion, maybe at that point you'll have even moved out of that magazine and into something a little more prominent."

I flinch but smile through it. Evan has always considered my career choice to be more of a hobby. Those were his words. I hate that he looks at it like it's less because it's a creative job. In the spirit of not ruining this night, I let it go.

He smiles wide, looking gorgeous.

"Okay, sweetheart, here it goes." He takes a deep breath. "I've been offered a position with Foster Grant and Spire in New York. It's a year-long contract and may be extended after that," he says, beaming with excitement as he mentions a very prominent firm.

Wait, what?

"I-I'm sorry?" I ask in shock as our dessert and champagne arrives, no diamond in sight.

He smiles even wider, oblivious that a thousand imaginary hearts just broke into pieces and shattered at my feet.

"Yes, I told you this was life changing. It's a huge opportunity for me," he says.

Not for us, for *him*.

I pull my hand away and take a sip of—okay, I chug—half the glass of champagne as I listen to him tell me how prestigious this is and once his year-long contract is up, he'll be able to come back here and have any job in Atlanta he wants.

"You've already accepted this?" I ask, my voice cracking.

His smile drops. "Of course, I thought you'd be happy for me, this is a big step. Like I said, life changing."

"Evan, you didn't think to consult me before you committed us to moving across the country?"

Evan begins to shake his head, something that almost resembles shock lines his face.

"I thought... Babe, I thought you'd just stay here; I know you're up for that promotion and I could fly back every other weekend."

WHAT?

"Evan... I..." I have no words. How stupid of me to assume this night was about us, a proposal. Our future. Something to look forward to. Evan is the type of man my parents always hoped I'd marry. To hear he isn't even thinking about it is... well, devastating.

"Plus, Brinley, I'll really need to focus when I'm there. If it's all the same to you, I'd rather you stayed here. We're both adults, we can handle a little long distance," he adds.

I recoil, leaning back in my chair.

I can't stop my eyes from filling up, and no matter how hard I try to stop the words from bubbling up, they come anyway.

"I thought you were going to propose to me tonight." I laugh like a lunatic through my tears, knowing just how pathetic and needy I sound, also knowing how much Evan hates when I cry. He dubs that kind of emotion dramatic.

Evan stares at me, and I feel the distance between us like someone just dropped a thousand-pound weight onto the table. We're on two completely different planets here and I have no idea how I didn't see it before now.

"Brinley, I—You're beautiful and sweet, but marriage just... it isn't on my radar right now. My career has to come first, and you'd have to... establish yourself more before my family would accept... that."

Ouch.

"By *that*, you mean *me*," I say quietly, using my napkin to dab at my tears. "I'm not good enough for you, you mean," I guffaw before sucking back the rest of my champagne and refilling it to the brim.

"Babe, you're making a bit of a spectacle in front of the entire restaurant," he leans in, speaking quietly. I barely notice because I'm spiraling.

What am I doing with this man? How did I not see this? Everything comes crashing down on me all at once. We don't have a relationship. We're... roommates. Really good roommates.

I down the other half of the glass and that's when it fully hits me. I'm sick of all of it. Sick of bosses who think they can push me around for three years, a selfish boyfriend who thinks I'm going to just wait around while he lives his dream and I get better at 'being better' for him. Because who Brinley Rose Beaumont is, apparently isn't good enough for Evan Radcliffe the second.

I stand and look down at him, every fiber of my being telling me to be strong and that this isn't absolutely crazy. For once in my life, I don't take the time to overthink. I follow my gut.

"I'm not willing to wait around while you decide if I'm good enough for you or not." I shrug, saying the words barely above a whisper. "So, I guess what I'm saying is... good luck in New York..." One fat tear slides down my cheek as I watch the years between us evaporate.

"Come on, Brinley, babe," Evan says, leaning back in his chair, but there's no real fight in him. He doesn't even stand.

I turn on my heel using every bit of confidence I have to keep walking. I hope he'll follow, I hope he'll tell me he's ready to give me a future, but by the time I've made it to the lobby and onto Atlanta's streets, it's obvious he isn't. I pull my phone out to get myself an Uber.

While I wait, fighting back more tears, I realize four things. I have no job, I'm about to have no place to live, I wasted a completely good piece of cheesecake, and this *entire* day officially sucks.

CHAPTER 3
Brinley

Two Weeks Later

I use the tiny umbrella in my drink to stir the sugary liquid around in slow circles, while I stifle back my tears. I cried the whole way here. I'm the blubbery mess in the corner even though the air in this club is happy. My mother would be appalled I'm even out in public looking like I just rolled out of bed. The night is alive in Savannah. It's only 9:30 p.m. and I needed to take a break from driving, plus I really had to pee. It was then I realized I'm in no hurry, I don't owe anything to anyone, and a drink after the two weeks I've had sure sounded good.

The rooftop patio at The Crystal Cave is bustling for a Thursday night—music plays, and twinkle lights mixed with greenery dance against the rustic wood pergolas overhead. Lanterns and flameless candles give the outdoor deck a moody ambience as they flicker throughout the space. It's dark and the beat of the song playing courses through my chest as I contemplate my next steps.

I still have a thirty-minute drive ahead of me to my home-town of Harmony, Georgia, the small-ish ,southern town I grew up in. Population 9,000, until today. After today it will be 9,001.

My parents vacant house is the only place on Earth I have left to go after I spent the last two weeks packing up my life and all my belongings that were in Evan's apartment in Atlanta. Almost everything was his. I was just an add on. Our life wasn't unpleasant, so I guess I stayed because it was expected... easy. I realize now that easy isn't always right, and that hit me when I hugged him goodbye and we promised to remain friends. I wasn't even sad, just a little angry that I didn't see it sooner.

I swallow down my piña colada. I wish I could have another but anymore and I'll be too tipsy to drive because, truthfully, I don't ever drink more than one.

I log into my banking app to view my dismal savings and severance, calculating how long that will last me. I'll need to get a job right away. And if design jobs aren't available, I could always pick up some shifts at the diner, if Mrs. Palmer still owns it—

"Jelly!?"

My childhood nickname is called from behind me. Yelled rather, with a squeal at a deafening level even over the thump of the music. I turn to meet the owner and my eyes instantly start to tear up. I stand, because she's coming toward me, fast.

"Oh my *god,* PB!" I don't even get the words out before I'm pulled into a crushing hug with my childhood best friend, Layla, the peanut butter to my jelly.

"What the hell are you doing here?" she asks as I take in her appearance. Layla looks different than the last time I was in town two years ago, and vastly different from our senior year in high school, but she's stunning.

Layla and I were inseparable when we were young, best

friends since we were eight. Now, she's ultra sexy, her long, naturally dark hair is almost fire engine red, and her entire arm is covered in tattoos. On top of her head is a makeshift sparkly wedding veil. She wears a sash across her chest that says *Property of Ax* and a massive pear-shaped diamond on her ring finger.

We look strikingly different, I imagine. Layla is small, only five-foot-two and tiny all around. I have a good four or five inches on her and my body is curvy—I could never fit my ass in her jeans. I'm not complaining, I'm proud of my curves and work hard to maintain them with daily yoga.

Where Layla is shiny and nightclub ready, I'm rocking my tights and my oversized Nirvana t shirt, no makeup, my long, dark hair in a big messy bun.

"I'm not sure why I'm here, prolonging going to an empty house maybe," I answer as three other women come to join us, chattering away.

They all look the same as Layla does, for the most part, and are all strikingly beautiful.

"I don't understand. You're going home?" she asks as I glance past her to the three ominous men behind Layla's shoulder. My stomach drops into my feet when I realize they're all together. It's impossible *not* to notice them. They're all leather-clad, tall, muscular, and they're gruff, with beards of various growth. One has a bandana covering his head and they all wear leather vests that tell me which motorcycle club they belong to —*Hounds of Hell*. They're a good fifteen feet away from me but I can smell their leather and smoke. As if on cue, one of them pulls a cigarette out of the pack with his teeth and lights it.

"Only you could be out in glorified pajamas and still look this beautiful," she observes, pulling me from my stare as she takes in my outfit.

I half listen to Layla as I eye the men behind her again and look back to her in question, *why are they here?*

She giggles. "Ignore them, they're harmless, just making sure we stay safe. This is my bachelorette party! My wedding is in nine days!" She smiles wide.

It's like a sucker punch to the gut to remember this after the couple weeks I've just had. I think of her wedding invite I turned down two months ago because Evan and I were supposed to be away with friends.

"Layla, what have you gotten yourself into?" I whisper with wide eyes so the other girls can't hear. They're talking to each other and have no concern for the dangerous men behind them either.

Layla can say whatever she wants but these men? Harmless? *My ass.*

"Brin, you know me, I wouldn't give my life to a man I didn't feel safe with, you're doing the thing the whole town does. Don't judge," she scolds me.

I shake my head, knowing exactly who the Hounds of Hell are. At least, I know everything I've always been told.

"You could say congratulations," Layla adds, looking a little hurt. I instantly feel bad for judging her. The thing is, Layla is usually a good judge of character so I can't wrap my head around any of this. I realize maybe I don't really know her that well anymore. I was so wrapped up in my life with Evan, wanting forever with him, wanting the life I thought I should have. Through all that, Layla and I just drifted apart. Partly because I stopped coming home after my mom died. It's hard to stay in touch the same way when you live hours away. Even though time has passed, Layla still picks right back up with me the moment I come home. I make a silent promise to spend as much time with her as I can.

"Right. Congratulations, I'm sorry," I say. Her friends stop chattering so she turns to introduce me to them. There's a super fit Asian girl with blunt bangs, full lips, and as many tattoos as Layla, named Amber, a blonde bombshell, Chantel, who seems like every man's fantasy with cherry red, glossy full lips and a diamond stud nose ring. Another blonde with wild, curly hair, who seems a bit older is named Maria.

I make small talk with them but can't stop eyeing the men at the same time. The sight of them this close to us makes me extremely uneasy. The men of the Hounds of Hell were a staple in town everyone avoided.

We've always been told they're extremely bad news, especially by our parents and people in our church growing up. I remember Sunday sermons laced with prayers for our town, we even prayed for club members, their wives, and local businesses. Some of the church elders even had rallies with signs that said, *"Keep the Harmony in Harmony"* outside the businesses the club had their hands in. Their presence casted a shadow over our otherwise safe and friendly town.

What scares me the most is that I'm gathering by their presence that Layla is Ax's property and Ax must be their property. I've never even met him, but if I remember correctly, I think this wedding came fast, and Layla has always been a bit of a rebel. But she's never been up to anything dangerous like this before—this is the first. I know I need to get my friend alone and make sure she's okay, not involved in anything that could get her into real trouble.

"Come sit with us, let's catch up!" she says, pointing to an entire corner of the rooftop that's sectioned off, there are decorations and food laid out, a few other girls dancing. It's like a little VIP area.

I try hard not to be afraid but I'm definitely hesitant because of her crew and Layla can tell. She leans into me. She smells like the perfume she's always worn. It's comforting and makes me feel like she's still the same girl I always knew.

"Trust me, you're safe. The MC isn't cut and dry. It's not what we were told," she says low enough for only me to hear. Her brown eyes meet mine.

I nod. I might not know this new life she's got but I know Layla, and I at least know she would never put me in harm's way. "For a few minutes," I agree.

For no other reason than I feel like grasping onto something familiar and comforting, I blow out a breath and follow the intimidating Hounds of Hell bikers and these women into the VIP area.

This is not at all what I thought I'd be doing when I woke up this morning.

"Babe, honestly, that sucks, but you know I always say it like it is. You would've been like a Stepford wife, so I feel like you were saved. You deserve better than that. Did you know a man knows if he wants to marry you in six months? He was making you wait... stringing you along," Layla says matter-of-factly almost an hour after I've told her all about the day that feels like an eternity ago, not mere weeks. "So, what, you're coming back to Harmony to start fresh?" she asks, sipping her drink.

"Something like that, more like because I don't really have a choice," I say, nursing my water, my drink long gone, while swiping the tears from my cheeks.

"Sorry, I don't want to rain on your parade with how depressing this is on your special night," I say as the other girls return after dancing up a storm. They gave up on my downer of a story thirty minutes ago.

At least I know for certain now why these men are here. Layla's fiancé is a member in the MC and I wonder, as she tells me all about him, how she could fall in love with a man like that and not worry for her safety. As wonderful as he may be, she has to know he is involved with the wrong kind of people. She's willingly giving herself over to a life of crime and danger.

"Pfft. I'm just glad I could be here. Fate for the win." She blows out a raspberry, takes a big sip and then her eyes light up. "This is perfect!" She smiles.

"What is?" I ask cautiously.

"You *need* a distraction! You're home. You have to come now!" she says.

I look at her, not understanding.

"My wedding, the one you declined!" she says, her pretty mouth turning into a frown. "You're coming. We'll dance, we'll have some fun, it's on Tybee Island, it's beautiful. We have Lighthouse Landing all to ourselves."

My eyebrows perk up. Lighthouse Landing is one of the nicest resorts on Tybee Island, right on the ocean. For some reason, I pictured this wedding to be anything but traditional. Maybe in one of the club members' backyards while people smoked various kinds of drugs and got black out drunk, some women dancing in barely there clothing.

Come to think of it, that's pretty much what I picture when I think of them—seedy, dark, sexual, ruthless. I know enough to know if you don't look too long and keep your distance, they'll leave you alone. If I go to this wedding, not looking is just impossible.

"Do you ever worry about what will happen if they get... into trouble while you're with them?" I ask, not understanding my own curiosity.

"Look, I'm not saying my soon-to-be husband and his crew are always innocent men. *Some* things are true. Like, if you get on their bad side, hiding wouldn't help you."

My stomach drops with the nonchalance she says these words

"But these things aren't so black and white, Brin. Our parents... they were assumptive and judgemental. They didn't know the truth. Don't you ever question *them?*" Layla asks, with a surety that makes me go over everything I think I know.

We all heard the rumors growing up. Dragging men who defy them behind their bikes down Main Street. Breaking limbs and branding body parts. I also think of what I witnessed. When I was eight, we stopped at the bakery for a cake for a dinner party and I remember seeing police and caution tape around the local diner across the street. When my mom got back in the car, she told my dad as quietly as she could that a fight had broken out and a club member threw someone through their front window and he almost bled to death. That's when my father said this town was being taken over by heathens. My parents used to talk about them like they were lowlifes, but I do have a few different memories. One in partic-ular includes a giant, gray-haired man holding the door for me and Mom once when we went into the bank. My mom had never looked so scared ushering me by him, but I remember how he smiled down at me as we walked by. He seemed almost like a gentleman.

"So... your future husband, aside from this life"—I glance nervously to the men joking and talking behind her, paying me no mind—"what does he do?" I cross my legs at my ankles and place my palms on my knees. It's hard to help but when I'm nervous I go full princess etiquette.

Layla looks at me like she knows I'm judging her and I hate

that I am, that's something Evan used to do that I always disliked.

"He's in the... importing and exporting business. It pays well." Layla shrugs, taking a shot. "His interests are spread all over Georgia."

She says it like he's any local businessman. I'm sure he is a man of business, but something tells me it isn't of the legal kind. She puts her hand over mine.

"Look, I've missed you, Brin. It hasn't been the same since you left. God, six years is a long time. Come on, you need a weekend to not think about your own problems. We'll have so much fun and maybe you'll see. They may be a little scary but they're not who you think. Say yes," she chides, her long fiery hair falling over her shoulders. She's still one of the prettiest girls I've ever seen.

"I should work on opening up the house. God knows what's waiting for me. Since Mom died and my aunt left a year ago, no one's been checking in on it."

I'm definitely grasping for excuses. Layla knows it.

"Brin." She gives me the look I know well from my youth. "Stop being so fucking responsible and proper for once and come have some fun. The rehearsal dinner is next Friday night at the club and then we're all heading to Tybee Island on Saturday morning."

I look up. "At the club? The Hounds of Hell *clubhouse?*" I repeat, eyeing one of the men behind her smacking another in the back of the head playfully. It's obvious to anyone they are essentially the bodyguards of these girls because no one has come to speak to us. A ripple of fear snakes up my spine. Even though I know it's wrong, something about the idea of seeing their world from the inside piques my interest a little more than it should.

"And your excuses are bullshit. You have all week to work

on the house and make connections for a job; plus, even if you don't get it done, all that work will be there for you after the wedding."

Layla hugs me again happily.

"Please say you'll come?" she squeals. "This is so exciting. We are going to be able to hang out all the time now that you're home."

I look to the men behind her. The idea of actually being sucked into this world of hers? *That's what scares me.*

She pulls back, and I force a smile. I've done the right thing for twenty-four years and where has that gotten me? Alone, jobless, and questioning everything. For the first time in a long time, I find myself feeling free and spontaneous.

"Okay. I'll come." I nod, which only makes her smile grow and she lets out another little squeal.

A rush of excitement runs through my blood.

"Yay! Can you believe I'm getting married?" Layla chirps. "And let's have lunch during the week." She turns her head. "Chris?" she calls to one of the men behind her. He's leaning on the small private bar in the VIP area, he has a patch labeled prospect. I recall that means he's not a member yet, just hopes to be. He comes over to her with few short strides. "Call the Lighthouse Landing and book my bestie here a room—one with an ocean view." She winks.

"Oh, I can't afford... fancy. I'll just do a basic—" I start to say.

"Nonsense, we're paying for our guests and that includes you." Layla looks back to the guy she called Chris. "Like I said, please," she says sweetly to him.

He nods and pulls his phone out of his pocket, making me wonder again just what kind of life my friend is living having these men at her disposal.

Visions of *Beyond The Law* or *The Gauntlet*, those old

biker movies my dad used to watch fill my head. But this isn't the movies, it's real life.

Hopefully, my friend telling me I'll be safe is true because unless I come up with a really good excuse, it looks like I'll be spending next weekend with Harmony's most notorious outlaws.

CHAPTER 4
Brinley

The sound of cicadas buzzing and birds chirping wake me from my sleep, which tells me it is no longer early morning. I pull my mom's comforter up over my face. Thankfully, when I got to my family home last night, I found it still in one piece and critter free. My parents' old house is massive. It sits on over an acre of land and is stately. It hasn't changed décor-wise since I was a kid, and it was definitely an eerie homecoming. The once warm halls, which used to echo with Mom's favorites—Reba McIntyre or worship music—were silent and sterile with everything covered in sheets. It felt more like the typical haunted houses you see in old movies. All my mother's clothing was donated, and her fancy dishes were packed in bins on raised shelves.

My aunt did a good job of hiring a preservation company to seal this place up before she moved away with her new husband last year. All the pillows and bedding were still vacuum sealed in the linen closet and almost still smelled fresh when I pulled them out and made the bed.

I did fear for my foot going right through the rotted boards of my wraparound front porch when I made my way up the old creaky steps last night. But aside from that, everything seems to be okay, which is a relief.

I rub my eyes and glance at the time. 10:30 a.m. I check my phone out of habit for any calls from Evan. There are none.

"Day one of a new life," I say as I blow out a deep breath and stand, pulling on my slippers. I plan to spend my day both unpacking and getting the house feeling like a home again. But first, I have to head to town, get some sort of coffee and grab a few things, including a dress for Layla's wedding because that is definitely not something I brought with me.

My phone buzzes with two texts from Layla before I even get out the door.

PB

I'm so glad you're here!

Let's do lunch Wednesday, you looked so nervous last night.

I did not

PB

Yes, you did. I'm thinking I should mentally prepare you for the scene you're walking into and the men, a little different than you're used to. Not bad, just different.

We had all that etiquette training growing up, but in this world it's useless. You need a whole new set of etiquette rules with the club.

Excellent. can't wait for class. These men sound like just what I've been missing.

PB

Maybe they are... I mean did that ex of yours ever even give you an orgasm?

I sigh.

Occasionally. Truthfully... not with out my help

PB

Exactly what I thought. Happy shopping today! Blue is always a hot color on you, and show off those tits. I'll expect photos of your choice.

Yes slutty mom

I picture the men with her last night. I can still recall the smell of leather and smoke. *No way.* Not my type whatsoever.

After my shower, I toss on a white tank top and tie a black and white flannel around my waist. I add a pair of worn in cut off jean shorts and my Birkenstocks. My hair is tossed in a clip before heading out the door. I almost put my foot through the front porch again.

"*Son of a—*" I start to say to myself.

"Probably termites," a vaguely familiar voice says to me from next door. My eyes snap to the direction of the voice and I recognize its owner almost instantly.

"Hi, Mr. Kennedy. It's been a long time," I say.

He looks older. I think he's close to eighty by now.

"Yep, but I'm still kicking." His white mustache wiggles and his weathered face is in a broad smile as he holds a trusty pair of clipping shears, working on his hedges bordering twenty feet from my driveway. "Are you back for good? Nice to see some life over there, honey."

He was always such a sweet man. His wife cooked for us for two weeks when my dad died.

"Not sure yet," I say honestly, yet I have no idea where else I would go.

"Well, I can give you the number of a local contractor to look at that porch, it's gonna cost you a pretty penny, though.

The mites are the worst. All you can do is hope they aren't in the house too."

Shit. I hadn't thought of that.

"Thanks, but my savings account doesn't warrant a pretty penny at the moment." I smile ruefully.

Mr. Kennedy stops trimming his hedges thinking for a moment.

"Well, if you fixed up that old truck of your dad's and put it up for sale, that may help." He gets back to trimming.

"*Alchemy Customs.* It's a garage on Bleeker. They do all types of bodywork. They're the best. Even have some famous clients. They could fix that rust up and give it a paint job, then you could probably sell it easily. Your dad always kept what was under the hood in tip top shape, if it needs any inside work, there's a garage right next door to *Alchemy.*" I look toward the garage; I hadn't even thought about the truck. "I reckon you could maybe even get upwards of twenty thousand. Unless you were planning on keeping it." He winks.

I was not.

That old 1950 Ford F1 was my dad's pride and joy. But it's been rusting for years. I know my mom had it started a few years ago, I just don't know if it would even run now to get to this *Alchemy Customs.* I thank Mr. Kennedy and make a mental note to try this week. I can at least get a quote. It's sad to let it go but the house not falling apart is more important.

Thirty minutes later, the June sun in downtown Harmony is striking as usual. Our little town is just as pretty as it always was. We get tourists in the summer with cottages on the lake and it's bustling. Our local coffee shop, *The Balanced Bean,* remains but now houses an outdoor patio with covered roof and twinkle lights. The block I remember empty last time I was here is full of small shops, save for a few vacant spaces. A yoga studio, boutique bookstore, a milkshake parlor, some restaurants. It's vibrant and pleasant.

I notice the design center on main across from the coffee shop. It has a peaked roof over the entrance to make it appear like a cozy front porch. *Crimson Homes,* the rustic sign hanging on two chains from the peak reads. But the reason I stop isn't to admire the pretty building design. It's the *Now Hiring* sign on the door. No details what they're hiring for. Harmony, Georgia may be the only place left on earth that still puts help wanted signs in the window.

I look down at my casual outfit. I don't have anything with me and I'm not exactly dressed to interview but I decide to go for it anyway. I pull off the flannel that's tied around my waist and put it on, buttoning it up and tucking it in then pull the clip from my hair and fluff it around my shoulders. Maybe I'll get lucky. I push the door open with a tiny ding and walk around. The space is vast and beautiful. Flooring, lighting, and tile samples adorn the walls and aisles—everything you could imagine for new home design and more.

"Can I help you?" a voice asks from behind me as I'm running my fingers over a rather pretty mosaic.

I turn to face it and smile wide as I'm met with Layla's older brother.

"Dell?!"

"Wow, Brinley!" he says as we stand awkwardly suspended in time before he moves forward to give me a little side hug.

"I didn't know you were in town. Are you visiting?" he asks at the same time I ask, "How are you?"

He smiles. He's tall, fit with dark blonde hair and he wears a button down and slacks.

"I'm here to stay. I think. That's why I came in. I'm a designer and you're hiring. What for?" I point to the sign in the window.

"Yeah, we are. I'm not the owner, I'm the on-staff architect. Custom builds division. They're great to work for, it's a really easy-going environment.The position they're hiring for isn't a designer per se, but similar. You'd be able to help people plan their dream homes. What are your qualifications now? You were taking structural design in Seattle right? I could put in a word?"

"I was but I switched to Interior..."

We talk for a few minutes about my experience, my degree, and their build load. As luck would have it, the owner makes his way back part way through our conversation. We chat easily for another ten minutes. I leave with the promise of sending my resume and the owner telling me he'll call me over the weekend after he reviews it.

I pop my sunglasses on and smile into the sun feeling pretty confident I may already have a new job lined up as I breeze out the door, waving goodbye to Dell as I go.

Home one day.

That's how it's done, I think to myself with a grin. With a new job possibly secured, maybe I will fix up my dad's old truck to sell after all. I could use some of my savings to pay for the repair then recoup it after, if it's not too much.

I hustle into the trendy coffee shop, humming one of my mom's favorite Reba songs and grab my latte before sitting outside in the sun. I scroll through truck ads resembling my dad's model and happily find they are going for even more than Mr. Kennedy thought when restored. I'm only part way through my latte before I hear them.

The low rumble of Harleys. It's like the town anthem. No one seems to look or care when the four bikes pull up to the next block of buildings. They park almost directly in front of me in a perfectly choreographed backed-in slant. I watch them from my periphery, the chrome and metal glimmering in the afternoon sun. They almost cause my wrought iron table to shake against the concrete with their final rumble before the engines are cut.

I don't need to see the back of their leather vests to know they're members of the Hounds of Hell but the wolf skull glaring at me as they park and pop their kicks just solidifies it.

I instantly recognize two of them from last night in Savannah. The one with the Enforcer patch and the other with the Gunnar patch. They're big men, the Gunnar has wavy hair pulled back in a type of man bun that looks anything but dainty.

Two more get off their bikes and pull their helmets off—one is skinnier, older, and has spiky blonde hair and his patch says Road Runner.

My eyes move to... the largest man in the group. As he pulls his helmet off I'm stricken, yet I can't look away. He's the closest to me, and he was definitely not in Savannah last night.

My palms instantly start to sweat as he hangs his helmet from his grip with his large, sculpted hands. He faces my direction and looks around, scanning the area like he's the arriving king, watching for any threat.

I glance up again, watching him move with a heavy grace, struggling to keep my mouth closed as I drink him in, almost in slow motion. He's tall, maybe six-foot-four or six-foot-five and he's wide and solid. He's a real Jason Momoa type—part Khal Drogo, part outlaw.

Normally, I would do the proper thing and turn my eyes from a man like this. I've been trained since the age of welve about the kind of man who would be right for me and the kind of man who would hurt me, but something about him transfixes me.

He isn't just existing, it's like the world rotates around *him*.

He wears a thin white t-shirt under what appears to be his leather club vest, his powerful arms strain against the fabric. Dog tags peek out from the neckline, glinting in the sunlight that suddenly feels so much warmer.

He's military? I did not expect that.

From what I can see, his body is a vast landscape, a terrain of rippled muscle, and, apart from his face, he's covered in ink.

The bold tattoos creep up his neck, over his hands, fore-arms, and fingers. A portrait of a woman done in a Day of the Dead style on his forearm is haunting and I wonder who she is before imagining all the ink I can't see because of his clothes.

His dark brown hair is pushed back, it doesn't seem overly long but what is there is secured at the nape of his neck, a few wisps have gone astray. His beard is a shade darker than his hair and groomed but gruff—like everything he does is on purpose.

His face turns to mine as he pulls off his sunglasses and strides up onto the sidewalk in front of me. I wish my pair was shielding my eyes instead of sitting on top of my head so I could watch him without shame. His cheekbones are high and straight, his jaw, wide and square. His eyes start at my sandals as he moves, slowly raking over me in the few seconds he glances at me. When they meet mine, I notice they're startling, almost inhuman and the lightest shade of gray I've ever seen. It's almost like time stands in a suspended still.

His gaze is hot, like a branding iron held too close to my skin, and he stares at me without regret, like he has the right to know exactly who I am and why I'm here.

I cross my leg over the other and force myself to break the trance he holds me in, doing my best to be casual and focus on the mural wall of the coffee shop, pulling my sunglasses down and willing my heart to stop beating so fast.

The group of them is close now and one of the other men speaks to him. I feel it pull his stare away. I breathe out deeply as he moves out of my direct sight. I can't hear what they're saying but there's no question to me that the man I can't keep my eyes off of is in charge. He commands everyone's attention and as he talks to the other men at the vacant building next door. I can smell his leather and spice scent mixed with a hint of smoke. I eye the patch on his chest when he isn't looking.

President.

The president's voice is deep and steady. They spend the next few minutes talking to a man in a suit while I drink my coffee and pick at my blueberry muffin. They move as they talk about the exterior of the buildings. When I see that they're heading inside, I stand and gather my purse to escape as fast as I can into the dress shop next door.

I blow out a breath and try my best to push the president's startling presence from my mind. Any questions I have about him will probably always go unanswered because I'll never ask them out loud.

He looks like the kind of dark mystery I would drown in.

I sift through the aisles and select some dresses for trying. As my breath returns to normal, I tell myself maybe I'm building these people up in my mind.

My parents didn't force a sheltered life on me, but they definitely preyed on fear to keep me safe. Fear of God, fear of unsavory people, fear of my own choices. Probably to keep me away from Hounds of Hell members or people like them.

I don't know why on Earth I do it, but I listen to Layla and go with a light blue dress, almost the color of my eyes. It's off the shoulder with long billowy sleeves structured at the waist where it flairs outward and lands at my mid thigh. It's shorter than I'd normally choose for my life in Atlanta but I feel sexy in it... and screw it, I have no one to appease but me. It's just the kind of dress Evan would have said is "a little inappropriate" and something about that makes me want it even more. The best part is the back, it's wide open to almost the center, and I hold my hair up in the mirror to see how it would look if I wear it up.

I select another for the rehearsal dinner, equally as short and revealing, but this time it's pale yellow and strapless, it makes my breasts look amazing and has a chiffon-like feel to it and a high-low hemline.

I thank the cashier and internally cry over the fact that the two dresses cost over two hundred and fifty dollars I don't really have. I remind myself that's looking up, since I might have just scored a job and maybe can fix up my dad's old truck to sell.

I push the front door open, stuffing the receipt into my purse, making a beeline for my car. I glance around but don't see the bikes or the bikers that were talking beside the coffee shop anymore. It's probably a good thing. As captivating as *he* was, something about his eyes shook me to my core. The last thing I need, for my safety and my heart rate, is to be on the radar of the Hounds of Hell president.

CHAPTER 5
Brinley

"You look *hot*! Wait—do you have a tan *already*?" Layla squeals as she looks over my yellow strapless dress I bought for the rehearsal when I knock on her door the following Friday evening.

"I've been doing yoga outside." I shrug, forcing the carefree tone to my voice. And I've been wandering the halls of my parents' barren mansion, getting through orientation at Crimson Homes after they called last Saturday and offered me the job, trying not to text Evan simply out of habit, and trying not to cry myself to sleep every night over my derailed future.

And more than I care to admit, I've been trying not to think of the haunting Hounds of Hell president who Layla told me was named Wolfe when we had lunch the other day. True story.

That's his actual name.

Layla smiles back, she can't know any of my struggles by my tone. I'm a pro after growing up with my parents.

I force a big happy smile and hug her. I don't know what I expected when she gave me her address to an older part of town, but it was not this. This little pocket of hundred-year-old homes on sprawling properties has been totally revived. It looks like new families have moved in and everything is up kept and very Hallmark-ish. Layla's house is no exception. It's a 1920's Craftsman style house and has been fully renovated. I'm pleasantly surprised and remind myself this doesn't look like the home of a criminal. Layla's house is rustic and girly but somehow still smells like leather even though her fiancé isn't here. I look over the photos that line the table in the living room. The man Layla is marrying looks like the other club members I've seen around town since I've been home. The only one I haven't seen again is their club president. And for some reason, I've been looking every time I hear the tell-tale rumble of a Harley on Main. If anything, just to show myself he isn't as captivating as I remember.

I smile at a photo of Layla and her fiancé where his arms are wrapped around her waist and he's biting her earlobe. Layla's man has her name tattooed under his left eye. It's small but that's commitment if I've ever seen it.

I toss my hair over my shoulder as I kick my heels off so I don't mark up their shiny hardwood floor.

I'm determined to push down my worries about where I'm going and just try to have some fun this weekend.

I called the contractor Mr. Kennedy gave me this afternoon and he flat out told me I'm looking at thousands to fix the porch.

It's just the type of problem I'm not prepared to worry about until Monday.

"Okay, we have time for one toast and then we need to go. I have to see what these boys did all day... God, I knew I never should've left Sean in charge of décor," Layla says nervously.

Something else I learned over lunch the other day is that

Layla's fiancé has a real name. Shockingly, he wasn't born as Ax.

"Shelly will help him and make sure it's beautiful," Chantel says.

Layla nods. "Yes, you're right. Okay, one shot then we'll go!" she calls out.

I can't help but notice how beautiful she looks tonight in pale pink silk. Her hair is upswept and she has glittery pins holding it in place. It's a shame her parents didn't live long enough to see her wedding day; although, I know they wouldn't approve of her marrying into the MC anyway, so maybe it's for the best.

I take my shot and knock it back the way the other girls do as we all take a seat in Layla's comfortable living room. The shot is surprisingly sweet and sugary. Chantel sets her shot glass down and asks me if I've ever been to a clubhouse before.

"No," I answer honestly. "I was always told to stay away from anyone associated with the club." I look at Layla. "We both were."

"That didn't work out so well," Amber says with a giggle as she fluffs her hair.

"Brin saw Wolfe and a few of the guys this week, though, and almost pissed her panties," Layla tells them. The girls laugh as they down another shot.

I groan. "It was... embarrassing, but I froze. I just sat there and stared at him. He looked me over like he was about to demand my personal info," I comment. "And he seems... terrifying, he stared right at me."

"He is," they all say in unison and laugh some more.

"But goddamn, he's fucking hot. BDE for sure," Amber snorts out.

"BDE?" I ask, and the girls laugh harder.

"You are innocent, aren't you, new girl?" Maria chuckles.

"Biker dick energy," Chantel fills me in.

Oh.

Hot? I've never looked at a man like that as hot before. Visions of him pinning me up against his bike overtake me. My body heats and I feel the pink creeping up my cheeks. I squeeze my eyes shut to force the vision from my mind.

"And trust me, he lives up to the hype," Chantel says, cutting into my thoughts like she knows firsthand.

I cross my ankles and play with the hem on my dress.

"I can't even imagine being with a man like that. He's intimidating, to say the least," I say, focusing on the hem like it's the most intriguing thing on earth.

"You can be afraid of him and still want him..." Chantel says. They all laugh, and now I think they *all* know firsthand.

"Forgive me for asking this but, have you *all* slept with him?" I ask incredulously.

"I haven't," Layla pipes up sweetly, arm raised. "The only member of HOH I've slept with is Sean." She giggles using the acronym the town does for the Hounds of Hell.

"On the first night you met him." Maria smirks.

I look at my friend.

"Couldn't help it, all he had to do was touch me." Layla smiles wistfully, and I feel a pang of uncontrollable jealousy.

I look at the other three girls as Chantel points between herself and the other two. "As far as not sleeping with Wolfe... we can't say the same, but that's ancient history. Like, years ago ancient history." They laugh and there's something about it— maybe the fruity shots I just inhaled—that makes me laugh with them.

"You all are a lot braver than I am," I admit honestly.

"Don't knock it till you try it. You hang around long enough, it's just inevitable," Maria says, spraying perfume down her cleavage.

"Hey, don't bust my friend's chops. She's had two years of mediocre and occasional orgasms." Layla winks.

I mouth the word "*asshole*" at her, and she grins. I love that our friendship is the type that picks right up where it left off even when time passes. Right now, I'm thanking my lucky stars I ran into her last week. At least I feel like I have someone. With Layla it's always easy.

Layla stands up and makes her way to the mirror behind us to primp. I follow her because sitting here makes me antsy.

"So... will he be there tonight?" I ask, hating myself for not being able to hold the question in, I lean in to apply lipstick in the mirror beside Layla. As soon as I do and see Chantel's smirk over my shoulder, I want to curl into a ball of embarrassment because she's totally on to me.

"Wolfe? Of course. Nothing happens at the club if he isn't there," Layla says. She bites her lip in thought as she pulls gloss out of her purse, using the same mirror I stand in front of to apply it before side eyeing me.

"You know, you could have some fun with him," Layla says, rubbing her lips together.

I scoff.

"Don't make that uppity face. If not him, then someone like him, someone different than the boring, bland old vanilla you're used to," she adds before turning to me. "Sorry to say, Brin, but what you're doing hasn't worked for you. You've always dated preppy goody boys. Maybe you need a *man*."

I shake my head. "I wouldn't have the first clue about what to do with a man like that." I turn to the room. "You all didn't care that he didn't want to, like, date? Just having sex with him, that didn't make it weird afterward?" I ask them all. I know how clueless I sound, but I genuinely want to know how this works for all of them.

They all laugh.

"I don't think Wolfe understands the concept of dating or a relationship," Maria says

"Or even has feelings," Amber adds with a giggle. "You know what you're getting into with him immediately."

"That man will be single forever. He has everything on his shoulders, and I heard him say once he doesn't believe in love," Maria says. "Hell, half the time I don't even think he believes in *like*. I went to school with him. Known him for twenty-two years, since we were ten years old. He's never had a girlfriend but always had a girl, if you know what I mean."

I register that he's eight years older than me. I knew he was older.

She laughs. "And to answer you, no, it's not weird. It is what it is. All the guys have their own demons, Wolfe, especially, but they're all safe. Wolfe never even kisses women."

"Why hasn't he kissed a woman?" I ask in shock, which makes the other girls laugh at my innocence.

"I'm sure he *has* kissed plenty, but he just *doesn't* kiss. I don't even think he's been with the same woman twice," Maria says with a shrug, like that's normal.

I picture that big, inked body hovering over me again this time on a bed, this time he's leaning in to kiss *me*. I blink to push the image from my mind. Too much of this fruity alcohol.

"He's not my type and I'm sure I'm not his..." I shake my head.

Layla locks arms with me as we prepare to leave and leans in.

"Maybe *not your type* is just what you need."

Chantel slips on her spiky black heels. "Come on, new girl, let us introduce you to the fun side of the town."

Well, shit. I have no idea if I'm ready for that.

Twenty minutes later, we're pulling down the half mile long driveway to the Hounds of Hell Clubhouse.

"Holy crap... so many people," I whisper to Layla, taking in the long line of pick-up trucks, SUVs, and of course, Harleys. *A lot* of them. If I had to guess, I'd say there are at least seventy-five bikes parked along the grass of the drive leading up to the house.

"Almost the whole family is here this weekend." She proceeds to tell me that members of HOH came all the way from outside Chicago, Boston, and New York to be here this weekend.

The property is huge. It seems to go on forever, with a wide creek running behind it. I can see a bonfire happening at the side of the property on a vast patio, the outdoor kitchen is fit for a king with what has to be a ten-foot peninsula with built in grills and a smoker. The smell of smoke and weed hangs heavy in the June night air and the lightning bugs are out in full force.

But the real party is in the massive pole barn style building in the center that houses the Hounds of Hell welded metal sign along with their insignia. I can hear the music from here—a Metallica song—and a lot of people are singing along.

Layla leads us around the tall building, and we enter through the side door.

The scene unfolding is not the scene I pictured for the clubhouse. Edison lights hang everywhere—so do paper lanterns—and they omit a soft glow over the entire space. It's smoky and warm, long tables fill the space, and the entire ceiling is exposed beam with greenery woven through. Each table is adorned with centerpieces and candles, and the dessert table on the opposite side has me drooling already.

People are everywhere, laughing, drinking beer, there is a wall of dartboards where it appears a big tournament of sorts is happening. It's happy—cozy— and feels like a family home. I can't make sense of it. This looks nothing like the dark under-world I pictured when growing up. Many of the men that wander around wear the leather vest I just learned on the way here is called a cut. The mean looking wolf skull eyes me down from their backs. Above it sits a curved banner patch reading *Hounds of Hell*, and below it, some of the men have an extra banner that curves upwards. It reads *Soldier of Bedlam* and I wonder why some have it and some don't.

Layla gasps and covers her mouth with her hands as she takes in her surroundings.

"I did good, baby? I've been working on it with the boy all week." A tiny little woman approaches. Her voice is loud for her size, just like her stark white hair teased up and her cherry red lips. She wears a black and white cheetah print dress. I instantly feel comfortable with her.

"Shell..." Layla leans in to hug her tightly. "It's so beautiful, I can't even believe it, thank you for making sure he did a good job."

The small woman looks right at me over Layla's shoulder and smiles.

"Who's this beauty?" She lets go of Layla and holds out both her hands, taking mine into hers.

"This is my lifelong friend Brinley, my jelly." She winks. "She just... came back to town, I told her she had to come and be a part of everything this weekend." Layla smiles, not divulging my shit storm of a life right now.

Bless her.

"Well, we're glad to have you, sweetie. Make yourself at

home. I'm Shelly. Think of me like the hospitality department. Anyone fucks with you at all, see me and I'll take care of them."

The look on her face tells me she will. I nod back at her.

"How the fuck do you expect me not to drag you into the hallway looking like this... *fuck*." A grizzly voice sounds.

Shelly swats the tall, muscular tattooed man from the photos in Layla's home. He's got a buzz cut and a bushy beard as he wraps his arms around Layla from behind and starts kissing a line down her shoulder like there is no one else in the room. I smile as I watch them, and that pang of envy hits me again with the passion he has for her.

"Don't gross your old mother out," Shelly scoffs.

That small woman birthed this mammoth?

Her bear of a son wears a club vest that bears the patch *Sgt at Arms*. I don't know anything about motorcycle clubs, but I've watched enough old movies with my dad to know a Sergeant at Arms is a top ranked man. Any thoughts I had of her future husband just being a low-ranking member of the club are out the window now.

"This is my Sean," Layla says as she pushes his face off her neck.

Sean looks up. "Hey, new girl." He grins at me.

"She isn't new, I've known her since I was eight. I told you she was coming."

Sean looks me over, and I start to worry I've done something wrong.

"She's not a cop," Layla adds.

Sean shrugs and shakes my hand like a perfect gentleman.

"Old habits. Nice to meet you..."

"Brinley," I say.

"Sorry, Brin." Layla rolls her eyes. "Anyone new... they get dramatic."

"Hope you brought your thirst and your appetite tonight,"

Sean says to me on cue as Chantel returns, passing us all shots of dark amber liquid. "Around here, we drink and eat well."

I take it from her as does everyone else.

"What is this?" I ask

"Don't ask, new girl, just drink. You'll like it," Amber promises.

I smell it first then look up at everyone in our circle.

"I like to know what I'm drinking. What liquors are in it?" I ask simply. They all look at me like I just proposed we sing a church hymn.

I relax my stance, trying to appear casual. It smells like cinnamon.

"It's liquid cocaine," Sean says with a smirk and a nod that says he doesn't think I can handle it. He laughs, my worry probably apparent.

"Jägermeister and Goldschlager," Layla says, swatting Sean. "No actual cocaine. You'll like it."

Sean raises his hand and even Shelly is ready to knock hers back. If this little old woman can take it, so can I, I decide.

"Try to relax," Layla whispers to me.

"To the beautiful woman who will promise to love and obey me forever tomorrow." Sean chuckles evilly, and Layla swats him before we all tip our shots back.

Damnnnn, it's like straight cinnamon fire burning down my throat. I make a face to keep from choking. I don't even have that one back before the next one is placed in my hand.

I take it, yet I question how much these people drink. I rarely drink, but I remind myself this is my weekend to let loose. I can be *anyone* I want to be here. They don't know Brinley the girl who watches *Friends* alone in her fuzzy pajamas on Saturday nights. And this new Brinley wants to feel a little less nervous, so down the hatch the liquid cocaine goes.

I screw my eyes shut as the fire slides down my throat and

the guitar intro to Guns N' Roses' "Sweet Child O' Mine" fills the air at a deafening level. Layla gives a whoop as I smile and shake my head.

Before I even open my eyes, I can feel the air around me has shifted. When I do, I'm met with that hollow mercury gaze that pulls me in, and the air shifts again, turning downright electric. My knees weaken as Wolfe leans against the bar not ten feet away, watching me. Perfectly fitted jeans, motorcycle boots and a black and white flannel Carhartt under his cut. Wolfe doesn't look away when my eyes meet his, he raises the glass in his inked hand up to his mouth. This close, I notice each finger has Roman numerals on them and vines weave through.

He draws a long sip from his glass of what looks like some sort of whiskey. His eyes stay on me over the rim, the same curious way they did the first time I saw him, slow, like he's taking in every inch of me. I can't tell whether it's the intense way he's staring or the liquid cocaine, but my body feels warm and dizzy under the weight. I place my shot glass on the tray at the bar without looking away from him.

"Wolfe, this is Brinley. I know you two haven't been formally introduced but she's my best friend from elementary school," Layla says.

Wolfe nods at me. His face remains expressionless, but his gaze is like velvet and courses over me in a way I've never felt. I nervously fold my hands and let them hang in front of me.

"Uh... You two already know each other?" Shelly asks as Wolfe and I just stare at each other in silence.

"We saw each other once. We don't *know* each other," I answer her nervously, pulling my eyes away from Wolfe's.

"We saw each other?" Wolfe asks in a deep timbre, the hint of a smirk playing at his lips, and I want to die. Of course, he didn't notice me the way I noticed him that day. And why would he remember *me*? I fold my arms across my chest awkwardly. I feel everyone's eyes remain on me, including his, when I do.

"Well, *I* saw you because... it's kind of hard not to notice four tanks rolling down Main Street," I bite out like I'm proving my point in debate class. "I would've been able to hear those bikes from the other side of town." I tilt my head and looking down my nose at him like I'm judging my opponent.

Sean starts to laugh at my reaction.

"Well, it's pretty obvious she's *your* friend," he says, kissing Layla on the neck.

I grin at Sean, my eyes flit back to Wolfe's. They're still on me, less amused. I fight the feeling that tells me I like his attention, knowing I *should not* want it with everything in me.

"Let's eat, ya bunch of fuckin' hooligans!" someone yells out over a megaphone.

Wolfe stands to his full height. I internally shrink as he walks straight toward me, his eyes never waiver as he approaches. The smell of leather and spice fills my senses; it grows stronger the closer he gets. I stand frozen, waiting with bated breath for him to pass but he doesn't. To my surprise, Wolfe stops dead in front of me. He towers over me looking down. The feel of his wide knuckles slinking down my forearm sends me into a sort of frenzy. My skin breaks out in goosebumps and my stomach somersaults. I know fear, I should feel fear now, but my body has other ideas. My pulse starts to race and heat creeps up my throat and over my cheeks.

Wolfe just looks down at me. Even in heels, I'm no match for his great height. He could swallow me whole. I suck in a breath, not knowing what to expect. I watch as his wide jaw ticks like he's annoyed at my simple existence. He angles his head to watch my rapidly beating pulse in my neck, his lips popping open as if he may just swoop in and take a bite out of me.

"Brinley..." His low voice is clear in the noisy room, and the sound of it has me feeling like I'm hearing my own name for the first time. "The good girl with the smart mouth?" he asks low, his knuckles still grazing my arm in a static connection. "If you aren't careful, little hummingbird, I may have to use that mouth to set you straight." He leans in closer, and my knees go weak as his lips hover over my ear. "But maybe that's exactly what you want... maybe you're sick of being good, yeah?"

"*Excuse me?*" I ask, my voice another octave altogether as I realize he just threatened me, at least I think he did?

"When you figure it out, come and find me," he adds as he backs away, giving me one last look and heads into the crowd.

It takes me a full ten seconds to blink and recover.

My stomach drops as I realize his threat doesn't scare me nearly as much as it excites me.

CHAPTER 6
Gabriel

Didn't really give a fuck about attending this party. I'm here only out of duty as Sean's lifelong friend. He's like a brother to me. I hate weddings and everything about them. Two people lying to each other about loving one another for eternity is simple bullshit we make up to make our souls feel less empty. The world would be a much better place if people just accepted that and embraced that truth. We'd be less distracted.

Problem is, everyone is hoping their lives will be like the works of literature my mother read to me over and over as a boy.

Those books are an excellent escape, no doubt. But there's a reason why they're called fiction.

The word fiction comes from the Old French word *ficcion* —meaning ruse. And that's what love is, a fucking ruse. Romantic love, at least.

Maybe I should be in a better mood, this is a party after all. I'm just too fucking tired to pretend I give a fuck that Ax has found his soulmate, when less than a year ago he was fucking his way through every sweetbutt who came into my clubhouse.

I focus on the necessary. That this wedding of his will prove useful to the club. It's the perfect, secluded place to take the piece of shit we've been hunting and get some answers from him before we gut him from the inside out for fucking Mason's underage sister. Brian "Gator" Freeland. We've been watching him at the safe house he's staying in, owned by the Disciples of Sin. They're our rival club and we've been keeping track of his movements there for over ten days, ever since we got word he was in Lakeshore—about thirty minutes from Harmony.

We've been learning his habits, who's protecting him, how to get in, how to get out. The mission we've planned to get him out tomorrow afternoon and to Tybee Island rests fully on me. If anyone is hurt, it's on my back as president. On the flip side, if we ruin Ax's wedding... again, I'm to blame, and that would be worse because I'll answer to Shelly on that one. No one wants to answer to Shelly, I've seen that woman shoot a man in the kneecap for accusing her son of stealing.

Ruin his wedding? I'm a fucking dead man.

Between nabbing our soon-to-be prisoner Gator without any of my men getting hurt, getting a new clinic supplied in Savannah by Saturday to make up for stolen product, and Kai and me finishing a custom paint job on a bike for a Braves player, all I want to do tonight is knock around the heavy bag, head to my shop to catch up on some work and maybe get some fucking peace and quiet.

I thrive on regiment. Routine and control. My men know I'm a very prepared leader, not easily surprised. I normally know every single person about to step foot into this clubhouse, so color me fucking shocked when I was on my way to the bar to congratulate the bride, and a little hummingbird flew into my crosshairs.

Brinley Rose Beaumont.

The woman whose pulse I can see thrumming away in her

slender, silky throat from here. The woman I haven't been able to stop thinking about since I first laid eyes on her sitting at the coffee shop over a week ago, turning away from me like I may corrupt her just from looking at her. It's highly fucking unusual I even remember her, because normally I don't think of a woman at all after I make the decision to either stop looking at her or pull my dick out of her.

Whichever happens first.

But this woman's mere existence, for some reason, just fucking thunderstruck me.

The moment I saw her, I had the uncontrollable urge to pull her into the alley, tie her wrists together with that shirt around her waist, and make her scream my name until she was begging me instead of snubbing me.

At first, I thought she was a tourist, but something about the way she didn't even really look up in surprise when she heard our bikes and the way her body tensed told me she knew my club and that she was local. That, and the Georgia plates on the car she got into when she left the dress shop. I forced myself to stop watching her out the window, the way she walked, unsure of her beauty, unassuming, probably tapped on the hand with a ruler as a child every time she got out of line. Shoulders back, quick little ladylike strides.

She screamed ballet lessons and cotillion.

I rationalized that I'd probably find out she's too young, boring as fuck, maybe had the same preppy boyfriend since she was in high school, but still, there was something about her I couldn't get out of my head. Enough to make me hand Kai her license plate number when I got back to the clubhouse and order him to tell me everything about her.

Turns out, I was right.

She is young—almost nine years younger than me—she is exactly who I thought she was, the daughter of an upscale

Atlanta real estate lawyer, her whole family belonged to the Crested River Country Club, she was a fucking debutant, and she does have a preppy boyfriend in Atlanta. So, I shouldn't give one fuck who she is or why she's brought her heart-shaped ass into my clubhouse.

Except now that she's standing here in front of me, I can't look away, and I find myself wondering how fucking stupid her Atlanta boyfriend is.

The answer is a special kind of stupid to ever let her come in here looking like this. He might as well have served her up on a silver fucking platter for my taking.

Her long, thick hair, as black as my soul, falls in shiny waves over her shoulders, she's got a classic vibe about her, everything is completely natural and wholesome, high cheekbones, wide blue eyes. The only unholy things about her? Her full pouty lips and the little dimple in her chin. Watching her nervously fidget in the dim bar lights, I find myself picturing all the ungodly depraved things I can do with those lips, particularly biting into them just enough to break the surface and watch them bleed before wrapping them around my cock.

I catch Brinley's gaze now and hold it. The pale yellow dress she wears is strapless and short in the front, offering me the supple curve of her inner thighs. All her upper back, slender arms and completely biteable neck are on full display. The tight bodice pushes her perky tits up, boasting the type of cleavage I would make a home in. I'm willing to bet there's not a shred of ink on her skin or even the hint of a piercing other than her gold hoops at her ears. Good girl to her core.

The way her eyes widen and fill with fear as I approach her drives me fucking wild.

"Brinley…" I speak her name and feel her skin turn to goosebumps under my knuckles. Her entire body is wired with electricity and it pulses through her to me. "The good girl with the smart mouth?" I assume. I smirk, wanting to toy with her a little more. "If you aren't careful, little hummingbird, I may have to use that mouth to set you straight." I feel the heat from her skin, hear the pant in her shaky breath. I lean in on a gut instinct so strong I couldn't fight it if I tried as the thought overwhelms me. "But maybe that's exactly what you want... maybe you're sick of being good, yeah?"

"*E-Excuse me?*" she stutters in that smoky voice that goes straight to my dick. The shock she wears isn't surprising but the second of longing I see in her eyes when I back up *is*. It's what tells me my gut is right. I won't force her, I'll let her get there on her own.

"When you figure it out, come and find me."

I can hear her panting behind me as I seek out a place to sit with a satisfied grin on my face.

Didn't give a fuck where that was going to be, until right this second.

Now, I just want to be somewhere where I can watch Brinley more closely.

If she turns out to be as bland as she is on paper, maybe I'll be able to stop fucking thinking about her.

I make my way to the center of the room, choosing a table, knowing wherever I sit, my brothers and their women will follow, and so will my prey.

CHAPTER 7
Gabriel

As expected, my men trailed through the crowd behind me, Layla and her girl gang following behind them.

The tables are large and each seat twelve easily. I watch as Brinley hesitantly takes a seat directly across from me, opening and spreading her napkin in her lap like she's at a state dinner.

The movement from her shaking out the fabric fans her scent over me. She smells like sweet summer blooms and fear. It's fucking intoxicating. She fidgets with her cutlery, rearranging it. I'm lost in watching her place her fork on the left, knife on the right, just as she's probably been taught. A good girl with manners, etiquette, and class. I should be bored as fuck right now but there's just something about her that continues to draw me in. Her first finger slides up the blade of her sharp steak knife, caressing it as she sips her glass of wine. I wonder why she'd pick the knife as her comfort while I sip my whiskey in silence. She continues as she looks around, not even realizing she's doing it, and my thoughts run wild with the possibility of what lies beneath her surface.

The table listens intently as Kai rambles on with a story like he always does. Fucking kid never stops talking. I shift forward in my seat, just enough that I can make out her scent in detail... I take in a heady breath and my mouth waters. Jasmine with a hint of honeysuckle.

The chatter is never-ending while more whiskey is poured, and dinner is carted out. The local catering company the club hired has been working all day in the commercial kitchen attached to the hall.

I watch Brinley listen intently to Layla ramble on about wedding details but I don't really hear any of it. The candle-light from the table casts shadows on her supple skin, her shiny lips are painted a glossy pink. She wraps them around the rim of the glass. When my cock pulses I know my plan to find her uninteresting is failing me.

She's completely out of her element, but she's curious. Looking around the room trying to drink us in, trying to make sense of why we seem so civil. We aren't but what she's getting is our club on best behavior for Ax.

"So, Brinley, you grew up here?" Kai asks, leaning forward onto his palm with a *fuck me* look on his pretty boy face.

She smiles at him in response and it's fucking earth shatter-ing. The way those full pouty lips curve upward over straight white teeth for Kai of all people serves to heat my blood.

As do those gorgeous dimples in her cheeks that appear for him. They match the one in her chin.

This fucking guy. His dick is still probably wet from the blonde he took into the pool hall earlier.

"Yes, over on the corner of Netherwood and Spruce," she answers in that raspy, soft voice. "I just got back to the house last week. My mom left it for me when she passed but I haven't been the best at keeping up with it the last couple of years."

"The McCurry boys gave her an insane cost to replace the

porch." Layla takes a bite of fresh bread. "You boys need to have a chat with them about it," she orders, nudging Ax.

Ax nods of course. He's a fucking slave for this woman.

"No, that's fine, termites are an expensive fix..." Brinley says. "I don't want any... trouble."

My men look around the table at each other and grin. She's Layla's friend so they'll be respectful. She probably thinks we're gonna go bang down their door and threaten them.

I mean, it's possible but the stereotype is amusing, nonetheless.

"The whole thing needs replacing. I just started working with Layla's brother at Crimson Homes. I'll have it fixed up by the end of the summer. No need for a talk," Brinley adds, resting her hand on Layla's arm, her pale pink fingernails shine in the dim light. The beast in me imagines what they'd look like with my blood under them after she tears up my back.

"I'm pretty good with wood, I could probably take a look for you." Kai gives her his best dazzling smile, and I grit my molars to stop myself from cuffing him up the back of his head.

Brinley smiles nervously and averts her eyes from his, her innocence taking over. I kick him sharply under the table without looking up from cutting my steak. Kai turns his attention to me. I lift my gaze to take my bite and shake my head slightly only once, no one else would notice. Kai nods and grimaces, understanding I'm telling him to back off.

My eyes flit to Brinley's and the moment I meet her gaze she looks away. I take another bite of steak and watch her talk to Layla. Every time I feel her eyes on me, I focus on her, and every time she looks away, pretending she wasn't looking at me.

It's a game I could play all night.

You can look away all you want, but you can't run from me, little hummingbird.

My VP and cousin, Jake, stands with a head nod and a

smirk to the table beside us. I follow his gaze to a sweetbutt and know he's about to hook up. He's always ready to party and is extremely impulsive which is why his father, my uncle Ray, nominated me to take over as president for him before he died. I didn't want to take it from Jake, but luckily for me, Jake didn't seem to care. He was happy to be VP. This way, he can drink copious amounts and party his life away. Two things I have zero interest in doing. I'll knock back a shot of whiskey or two but aside from that, my body is my fucking temple.

I grab his arm. "Be back here in thirty minutes, you aren't missing toasts," I say, and he nods before stealing out the club-house door.

Jake listens and slides back into his seat twenty-five minutes later just as Shelly starts the rounds of speeches after dinner and has all the girls at the table tearing up. Ax's father was my uncle's Enforcer and his father before that was Sergeant at Arms for my grandfather. The club is in all of our blood, and Ax and I already have an unbreakable brotherhood. We served three tours in the Middle East together. That shit bonds you like nothing else.

I watch Ax now as his mother talks and Layla tears up, he's all in for this fucking woman or so it seems.

Layla is cool, I'll give her that, but as I listen, all I can think of is Ax on his knees before he met her, no more than a year ago, on the middle of the pool table while two brunettes traded sucking him off in front of everyone. A competition to see which one would earn his cum down their throat first.

He tried to pass them off to the rest of us after, to which I gave him a hard fucking no. I'm all for fucking women but there isn't a damn thing they could do to earn my cock down their throat. Especially the ones who hang around here. No clue where their mouths have been.

I watch the two lovebirds across the table now. Ax has his

arm around Layla's neck and he kisses her on the lips like he is actually committed to her for all eternity.

Layla champions all her girls for more shots, and after speeches the party gets going. I take a few minutes to do my diligence of making my way around the room and talking to everyone important. We have several members from different charters here and some of their ol' ladies. Not all the men bring them along, some of them treat events like this as a release from their constants. Ax and I also have ex-military buddies who have shown up for us. Men we spent time with in Kuwait and Afghanistan. Seeing these men here tonight brings back all sorts of memories from both ends of the spectrum. I make my way back to the table to find Brinley and Layla acting out some sort of choreographed dance while seated at the table, and I keep on eye on the proper little hummingbird that seems to be loosening up.

"We did at least ten of these over the years for our church youth groups," Brinley tells the girls.

"Do you still remember every single one?" Layla asks her, laughing as I rejoin.

"I cannot see you as the little girl in the front row every Sunday..." Chantel says to Layla as she laughs, gulping back a shot—probably her tenth. I've seen that woman drink men under the table on any given night.

"New girl, I could see," she says, pointing to Brinley to which they laugh again—all of them but Brinley, which just solidifies to me she may not always enjoy her good girl persona.

Before Brinley can speak, I sit. She straightens right up, and her eyes nervously focus on anything *but* me, instead paying attention to her half-filled glass, people talking and milling about, the girls.

It's okay, I have a big enough ego to handle her evasiveness. I already know her secret.

She *wants* to look at me.

My phone buzzes on the table just as we're all through toasting Chantel and her maid of honor's speech. No sooner does mine buzz, but every one of my men's start buzzing and dinging simultaneously.

I'm instantly on high alert, my hand covers the gun concealed under my cut at my hip, and I look around the room for threats. I open the text, it's a photo from an unknown number, of myself, Kai, Ax and Jake in Jake's dad's old Silverado yesterday at a stop light leaving Lakeshore. DOS territory.

We were there to stake out across from the coffee shop watching for Gator's men picking up his weekly Percocet. You can't even see us through the tinted windows. I can't understand how they knew we were there—Jake's truck isn't registered to him. There's no way they would've known it was us—

The entire building shakes as an explosion rocks the outside of the club house. It's instant pandemonium. Women scream and people get up and start running for shelter. I stand without thought and get to Brinley in one stride. I wrap one arm around her waist. She gasps and tips her head back, looking into my eyes, her face just a few inches from mine. Her eyes fill with fear as I pick her up in a rag doll carry and following Ax and Layla, we burrow the girls into a hallway alcove for safety.

When I set Brinley down her mouth pops open, but she doesn't speak. She breathes in shallow breaths, the way the body does when it's dipping into fight or flight.

"Stay," I order.

She closes her mouth, gulps and nods. Her ocean eyes and the way her throat works to swallow threatens to hold me, but I know I have to go.

"Don't leave them for one fucking second! And no one

leaves this building!" I yell to Mason over my shoulder, then turn to Chris, one of our prospects. "Lock it all down, now!"

It's only been twenty seconds, but I'm already running to the front door forty feet away. I see the Silverado is engulfed in a mass of flames and smoke in the parking lot near the hall. We fly through the clubhouse door. I don't even have to turn to know Jake, Ax, and Robby J—one of my most trusted and long-est-patched members—are behind me.

Mason, Kai, and the grandpa of our group, Flipp, stay inside and keep the room as calm as possible. Out here we're poised and ready to attack whoever the fuck somehow got through our security system and our gates.

Ax and I are first. We move like trained operatives, orga-nized and stealthy. I'm searching for something, anything I can shoot at. I two-finger point to Jake and Robby J then to the woods beyond our premises. A couple more of my men are outside now, putting out the blaze with the two-hundred-foot hose we use to spray down our metal building.

My boots are quiet on the gravel. I hear something near the gate and turn and aim my custom 1911 at the sound. I see the fucker instantly behind a stack of pallets at our gate. His cut tells me he's a Disciples of Sin prospect and that he just failed.

He's probably going to die, but not until I get all the intel out of him that I want. I'm seething as I move toward him. I want to know how the fuck he got past my security gate. He moves his hand behind his back when I approach him. He knows there's no point in fighting. If he runs he's dead.

"Don't fucking do it," I warn him. He tries to pull out his heat and take aim at me, but I'm faster. I take my shot and it hits him in the hand, blowing two of his fingers clean off. His gun drops to the dirt below and he howls in pain.

"Move an inch you'll lose the rest," I say, unmoving and calm. Once I make it to his kneeling body, I see he's frantically squeezing his two severed fingers in an attempt to stop the bleeding. I pull his skinny ass up by the cuff of his shirt and rip his cut from his body in one clean movement, dropping it to the ground and spitting on it. He'll never put it back on. I signal to Ax as I haul this pain in my ass to the cargo van at the side of the clubhouse.

Motherfucker.

Can't even get one fucking night off.

CHAPTER 8
Brinley

"What's going on, Layla?" I whisper. My voice sounds foreign in my own head, panicked as I ask the question. We've been behind one of the big scary members since Wolfe scooped me up and sent my heart into my throat before he dropped me here.

"You can move, Mason. I think we're safe," Layla says, not at all fazed and sounding more than a little annoyed that this happened in the middle of her rehearsal dinner.

I look up under hooded eyes at the man she calls Mason. I don't want to stare but he scares me nearly as much as Wolfe. He's almost the same height and he's solid. He wears a black bandana around his head and has a scruffy goatee and mustache, yet he doesn't appear much older than me. His jaw is wide and permanently set in a straight, grim expression. It isn't his looks but what's behind his eyes that scares me, like nothing would phase him because he's seen and done it all. I've only heard him say about five words up until now.

"I'll move when someone *tells* me you're safe," Mason says in a deep voice, looking down at me and I look away. "Don't look so scared. They aren't getting in here, new girl. This place is built like Fort Knox." He pats the concrete wall behind him.

My eyes flit to his briefly but I'm sure to look away as fast as I can. I'm unable to understand what I see there. I swear I hear gunshots ring outside and I feel like I'm about to pass out. My breathing increases.

"You're safe," Layla says. "Sean and Wolfe were Force Exploration, although I never thought we'd need their skills at my rehearsal dinner!" She narrows her eyes at Mason like it's his fault and as if she isn't even afraid of him. Desensitized is what she is.

"Just some after dinner entertainment for us," he says to her with an evil smirk that tells me he'd enjoy toying with whoever is out there.

I shudder.

"Force... exploration?" I ask, partly to distract myself, partly because I'm actually curious. I must look at her with a blank stare of what the hell are you talking about because Mason leans in.

"Marines. Both of them. Three long ass tours," he says. "A little explosion won't shake them in the slightest, it's just enough to get their blood going."

I gulp and nod, still terrified but somehow, I feel better knowing Wolfe is the one out there.

Twenty minutes later, someone has turned the music back on and people have started to drink again like nothing was even wrong. Mason pulls his phone out and reads a text then stands.

"You're free to go, there's no threat. Just one thing. You can't leave the building tonight. You have to wait till morning." He looks to Layla. "And you'll be escorted to your house to get what you need before we leave for Tybee," he says.

Layla isn't bothered but I feel like I might throw up.

Not a chance I'm sleeping here.

"No way, that wasn't part of the deal," I say to Layla, my voice a full two octaves higher than normal. "I don't even have anything to sleep in," I say which gets Mason's attention.

Getting the hell out of here was my first plan the moment we got the go ahead.

"Shelly will have everything you need. It's just a precaution, new girl. Don't need people coming and going while we're carving someone up out there," Mason adds with a pat on my shoulder. I can't tell if he means it.

"He doesn't mean that," Layla says. She must notice I'm terrified. The thing is, she says that but doesn't look convinced herself.

I watch Mason walk away and ask myself how someone becomes that way. Goddamn terrifying is what it is. I follow Layla blindly, still a bit buzzed from my pre-dinner shots and wine. I'm pretty sure that alcohol is the only thing keeping me standing. We meet up with Chantel, Maria, and Amber on the way back to the bar and they also seem unfazed.

I guess gunshots and things blowing up are normal around here?

I mentally scold myself for allowing myself to come.

"Have another drink," Layla says, handing me something fruity looking.

"Breathe. It's just a daiquiri. Remi makes the best ones in the entire town." She sends a friendly wink and smile to the redheaded woman behind the bar as "Seven Nation Army" by The White Stripes begins to play over the speakers.

I look around at the party in full swing, outside dramatics long forgotten. I try my best to force my body to return to its normal pace. My heart has been beating rapidly and I've been clammy for the better part of a half hour. Less than a month ago, I was watching *The Real Housewives* on my sofa in

Atlanta eating ice cream. I take a sip of the daiquiri that goes down super easy and actually *is* really good.

When the lyrics *Hounds of Hell* play through the speaker, the whole crowd sings along.

I shake my head as I look around, resigning myself to soak up some of the energy of the rowdy, carefree crowd. There's no question I'm in some sort of alternate universe here.

Screw it. I take another sip. If I have to stay here all night long, I might have another six of these daiquiris. It certainly seems easier than coping with the danger lurking everywhere I turn.

CHAPTER 9

Gabriel

I watch as Rick, our club's resident doctor, wraps the piece of shit DOS prospect's hand. I don't need this fucker bleeding all over the place.

"Knock me out..." he whines around his gag. *Pussy.*

"It's just a couple fingers." I clap him on the back and lean forward. "You have eight more. Wait until it's your kneecaps. You'll be ready to die then," I add.

He starts to hit his head against the interior wall of the van —trying to knock himself out, I presume.

I roll my eyes. "Jesus Christ, that won't work, dipshit." I turn to Rick. "Got something to help put the baby here to sleep? I don't want to worry about him for the rest of the night. I've had a fuck of a long day already."

"Will do." Rick nods, heading to his medical bag.

"This all has to happen the fucking night before my wedding?" Ax asks as he approaches, acting appropriately annoyed. I know he secretly lives for this shit. He stops to tuck his gun into his holster at his back. "The rest of the perimeter is secure. I have no idea how this fucker got in... but you're going to tell us, aren't you?" he adds before grabbing the intruder by the hair. "There could've been women or kids out here, you motherfucker." He bounces his head off the side of the van wall.

I shake my head. Exactly what the dipshit wants.

"We're going to get the answers we want out of him... but not until tomorrow," I say, mostly just pissed off that he is pulling me away from my little fixation I was just starting to get to know.

I turn to my prisoner. "You spend the night dreaming of how loyal you plan to be for a club you don't even belong to yet."

He whimpers behind his makeshift gag.

"And don't worry. Tomorrow, you'll have some company. You play your cards right, maybe you'll live." I let him in on the little secret we're bringing in a friend for him.

"Wolfe," Ax says from beside me. "Kai is already getting what you want, and the party's back on."

I nod.

"No outsiders leave here until tomorrow, if brothers want to leave that's fine, but anyone who can't protect themselves stays," I announce, not chancing anyone getting hurt on the way out. My mind specifically goes to the woman I just pushed behind Mason in the hallway. I blink and shake it off.

"It'll be easier to see what's what and scope our surrounding woods in the light of day," I add.

"That's going to be at least fifty people," Ax says.

"It's fine. We have the space," I say casually with a shrug. "Tell Kai to start letting people know."

I look toward the back of the van.

"You're here for the night; as soon as he starts to stir, give him another," I say to Rick as he injects the prospect. "He can stay asleep straight through until after the wedding. This is a tomorrow night problem."

It doesn't take long for the shot to take effect and the prospect passes out, his head hitting the floor of the van with a sickening thud.

"And... by the way, we've got you," I add, letting Rick know he'll be getting a bonus for keeping twenty-four-hour watch over my prisoner. "You need a break, Chris has got you covered," I say

Rick nods, and I signal for Ax to tell Chris.

I check to ensure the fire from Jake's pick-up truck is in fact out, and text my contact at the sheriff's office. The police won't come out here anyway, unless something astronomical happens but I like to be sure and get ahead of it. If anyone saw the flames, they may have called.

I turn to Ax. "Gather the guys, emergency chapel right now, and"—I look down to my clothes covered in this asshole's blood and soot from the flames— "then I need a fucking shower."

Ax grins wickedly and pulls his dick from his jeans, pissing all over this shit head's boots that hang out of the back of the van into the grass.

I shake my head and chuckle.

"Fucking goon," I mutter.

Rick doesn't even glance up. He's been at our beck and call for years and he's used to us.

I leave them under the watch of our prospect, Chris, for the night and make my way back inside. I need to see the security footage before chapel and I need a fucking drink.

It's going to be a late one, and my little fixation, unfortunately, is going to have to wait.

CHAPTER 10
Brinley

I'm drunk. Drunker than I think I've ever been.

Is it a good idea to get this drunk in the face of something traumatic? Probably not, but I did anyway against the better judgement screaming in my head. The good thing about being this drunk is that it's a lot easier to tell that voice to shut the hell up.

We've been dancing for hours, or so it feels like. I haven't seen Wolfe or any of the other guys that were at our table for a while. I'm sweaty and I have to pee. Another drink wouldn't hurt either.

"Where's the bathroom?" I call to Layla over the music. She just smiles and gives me directions. I repeat them in my head so I don't forget. Fourth door on the left... or was it right?

It's loud now and there are people everywhere. I can't make sense of this night or how I'm in this situation. I'll just make it through, and tomorrow the familiarity of home will make me think straight and I can make an excuse to Layla to avoid her wedding. There's not a chance in hell I'm going.

I stumble through the bar area in search of this elusive

hallway to the bathroom. I smooth out my dress and hair, trying to walk as straight as possible. I'm either seeing things or crazy shit is happening around here. There is a woman laying on one of the pool tables as I walk by and another is taking a lime out from between her breasts with her teeth and people are making out... everywhere.

I watch a sitting man slide his large hands up under a women's black leather skirt as she stands in front of him. He squeezes her ass. I can't see him behind her body, only his big hands that seem to take up all of her flesh. He lifts her skirt right up over her ass and he slides her thong aside as she tips her head back and moans, absolutely zero shame. He pulls her closer and slides his legs between hers, two boot-clad feet holding her legs apart then shoves two fingers into her pussy right out in the open.

My mouth falls slack as I watch. I need to look away but I... don't. I feel heat start to coil between my legs at the vision before me. My hand travels slowly up from my chest, over my throat to my lips, I try to feel the shock I know I should, but I don't. This is wrong. I shouldn't be watching them. But I simply can't help the heat rushing over me.

The woman moans as he viciously thrusts his fingers into her, and I think I hear him tell her to *take them like a good little slut.* When his face comes into view over her shoulder, I'm shocked to see that it's Kai. The sweet, clean cut looking one? He grins... and damn. I did not expect that.

"I've got another hand, new girl, if you're interested," he says as I blink, realizing I'm standing right in front of them, staring.

He chuckles as I begin to move quickly toward the only hallway I see and push through a swinging door to get to it. It's quieter here and darker. Four doors down for the bathroom or five? It's a little fuzzy. I decide to push open every door along the way. I'm mostly greeted with unkempt spaces that look like bedrooms. I find the bathroom mercifully. I probably couldn't have held it much longer.

I wash my hands with what is actually really nice soap. I giggle.

Things you notice when you're drunk for a thousand, please.

I fix myself up as best I can before heading back out to the hall. Miraculously, my makeup is still fairly intact. When I get into the dark hallway, I look both ways trying to remember which direction I came from. I hear moaning in the distance and the heat continues to flush through me. What the hell is wrong with me? Why is this torrid place turning me on like this?

I decide to go right and pass the first doorway. It has a licence plate screwed to the door that reads, *"For those who like to fuck"*.

Apparently, the people inside like to, judging by the sounds.

A light catches my eye in the otherwise dark hall. It's coming from underneath a door at the end.

I don't listen to my conscience, instead I listen to the little dark voice in my head telling me to go as I push it open. The space is large and spotless. A massive American flag with an eagle in the center graces the wall. It's pinned straight and taut over a comfortable looking, worn in leather sofa. The floors are dark wood and shiny clean. It smells like cedarwood. There is a kitchen area at the back, it's almost like a studio apartment of sorts. The other side of the wide open space has a solid wood divider.

I venture behind like I have permission, telling myself it's perfectly fine that I'm snooping in this stranger's space. A bigger than normal king-size bed made impeccably with dark gray bedding and ten feet of bookshelves lined with books catches my eye. My mouth falls open as I move toward them and take in some of the titles, running my fingers along the spines as I go. As a girl who always liked to read the classics, this is impressive.

The Art of War
Fire in The Belly
A collection of very old looking Machiavelli's.
The Great Gatsby
The Beautiful and Damned
1984

And the shelves continue, lined with classic works of literature. I stand there running a finger over them taking in the other items. Photos catch my eye. They're of Wolfe and Sean and other men in beige fatigues head to toe. Even their helmets are beige. I flip them over to see if there is any info on the back.

Field Lights 2009, Roaring Lion 2010, Eagles Trace 2012
All of them say 2nd Battalion 9th.
Missions?

Some are in casual settings; some look like they're on-duty photos. I trace a line down Wolfe's face in one of them, white t-shirt covered in dust, he's so tan his skin looks unrecognizable, and he holds a very scary looking gun on a table in front of him like he's cleaning it. He has a lot less ink in these photos than now, but that same emotionless gaze haunts his eyes.

The gaze of a man who's seen it all.

I move on and pull a copy of *The Great Gatsby* out and skim my fingers over the weathered spine, flipping it over. The eyes in the solid blue cover pierce mine. I haven't seen this edition before and I instantly know it's very old. I open it and read the handwritten note on the inside cover

"To my fierce protector, always keep your world view bigger than our backyard," and a heart under it.

"Why are you here?" a deep voice booms. *The* deep voice that sends shivers up the back of my neck.

I spin around and fall backward against the shelf, making it rattle.

Wolfe stands just ten feet away from me. He's freshly showered, his hair loose, touching his ears in wet strands, and he's wearing a clean black t-shirt and black jeans. He holds his cut in his hand. I take in his corded inked forearms, rippled with veins as he swipes his hair back.

I open my mouth, but I have nothing to say. There's no way around this, I'm totally busted snooping in his room.

But honestly, who am I kidding? I knew the moment I saw the photos this was either his space or Ax's. I'm still holding his book, for God's sake.

"I asked what you're doing here, I don't ask twice," he repeats, tossing his cut onto his bed in a slow intentional drop, his voice a deep velvet that both speeds my heart rate up and calms it all at the same time.

"I just... um, the light was on, I thought it was the way out," I offer lamely as a flush creeps up my neck. "I mean, you're the one who left the door wide open so it's kind of your fault," I add, trying to sound as confident as I can.

Wolfe moves toward me before I can say another word, closing the short distance between us in just two strides. I glance up at him towering over me. So close. Dangerously close.

He raises a hand, and I can't help it, I flinch, afraid he might hurt me.

Wolfe studies my reaction with a hint of a smirk and embarrassment floods my chest, yet he continues, letting the back of his knuckles run over my cheekbone then down to the column of my throat. He's touching me. I just met this man today and he's *touching me.*

He pauses with his knuckles at the nape of my neck, feeling my thundering heartbeat under his fingers.

"There's that smart mouth again. You use it freely, yet you're terrified, little hummingbird." His eyes meet mine as he flips his hand and grips my throat. His palm covers all of it and I understand instantly why he's given me that name... he can see and feel my heart beating a million miles a minute. His fingers slide back into my hair, the pads of them trace my scalp before he grabs a fist full and pulls my neck taut, bringing my body forward to him so we're flush, and I have nowhere to look but into his gray eyes.

Does he think I came here to have sex with him? Instinct takes over and I reach up and smack him in the face. The sound tells me it was hard, but I think it hurts me more than it hurts him, because he doesn't even flinch.

He grips my hair tight enough for me to cry out. It burns like he's ripping it out at the roots.

"And here I thought you were ready to shed this perfectly practiced little exterior... but now, I see. The hummingbird just wants to fight..." he growls, a sadistic light fills his eyes and for the first time I see emotion there.

I swing again, knowing he will just retaliate but I can't help myself.

Some dark action inside me takes over. His hand slides back to my throat, encompassing all of it as my hand connects with his cheek in the same spot it just did moments ago. He squeezes only the sides of my throat so controlled and practiced I instantly see stars.

He's right, I am terrified but something else is happening. Something I couldn't understand if I tried. I squeeze my thighs together as my core begins to ache, even under his unpredictable touch.

It sends my blood racing, causing me to let out a tiny moan

I have no control over. The feel of him touching me is everywhere all at once. The warmth from his lips comes so close to mine as he leans in, his cedarwood and spice scent mixed with fresh, clean soap singing to me.

"*And he looked at her the way all women want to be looked at by a man,*" Wolfe's deep voice says evenly as he keeps his hand tight to my throat while grazing the knuckles of his free one down my body, over the peak of my hardened nipple.

I'm helpless and I shudder.

Wolfe doesn't stay at my breast. He continues down over the curve of my waist. His fingers graze my forearm slowly until his hand wraps around the book I'm still holding. He pulls it from me roughly.

"Nick Carraway," he says, holding up *The Great Gatsby*, as if I didn't know that was the narrator's name. He places the book back in its home on the shelf without loosening the grip on my throat.

"This isn't a library. So when you realized this was my room, tell me why you stayed, Brinley?"

I hate that I love the way my name sounds rolling off his tongue.

"Please, just let me go, I'm sorry I came in here, I didn't know it was your room. I saw the books... I was curious," I say between gasps.

I begin to claw at his hold around my throat to no avail, claustrophobia setting in. I scratch at his forearms in my tipsy state as he holds me tight enough that it's hard to breathe but not impossible.

All the while, the sensation of my pussy throbbing continues and I seriously question my sanity.

Those gray eyes are stormy now and dark staring into mine. I'm surprised when Wolfe's grip loosens and his thumb begins to move back and forth over the center of my throat, sliding upward so it rests below my ear. The graze continues there.

"I think you knew it was my room the moment you came in and you wanted to be caught," he says, coating me in truth from my head to my toes. The sensitive spot he's touching with the calloused pad of his thumb in slow circles almost has my eyes rolling back.

"You think you *should* fight your desires. The world has been telling you your whole life you should fight, but you don't *want* to. You *want* me to touch you like this." His eyes roam over me as if he's trying to understand me.

I watch as a decision is made, and he begins to slide his other broad palm up my outer thigh.

Wolfe is a man in control, his breathing is calm and even, but his normally light eyes are so dark I can't help but lose myself in them. I'm totally at his mercy. I pant faster as his eyes continue their search.

"Having my eyes on you excites you," he observes.

I clench my thighs together as his grip around my neck deepens and heat spreads through my core with every word, every touch. I fight it with everything in me. "Let me go." I croak out a final attempt, my inhibitions lessen by the second.

"You can fight me if you want to, little hummingbird." Wolfe tilts my head back, exposing the column of my throat to him. He brings his lips down to my pulse point and kisses me there, just once and I cave. Everything is heightened, the scruff of his beard and the contrast of his soft lips when they connect to my skin is like the static of an electric shock. I feel everything. My aching clit, my clothing against my skin, the air around me, startlingly cool as the warmth of his mouth dissipates, and his delicious breath draws me in.

"Fight," he commands in an even deeper baritone. "And I promise, it will only make your pleasure sweeter."

We lock eyes for only a second as I decide, a flurry of activity and dark fantasies takes over without a thought in my mind. I try to knee him, but he blocks me and winds his hand back in my hair. I smack him again, but he lets go of my hair and quickly lifts both my wrists overhead gripping me one-handed with the same strength he held my throat. I'm no physical match for him but I have to try, don't I?

His words settle with me... *I'm fighting because I'm told to.*

Because I've always been told a man should *earn* the right to touch me like this. Wolfe is right about that, but he's also right when he says I *want* him to touch me.

I do.

Holding my hands hostage, Wolfe uses his heavy knee to push my legs apart and presses his body into mine. The wood of the bookshelf bites into my shoulder blades.

"You can pretend you don't want me. But your body tells a different tale. See..." He trails a thumb to my throat where my pulse continues to hammer thunderously. The inability to move is too much. I squeeze my thighs without thought around his leg, it offers me a slight friction that makes my pussy ache even more. He bends down and lets his teeth graze the skin of my neck.

I hear the lowest groan come from him as he mutters, "*fuck.*"

I whimper in response, my chest heaves with heavy breath, pushing my breasts right into him with every inhale.

"Your heart flutters like this whenever I'm near you. You *want* me to slide my hand right under this dress."

Do I?

"You *want* to find out how much faster I can make this fluttering heart beat."

"Fuck you!" I spit out as best I can, the word I never really use feeling foreign on my tongue, but I have no hands left to claw him with.

His skin has scratches on it from my nails and his cheek is red, but he doesn't even seem to notice.

"My heart beats faster because... I'm afraid of you," I say honestly, looking into his eyes, hoping he will feel badly enough to let me go and wishing he wouldn't all at the same time.

"I know," he growls. "I fucking *love* it."

"Please..." I whimper, half in ecstasy, half in terror.

This man gets off on scaring me and I have no idea what he's capable of.

I stare up into his violent eyes, his godlike face seeming completely devoid of empathy. He's a hunter whose only purpose is to trap his prey, and right now his prey is me.

"I bet you've always done everything right, haven't you?" Wolfe asks as his free hand slides to the zipper at the back of my strapless dress.

'Y-yes," I stutter.

"Did you know humans are the only species that relates permission to anything sexual? For every other species that roams this earth, it is simply taken."

He pulls my zipper roughly, and before I even realize what is happening my dress pools at my feet.

"Desire and primal need are the only rules that are followed," he says.

I gasp as my nipples pebble even more when the cool air hits them. This earns a growl from Wolfe before he dips his head and pulls one into his hot mouth, toying with it against his tongue. I want to fight but...

Holy shit. That feels so good.

I lean my head back against the bookcase and let out a ragged moan, I absentmindedly push my hips toward him.

"It's quite simple. You just let your body take what it

wants." Wolfe's teeth graze my nipple before his tongue rolls over it and I quiver beneath his lips.

"You don't know... what I want..." I pant out. He moves to my other breast and plays with that nipple in his mouth for a moment and I may combust with a pleasure I've never felt.

"But I do...I already know you." His lips trail over me as one hand still holds my wrists and the other circles my waist, gliding over all the skin he can manage.

"You *want* to know what it's like to be properly handled by a man. A man who can satisfy every dark craving you've ever had but have never admitted."

"I've had men that can do that," I lie in pathetic defense. My words come out garbled and trail off in a moan as his lips skim my breast and his tongue flicks against the peak of my nipple. My drunken courage only seems to piss him off. Wolfe bites down on my nipple and I cry out as tiny zaps of pleasure rush my core.

It hits me as I angle my hips closer to him without shame that this *is* what I want. What I always wished for with Evan, but I know now Evan wasn't capable of this. I never thought any man was...

"No, little hummingbird, you haven't, because you only just met me today." He moves his head down to the skin beneath my earlobe, my hands start to lose sensation under his clasp. Wolfe takes his time to breathe me in, running his nose along the column of my throat. "It's not wise to test that smart mouth with me. I'm already testing every bit of fucking patience I have with you in my space," he snarls, biting down hard on my earlobe.

I whimper in pain but outwardly, it sounds like pleasure.

"Pain doesn't scare you..." It isn't a question, it's an assessment, but I don't miss the tone of surprise that lines his voice. No, pain *does* scare me, I want to say in protest, but I don't. My body isn't listening to my mind like it should and right now my body is winning, hands down.

Wolfe's hand slides over the thin cotton of my panties and with a flick of a wrist he adds a slap to my pussy. I must be having an out of body experience because I moan again, *loudly*.

"You get off on it," he growls, his brow knotted in frustration,

"Why does that make you angry?" I ask breathlessly, silently begging for more.

"Because I want to do bad things to you.Very bad things. And knowing you won't try to stop me? It's dangerous for you."

Using his boot to kick my feet apart even wider, Wolfe holds me in place with his powerful body. His hardened cock presses against my hip, it feels just as big as his attitude portrays and it ignites me as I imagine it filling me in ways I've never been filled.

If I could use my hands, I'd slide them under his shirt just to see what this kind of man feels like. Just once.

Wolfe tears my flimsy panties off like they're made of tissue paper in one swift action, and I gasp, standing fully naked before this man I've just met, while he remains fully clothed, in his element, in control.

He holds the power.

Call it fear, call it alcohol, whatever you will, I'm so wet I'm dripping down my thighs.

"*Please*," I whine, then moan again, angling my hips toward him, not really knowing what I'm asking. The moment the word leaves my lips the faintest growl rumbles through his chest pressed against me.

"The fucking sounds you make, you might as well be asking me to eat you alive." Wolfe drops his lips to my neck, my collarbone, my shoulders, my breasts, trading between biting me and ravaging me with open mouthed kisses. As his palm slides further down my belly to the apex of my thighs, I wait with anticipation like putty in his hands.

Finally, the pad of his middle finger finds my clit and what little fight I had left to get away from him dies.

Instead, I close my eyes, push myself closer, let my body take over and beg him for more.

CHAPTER 11

Gabriel

I don't kiss women. Never thought the act was worth anything. When I was young, it was a necessary step to get me what I wanted, which was to come. When I stopped having to use it as a tool to get there, I just never did. There's never a need for niceties when women just take their clothes off and ask you to fuck them.

But I fight the need I feel to kiss Brinley now. Not to feed into her feelings or because I crave the softness of it. No, this is a carnal need I can't seem to shake. It has me wanting to bring every single part of her to my mouth so I can devour her, and then feast on the remains until there's nothing left. My fingers slide between her legs, and I groan against her mouth, still denying myself the kiss.

"Mmm...This soaking little pussy... all for the man you're afraid of?" I note.

She mewls into me with a quiet "*yes*" as two of my fingers sink into her hot, tight cunt.

So fucking tight it's like she's never been fucked.

"You're dripping down my hand, you want my fear and pain."

"I-I don't know," she murmurs softly as my fingers stretch her.

"Yeah, you do, you're making a mess, Brinley soaking my hand like this..." Just her name on my tongue has my cock begging. "*More,*" I tell her

She whines again as I try to make sense of this woman and her hold on me.

My dick throbs against my zipper. I haven't wanted like this in *so* long, maybe ever.

Her eyes grow wide as I stand over her, taking in the sight of her naked flesh while my fingers strum her clit, then slide into her at a slow, steady pace while I savor her every sound. Her body is perfection. She's all soft, silky and curvy with so many enticing places to grab that my mind can't settle on where to touch first.

Her little whimpers as I fuck my fingers into her admit what her lips refuse to. I run my tongue down the column of her throat, enjoying the foreign feeling of being turned on like this, simply by my mouth meeting her skin.

I wrap my lips around the hardened peak of her nipple, letting my teeth tug it lightly. She shudders and angles her hips up to me.

I smirk.

Doesn't want me, yet so greedy, so eager.

"I don't do this... I can't," she moans, totally out of control now as I start to work my fingers faster, sliding in and out of her arousal with ease as my thumb begins to offer her swollen clit friction.

"Yes you can. You already are," I encourage her. "*Take what you want.*"

I stroke her g-spot, and the way her eyes roll back tell me

she's never felt this before. The sounds of her wet pussy as my fingers work in and out of her is intoxicating while she gives me breathy little moans from the back of her throat.

I continue to flick my tongue over her pretty pink nipple. I can't get enough. She tastes as sweet as she smells.

"I don't even know you...please, I need..." Brinley's protest conflicts with her bucking hips as I once again curve my fingers to the place inside her that she needs to come completely apart. My eyes remain on hers as her pupils dilate and the flush of her cheeks grows. The sounds she's making, the way she's looking at me tells me this experience is all brand new to her. It makes me want to devour her even more.

"Please what, little hummingbird?" I toy with her as frustrated little whimpers leave her lips. "Tell me what you want from me. You want to use my fingers to come?"

"Yes." She gives, another jolt of electricity to my cock.

"Then, ask, use that smart mouth."

"I want to use you. Can I please use you?" she whispers shyly. It sounds like begging.

Fuck, this woman's sweet submissiveness was made for me.

"If I let you use me, you better do it right... make a *fucking* mess," I command as I continue fucking her with my fingers.

I let go of her wrists that I held above her head, and she doesn't hesitate for one second. Her hands slide under my shirt across my lower back. The feel of her soft, warm fingers against my skin sends fire through my body. I don't stop, I don't give her any reprieve as I press her deeper into the bookshelf. The second I feel her tight cunt clench around my fingers and her nails digging into my flesh, I pull my fingers from her and lay a tight slap to her clit and then smooth over the pain.

I force Brinley right to that edge as I slide three fingers back into her, her legs begin to shake as she starts to fall apart, and I almost come like a fucking school boy from her sounds.

She lets go and cries out as the orgasm is wrenched from her.

"Wolfe, *oh my god!*" Brinley moans and shudders, letting go. I hold her up while her legs shake and she drips down my hand.

Her breathing slows and her moans grow softer. I pull my fingers from her and slide her cum up over her clit. She shudders, so sensitive, so boneless in my arms. Bringing my fingers to my lips, I suck them clean one by one and then go back for more. She's so fucking sweet, I want every drop. I bring my hand back up, and spread her mess all over her lips, her chin, pressing into that little dimple, without thought I lick her there, tasting her.

Fucking Christ, it's like I can't get enough of her. I paint her plush, pillowy lips with her cum.

"Taste," I command, just wanting to watch her discover herself. Brinley licks her lips and her eyes flutter closed. The shred of control I'm holding firm to starts to waver as her tongue dusts across her lip again and the need to kiss her overwhelms me.

"Uh, Pres, so fuckin sorry, but you need to see this. *Now.*" I hear Jake's voice beyond as his fist pounds against my door.

Jake would never come to my private space if he wasn't desperate, but I still might put a bullet in his head regardless.

Brinley pants beneath my hands for a few seconds. I look down at her, sobering up from the heady air that hangs over us.

"When I make you come, *I* am your god. The only name you cry out is mine. Remember that for next time," I tell her.

"N-next time—" she starts, and I touch her lips, silencing her.

"Stay here."

She stares up at me wide eyed and I feel the pull from her

again, like she's trying to see into my soul. That is not a place she wants to go.

I don't say anything as I simply pull my cut off the bed and leave her standing naked in the middle of my room, the sweet scent of her pussy still coats my fingers, my taste buds. Without glancing back, I open my door and lock it from the inside, closing it behind me.

"This better be fucking life or death," I tell Jake, and I've never meant anything more.

CHAPTER 12

Gabriel

I pull the blanket down over my head to cover the noise. Things are breaking again; Mom is crying again. I start to hum to myself, the song Mom taught me. "Hotel California" over and over.

"Sing this to yourself when you hear him like that. Close your eyes and it will all be over soon, little warrior," she would tell me.

The party still sounds in the background, people shouting, why don't they stop him? Why don't they protect her? I hear the sickening thud of his fist hitting her face.

"You let him fucking look at you? At what's mine?"

"No, I didn't, Shamus." Another thud.

"Don't lie to me, bitch." I hear my father's angry voice. The one that tells me Mom is going to get hurt. I squeeze my eyes shut and sing louder to myself but it doesn't drown them out.

My mother falls to the wooden floor and I see her staring back at me, she smiles, her one eye is already swelling.

"It's okay. Close your eyes. Sing, baby," she croaks.

It's then that I see him climb on top of her and before I can stop myself I'm crawling out from under the bed and rushing to plant myself on top of her between them. I've never been so scared.

I look up at him, maybe he'll hit me a few times before he hits her again.

Dad's fist is raised to come down but he looks at me, like he's looking right through me. The door opens and my uncle comes in.

"That's enough, Switch." The deep voice of my uncle echoes in the quiet room. He uses my dad's nickname.

My dad drops his fist. I try not to cry, happy my uncle is here. Dad never disobeys my uncle. He smirks at me and it makes me wish I was strong. Strong enough to hurt him. I try so hard not to cry. If I cry, he'll hit me. I wish I could make him bleed the way he makes her bleed.

"You'll get your chance, little wolf," my uncle tells me like he's reading my thoughts.

I know he's the boss. They call him Pres. My dad is VP. I look back at my uncle as my dad gets up off my mom and shakes his bloody fist out.

"Stace," my uncle calls out to my aunt. "Come and help clean Theresa up."

"She was letting Tank stare at her ass," Dad offers, but my uncle doesn't waste one second, he punches my dad in the face and blood spurts from his lips.

"You can rough her up, you can't fucking render her unconscious. Get some fucking self control." My uncle is the only man on earth scarier than Dad but I know he'd never hurt me. The blood trickles down my dad's chin. It makes me... happy.

I smile at the same second my dad's eyes look to mine. He makes his way over to me quickly and grabs my pajama shirt in his fist.

I whimper.

"One day, you'll be old enough for me to wipe that smirk right off your face, you little shit."

My smile fades with his words. He always threatens me when he drinks this much whiskey.

All I can think is when that day comes, I'll be ready.

"Warrior," my mother says as she puts her hand over mine beside me. "Gabe. My little warrior."

I sit up in a cold sweat and rub my eyes with the heels of my palms. 5:45 a.m. It's been twenty-four years, and I still dream about the night I vowed to make my father suffer. These dreams reoccur, mixed with the day I watched the life drain from her eyes—all because of him.

The sound of thunder rolls out the window. It's pitch-black outside and I'm still in the chapel with my men; it looks like the sun hasn't even come up yet. I focus and take in the sight of Mason and Robby sleeping sitting up on the sofa across the desk from me. Kai sits awake at the desk watching the security footage at the DOS safe house, drinking a coffee from a paper cup.

We went in shifts, rotating between watching and sleeping. Word that they'd pull Gator from the safe house after finding us in Lakeshore yesterday spread last night, and we've got members on watch in person while we stay posted here, watching the cameras, ready to move if they do. On the flip side, Kai finished up a loop that will run to their feed when we go today, exactly at noon, to get him when he's the least protected. As much danger as they think he's in, we're betting on his detail's weekly need to get his dick wet.

"Morning, boss," Kai says to me. "Sleep well?" he asks, knowing I fucking didn't.

"As well as you did," I say, my voice thick with hardly any sleep.

"I'm going to get some time in with the bag," I tell him. I

need it. Our clubhouse has a gym with heavy bags and weights, it's nothing like my usual space but it does in a pinch when I've got a million things on my shoulders and I'm already fighting the memory of Brinley from hours ago the moment I fully wake up. I'm instantly hard again with no outlet. Fucking shit is painful, and I'm not used to it.

I want nothing more than to go fuck that tight pussy I've been dreaming about since I saw her at that coffee shop ten days ago, but that will have to wait. I can't be distracted for even one second today.

I clap him on the shoulder. "You good here for a few?" It's a rhetorical question. I know he is.

"Yeah, I'm gonna wake Robby soon and I'll sleep for a bit."

I nod, then stand and stretch, wondering if Brinley listened and stayed in my room. There's a part of her that wants the darker side I can give her. I saw it in her eyes when she came all over my hand. I know now I won't stop until I unearth it completely and absorb it all for myself. Her torn panties burn a hole in my pocket as I stake my claim.

Once I make a decision, I never waiver or ask myself why. What I know is, I want Brinley Rose Beaumont in a way I can't comprehend, and I'm nowhere near done uncovering the darkness in her.

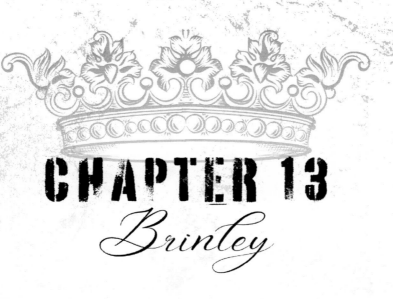

CHAPTER 13
Brinley

Ow... I open my eyes to the sound of my phone buzzing on the floor.

I think I passed out. I quickly close them when I realize it hurts to look... anywhere and I'm in a stranger's bed. Oh my god, everything starts playing through my mind like a movie—a horror movie I let myself be a part of. I didn't stop it, I didn't make him stop, I *wanted* him. More than I've ever wanted a man and I have no idea why. I just know I need to get out of here.

> Sorry I fell asleep in a bedroom. I don't know whose it is.

I lie, embarrassed to have been Wolfe's toy for the night, or *one* of them.

PB

> Liar. Wolfe is up and, in the gym, he said you stayed in his room. Excuse me while I pick my jaw up off the floor Miss "How could you be with a man like that?"

Shit.

> We didn't have sex. I was so drunk.

I flip over quickly in a panic and realize the door is still locked. I don't think he's been in here since he left. My poor head is pounding but I don't have time to think about that. I scramble. The last thing I need is for Wolfe to come back and have to do the walk of torrid shame past him to get out of here. It hits me then that I questioned Layla on her involvement with Sean, and yet I walked right into Wolfe's room, into his trap, without question.

I pull my dress up over my still naked body. It's only 7:30 a.m. I don't remember anything after he left other than passing out cold in his bed. I search frantically for my panties but they're quite literally nowhere to be found and then I remember they were torn from my body. I start to rummage through the cabinets in his small kitchen area desperate for some sort of helper for my headache, all I find are supplements, vitamins, electrolytes. Who is this man?

Everything is neat and organized. I find myself wondering if he lives here all the time. I move to his private bathroom, it's barren and neat also. I manage to score regular Tylenol in the medicine cabinet and gratefully swallow two down with a bottle of water from his compact fridge.

I throw my heels on with one hand and grab my purse with the other, flipping the comforter up to see if I can find my ruined panties. I don't.

I open my app and order an Uber. The sooner it gets here, the better. I need to sleep, and I wanted to take my dad's truck to *Alchemy Customs*. On the upside, I will have the whole day to do it because there's no chance I'm going to this wedding. Layla is just going to have to understand.

"You don't have to lie. I think it's good for you to dig your heels into some life experience, and he just went into town with Robby, so you can stop looking around for him," Layla says, thoroughly enjoying this as I walk into the main hall of the clubhouse.

The entire party from last night is cleaned up and everything is back in order. It smells like bacon and eggs. My stomach growls, but I know I have to get the hell out of here. I look around the table at the girls enjoying a leisurely breakfast.

"We did not have sex, I wasn't lying," I whisper-yell to her while the other three girls in her crew snicker. I check on my Uber to pull my gaze from theirs.

"But he definitely gave you a life altering orgasm," Amber states, leaning back in her chair.

I look at her. "Do you guys just share everything? And I am being honest. No sex—none, zip, zero." I make the zero hand motion and eye Layla's coffee. It smells so good.

"I didn't say sex. There's no way you slept in that man's bed, because *no one* sleeps in his bed. I actually don't even think anyone's ever been in his *room*," Amber says as she looks at the other girls for confirmation.

"That's how you get your tits ripped off." Maria snickers

"Exactly... so don't tell us he didn't make you come. Hell, there are times just looking at him almost does it for me," Chantel says with a grin.

I don't know why but I don't like her talking about Wolfe like that. I have no claim on him after one orgasm. Okay, one *really* intense orgasm.

The best I've ever had.

My face contorts as I try yet again to understand what it was about him that made me leave every value and moral I'm proud of at his bedroom door.

Maria takes in the look on my face and starts laughing. "Told you."

"Oh god." I put my head in my hands. "Never again. Seeing him tonight will be humiliating," I tell them as I steal a piece of Layla's bacon and start nibbling nervously.

Layla reaches out and grabs my forearm. "Hey. Snap out of it," she says, backhanding me in the arm.

I nod like a nervous schoolgirl.

"You aren't some weak woman who got tricked into anything with Wolfe. If you were attracted to him, that's okay. If I'm guessing right, and I know I am by the way, you kept looking at him last night too. It was hot, whatever happened—"

"Her really good orgasm she definitely didn't have." Amber giggles.

I look at her and half smile in defeat. These girls are just so free and although I'm not used to it, it's kind of nice not having to feel bad about myself all the time or trying to be 'better' because I think someone expects more from me. It's nice to be me, mistakes and all.

"It was really, really good," I give, and all four girls laugh hysterically.

"You deserve it. You don't have to worry about it being weird at all. He isn't the relationship type, I told you that. He isn't going to want that from you," Layla says.

"Hell, you'll be lucky if he even remembers your name, new girl." Chantel snickers. It stings me just a little even though I already knew it. But what can I expect when I just gave my body over to him so easily?

"You *are* coming to my wedding. I see that look on your

face. Don't think you're getting out of it. I want you there, it's not a mistake that you're home now, Brin. Let's dance, have fun, and maybe you'll go back to your room alone, maybe you won't. But this space"—Layla uses her hand in a circular motion to all the girls—"it's a judgement-free zone. So you hooked up with Wolfe a little? *Own* it. Go home, take a shower, for God's sake, clean yourself up, you smell like vodka. I walk down the aisle at sunset," she says as happily as she takes a bite of toast.

I laugh, feeling oddly better.

Looking at Layla, I realize she's right. For the first time in my life, the only person I owe an explanation to this morning is me.

"Own it," I repeat. "Just like that, no big deal?"

"Just like that. You've got this," Layla confirms. "Act like he was lucky to make you come." She winks, and my mouth falls open as she laughs. "Embrace what *you* want, Brin. Stop berating yourself."

"Okay, yes, a mistake like that is fine as long as I learn from it." I mentally cringe, sounding just like my mother.

"Or don't learn from it and just be glad you had fun." Layla grins, shoving eggs into her mouth.

My phone dings and I see that my Uber is here. I smile at them and give Layla a hug, motioning goodbye to the other girls before nabbing a piece of road bacon.

"Hey, Brin, make sure you look hot," she calls over her shoulder as I make my way to the door. "Make him eat his heart out. You have the pussy. You have the power," Layla yells way too loudly considering the amount of people milling about.

My cheeks turn a bright shade of pink as I steal out the clubhouse door into the pouring rain and into the back of the Uber. I slink down in the seat as I greet my driver, breathing a sigh of relief as he three-point turns his way out the driveway.

The last thing I see before we cross the gate is Wolfe getting out of a gunmetal black Dodge Ram with Robby, who's holding a tray with a bunch of large sized coffees in it.

Wolfe looks right at me.

It's obvious I'm fleeing the scene and I want to die a slow death from embarrassment. I lean back in the seat.

He's definitely a bad decision, maybe the worst one I could make at this time in my life. But something about the way he looks at me has me wanting to make it.

Over and over again.

CHAPTER 14

Gabriel

I pull my mask off and inspect the paint mix Kai has just tested. It's for the Harley gas tank I'm hand-spraying a hexagon pattern on the base. We snuck into the garage to get it done before we go get Gator when his protection leaves for his Saturday whore call. Not exactly conventional when we're planning something like we are today, but sometimes the line between keeping my legal business running while dealing with all the day-to-day of my club is a struggle.

I'm already later than I hoped because chapel ran late and I had to have a talk with Mason, reminding him he can't kill Gator the moment we get him into the van. We need to know who gave him the order to seek out Mason's little sister and who ransacked two of our Atlanta clinics over the last month.

We're sure we know, but we need that confirmation so we don't start a needless war that puts my club at risk.

"Needs more sheen," I say to Kai, knowing exactly what my client wants. He's fussy, and with any luck this job will be done today and be one less thing I have to worry about. "He wants it like a glossy lipstick—the exact shade his fiancée wears." I hand him the image of the color again so he can match the sheen.

I picture the shade on Brinley's full lips, and my cock swells at the thought. The irony isn't lost on me that I'm usually pushing women out the door, but the one I actually let stay in my room last night snuck out and hid from me in the backseat of her Uber this morning.

Something I'll be teaching her? She doesn't leave until I tell her she can leave.

Kai takes the card with the lipstick shade and puts it in his coverall pocket.

"That's fucking sick, by the way, man." Kai nods to the work I'm doing.

Airbrushing hand drawn, intricate designs is my specialty. This one will have the beehive pattern and the Harley logo embedded into it when we're done.

I'm just about to get back to it when what sounds like a loud backfire echoes outside the garage. It makes us both flinch and drop what we're working on. I shut off the compressor my airbrush is hooked up to and stalk toward the half open, overhead door. I pull it up wide, knowing it won't be anything too threatening since we're in the middle of downtown Harmony.

I can't say what I was expecting to find in my yard, but anything else isn't comparable in the slightest to what actually greets me.

My little hummingbird. In the tightest cutoff jean shorts she could mold to her body and a loose black tank top. She's focused and struggling to lift the hood of a rusted-out piece of shit Ford.

She might as well be wearing a big red bow and a gift tag addressed just to me.

I hold my hand out across Kai's chest to block his fast approach. I don't fucking think so.

He smirks and chuckles before turning around and heading back inside. Brinley gets the hood up miraculously and pins it in place. I watch as she waves smoke out and her tank blows around the dip of her curvy waist, enticing me to rip the shorts from her body and devour the fucking sweetest pussy I've ever tasted. And I would do it right here in the middle of my parking lot.

I stand for a minute while she doesn't realize I'm here just watching her, wondering who the fuck's truck this is. It's not in that bad of shape for being original but it definitely needs some work. I pull my mask down from my forehead and let it dangle around my neck, wiping the sweat from my brow with the sleeve of my t-shirt.

I've seen enough of the back of her, now I want to see the front, so I clear my throat.

She spins around instantly and when she realizes it's me, her mouth falls slack.

Her hair is in a high ponytail and her pretty heart-shaped face is center stage.

Motherfucking thunderstruck.

Brinley makes an effort to close her pouty lips. *Shame.*

She's a goddamn smoke show.

"*What the...* seriously?" she asks under her breath as she puts her phone in her back pocket, her breathing shallow.

Her polite annoyance fuels me further. I fucking love how flustered she is.

I want more.

"I just..." I watch the pink start to creep up her throat and I almost feel her pulse start to increase. "I barely got this thing here. How are you *everywhere?*" she asks,

"If by everywhere, you mean the town I live in and the business I own, I think it's obvious," I deadpan.

"Right, my neighbor said you were the best," she says as she folds her hands in front of her. I'm starting to recognize this is Brinley's way of centering herself when she feels like she's over-stepped or when she's nervous, another thing she's probably been trained to do.

I can't wait to retrain her to never fucking apologize.

"We are," I tell her. "Custom body work and paint—which you clearly need. Next door, Big Mike's does everything on the inside, which you also seem to need," I say, eyeing her steaming truck.

"I don't think... I can just take it to Taylor's. That's where my dad went, I only came here because Mr. Kennedy seems reliable—"

"Taylor's doesn't do body work anymore," I interrupt her. "And why wouldn't you want the best?"

"It's just, well... dammit." Brinley straightens her shoulders before speaking like she's answering a question in a beauty pageant. "In case you haven't noticed, this isn't easy for me. I don't do things like what we did last night. And I don't have a lot of money." Her eyes meet mine and I shamelessly stare. "Plus..." she starts.

I let her stumble over her words.

"I need the work done on this truck to be above board," Brinley says, looking up at me, interrupting my hungry roam of her body with my gaze.

I raise an eyebrow and pull my gloves off, moving toward her, eating up the ten feet between us to get a closer look at her truck and fuck, I just want to smell her.

Brinley backs against the hood as I approach, not knowing what to do, the pink starting to return. I breathe in her jasmine scent and reach out, grabbing her belt loops with my first two fingers, tugging her to me. Her mouth pops open and I almost turn savage with the need to stick my tongue into it.

The fuck? Get it together. Jesus Christ.

I wait a few seconds just enjoying her struggle then drop my hand.

Her breath hitches like she thinks I may hurt her. If she keeps looking at me like this, I might, but I'd make sure she fucking loved it.

I reach into Brinley's front pocket and pull her keys out. I let go of her and she moves quickly between her truck and the car beside it, trying to get out of my way. I have a quick look at the disaster in front of me.

"What you brought me is a half eaten electrical system. Probably mice, I don't even know how you made it here."

"Crap," she mutters, looking down then back into my eyes.

"It's not normal for a truck this age to have this wiring. Did someone restore this?" I ask as I continue to inspect.

"My dad," Brinley answers, tightening her long ponytail.

I watch the worry grow on her face, seeing the dollar signs add up as I tell her all the things she's going to have to replace.

"Big Mike will give you a detailed breakdown, but..." I think for a second. "Are you planning on selling it? Is that why you want to have it fixed?"

"Yeah, I was thinking about it. For the front porch Layla mentioned last night."

"We can work something out," I tell her, closing the hood. I crouch down and start at the front of the truck, running my hand along to scan the body,

"I, um... just don't want to be involved in anything... less than above board," she says.

This woman really has no idea what it means to be socially aware. She's basically insinuating I'm a criminal. I mean, I am, but still.

I stand and start to make my way to the back of the truck, sandwiching her against the truck. She backs up, as if she could disappear into it but not before every part of me grazes every part of her and that fluttering pulse lights up at her throat. I pause against her just because I want to feel her.

"You don't know me and you don't trust me," I tell her the obvious, caging her in with both my hands on either side of her. "But we'll get one thing straight right now. I don't like being an assumption. This *is* an above-board business you're at."

"Okay," she says. "S-sorry I wasn't sure."

"Because I run a motorcycle club, you think I'm going to rip you off?" I ask her.

I push off the truck and uncage her, putting space between us. Brinley takes a deep, shaky breath, but she doesn't move.

I pop a glove back on and run my hand across the bottom part of her door. Rust falls off as I go. "I'm less likely to rip you off *because* I run a motorcycle club. Street sense 101. We have integrity," I tell her.

"Of course." Brinley agrees but only out of fear.

"How bad is it?" she asks, changing the subject, watching me check the rest of the truck over. I stand and stuff my gloves in the back pocket of my coveralls.

"It's rough. It's a lot of work to restore the body. That hasn't ever been done before, has it?"

"I don't think so," she says, confirming what I already know.

"We'll make it the same robin's egg blue it's supposed to be now."

"How much will it be?" she asks, blocking the sun from her eyes with her hand.

"Like I said, we can work something out." I move closer to her. "You don't pay me or Mike until you sell it. You'll get double the restoration cost. I can guarantee it. I even know some people who may be interested in buying."

Brinley drops her hand, and her eyes hold the sun. It turns them such a light shade of blue they almost take my breath away. She looks at the truck then back at me.

"Can I think about it?"

"Nope." I drop her keys into my pocket. "No one else will look after you the way I will. It would also be a safety hazard for me to just let you drive it home."

She gives a haughty look to deter me but it only serves to show me the smallest spark of fire I know is lurking under her prim and proper surface.

"I wasn't going to drive home. The neighbor I was telling you about? He offered, he's picking me up—" she says at the precise moment a little beige sedan pulls into the parking lot.

I'm ready to tell her I'll be driving her home, not some fucking guy I don't know, when I see he's about seventy-five years old. He waves at her with a wrinkly smile and then at me and I realize he's a customer of Mike's.

"Yeah okay, give me your phone," I tell her, waving at him.

Brinley looks as if she's unsure, and I start to lose a little patience.

I hold my hand out. "You expect Mike to call the price out to you down the middle of Main?" I ask her gruffly.

She reaches into her pocket without looking away, unlocks it and hands it to me, folding her hands in front of her while she waits. I add my information to it, text myself and hold it back out to her. She goes to take it and I pull it away.

Brinley scoffs and that little spark surfaces again as she reaches.

"We're not ten, just give it back." She looks back at her happy neighbor. "I don't want to make him wait."

I decide I like Brinley Beaumont a little annoyed and fired up.

"Make sure you answer it when I call," I tell her firmly, unmoving. She looks up at it then back at me. "Fine," she says, reaching for the phone. I let her take it and she practically runs from me to the passenger side of the old man's car, stuffing it in her pocket.

"Goodbye, Mr. Wolfe," she says in a tone that's meant to be businesslike but makes my cock twitch as she slinks into the front seat.

See you soon, hummingbird. Real soon.

CHAPTER 15

Brinley

I can't shake this man. He owns the only body shop in town? Aren't outlaws supposed to do like, outlaw things as opposed to working a nine-to-five job like everyone else?

I must be losing my mind because I left my dad's pride and joy—albeit rusty pride and joy—with the biker president who sucks all the air from my lungs. Especially when he's all masculine and dirty from working with his strong hands and bike parts all morning. I'm putting myself into an environment where I will see him *again* tonight.

I text Layla as Mr. Kennedy cruises through town singing to John Prine on the local country station.

> I thought you said he'd be ignoring me by now?

PB

He should be.

> Well, he's not, in fact he seems to want to unnerve me every chance he gets

PB

Interesting. I've never seen this before. You're like a shiny new toy.

I roll my eyes

Lucky me.

PB

A science experiment of sorts one would say.

This isn't funny, he has my dad's truck. He better not use it to whack anyone.

PB

Oh my god, I promise he won't whack anyone.

Now can you please just take your pretty ass home and get packing? You should be leaving to come see my stunning royal self in less than four hours.

I barely have myself packed when I get a phone call from Big Mike himself an hour later confirming the price to fix my truck. I'm not even finished that conversation when a text comes through.

W

Change of plans. Pack light and do not leave on your own, understand?

I pull my phone back from my face to look at the text as I finish my conversation with Mike.

I just stare at it for a solid minute after I hang up. I start to type but then stop myself. I've seen too much of him in the last two days. I need a little distance to think clearly.

I flip my phone over on the kitchen counter.

I know it's childish but it's easier to just pretend I didn't see it, and besides, I don't have to answer to him anyway. As I finish packing, I remind myself there will be women everywhere tonight—lots of them. More than enough to steal his attention. As I make sure everything is clean and ready for me to leave for the night, I settle with the idea that Wolfe is just paying attention to me because I didn't fawn all over him this morning. And maybe the big, all-powerful president isn't used to that.

No matter how much I try not to think about him, his words echo in the deep baritone of his voice this morning when he told me to make sure I answer his call.

Whatever. I think I'm sort of done doing *every* single thing everyone tells me.

He'll get over it.

CHAPTER 16
Gabriel

There's a type of adrenaline, a rush you get from planning something and executing it perfectly, managing to keep all your men safe.

Robby cuts through the fencing at the side of the DOS safe house. We've received word that one of Gator's protection backups has just arrived at his regular escort's motel room. Gator's never alone but this is the closest he'll get.

He's hiding out like a fucking bitch.

I should be laser focused. I should have a one-track mind to get in, grab Gator, and get the fuck out, but I don't. I'm goddamn distracted by the woman who hasn't answered my text all morning, after I specifically told her to and it's pissing me off.

"How are we?" Robby asks Kai over the walkie. Kai is in our service van on Country Road 3—the only road that leads to this dilapidated piece of shit house.

"Clear," Kai says back. "Loop is still up and running on their security system, so be quick."

Robby, Ax, and I squeeze through the gaping hole in the

fence that's in the woods at the back of the property and we wait. We've been studying these grounds for almost two weeks, we've got the land deeds, and we know every single person coming and going. We're ready and we're not leaving here without the man who stole Mason's little sister's innocence. One rule we live by? Women and kids are off fucking limits. Break those rules, you die, no matter who you are.

I listen for sound, for movement, anything, but there's nothing. Just insects and nature. The rain from this morning has been gone for hours but the grass is still damp under our boots.

"Go," I tell Ax, pointing in the direction of the house that's over a hundred yards away. We take off, moving steadily through the trees and pop out near the backside of the house. My gun is a comforting and familiar weight in my hands as we make our way through the clearing between the woods and the back of this shithole they're calling home. The moment my boot touches the edge of the clearing gunshots fill the air. We expected that.

I look back to Robby to check that he's still good. He ducks behind a barrel, while Ax and I duck behind the deck rail. The deck is cluttered with furniture and old tires for us to take cover. We assess the direction the bullets fly from and how many shooters there are. Time moves oddly slow when you're in a combat situation.

It's the body's way to fight for survival. Your training kicks in and you begin to run on autopilot and instinct. You become hyper aware of everything around you—the way the trees move, any creak in the floorboards, the wind. Everything.

I take aim and blast an empty beer can on the opposite side of the deck from where I am, hoping whoever is inside of the house isn't as smart as I am. I'm happy to find out he isn't as he pushes the door open and shoots. I snipe him behind the ear and he drops lifeless to the deck, and I wait. I knew him, he was a rank-and-file member—sloppy, always high. There's usually two of them here at this time of day, so we wait for the second target for a few minutes, even though we know we only have a forty-five-minute window before number three is back. The absence of our second shooter makes me nervous.

I get my eyes on Robby and point to the side window. Not a chance we're going in the back to be sitting ducks for Gator. I creep along the side of the deck until I'm under the window and pull a small pocket mirror out of my cut, using it to see inside. A shaky hand holding a Glock 17 points toward the back door. I wait.

Call it a side effect from growing up with my father. Patience. The ability to stay calm in an intense situation. I *could* go off half cocked and shoot the gun out of his hand or I could wait for a better shot and determine if this is, in fact, Gator shooting at us and if he's alone. He doesn't know I'm here, so I have the advantage. He inches forward, and I confirm it is Gator. He's seen better days. Hole yourself up virtually alone in a cabin with various painkillers and booze, and I suppose you'd look the same—dirty, skittish, afraid.

It's why I've never put that garbage in my body. It's a weaker man's escape.

The moment I get a clear shot through the window, I take it. I don't want to kill him. Yet.

We're gonna have some fun with him first and help him understand exactly why fucking with a sixteen-year-old is a bad fucking decision.

My shot hits Gator square in his right shoulder and he drops his arm, his gun clattering to the floor. I look back to Robby, then to Ax who's still behind the deck rail and point to the back door. Ax takes off to climb the deck and I cover him. If Gator manages to reach for his gun, he'll be down a hand before he ever picks it up.

I signal for Robby to move. He busts through the front door and kicks Gator's gun to the other side of the room. I keep my eyes firmly planted on Robby's figure through the window as he moves through the tiny house.

"Clear," he sounds to let me know we're good to go.

I pull my walkie out of my back pocket. "Still good?" I ask Kai. "We're securing the package now."

"All good," Kai responds.

Minutes later, after I've gagged and dragged Gator's heavy ass almost all the way across the property, a bike speeds down the old drive of the house and its young rider hops off it in seconds, firing at us. I turn to face him and hold Gator like a human shield. Like I said, I don't want him to die yet but if it's him or me.

New guy runs toward us trying to dart behind junk throughout the yard. I'm pretty sure he's a prospect. He's nervous, it's obvious by the way he shoots, everything is going wide or high and the closer he gets we can see he's shaking.

Someone just sent this kid out here at the wrong time. *Should have just kept on driving by, kid.*

Robby takes a shot and hits the kid in the right shoulder. He drops to the ground, and we make it to the treeline with his garbled sounds echoing in the distance just as Kai and Mason bust through the trees for back up.

"Going soft?" I chuckle to Robby as I stuff the feet of a whining and roughed up Gator in the back of the van. It's still covered in the prospect's blood from last night and he's out cold in the back. Gator's eyes grow wide when he sees another member of his club and that adrenaline I always chase courses through my veins.

"He's a kid, man. Fuck, can't be more than seventeen. Jesus, what the fuck is going on with this club?" Robby asks rhetorically, smacking Gator's head into the van wall.

"I hear ya," I say. "The kid will tell the club we took you," I say to Gator. "Maybe they'll try to come and save you." I chuckle knowing they sure as hell won't.

Gator mumbles something against his gag. He's scared shitless, he knows he's fucked.

"Try not to bleed too much on my shit," I add before slamming the door shut.

"That was easy. I was hoping you would've had to blow out one of his kneecaps to get him here," Mason says, looking around as we move up to the passenger's side door to tell him he and Kai are good to go.

I shrug. "Sometimes it's easy, sometimes it's not." I pat him on the arm. "Patience. We've got him and he's all yours."

I look around, no one in sight, still fifteen minutes before his number three is back.

Ax, Robby, and I get into my truck behind the van.

"Time to gut some squids, boys," I say over the walkie to Kai's van. The men in my truck and Kai all shout out their own forms of "Fuck yes." And I grin.

Today's major problem is down.

Now to school my defiant little hummingbird in the art of doing what she's told.

CHAPTER 17

Brinley

By exactly 2:15 p.m. I'm ready to head out the door in my standard skinny jeans and Chucks toward my car when I hear the rumble of bikes. I grab my bag, shut everything off and rush, determined to get out of my driveway, just in case. But by the time I get to the porch it's apparent something is already blocking it. A Harley. A rather fancy one I didn't see the first day I saw Wolfe downtown. This one is a soft matte black and looks like a beautiful custom job.

But the bike isn't what has my attention now. It's the man leaning against the seat. The very man I've done my best to avoid all day, looking like heartbreak and the most dangerous kind of sin.

For the first time since I laid eyes on him, I admit it openly to myself with no hesitation.

Wolfe is so gorgeous it's almost suffocating, and for some insane reason he's sitting in my driveway waiting for *me*.

"I guess owning the best body shop in town has its perks?" I ask, nodding to the bike.

He's wearing another pair of black jeans that fit him perfectly and a black t-shirt under his cut. Wolfe doesn't answer me; he just settles in, so I try to coax him again.

"You lost?" I ask, trying my best to appear cool and collected. I'm clearly not cool or collected any more than he is lost. In fact, Wolfe looks completely at home in my driveway. I stand frozen as he unfolds his arms, and I wonder why he's insisting on being here right now.

"I told you to answer me," he says, sounding irritated. His eyes bore into mine. "Good thing I'm early. You clearly were just about to leave alone."

I shrug. "You didn't call, you texted, and you're not *my* president."

As soon as the words leave my mouth, I regret them. I don't know what it is about him that makes me have no filter and put my foot in my mouth like this.

I shrink right into my chucks when he lifts off the bike to his full imposing height and strides closer to me. His jaw is set so hard it looks like he's about to pop a tendon.

"Do you remember what I told you about that smart mouth?" he asks,

Visions of us together begin to fill my mind. I nod.

"Next time, you *will* answer me. Now. Let's go." His jaw sets again.

"Go?" I ask, unmoving.

"You're riding with me," he says.

I look at the bike behind Wolfe then back up at him.

"No, I'm driving my car. After last night, I think I'd like to be able to get away if something else blows up." I look up at him, now only a few inches from me, and try to figure out the best way to be honest with him. I nervously tap my foot when he says nothing because he just makes me so on edge.

"I've never even sat on a bike before, let alone ridden one and I don't plan on starting today. It just isn't me. I think we can both admit we're not each other's types. What happened last night was a one-time thing. I had too much to drink," I say in one continuous sentence as bravely as I can.

Wolfe looks down at me, almost in amusement.

"Mm-hmm. You mean, when you begged me to let you come?"

I ignore him. Even his dirty words make me feel all sorts of want I can't understand, so I just continue.

"You have your lifestyle, and I have mine and mine is not... like yours. I just don't fit in with—"

Wolfe rolls his eyes and grunts, losing patience with me. "Enough," he says in a no argument kind of tone. "After last night's threat, you're not going to Tybee alone. No one is." He gives a practical excuse I wasn't expecting. I open my mouth to speak but nothing comes out.

His eyes drift there in response and I watch his throat work to swallow before his eyes meet mine again. He leans into me; his voice gets lower, and my mouth turns to sand.

"It's not negotiable and I'm getting tired of you not listening to me." He simply motions his head toward his bike.

"I..." I start to speak but I have no words. I can't believe he gets away with speaking to women like this. I look at the road, then back at him, pushing myself to be bolder than I was yesterday. He isn't going to hurt me in the middle of my quiet family orientated street.

"I'm not going to just let you command me, I don't like it."

"Then don't fight me," he says like it's a no brainer, sensing my obvious hesitation to go with him. Wolfe puts his hands on each of my shoulders and leans down over my lips, momentarily stunning me into submission.

"Get on the fucking bike, Brinley." This tone is lower and more commanding than his usual velvety one. As soon as he uses it, I know my fight is over because despite all of my internal protests, the way he orders me around, in that deep octave, sinks beneath my skin as if its only destination is my core. He doesn't wait for me to answer him, he simply slides his hands down my arms and turns and walks away, like he has no doubt I'll follow.

And, of course, I do.

One arm reaches out to me as I approach, taking my small bag from me, securing it with his on the wide bike. Wolfe turns, analyzing me. The only thing I can do is stand nervously and let him. I fold my hands in front of me.

He looks down and notices, then surprises me by reaching out a hand to separate them as his brows knot. Looking back up to my face, his hand reaches around to the back of my head and he pulls the claw clip I have out of my hair. His eyes stay on mine as all my hair tumbles down around my shoulders, but I don't move, taking in the way he looks at me, almost like he's angry as he stares down at me. Something as simple as pulling out my hair clip and I'm pooling in my panties for this man. Wolfe lifts a smaller black helmet up and sets it on my head, clipping it in place under my chin, tightening the strap with his big fingers until it's a perfect fit. Then he adds the matching jacket off the back of his bag. I shrug it off as he tries to place it on my shoulders.

"How many women have you lent these to?" I ask, wrinkling my nose. I can tell I'm pushing him because the sound he makes in response is like a type of frustrated growl.

"Little brat," Wolfe says as he pulls the jacket back down around me firmly, forcing me to put it on. In truth, it's light and so soft and fits me perfectly as he zips it up. "This is a day of firsts for both of us," he says, looking down at me all dressed in his leather.

"Oh?" I ask

"You've never been on a bike, which was obvious before you told me," he says curtly. "And no woman has been on mine —ever."

My mouth falls open as he climbs onto his bike and directs me to my place where I'll sit behind him.

"Keep your feet here." He points to the foot pegs. I struggle to straddle it but manage.

"Assume everything is hot," he says over his shoulder as I settle on the bike, taking my place behind him. God, he smells so good. Leather, spice, and that hint of smoke from the clubhouse.

Fight it, Brinley runs through my mind but my body isn't listening.

Traitor.

I make an awkward little dance of trying to place my hands on his shoulders then his side, but Wolfe isn't having it.

"You hold me here," he says, securely wrapping my arms around his waist, giving my hands a squeeze when he's happy with where they rest against him. I'm helpless to fight him as he reaches down and grips both my thighs, pulling me forward until I'm snug against his back.

"Don't let go, little bird," he says low over his shoulder.

The roar of the bike coming to life between my thighs sends a kind of rush I've never felt in my life through my blood.

As Wolfe backs out of my driveway and onto my street, I see Sean with Layla, Jake, and Kai on bikes of their own. Kai waves with a big goofy grin on his face. I wave back, he's the happiest one in the group but the brutal way he fucked his fingers into that woman last night without shame tells me he's still one of them. I make eye contact with the bride next. I might kill her for not warning me I would be getting an escort to her wedding.

Wolfe takes his place, front and center and leads the rest of the pack behind him. It only takes ten minutes to get through town. When we hit the outskirts of Harmony and Wolfe's speed picks up with the open highway before us, I grip him so tightly I must be cutting his circulation off, but if I am he doesn't seem to mind. I lean my head on his back as we reach a travelling speed.

The wind whips my hair, the only scent I breathe is him and his bike and I smile wide. I anticipated hating this, but I've never felt so free.

Our drive passes fairly quickly; we ride through another small village on the way to Tybee. People around these parts seem used to seeing HOH riding through, so no one pays us any mind aside from a few cautious glances as we cruise through the small Georgia town, passing pecan stands and farms on our way. We only stop once at the town's main light but when Wolfe slides his hand back and rubs the side of my thigh it feels almost as if he's checking in on me. The way his large, chiseled hand looks on my leg doesn't help to keep my panties dry with my arms wrapped around his thick torso.

There's something so sure and confident about Wolfe, it trickles down to everything he does, even the steadiness with which he rides. Like he never has a single thought of self doubt run through his mind. It's such a different feeling from any man I've ever been around. I know he has no qualms about violence. I know he has to be ruthless to run this club. But right now it's so conflicting because I can't help but feel safe with this man that I shouldn't. At this moment the only things I feel are protected and thought of.

When we reach the resort, I'm stupefied. It's absolutely stunning in person. The sun is bright, like the whole sky has opened up above us. The ocean sparkles in the background of the sprawling white estate. It sits on acres of secluded wooded property with multiple docks that stretch from the main building to the ocean. One enormous main building, that appears to be made mostly of windows, gives way to so many little cottages behind it that sit at the base of the ocean. There's nothing else around for what feels like miles.

I climb off his bike and remove my helmet, taking it all in. The air smells salty and fresh. My hair moves around my face in the ocean breeze as the sun sits over the water. The roar of the waves seems like the only sound.

"Breathtaking," I mutter, absorbing it all.

Before I see him, I feel him, smell him.

"Mm-hmm," Wolfe murmurs, coming up behind me.

I look up and he's looking down at me.

"You liked all that power between your thighs," he assesses, looking from me out to the water as some of the other guys start to close in on us.

I can't help myself. My mouth turns up into the slightest grin, but I keep my eyes focused on the ocean, so I don't give him too much satisfaction.

"It wasn't terrible." I shrug.

Wolfe leans down so only I can hear him. "Fuck yeah, you look damn good in leather, hummingbird."

"Ready, boss?" Robby asks.

Wolfe looks at him and points to the other guys then leans down over my ear. "You feel a little less like a good girl now, yeah?" he notes, not leaving me room to answer as he turns, then looks back at me over his shoulder.

I watch him go, a little breathless and a lot turned on from just the deep rumble of his voice in my ear. I'm not alone for more than a few seconds before Layla comes bounding up, fresh off the back of Sean's bike. Her jacket is different. It's got the club insignia on it and says *Property of Ax* on the back.

"How was that for *not your type?*" Layla grins

"You could've given me some warning he was coming," I say to her. "Happy wedding night, by the way, PB." I hug her, she smells like the same perfume she's always worn but today it's mixed with leather.

Layla 2.0.

"If I would've warned you, you would've backed out and hid in the closet while he rang your doorbell. It's been years but I still know you inside and out, Brin, and I wanted you here."

"Hide in my closet? Says you," I grunt, kicking at a weed with the toe of my shoe.

"Yeah, says me," Layla replies. A slow grin creeps across her face. "So, did you hate it?" she asks.

I look in the direction Wolfe went and breathe out a sigh watching as he speaks to his men.

"Oddly, no," I say.

"I think he likes you," Layla observes as she glances back out at the water.

"He doesn't *like*, remember? That's what you all told me."

"True, but I've never seen a woman on the back of his bike," Layla says.

"So he told me," I add quickly.

"Like I said, science experiment." Layla laughs as an SUV pulls in and parks near us, blaring Joan Jett.

Chantel, Amber, Maria, and one other woman pile out. They carry beauty boxes, hair styling tools, and garment bags.

Layla's wedding day mobile beauty salon has clearly arrived.

Layla locks arms with me to start moving in their direction.

"Hmm," she muses. "Something just occurred to me."

"What?" I ask, just waiting for it. I know it will be cocky, that's how Lay operates.

"You could've come up with the girls, but yet he made sure you came with him, so the plot thickens"

I scoff. "Whatever, like I said, he's just not my type *at all*."

"How many times have you told yourself that?" She giggles. "Enough to believe it yet?"

CHAPTER 18
Gabriel

When Mason and Kai arrive an hour after us, we get them to bring the truck down the dirt path to the maintenance cabin on the resort property. It's empty and hidden back behind the tree line of the woods, quite a ways from the main buildings where the wedding will be held—just like Ax said—and we have it ready. No one knows we're here, so if we have to put these two in the ground in the woods, it will be the last place anyone ever looks. But, we're bringing them in with their faces covered just in case we let the prospect live.

It's a large space with two rooms, a kitchen, dining area and a bedroom. Hasn't been used since the seventies and is almost decrepit now that the resort has live out staff. It's devoid of furniture except for an old wooden kitchen table. We've already got the eight fingered prospect from last night gagged and handcuffed to the radiator in the bedroom. If he's smart and tells us what we need to know, we'll let him live to deliver a message to his pathetic club.

Gator is out cold right now, sedated thanks to Rick, but he

should be waking up somewhere in the middle of the reception which serves us just right.

Mason is foaming at the mouth to start peeling back his fingernails and after riding up here with Brinley at my back, I'm in the mood to get a little aggression out too. I felt every single one of my men's stares this afternoon when Ax suggested Chantel and the girls could pick up Brinley and I said no.

I know it's out of character for me to pick her up—or any girl, for that matter—myself but I don't give a fuck what they think. I can't give them a reason as to why she seems to have this hold on me, nor do I owe them one. There's no logical reason I should be thinking about her every waking second. The shared energy that tethers us in a way is unexplainable and the way her pupils dilate when she focuses on me tells me her truth and I'm becoming desperate to uncover it.

We bind Gator's feet where he sits in the center of the kitchen. He's gagged and his arms, like the prospect's, are also zip-tied behind his back.

Gator has pissed himself somewhere along the way and is sleeping off his sedative with his mouth hanging open. Mason grits his jaw, and I just know he's thinking about the way his sister looked when she learned those videos went out club wide through the Disciples of Sin.

"Fuck this," Mason seethes, pulling his Bowie knife from the sheath at his hip. He looks up at me with the need for revenge burning in his eyes.

"I know he's out, I know he won't feel it, but I will. And he'll feel it when he wakes up," he pleads to me. "I want the fingers from his right hand, the first two," he says, then grits his teeth.

I know why he needs this.

I nod only once and his eyes light up with the anticipation

of blood. Sometimes, I think Mason is even more unhinged than I am.

He makes his way over to Gator and kneels onto his arm, spreads his fingers wide and hacks them clean off. Gator's hand instantly begins to bleed profusely on the tarp covered floor. Mason uses one heavy boot to stomp the severed fingers, the sound is a sickening crunch, then he tosses them into Gator's lap and makes his way over to me.

"It's a start," he deadpans.

I put my arm around him. "Feel better?" I ask with a chuckle.

"I'll feel better when he's the dead man who fucked my baby sister instead of the living one."

I look back at Gator, his mangled hand bleeding all over the place, and instruct Rick to just leave him. He's a dead man anyway, and that thought gives me peace. I don't take a life lightly, but there are some things that just can't be avoided. Even if it were one of my men that went after underage pussy, I would personally hand them this same fate without remorse. The difference is, most of my guys are soldiers and stand-up men. They might get around and a little outta control but none of them are creeps that prey on children. DOS has been known for patching in all sorts of characters lately, and they're never really able to keep a good handle on their so called 'disciples.' That's probably because the club Pres snorts his weight in coke and is always out of fucking control, just like the rest of them.

Monkey see, monkey do.

One day, we'll either take them down or patch them over, and the area of Atlanta they peddle their dope in will fall to one of our sister clubs.

Until then, I'm okay to pick them off one at a time, especially if it means no young girl will ever fall victim to pieces of shit like Gator Freeland again.

"Got that out of the way. Think I can get married without a catastrophe before you fuckers carve this turkey?" Ax asks as he breezes between us, gripping both our shoulders.

"Can't promise anything," I tell him honestly.

"We'll at least try to get you through the ceremony, Lover-boy," Flipp calls from behind us.

Fucking boys. Never a dull moment.

CHAPTER 19

Brinley

I've lived in Georgia my whole life, but I haven't been to Tybee since I was a little girl. I'd forgotten how magical it is.

The inside of the sanctuary where the wedding is taking place has been transformed to a rustic, white floral dream. Much like last night's rehearsal dinner, greenery, lights, and lanterns hang from every surface, candles are everywhere, and the entire back wall of windows faces the ocean.

The sun is just starting to sink when the organ plays and all the club members begin walking in, not in suits, but in the same black jeans, long sleeved, black button-down shirt and their cuts. The ones who wear rings have them on and the men are cleaned up, hair pushed back off their faces, those with longer hair in the back. There must be fifty of them and they all come in together. It's almost hypnotizing to watch them. I can't imagine being so invested in anything or having that much of my heart committed to something.

I shake my head, realizing that I'm romanticising all their probable illegal activity for one reason and one reason only, and that reason just walked in with the groom. Wavy hair, loose just behind his ears, Wolfe looks... incredible. It hits me that I don't even know his first name.

Wolfe's eyes lock on mine and I try my best to fight the pull. His powerful shoulders flex as he looks away, releasing his hold on me as he shakes a few members' hands.

He strides to the front to shake Sean's hand in congratulation, and I see him smile for the first time as he gives Sean the manliest hug I've ever witnessed, the kind where they clap each other on the back only once. Wolfe always looks incredible, but this smile, it's the vast transformation between a cold and emotionless man and one who feels deeply for his men. In less than one second, he pulls me in like a moth to flame.

I wait for his eyes to come back to mine and as I do, a sort of nervous elation washes over me, like I'm inching my way up a really high roller coaster, anticipating that drop.

They search... lock to mine... hold me... *Drop.*

Wolfe turns to stand at Sean's side as the music begins to play, and one by one the bridesmaids make their way down the aisle. Their dresses flow in a silky cascade, each woman filling out her black floor length dress in her own beautiful way. Everyone's breath catches as Layla rounds the corner on the arm of Dell. I smile when I see him, and he gives me a small wave. It's nice to find a friendly face in the crowd and he looks great.

The ceremony goes by quickly, officiated by a club chaplain from Rochester. It's not religious in any way and we listen as Layla and Sean recite their own vows, Sean adding in that he promises to obey Layla as much as possible and Layla adds that she promises to disobey him, which makes us all laugh. It's an oddly sweet and endearing ceremony, and as the sun says it's final goodbye to the day, they're announced husband and wife. They kiss amidst a roar of cheers and flashbulbs from the photographers.

By the time photos are over and we're all ushered into the equally beautiful reception room, I'm feeling relaxed and actually glad that I came. Layla said there are times when club life gets hectic, maybe I was just unlucky enough to witness it on my first go around last night. I'm amazed once again how different this group is than I expected.

"Funny meeting you here," Dell says from behind me as I stand at the bar.

I turn with my drink in hand, offer him the standard, "hey" and a friendly side hug.

"Not my usual crowd, where are you sitting?" he asks.

"Table six." I smile.

"Me too, glad I'll have someone I know to talk to." Dell smiles. He's always been handsome in a preppy, clean cut sort of way. Totally my normal type if he wasn't Lay's brother. His hair is shiny and swept to the side like he took the time to style it.

"Same here." I smile, actually meaning it.

Dell was always like an older brother to me when I was younger. And now that we have the connection of work, it seems easy and safe. He grabs a drink, and we begin to make our way to table six together, chatting about work and Layla. He tells me he was hesitant at first about Layla's new life, but he knows how much Sean loves her and how good he is to her.

"I have to trust Lay. She's always been a good judge of character. And it's not like she'll listen anyway..." Dell shrugs, taking a drink from his stein of beer and, leaning in, he smiles wide. "Also, well, he could definitely kick my ass so I just keep my mouth shut." He chuckles which in turn makes me laugh with him.

"At least you're honest about it." I pat him on the arm.

We haven't even been talking for a full minute, before Kai is at my side at our table.

"I think there's been a misunderstanding on the seating arrangement. Layla requested you sit at her table," he says to me, while offering Dell a big friendly grin that says *I'm a nice guy but I could break you.* I have no idea how he does that so well.

I look back at Wolfe—who's sitting now, two seats down from Layla and Sean at the head table—staring straight at me, sipping an amber colored whiskey.

"No, thank you. It's fine I can stay here," I say politely, not breaking eye contact with Wolfe. I was actually comfortable with a familiar family friend and it's obvious to me what's going on here. He may be used to getting whatever he wants but I won't be at his beck and call. Not to mention, staying away from Wolfe is in my best interest because when he's too close I just don't think straight.

"Please, go tell *Layla.*" I emphasize her name because I know damn well it's not her that wants me to move. "I'm going to stay *here.*"

Kai smiles even bigger. "I wouldn't disappoint the bride on her wedding day, would you?"

I look over and she's sitting at the table, waving at me excitedly. She's so beautiful in her princess gown as she called it. It's a white classic A-cut number, but around the bodice and dancing down the train is the most delicate black lace. I remind myself it's her wedding day and I won't start any drama with her infuriating club president.

"Fine," I say, standing to follow him.

"Sorry, Dell." I put my hand on his shoulder.

He waves me off. "No worries, Brin! Dance later?" he asks, standing, completely oblivious.

"Of course," I say, giving him a friendly side hug.

I follow Kai, shooting daggers at the smug face ready to greet me.

CHAPTER 20
Gabriel

It took about five seconds of me watching Brinley touch Layla's preppy brother to know that wouldn't be happening all night long. Dell might seem like the straight-laced man she thinks she belongs with, but that's because he gets all his fucked up fetishes out in his spare time. There are mommy issues like I've never seen in his internet search history.

Brinley will sit with me because I might go fucking postal if I have to spend one more goddamn second not breathing in her sweet scent. She's probably not going to come willingly but, whether she likes it or not, Brinley Rose Beaumont is already mine. Something about this woman has me wanting to strip her down, defile her and put the pieces back together in a way that suits only me, as if there was her life before she came apart for me and her life after, and that takes more time than just one night.

When Brinley reaches the table, it's obvious there's only one available chair. It's to my left, in between myself and Layla. I don't look up; I just pull it out for her. She sighs and I can practically hear her roll her eyes at me.

It's fine. She can be mad at me while she does what she's told.

Layla looks at her and smiles. "You're sitting with us? Cool."

Brinley smiles back at her, rosy lips parted, her dimples on full display in her dewy cheeks and I'm bewitched. I've never seen any living thing look so fucking beautiful. The dress she's wearing tonight is the same shade of blue as her wide, almond-shaped eyes. It's the lightest, most enticing blue I've ever seen, and it hangs off her spectacular shoulders and then drifts down over her slender arms as if it was made to personally torture me.

When I came into the chapel and saw her standing there, long tanned legs on display, the open back of her dress, thick, raven hair in soft curls held up halfway by the twist of a pin, I nearly bent her over one of the pews. I will openly admit, the depth at which I'm thinking about this woman is enough to make me question my own fucking sanity, if that was something I did. But I don't. I simply want her and I don't care why.

Brinley's eyes meet mine and the smile falls from her lips. She reaches to the center of the table and grabs the bottle of red, pouring herself a hefty glass as the first appetizers are wheeled out for dinner.

"Dell is such a sweetheart, Lay. I'm so happy to be working with him," Brinley says without looking away as she pours her red. The smug little smirk on her face is a toy I'm about to start playing with.

"You two were cute over there, he likes you," I say, and the underlying tone of sarcasm doesn't go unnoticed by her.

I feel the eyes of my guys on me, particularly Jake who's sitting beside me listening attentively.

Layla laughs. "No, they're just comfortable, they've known each other since we were kids," Layla says, speaking for Brinley before turning to say something to Ax.

I lean in so only Brinley can hear me. "Come to think of it, you're not really his type." My lips hover over her earlobe "We know everything about everyone, remember? And to be his type, you'd have to be *much* older and be ready to spank him if he doesn't follow your every order."

Brinley's mouth goes from smirk to slack in one second and she looks to Dell then back to me. I lean back and sip my whiskey.

Her smug smile is gone, replaced by that flustered blush of her cheeks.

Much better.

CHAPTER 21
Brinley

"You're not hungry?" Wolfe asks as he carves his own steak.

I've been pushing my food around on my plate and listening to everyone at the table talk about random things that show just how well they all know each other.

"Just wondering why I'm here is all," I say, looking up at him. "Every woman in this room has their eye on you." And some bold ones have already approached him, to which he's said *"no,"* and if they don't listen, *"fuck off"* but I don't bring that up.

He chews and swallows his bite, pondering what I asked.

"Do you ever say no, Brinley?" Wolfe asks, observing my expression as I blink at his question.

"Do you ever answer a question without a question?" I ask, taking a bite of my salad.

"Yes," he says pointedly. "Now your turn. Do you ever say no?"

"Yes," I answer immediately before I even consider it.

"You're either misunderstanding me, or not answering honestly," Wolfe says with an all-knowing smirk as he pulls a bottle of whiskey over from the center of the table and pours some into my glass, then his own.

"How so?" I take a sip, needing something—anything—to take the edge off.

"When people who are important to you—your parents, your friends, a boyfriend perhaps, maybe a coworker—if they asked you to do something, something you don't necessarily want to do. Something that would make them feel happy or more comfortable, but compromises what you want, would you say no? Or would you say yes, only because you think you should do what you're told?"

I look up in his hypnotizing eyes, the candlelight reflecting off their silver flecks, and for some reason, I answer honestly.

"I would probably do it so I didn't disappoint them, but..." I start to defend myself. "That's what you should do for people you care about."

"Maybe," Wolfe says, picking up my unused knife and toying with the sharp tip against the table.

"Sometimes you can say yes to help out, I suppose. But if you *always* do it, you start to lose the person you are and you start living for them. You aren't your true self anymore, you're who *they* want you to be."

"And your point is? I like being nice," I retort, my glass of wine and half a glass of whiskey giving me a little fuel.

I lean back in my chair, cross my ankles and fold my hands in my lap. I watch his eyes follow my actions.

"When you knew I wanted you to come and sit here, you didn't hesitate to deny me," Wolfe says, angling the point of the knife against the rustic wood table, the light glints off the blade as he speaks. "You said no right away, even though I'm sure you understood that I *wanted* you to sit with me." He sets the knife down and waits for me to answer.

I gulp and think for a moment, trying to grasp at what he's getting at so I can get ahead of it.

"I don't know you, I guess I don't feel like I owe you anything," I say boldly. Looking up from the discarded knife, I lift my chin.

Wolfe smirks, and his eyes never leave mine as he grips the bottom of my chair with both hands and pulls me to him in one swift motion. My breath hitches when our knees touch.

He leans forward and places his broad hands into my lap over both of mine, without looking away from my gaze he separates them, leaving them to rest against each thigh all on their own. Without thought I take a deeper breath.

"Or... maybe with me, you simply aren't afraid to be yourself, even if that looks a little different than everyone else expects."

I look down feeling flustered, then back up at him.

"Okay... so? Even if you're right, what's in it for you if I am different from what people expect? Why do you care?" I ask, looking up at him then letting out what I really want to know.

"Why *me*?"

He smiles like he knows a secret I don't. It seems he's just about to say something as Jake taps him on the shoulder, muttering something low in his ear.

Wolfe nods at Jake but says nothing. I watch as Jake stands and nods to the door at Kai and Robby.

Wolfe looks back at me as if he's thinking through his next words carefully then leans in. My heart beats thunderously and I wonder if that will ever *not* happen when he's this close. He replaces his hands over mine and my stomach drops.

"I want to find out who Brinley Rose Beaumont is when, for once, she chooses *herself*. I want to be there when she finally lets herself be as wicked as she craves."

I blink and my mouth falls open, registering how he knows

my full name, not that I should be surprised. He said he knows everything about everyone, obviously that includes me. Wolfe lets go of my hands and stands as the crowd's chatter grows louder with the end of dinner. He looks down at me before leaving the room with most of his men.

Sean whispers something to Layla as the DJ starts some music up.

"He'll be right back," she says to me in explanation.

I nod, still processing that entire conversation.

Is he right? Am I not myself because I aim to make everyone else happy first?

Layla moves to pull me up to the dance floor, and instead of questioning my life's existence, I pour myself another shot of whiskey from the bottle still in front of Wolfe's seat, knock it back, and go with her. I wonder for a brief moment where half the club went in such a hurry. But just as quickly, I remind myself it's not my business, this isn't my world, I'm just visiting.

In order to force myself to forget how much I liked the thought of being called wicked, I start to dance with Layla and her girls and that's how we spend the next two hours. The crowd is thick and Sean is in and out periodically to check on Layla and talk to guests. Dell even joins us as we dance to all our favorites.

I don't see Wolfe or any of his men again aside from Sean, and by midnight I'm ready for some fresh air and some water. I grab a bottle from the bar and tell Layla I'll be right back, just needing the cool breeze.

I exit the side door of the dance hall, crack my water and chug, lifting the hair off my neck. The cool ocean breeze feels incredible.

I look around. The moon is full and the sky clear. I watch the water lap the shore below and I swear I can hear dolphins. I begin to walk, just to clear my head. There isn't a soul out here, but I hear a crew on the outdoor patio on the other side of the building and I smell their cigarette smoke and weed. I wonder if Wolfe is there, I haven't seen him since dinner.

Before I even know where I'm heading, I'm moving aimlessly toward the water, thinking about the person I am, and Wolfe's words telling me to be who I *want* to be. In truth, without Evan, I don't even know who that is now, aside from who my parents trained me to be. Who Evan wanted. Even who, once upon a time, the church wanted.

The water lapping at the shore and the thousands of stars overhead call to me, and it seems this little path I'm on will lead me all the way down to the water's edge.

I pass multiple cabins on my way, some have people partying in them. A woman's moans sound through an open window as I pass by. I wonder if all the HOH members are the ones staying in these. The sounds finally fall silent as I make it all the way down the hill to a trail at the edge of the woods. It's here, just before I bend to take off my shoes and walk barefoot in the sand, that I hear it.

The kind of blood curdling groan that instantly makes your stomach turn because you just know something is horribly wrong with the person it came from.

I snap my head to the left to see a flicker of light just beyond the first veil of trees. I wait, but hear nothing as the waves crash into the rocks and shore in the distance. The water retreats to the sea and I, once again, hear the muffled cry and voices. It was definitely a person and they're hurt in that cabin. I begin to move toward it as fast as my sandal clad feet can carry me. Who would even be staying out here, way off the beaten path?

A sickening crack fills my ears as I approach and then that sound again and more voices. The cabin isn't even elevated, I walk right up to the open screen door and my blood runs cold as I peer inside.

The stench of burning flesh fills my nose, making me gag.

I fall to my knees because there are just no words for what I see before me.

If I had to try, I would say... Carnage. Bloodlust. Torture.

Two men are on their knees, shirtless, one of them beaten beyond recognition, blood-filled saliva running out of his mouth as it pools on the wet, red tarp beneath his body. Both of them are missing fingers. Their faces are swollen, and someone's teeth are on the ground. The bigger one is cut open in so many places that my mind can't fully register all the wounds. He's bleeding from his ears, his eyes... between his legs. *Oh my fucking god.*

And the man standing before them both, like a gloriously dark and terrifying god, is Wolfe.

He stalks forward and stands over them, looking down at their broken bodies from his full height, holding some sort of butane torch. He has an evil in his eye as he fires it up, and flames flow in a thin jet from the tip.

I watch, frozen in horror, as he grips the bigger one by the hair and yanks his head up. Wolfe slowly brings the torch to the man's neck, and as his garbled screams fill the air, he burns off the flesh all the way from the ear down to the collarbone. Erasing a tattoo. He's concentrating like the man's pain means nothing. It's like he doesn't even hear his cries.

The man whispers something I can't hear, and Wolfe turns down the flames for a moment to listen.

I would almost think the man had just fallen unconscious if it weren't for the tiny whimpers that leave his lips. His skin still sizzles, as more of the thick, pungent smell fills the air. You'd think I would get up and run but I can't.

I can't look away from what I assume is a tattoo associating him with whatever club or gang he's a part of, now grossly destroyed by Wolfe, chased away by his own charred flesh.

I'm breathing so quickly and so silently I'm not even sure air is making its way to my lungs. My brain screams again to get up and move out of sight but I'm frozen like a deer caught in headlights.

I should be disgusted. I should be in shock.

But all I see is the dark power of the man standing before me. He knows exactly who he is without any shame, guilt or remorse.

It's... hauntingly beautiful.

I'm so consumed by the horrific feelings rushing through *me* as I choose to stay there, that I don't even notice Kai's eyes on me as I kneel outside the cabin door, the grassy dirt is cool against my skin. Wolfe sets his torch down but there's no regret on his face for what he's doing. He doesn't speak. He just draws his gun.

I feel ready to pass out.

Someone is crying.

"Wolfe." Kai nods his head in my direction. My eyes flit to him when I hear his name. He turns and his gray eyes snap to mine, holding them for the longest ten seconds of my life.

His gaze is my anchor, and I realize it's me who's crying.

"I've heard enough," I hear Mason say.

I see Wolfe's mouth move but I don't hear what he says. Then he takes a single shot—

A shot that hits the bigger man square in the middle of his forehead. He falls lifeless to the floor and there's a sickening thud when his head meets the bloody tarp.

I scream and then somehow, I'm on my feet and running. I don't get very far when I register the words, he mouthed to me were "*don't look.*"

Too late.

CHAPTER 22
Brinley

I never thought that in facing my death, I would face this type of disbelief. Like this can't be real, there has to be another way. This can't be all I was put here on this Earth to do. Something or someone has to save me, don't they? Did every action, every choice I've ever made lead me here, just like my parents always told me? If I had stayed with Evan, I'd be home safe on my living room sofa instead of trying to outrun a psychopath. All these thoughts crowd my mind as I bolt for the woods. My lungs burn as I run without stopping, uncontrollable sobs wrack my body and adrenaline courses through my veins.

He murdered that man. And by now he's probably murdered the other one too. *Murdered.* And they had been tortured for who knows how long? They were missing body parts. Fingers. Teeth. Genitals? Images flash through my mind as I finally register them. The way the bigger man's stomach was cut open in several places and leaking blood, the cuts deep, his one eye swollen shut. The smaller man's arm was broken in more than one place and hanging limply in front of him. I blink to rid my mind of the memory, and more tears fall.

That's where he went after dinner. To torture and murder those men. And it looked like it was second nature to him. *Because it is.* The voice in my head reminds me.

This man, I let him *touch me.* I wanted *him.* And even as he stood over them like their own personal reaper, I'm ashamed to admit I *still* wanted him.

And now he's going to kill me too, and probably bury me with them.

Time passes in a blur. I'm covered in cuts and scrapes; I've fallen numerous times. I don't know how long I've been running. I keep praying for a road, or a break in the trees so I can scream for help but there is none. I have nowhere to go and the sound of heavy boots on the ground behind me tells me to keep running, but I'm so tired. I have to stop.

"Brinley." I hear Wolfe's deep voice echo off the canopy of the woods, he doesn't even sound winded. He sounds calm. I freeze, my back scrapes against rough, cold bark as I do my best to hide behind a tree. I can feel the sting of dirt in my scratched-up skin as I pant, so quietly I think I'm barely breathing.

"Running is pointless, I can fucking smell you, humming-bird." His voice booms through the woods, closer this time.

I take off and run for as long as I can, almost twisting my ankle in the rough terrain more than once. Twigs snap under my wedge sandals, and I know I can't go on much longer. All the while I can hear him; the sound of his even and steady boots crushing the dead leaves underfoot as he stalks me through the woods, is almost enough to make me scream. But screaming wouldn't help me now. I'm not sure anything would.

I pause as I see light through the trees and desperately hope it's a road or another cabin, anything with people and the possibility of safety. I bolt towards it, moving my sore and tired feet as quickly as I can, begging my breath to be quiet so he doesn't hear it.

I see a large tree about twenty feet away and make that my destination, but before I can get more than five steps, a strong hand circles my throat and I'm being slammed backward into the thick trunk of a live oak. His other hand behind my head stops me from hitting it but the bark bites into my shoulders.

"Stop fighting me," Wolfe bites out.

I don't listen, I start to fight, scratching at him in protest. The fear of my imminent death fueling me.

"*Don't* fight me," he says as I cry out. He moves his hand from behind my head and snares both of my wrists, holding them captive in front of me so I can't continue scratching him and places his other large palm on my chest.

"Breathe," he says in a way that almost feels soothing.

I try to suck in a deep breath, understanding how predators calm their prey before they murder them. "You're going to... You killed..." I sob. "Those poor, innocent—"

"Don't you fucking dare. Don't you *ever* call those men innocent," Wolfe snarls in a low voice as his palm slides up over my heaving chest to grip my throat. Even in the dark, I can see the gray of his eyes boring into mine. He's angry, yet I don't feel as scared anymore. I am what my father would've called a masochist. Stupidly soothed by the man that is about to hurt me.

The hand on my throat loosens so Wolfe can gently graze his knuckles over it as if he is trying to decide between choking me and soothing me. It's a dance I can't make sense of.

"One of them blew up Jake's truck the other night. Anyone could have been standing there, been inside it, and that man isn't dead. He's going to deliver a message for us to his piece of shit leader."

My breath hitches as I try to catch it.

"The other one. The fucked-up bastard I shot—he groomed, drugged, and raped a sixteen-year-old girl almost a year ago, then shared photos and videos of it. He practically ruined her life. She wouldn't even leave her house for two months."

My stomach drops as time seems to stand still. Suddenly, I feel just as angry as he looks.

"And she's family. One of my men's little sisters." His palm leaves my neck and presses back into my chest as it rises and falls. "It was a rival club. They weren't happy. We did something that hurt their crank business in Atlanta, in one of their most profitable areas."

"I can't hear this. I don't want to hear this." I panic.

If I hear this, I'm dead.

"The girl was Mason's little sister—it was a retaliation of the sickest kind, and it goes against everything men like us stand for. So, did I let her brother do unfathomable things to him? Yes."

Mason's sister? I shudder, thinking of Mason angry. I find myself wondering if this girl I don't even know is okay.

As he speaks, Wolfe flips his hand over on my chest and his knuckles begin another leisurely graze over my collarbone, then to my shoulder, as his other still grips my wrists and I realize my breathing has involuntarily slowed. His hard body presses against mine and some fucked up part of me wants him here, feels safer with him pressed against me.

His lips come down to my neck and he shocks me by licking a slow trail upwards, tasting my sweat as he goes. I fist the bottom of his warm shirt with my still clasped hands under his cut without thought.

"And after I let her brother torture him, and get everything he wanted from him, did I shoot him in cold blood?" Wolfe releases me, moving both of his hands down to slide up the outside of my thighs, taking my dress with them, over my panties to wrap around my bare waist.

My deranged body ignites with this soft, intimate touch. It's a moment I'm sure I'll remember as traumatic for the rest of my life, but I pant as his thumbs trail over my lower belly.

"Fucking right I did. And I'd do it again. I don't regret it. Not for a single fucking second. My only regret is that we couldn't torture him for *longer*," Wolfe growls, that ominous tone coursing through me.

I whimper as Wolfe pulls me tight to him, holding me up with his hands circling my waist. His lips find my throat, then my collarbone, as his tongue sweeps across my skin. I grip his shirt tighter, but I can't tell if I'm pushing him away or pulling him closer. Is there any point in struggling? I fall completely slack against him, defeated. His mouth searches my shoulders, nipping, sucking, biting, like he can't control himself any more than I can. My hands slip under his shirt and I whimper. His hard muscled body feels warm against my palms.

He's too strong and if I'm going to die anyway, being handled like this, with more passion than I've ever felt in my life, is the way I choose to go. He's touching me with a hunger I've never felt.

I can't explain it. I can't understand it. Hell, I can't even process the reality that this is actually happening. I don't even ask myself why I shiver with desire as Wolfe grips my cotton panties and tears them from me, just as he did last night. Only this time he brings them closer to his face. I know they're wet with all the evidence he needs to prove that, however fucked up this is, whether I want to admit it or not, I *want him*. Darkness be damned.

He closes his eyes and breathes in, then slowly exhales with a deep groan, rubbing the damp cotton between his thumb and his first two fingers, as if he's assessing how wet they are. I watch with fascination as Wolfe pulls them to his mouth like he's about to suck my arousal from them, and that's exactly what he does. I'm helpless to do anything but watch as he turns his eyes to me and grins wickedly.

"You understand what it means that you just witnessed my club's business?" he says as he places my soaked and torn panties inside his cut.

I give a shallow nod, knowing this is the end. I begin to spiral.

"I won't say anything, I—"

"Shh," he says, running a thumb over my bottom lip, instantly calming me.

I silently pray that there's no pain.

"Listen to me now. You have two choices, little humming-bird. You die in these woods, or you become mine in these woods."

I blink, my eyes moving to his.

"When I say mine"—Wolfe steps back, unbuckling his belt. I have no idea what he's about to do but he surprises me by removing a large, sheathed knife from it. My breathing acceler-ates, turning frantic again as his hand moves back to my thighs —"I mean everything I did tonight is your cross to bear too."

"Why? why would you want—"

"Don't fucking ask me why." Wolfe presses me into the tree, his voice is frustrated and full of gravel. The bark gnaws at my skin.

He gently brushes my hair from my damp forehead and closes his eyes momentarily, as if to calm himself.

"I have no fucking idea *why* I can't stop thinking about you. No idea *why* I crave you the way I do," he says evenly.

Gripping me tight around the waist with one arm, the other yanks the top of my dress down exposing my breasts, and I moan as my head falls back against the tree. His hot mouth finds my nipple and he bites down, my pussy throbs with the pain. Before I can even cry out, he's pulling it back into his mouth, swirling his tongue over it and soothing the sting, setting my core on fire. I fantasize, once again, about what it would be like to have his mouth on mine.

"Why would I choose not to end you right here? Why do I want to take you and mark you and keep you for my own?" Two large fingers slide through my embarrassingly soaking slit as he holds his knife in that same hand. I feel the handle press against me in time with his fingers. The fear coursing through me with the thought of what he might do ignites me. A deep growl leaves his chest as he pushes his fingers further into me.

"It's the same reason you're fucking soaked...soaked all for me." Wolfe murmurs as he brings his fingers up and spreads my arousal across my bottom lip then moves back down to make slow sweeps against my clit with his knuckles.

Wolfe sucks my bottom lip into his mouth. I taste myself on his lips and realize how messed up it is that I pray for this murderer's kiss.

"The poetic justice is that we always crave what we're not." He bites down, and I whimper, suddenly understanding that while I crave his darkness, in some way he must crave my light. I push my hips into his hand, anything for more friction, for more of him, more of this.

The expert way he trades between strumming my clit and fucking into me with his fingers has my pussy clenching tightly to him, threatening to fall apart within seconds.

"I live to take what I shouldn't want, what I shouldn't deserve. I never question why I want things." His deep, velvet voice washes over me as my pussy clenches around his fingers, the sound of cicadas and my desperate moans fill the air, echoing off the trees like a soundtrack, the soundtrack of him playing my body like the most intimate instrument. "If you choose death, you'll never know..."

I'm so close to coming all over his fingers.

"Wolfe..." I whimper.

"If you choose to be mine, you will learn how easy it is to accept who you are..." He pulls his fingers from me abruptly and notches the smooth handle of his cool knife against my pussy, sliding it up and down through my slippery arousal. My brain begs to protest.

Inside, I'm screaming.

Outside, I grip his cut tighter and pull him closer.

"The same way your heart doesn't ask why it beats faster for me, I don't ask myself why I want you. I only take, hummingbird."

He clutches the leather sheath of the blade and slides the handle into me further. I cry out at the intrusion but still, I don't tell him to stop. I can't tell him to stop.

"I'm sorry I saw..." It rushes out of me. "I won't tell anyone." My eyes widen as he pushes the handle into me further.

"I don't need you to be sorry," Wolfe says as he slips the handle in another inch. "I need you to be an accessory," he growls as he pushes the smooth handle all the way in, and I gasp at the feeling of it fully seated inside of me. He slips it back out and begins fucking me with it at an all-consuming pace. His other hand leaves my waist as he brings his thumb to my clit and begins circling it with perfect pressure, giving me exactly what I need. I quiver as ecstasy and adrenaline rush through me.

"I need this pussy to crave me. To beg for me to take it any way I choose."

I hear him but I feel like my soul has left my body. His unhinged actions are sending me to places that have only ever haunted my darkest dreams.

"I need you to crave me the same way I crave you."

He looks back at me and smirks, his pupils blown out wide and filled with a frenzied bloodlust.

"Make the right choice, Brinley, so I don't have to flip this knife over and slit your beautiful throat with it."

My legs begin to shake, and my protest dies before it reaches my lips as I give in to him. My orgasm is inevitable, and I'm lost to whatever this is, whatever I am, with him.

My heart thunders in my chest as the slightly curved handle pulses against a place deep inside me and I feel like I may explode or lose control of my bladder—or both.

I tip my head forward and meet his gaze, reaching my hand up to the side of his strong jaw, running a thumb over his cheekbone.

"I don't want to die," I moan softly.

"Then come, little hummingbird, and say my name while you do," he commands.

My hand feels small against his face and the gentle touch I'm offering him in this moment feels wrong, but his eyes take in the look of desire I'm surely wearing and grow dark, like he might devour me at any moment.

"I don't know your first name," I say breathlessly. "Tell me," I add as the tight coil of heat takes a deep hold within my belly, my thighs, my soul.

"Gabriel," he answers softly against the shell of my ear.

"Gabriel..." I whisper his name for the first time, and the sound he makes is animalistic. It's enough to hurl me over the edge, to fall into the dark, stormy depths of him as I unravel around the handle of his knife.

"Gabriel," I cry out again, louder this time and his answer is a deep growl that rumbles through his chest.

"Again," he commands, and I do what he says, calling his name as the euphoric release of an explosive orgasm rushes to my center from every cell in my body and I come harder than I ever have, soaking the handle, his hand and his forearm.

With no end in sight, I call his name again along with some form of *please, more* and *don't stop,* all while hating that I want him, this man I don't even know with the hollow gray eyes.

When I open my eyes finally to the sound of our breathing, the only thing I see is treetops, my shame, and the stars.

Who am I in this moment? Who is this woman who just came without abandon all over the blunt end of this murderer's knife? And where is the torment I should feel?

Gabriel pulls his knife from me, and I look down, finding he's gripped the sheathed blade so hard it cut his hand through it and his blood drips from his palm into the grassy earth. He replaces the knife at his hip and skims his fingers into my pussy, pushing his blood into me, smearing it all over my swollen lips. It feels like a marking, a type of claiming. He slowly pulls them out, moving his hand up to my face to spread his blood and my cum all over my lips, like he's painting his masterpiece.

"I live inside *you* now, little hummingbird," he says as he leans in, staring down at me, his mercury eyes focus on my lips and all I can hear is his breathing. A battle wages in his eyes as his hand slides to the back of my neck where he grips possessively before his control snaps and he violently fists my hair. He pulls at my roots sharply, tilting my head back just before he captures my lips with his own, kissing me deeply.

I lose my breath, unprepared for the kiss I never thought would come. I'm docile and molded to him instantly. Wolfe kisses me as if he's desperate to taste me. His lips press into mine, and his tongue plunders, hungrily. I meet it with my own, just as eager as he is. The taste of copper and my own arousal washes into my mouth, and he groans into my lips before releasing me, leaving me completely unraveled.

He feasted on me for mere seconds, but it was the most

incredible kiss I've ever experienced, one that commanded my entire body.

I realize as I watch him try to compose himself now that there *is* a part of him, however small, that is fully capable of losing control.

"*Fuck—*" he says, turning his face from me. When he returns his eyes to mine, his pupils are contracted. They're controlled again, devoid of any emotion. He grips my throat.

"You do what I say now, and you stay alive," Wolfe says, his voice low.

He turns and begins to walk, expecting me to follow, and I ask myself what just happened. How he goes from so intense to cold and emotionless so easily. The rush of fear returns almost instantly. The haziness from my orgasm and the kiss evaporating by the second, making things clear once again.

I realize I truly have no idea what it means to be his and the thought of finding out terrifies me. As I follow Gabriel out of the woods, I know that the woman I was before we met might as well be as dead as the man he just murdered.

CHAPTER 23
Brinley

"I'm going to get an infection from that knife," I say as wooden stairs creak under our feet while we climb them.

Gabriel unlocks the door to his private cabin and ushers me in. I realize I prefer his first name, the only reason why that I can fathom is because it somehow makes him more human than his last.

"I just finished gutting a man with it. It was completely sterile. Sanitized. Twice. Hospital clean." He leans in and the scent of him overwhelms me again. It doesn't even seem like the endeavor in the woods caused him to break a sweat. "And I wouldn't put his blood anywhere near you," he says gruffly.

"But yours is okay?" I ask, kicking my muddy wedge heels off. I'm lucky I didn't break an ankle trying to run in those.

"My blood is clean," he says, stalking toward me after he turns on a light. Gabriel stands over me looking down into my eyes. He grazes a knuckle over my pulse like he measures the beats. "And I'll put it anywhere I please. In you, on you, mixed with your own. If I want you to drink it, you will. You owe your life to me. You *should* be saying thank you."

Rage fills me and I fight with everything in me not to cry. I force myself not to give him the satisfaction of my fear.

"Thank you," I say evenly.

"Time to clean up." he says, moving to usher me toward the only bathroom. I have nothing with me. Even my phone and purse are in the reception hall on the table.

"I need to go to my room and get my things," I tell him "I have nothing."

Gabriel pulls out his phone and starts to text. He finishes and puts it in his pocket.

"You'll stay with me. It's not safe for you to be alone until I explain our arrangement."

I.e., his club might try to kill me for seeing what I saw.

"Undress," he says as he turns the shower on, placing his hand under the water to feel the temperature. "Your personal things are on the way."

"My room number is—" The look he gives me tells me he already knows.

"Your things are on the way," Gabriel reiterates, leaving me no room to protest. "It'll work out a lot better for both of us if you stop second guessing everything I say. Then I won't need to fucking repeat myself," he adds.

His phone rings and he looks down before stepping through the bathroom door to answer it. I take the opportunity to close it behind him and lean back against it, already knowing better than to lock it. If he wants to come in here, the flimsy handle lock wouldn't stop him anyway, so what's the point?

I take the time while he's gone to use the toilet, praying his knife was as clean as he promised. I'm tender and swollen and wishing for the solace hot water will offer. I grab fresh towels and a washcloth from the shelf then strip my clothes away and stare at myself in the mirror. The makeup I worked so carefully to apply hours ago is smudged, the remnants of my mascara is dark beneath my eyes and tracks down my still flushed cheeks in washed out black lines where it had mixed with my tears. My hair that I had curled and pinned up is in disarray and hangs down my back in waves, tiny sticks and brambles caught up in the knotted mess. There's mud streaked across my skin and what looks like the start of bruising around my neck from him holding me against the tree. I turn and see the scratches that line my shoulder blades. They aren't deep but...I am a marked woman.

The deep timbre of Wolfe's voice echoes through the hollow door as he speaks to someone on the phone.

"You do what I say now, you stay alive," he had said and meant it.

All I have is my sovereignty.

And not the sovereignty of my body because that clearly belongs to him.

All I have is my choice.

I can choose to be either an open or a closed book when it suits me. I can choose not to indulge in his world until I understand it better.

I can choose to forgive myself for wanting him. I only owe myself.

There's also the possibility that he'll grow tired of me and let me go quietly. It's small, but at this point, he hasn't even tried to claim me with his cock, which goes against everything the people around him say about what kind of man he is.

It tells me that maybe I'm just as out of the ordinary for him as he is for me. That light to his dark.

The mirror begins to fog, pulling me from my thoughts and reminding me to step into the steamy shower, just as Gabriel re-enters the bathroom.

He leans back against the sink and stares as I let the water fall like rain over my skin, the heat soothing my aching muscles that are still coming down from the adrenaline. I almost fold my hands in front of me, partially out of habit and partially to stop his stare but instead I push back against my fears.

I lift my arms and face him, tilting my head slightly and skimming my hands back over my hair, staring right at him while I'm naked and on display.

"Must you sit there while I shower?" I ask as I rinse hotel-smelling shampoo from my hair. He's already seen all of me. It shouldn't really bother me that he's watching the water run down my naked body, but still, I have to ask.

"Yes," Gabriel answers simply, settling in.

My choices. My thoughts.

I will choose how to be his captive. I won't give him the fear he seems to crave unless I want to. I've seen everything he's capable of now, so as odd as it sounds, I have nothing left to fear.

"Suit yourself," I deadpan with a shrug, placing a hefty dollop of conditioner in my palm.

I don't miss his smirk as I work to wash away all the sin from this night. He settles in and folds his arms over his chest.

I'm vulnerable before him, yet the way he looks at me—how his normally light eyes turn dark and trace my body, absorbing my every move—only makes me feel powerful.

More powerful than I've ever felt.

CHAPTER 24

Gabriel

I watch Brinley behind the shower glass as she rinses her hair. She has no idea how close she came to death. How lucky she is I saved her life...

"She has to die. You know that?" Jake asks

"Clean this up," I tell Robby and two prospects, gesturing to the pathetic corpse face down on the tarp. "And send this one back with the extra set of balls in his mouth, sew them in then safety pin the note to his lips, let them all know this is what's coming to them if they touch anyone we care about again."

"You want me to go after that little sprite, boss?" Kai asks, nodding his head toward the woods where Brinley took off. I don't like that he calls her sprite—a good girl. Something about their assumptions just pisses me off.

"Fuck, she's Layla's friend," Ax says.

"It's gotta be done," Jake tells him.

"Fuck." Ax runs a hand over his beard. "If you have to do it, do it quick."

I shake my head. The only thing I can think is, not her.

"No. No one touches Brinley," I order. "She's mine to

handle," I say over my shoulder, making sure every one of them nods before I push through the screen door and go after her.

The sigh Brinley lets out in the steamy bathroom pulls me back to reality. For the second time in forty-eight hours, I've witnessed her face something traumatic, and yet here she is, standing before me in all her naked glory like it hasn't fazed her.

Her body is something I simply can't look away from. I didn't plan to stay when I came in to check on her after I ended my phone call with Ax, but the moment I saw the water rushing over those perfect full tits and down to her soft, curvy waist, I knew I wasn't going anywhere.

My eyes feast and catalogue every single curve, every part of her. Shapely thighs that filter up to the prettiest pussy I've ever laid eyes on, and a full, perfect ass that curves up to her lower back with a soft dip that begs for my hands. And just as I suspected, not one tattoo, not one piercing.

She's a blank canvas. One I will mark up, repeatedly, in every place I can.

My cock throbs against my zipper as she wrings out her hair, smoothing her hands over her body, her perfect pink nipples hardened to little points begging for my teeth. Brinley squeezes hotel body wash into her palm and begins to wash her shoulders, suds skimming over her, clinging to her the way the ocean outside laps at the shore. My brow furrows as I realize it's going to fuck up the way she smells and I hate that.

As she lifts her gaze to me and runs both hands over her tits, chasing the suds away, I unbuckle my jeans without thought. I've known full well since the first second I laid eyes on her that this woman is in unchartered waters for me. The moment I allow myself to cum with her name on my lips, I will be fully giving in to this obsession, and that time is now.

I free my cock, it bobs out from my boxers and points

straight at her. I spit into my palm and grip it before she even notices what I'm doing. And notice she does the second she shuts off the shower and looks over at me. My cock has never been harder or angrier after her visual torture. Her eyes take in my size first, then move with wide curiosity to the wrung of six barbells that line the underside of my shaft, forming a ladder. I instantly know she has no idea what to do with it or why, but she'll understand soon enough. Her eyes show her interest and tell me she's never seen any kind of a piercing on a man before and I'm not surprised. I wouldn't expect anything less.

"Come here," I demand as she wraps a towel around her body. Her face appears unsure, but her eyes tell a different story. Her eyes tell me she wants whatever I have to offer her, but her proper upbringing makes her fight the urge to look at me.

"Look," I tell her, nodding down. "Look what you do to me, Brinley Rose," I say, slowly pumping my rock-hard cock as she stands in front of me.

Brinley's eyes widen even more as she watches and the blush I crave slinks up her throat. I look down at her, so vulnerable, so clean in front of me that the urge I have to dirty her right up takes over as I run my thumb along her juicy bottom lip.

"That *must* have hurt, why do you have those?" She asks about my piercings, not understanding that pain is not something I shy from, in fact, I crave it. Her eyes have the hint of sass I'm starting to make my life's mission to bring out of her.

I smirk back and slide one finger between her still slick breasts, unhooking the towel from her. It lands on the floor as I continue working my cock. She licks her lips, and pre-cum begins to leak for her at the sight.

"The pain *is* the point. Someday soon, when I let your tight little cunt take my cock, you'll understand the reward for that pain."

She swallows, her smug little smirk gone, her face serious, and the fear I crave is back in her eyes. All of this combined is too much for me.

I use my boot clad foot to spread the towel out and then tap it twice with my heavy boot and wait. It's been... fuck, I don't remember the last time I had my cock in a woman's mouth. The idea overwhelms me as Brinley understands me instantly and drops to her knees.

Brinley shivers, cold from exiting the shower and her nipples pearl even more. She lets her gaze move up and down my cock slowly, then back up to me.

"Guess I'm just here to serve you then, *master?*" she says, her darker tone spikes my blood, like a hit to the vein, and I know this woman is fucking dangerous for me—she wants my wrath.

Brinley takes my cock in her small hand and runs a finger down the barbells, one by one. I slide my thumb down to her bottom lip, holding it open, her tongue moves involuntarily, and her big blue eyes look up, focusing on me through her lashes. The sight pushes me over the edge.

"There's the wicked girl I want," I say back, and she moans, confirming how eager she is.

I tap the head of my cock against her pillow soft lips, my voice growing even more commanding. "Open."

She slips her tongue out, licking the pre-cum that waits for her. My eyes threaten to roll back.

"Now suck," I order.

Brinley listens, attempting to play with the crown of my dick, and I groan as her tongue darts out, swirling over every single barbell. I feel her moan and it hums through my entire body. I look down at her, noticing the way she squeezes her thighs together and clenches her free hand in her lap. I grin, someday very soon she'll admit, out loud, how badly she wants me.

"You haven't given much head before, have you?" I ask with a smirk, because it's obvious. When her eyes look up to mine, she shakes her head slightly with my cock still in her mouth.

Fucking Christ. I'm happy as fuck to teach her.

"Hollow your cheeks out." I give a light tug to her jaw. "Loosen up here. Don't just lick. Swallow my cock, humming-bird," I say, my voice full of gravel and lust. She has no idea what she's doing but it's still the best blow job I can remember.

She does what I say, her tongue making intentional, languid flicks as she attempts to take me deep. I hit the back of her throat at the halfway point. She gags and sputters around me. Her hand sits at my base, her fingers barely touch, and she can't even get her mouth to meet her hand.

The sight of it urges me to fill all her holes that I know I'm too big for.

"That's it, use your tongue," I tell her as she gets herself into a rhythm. I slide my hands into her hair to help her. Brinley gags again, drool leaking down her chin when I hit the back of her throat.

I'm done attempting to take it easy, I'm too far gone. Her hot mouth wrapped around me is my kryptonite. Using the grip on her hair, I allow my thumbs to slide down her jaw and hold it open as wide as I can.

Brinley gags and I love it. I only grow harder with her struggle.

"Get used to taking all of me," I grunt. "Your pretty little face while I'm fucking your throat just became my new favorite view."

Brinley sputters more, she chokes, but I don't let up. I hit the back of her throat again and again without ceasing. For how long? I have no idea. I continue to pull myself out slowly then drive back in, just to revel in the feel. I'm desperate to last even one more second. Every thought I've had of her since the first moment I saw her sitting in the sun brims to the surface, the mix of fear and want in her eyes. There is no line between them.

She moans and whimpers, moving her body, rolling her hips and squeezing her thighs as I hold myself at the back of her throat for a beat.

"Slide your hand down to that sweet pussy, use yourself. You *will* come when I do," I tell her, knowing it won't take her long. Brinley's eyes grow wide, and fuck, it's enough to make me want to come all over her. I watch entranced as she carefully, almost gracefully slides a finger down her core and pushes it into her dripping cunt.

"Don't be so fucking polite. Take what you want. Add another," I tell her.

She moans and does what I say, adding another finger then swiping it up to add pressure to her clit in small circles.

"Attagirl," I say, sliding in and out of her throat as she finger fucks herself. I can tell she's new at that too, but she knows what she wants, she just has to have the confidence to take it. I slide out, allowing her to take a breath, trying to control my need to ruin her. She doesn't even fully inhale before I'm thrusting back in, but it's what she wants. The sound of her soaking pussy fuels us both as her hips continue to move, bucking into her own hand as she closes in on her high. Drool trickles down her neck and my balls churn and tighten. I grow deeper down her throat as my release licks up my spine.

A ragged moan from her as she comes with my cock in her mouth is what does me in.

I pull back slightly and tap the swollen head of my cock on her lips, she just naturally sticks her fucking tongue out. I'm done for. I come, hard. She closes her eyes in anticipation as hot ropes jut out against her lips, her cheeks, her neck.

"*Fuck,* Brinley..." I growl. My cum drips from her swollen pouty lips and Brinley looks up at me. I'm still hard as fuck and leaking. I swipe the cum from the head of my cock with my thumb and shove it between her lips. She looks up at me with glassy eyes but sucks my thumb into her mouth.

My breathing shallows as I watch her. I don't remember the last time I came this hard.

It's not enough, the way she looks right now, I'm already desperate for more.

"My wicked girl, Brinley, you take every drop I offer. *That's* what it means to be mine."

CHAPTER 25

Brinley

Gabriel's cum still rests against my cheeks, my lips, my tongue, along with his thumb, and a deranged part of me begs silently for him to fill me with it. I suck it off and look up at him through my lashes. I knew I was lost to him the moment he bit his bottom lip and groaned my name. Then, when he withdrew from my mouth and came in a way I've always thought was degrading—but instead I loved—I knew there would be no turning back.

I'll continue to crave it, crave him. And knowing that scares the shit out of me. My damp hair clings to my skin, and I clench my thighs, still desperate for more. I want it all.

"Boss," a deep voice booms through the cabin door.

Gabriel pulls his thumb from my lips with a tiny popping sound. "We've got her things here for you to get rid of and, uh, we're ready," the voice says.

Get rid of? They think I'm dead?

Gabriel tucks his still hard cock into his boxers and does up his jeans. I don't have a lot of experience with men, but the few I do have been nothing like him. He has the most beautiful and terrifying cock I've ever laid eyes on. I've never seen a man this big or with any kind of piercing before. I honestly don't know how he could even fit inside me. What could he possibly feel like? Will it hurt? *Will I find out?*

His large hand reaches downward to help me up. I take it. He turns silently and runs a washcloth under warm water and then uses it to clean me up, making sure to swipe over every place his cum rests on my skin.

"Get dressed." he orders, his voice resolute and calm again. My legs are stiff after kneeling on them and running through the woods.

Gabriel looks me over as I stand, waiting naked in front of him. I fight the urge to fold my hands in front of me.

"Clothes. Now," he reiterates "One more second of you standing there, looking like that and I'll be fighting a battle to stay here with you before seeing to the needs of my club."

I nod, but my stomach drops and heats all at once.

He hands me back my dirty dress. I slink it over my head and sit down on the chair beside the bed. Gabriel takes one last look at me, like he's making sure I'm fully covered and then pulls the door open wide.

Jake stands on the other side of it, he's bloody from head to toe. It's dried onto his shirt. I can see it in the dim light. His hands have been washed but I can still see spatters of it on his neck, and arms. It's a stark reminder that the man I just gave a blow job to, took a life tonight and these men think nothing of helping him clean it up.

Jake looks at me then back to Gabriel. His eyes are asking why I'm still alive.

"You want to go somewhere?" he asks.

"Where's Robby and Kai?" Gabriel asks.

Jake looks at me again, I look away.

"They're... in the woods already..." Jake looks back at me. "Busy."

Gabriel hands me my bag. "You can change now."

"Let's talk outside," he says to Jake, turning and closing the door behind him.

I make my way to the bathroom. The moment I shut the door, tears fill my eyes but I'm too afraid of him to not listen. I just move like a robot and do as I'm told.

I begin to change into tights and a t-shirt, bringing my brush through my hair and let it hang long and loose to finish drying. As I splash some cold water on my face, I can hear Gabriel and Jake's voices echoing quietly from the porch when I shut the water off. It isn't easy to hear them but if I concentrate I can.

"You got him ready?" Gabriel asks. I'd know his voice anywhere. In the short time I've known him, it's become ingrained in me.

"Yeah, I'll deliver him," Jake answers,

"Take someone with you," Gabriel commands.

"Nah, it brings too much heat, and you need all the guys to get this shit head six feet under. The ground is solid fuckin' clay. I'm fine to go alone, he's out cold right now."

Tears come. They're burying that man out there right now. His brain matter splattering against the wall behind him flashes through my mind and I feel instantly sick. I move to the toilet and hang my head over it, waiting for my stomach to empty any second.

"Ax went back to the party. We told him to. He can't be absent from his own wedding," Jake says.

"Good," Gabriel says. I hear the amusement in his voice as he adds, "Give him the night off."

"We'll put him in the ground. See you back here in two hours, yeah?" Gabriel confirms.

"Yeah, man, give or take a few, depending. I'm gonna take

the backroads in the van, and hey, uh, you gonna take care of that in there? Need any help?" he asks.

Fear ripples up my spine with another wave of nausea when I realize he's talking about me. I'm *that*.

"I've got it covered," Gabriel answers.

I hear Jake chuckle. "Fuck, it's not like you to let pussy cloud your judgement. She watched you pull the trigger and she's a prim and proper little sprite. She'll go straight to the cops."

"Enough," Gabriel snarls angrily. "I said I've got it."

"Yeah, yeah, gotcha, bro. Just gonna have a little fun first?" His laughter booms, but I don't hear Gabriel's response.

I throw up violently. I could make it off this island alive, but what I'm hearing is that they still want me dead. They don't trust me at all, and I know that means I'm a threat.

I flush the toilet and lean against the cool bathtub. It soothes me.

Fire like I've never felt rises in my belly.

I will not go down without a fight. I will figure this out.

I stand and brush my teeth, then take a deep breath as I hear the rumble of Jake's van or truck or whatever is out there.

I swipe my tears from my face and smooth my hair, holding my chin up as I exit the bathroom. When he sees me standing in the doorway, Gabriel looks up from placing a rather scary looking gun into a holster at his waist. He pulls out his phone and focuses on it, speaking to me without looking up.

"Stay here. I'll be back. Chris will be outside the door."

I speak in monotone. I shouldn't ask him, but I need to know. "How do you not think about it? The image of him dying plays in my mind over and over. I can't unsee it," I bite out.

I close my eyes as it comes again. The way the back of his head opened up. The sound his body made when he hit the sticky floor. It's not like the movies. It was like his face exploded. I open my eyes.

"I'll never forget it," I tell him, my eyes wide in horror as one tear slides down my cheek.

Gabriel moves to me in two quick strides. He pulls my head forward by the hair at the nape of my neck and swipes my tear away with the other hand.

"You *choose* to be stronger than this," he pushes out. "People live and people die. Understand right now that he was a waste of skin. Never give him another thought and don't you dare shed a tear over him. You just make the choice. Got it?"

I reach up to his hand in my hair and grip it as hard as I can while tears fill my eyes. "It's not that easy—"

"*Stronger,*" Gabriel says in the deepest, calmest tone.

He's holding me so tightly, I can't look anywhere but into his eyes, and the rest of my body is held with no hope of getting free. I try to claw at the hand holding my hair, he's pulling it so hard. He smirks at me with a sadistic grin.

"If you're trying to make me hard again, it's working," he says.

My breath increases and I squeeze my eyes shut. He releases my hair.

My captor. I want to hurt him and savor him all at the same time.

The cabin door isn't even fully shut before I pick up a vase and toss it against the wall in frustration over the impossible situation I've found myself in. It shatters. Good. I hope Gabriel slices himself open on it when he comes in, maybe that will make him hard too.

The back of my head still aches from where he held my hair, but I simply take my tights off, turn the light out, and crawl into bed. Then I let the tears fall.

CHAPTER 26
Gabriel

It's sometime after three in the morning when I finally meet up with my men deep in the woods beyond the maintenance cabin. I walked here alone so I could clear my fucking head.

I was focused before her. I was calculated. Right now, my head is a fucking mental shitshow of her face, her clenching cunt, her voice, and the fire I see in her eyes. The fucking *want*. She should be dead but the only thing I could think when Kai offered to go after her tonight, was that not one single hair on her head would be touched by anyone but me.

The wedding reception has wound down, although people were still partying in various cabins around the property when I walked by. Ax is gone for the night so we're short one man. Kai, Robby, Mason, and Flipp have a couple of feet dug out already. Four more to go. Digging doesn't happen quickly by hand. Especially when it's Georgia clay.

They all stop when they see me approaching. I observe what's left of Gator. He's laid out on a tarp and all of his missing pieces are scattered around him. He's already beginning to stiffen.

"Boss, you got a plan we don't know about? Something you wanna tell us about you and that little sprite?" Kai asks.

"She's still alive... so, do you have ideas you aren't letting the rest of us in on?" Flipp asks.

Fucking Jake must have told them.

"She saw it. She has to go," Robby adds.

"She's a rich man's daughter. A good girl, a liability," Flipp mutters, his weathered face crumpled into a scowl.

"Enough," I growl. "She's an accessory, yes, but she's *my* accessory. Understand?"

Every single one of them nods in understanding. Brinley is off fucking limits. Only *I* choose if and when she dies, and until then they'll treat her with the same respect they do me. The mood shifts as every one of them accepts without further explanation that it's now their job to protect her. I pick up a shovel that's leaning against the maintenance truck bed.

"Anyone have any issues?" I ask.

"No, boss," they all mutter.

"Then get back to work. All of you," I say. I move toward the shallow grave. I try to rationalize not killing her as I work in silence with my men. I don't know what to do with this blinding need to protect her, because I've only felt the need to protect one other woman. And that woman died at the hands of my father and this very club.

I *should* kill Brinley. If I wasn't such a selfish motherfucker, I would.

But I am and it's too late. I'm already addicted.

Three hours later, Gator has been committed back to the earth, where the worms can feast on his flesh, or what's left of it. I make my way into the cabin and pull my muddy boots off. I take one step and something sharp pierces the bottom of my foot. I silently curse while pulling it out, slicing my finger and thumb in the process, and then look around the room. Glass, all over the floor.

I can't help it, I grin. My little hummingbird has a temper after all. The shards glimmer in the dim light. I put my boots back on. Brinley will be cleaning that up in the morning. It's a teachable moment. Temper tantrums have consequences.

I'm caked in dirt, but I really don't give a fuck. I drop into the chair that's sitting across from Brinley as she sleeps soundly, breathing in the scent of her clean skin, but something isn't right. It smells too much like hotel soap mixed with the smoke and cologne of me. I don't like it and it just won't do. I glance around the room looking for her bag and make my way to it without thought, fishing inside for her perfume. I grab it out of a small floral cosmetic bag and twist the cap off the roll-on bottle. I breathe in the sweet jasmine scent before rolling some onto my thumb, it mixes with my blood and stings, but it feels like a part of her is seeping into me. Making my way back over to the bed, I sit on the edge and gently roll the perfume along her pulse point, and down her collarbone. I bend down and inhale, she makes a little sound, shifting, and starting to wake. I can still smell the hotel soap. It's not perfect, but it's better.

Brinley's hands are folded under her pretty face, her mouth is slightly parted, and her onyx hair is splayed everywhere. I simply watch her like this for a time, studying small things about her—that tiny dimple in her chin, the way her long lashes rest, her pouty lips and how they completely hypnotize me.

I flex my fists and struggle to understand why a strange feeling that I can only relate to peace has quietly surfaced in my cold, lead heart when I touch Brinley. I have no idea how long I just watch her sleep like this, stroking her neck, her jaw. Her eyes flutter open and a tightening in my chest takes hold as her gaze meets mine.

She's too good. She's too pure, and all I want to do is corrupt her.

The moment I bury myself deep within her and claim her, I'll be altered. Maybe forever. And I know it with every single part of me. But I'm not very good at denying myself what I want, so time isn't on her side.

CHAPTER 27

Brinley

A gentle hand on my face, and a soft touch with a warm calloused thumb wakes me from my nightmare. The nightmare I quickly remember is real. My eyes flutter open, I shoot up in bed and suck in a breath. I'm not used to the man Gabriel is yet. Especially like this. He's close, watching me intently. Every part of him is brooding. And at the moment, he's filthy dirty, which makes him even more intimidating.

"How long have you been there?" I croak.

"A while," he answers, standing and moving to the Keurig on the desk. He places a cup under it.

I watch him. He looks so out of place performing such a simple, normal task that I'm not sure what to do with it. Guess murderers need their coffee too.

"Your phone hasn't stopped. Layla and Evan," Gabriel says as the cup fills and the scent of coffee fills the air.

I reach over to my phone. Ten calls from Lay this morning.

One text from Evan that's readable on my lock screen.

EV

Hope you're settling in at home. Call me if you want to catch up.

I feel my face contort. My life with Evan seems so far away now.

Surreal.

I message Layla so she doesn't send out a manhunt and ask myself if she truly knows the life these men live. The life her husband lives.

I'm perfectly fine. See you in the dining hall.

PB

You spent the night with Wolfe, didn't you?

Shouldn't you be naked with your husband?

PB

My poor battered vagina needs a break sometimes

TMI

PB

So…you're with Wolfe?

No

PB

Chantel went to your room this morning to get you for the spa. You weren't there

Just because I wasn't there doesn't mean I'm with him

PB

Yes you are. See you at breakfast. Work up an appetite 😉

"What are you going to do with me now?" I ask openly, setting my phone down.

Gabriel looks me over as he adds cream to the cup of coffee, no sugar, then makes his way to me holding it out. I take it from him and my eyes meet his.

"When I said I know it all, I know *it all*," he says.

I can't decide if I'm creeped out by this or turned on.

"Then you already know who Evan is."

"Yes."

Gabriel leans against the wooden hutch as he starts to brew his own coffee. I let my eyes trail over the flexed muscle and veins of his sculpted arms.

He shrugs. "I wanted to see if you were still hung up on him. If he's going to be a problem. Figured I could tell by how you looked when I said his name."

"And could you?" I sip my coffee.

"Yes," he says simply.

Even though I don't love Evan anymore, I don't want him involved with this in any way. "That part of my life is long over. I think he just texted me to check in on me."

I wait as Gabriel studies me.

"You didn't answer me... about what you're going to do with me," I say, growing more self-conscious by the moment as I sit here in just a t-shirt with his heady stare on me. My nipples harden when this man simply looks at me, for God's sake. My body is a lost cause.

"Because I don't know what I'm going to do with you yet," he answers honestly.

"Does Layla know?" I ask. "What you all... do?"

His eyes narrow, and he turns to remove his coffee. He adds nothing. Of course he doesn't. This man screams *I take my coffee black.*

"You don't know what we do just because you witnessed one night," he retorts.

"I think I have a pretty good idea," I say, in a more snappy tone than I intend.

"You have *no* idea," he says.

I don't argue, only because the way Gabriel says it tells me maybe I don't.

"There are two ways members deal with their ol' ladies, or in your case a woman under protection."

"Captivity," I correct.

He shrugs. "Semantics."

I watch as Gabriel wraps his perfect lips around the rim of his paper cup as he sips. "Most of them either tell them everything or they tell them nothing."

"So Layla doesn't know much," I whisper, looking down at my cup.

Gabriel nods, confirming.

"Would he tell her if she wanted to know?" I ask, genuinely curious.

"Depends. Every man handles their ol' ladies' knowledge differently. He may not want her to know, or she may not be able to handle it."

"I would want to know all of it. I would never tolerate that," I say matter-of-factly, sounding very much like my mother. I internally cringe. "Hypothetically, of course," I add.

Gabriel smirks and I soften. I don't have a clue as to why this dirty, bloodied version of him is doing it for me, but here we are.

I take a big sip of my coffee and smooth my hair. It's wavy and knotted from letting it air dry while I cried myself to sleep last night.

"Will I go home?" I ask, feeling weak and at his mercy. I hate it.

Gabriel swallows a big gulp of his coffee, probably the whole cup.

"I can't trust you yet." He looks me over as he says it but it's no answer as to my fate.

I finish what is in my cup.

"Go meet your friend." He points to my toiletries and clothing under a mirror that hangs on the wall. "I'm going to take a shower. I have club business and then I'll be at breakfast with you"—he grabs fresh clothes from his bag as he speaks—"and clean up that glass. Don't do that again, losing your temper won't serve you."

"I'm not a child," I tell him with more attitude than warranted and self-admittedly like a petulant child. I look down and see his foot covered in white gauze.

"Then don't act like one," he says. "Chris is outside. He'll walk you down to the main building," he adds.

"Am I not safe because of what I saw last night?" I ask, just before Gabriel steps through the bathroom door, but he stops in his tracks. He turns and makes his way back to me, climbing onto the bed and grabbing both my thighs. My breath hitches as he pulls me down under him and hovers over me. He smells like campfire and leather mixed with whatever his aftershave or cologne is.

It's enough to make me crumble.

"You're not safe because you're mine, not because of what you saw," he says.

My pulse accelerates with his words and proximity. Of course Gabriel notices. He focuses on the flutter in my neck and then looks back up at me in question.

"What scares you? When I say that you're mine or that you aren't safe?" he asks in a low voice.

"Both." I gulp. "I'm not sure what scares me more. Being with you or being away from you," I answer honestly.

Gabriel's eyes move down to my lips. His Adam's apple bobs and tension lines the scruff of his jaw. He leans down, and his lips brush mine.

Just a single second of his soft kiss breathes life into every cell in my body. I'm alive and singing as he lingers for one more moment, then backs away. It takes me yet another to open my eyes.

"Good," is all Gabriel says before lifting himself off me and heading toward the shower. The lock of the door behind him says everything loud and clear. I am his to see, to use, to mold, however he wants.

But he's not mine.

I breathe in deeply and lay back on the bed. I can't even tell Layla what this is. She doesn't know what this club is capable of. She doesn't even know the man she married, or maybe she does but turns a blind eye?

I can't trust you yet. Gabriel's words repeat in my head.

I have a feeling I'm not done fighting this man yet, because there's not a chance in hell I'll be living in a motorcycle club-house. Gabriel might as well put a bullet in my head now if he thinks that's going to happen.

"There you are!" Layla winks, her massive diamond glints on her left hand. She's at a table in the main dining hall of the resort with the girls. This place is full. Club members are every-where, milling about and talking. Some are piling food onto their plates from the buffet.

I head over and get myself some food, but nothing seems all that appetizing. I get juice and coffee. Ax wanders up to the table at the same time I do, we both sit on opposite sides. His eggs and bacon take up all the real estate on his plate.

"Morning, new girl," he says like nothing happened last night. "Forgot salt and pepper, wifey." He kisses Layla on the head and heads back to the buffet for it.

"Sleep well?" Layla asks in a low voice.

"We did not have sex," I say to her automatically.

All four girls look up.

"Two nights and no sex?" Chantal asks. "What *are* you doing then?"

"I don't know. Arguing mostly," I answer honestly, swirling my juice in my glass.

I lean into Layla. "Can I talk to you without you asking any questions?" I whisper. She must see the look in my eyes because her expression grows serious instantly.

Layla nods and stands. "Sure, let's go to the ladies' room."

As we start to walk, I see the shape of Gabriel come through the door to the dining hall but I disappear behind the bathroom door before his eyes lock with mine.

"You're scaring me, Brin. Are you okay?" she asks the moment we get behind the safety of the door.

I break. It's unstoppable. The tears start to come. She pulls me in close and hugs me tight.

"What happened? Did he hurt you? I'll fucking kill him if he did."

"No." *Not really, anyway... not that I didn't enjoy.*

"Then what?"

I sniff. "I can't say. I just need a hug, I think."

"Brin. Did you see something that scared you?"

"You don't know, Lay? What they... do? You really don't?" I ask, knowing I'm going to be in trouble for even bringing it up.

She smiles and swipes my hair off my forehead.

"I know plenty, babe. But there's a difference between

181

wanting to know or asking what the club does, and just knowing. You can't be the wife of an HOH member and be delusional. Of course I've seen and heard some things. I know you might not believe me now, but these guys are better than whatever you saw or heard."

I scoff. "Is it normal that they keep someone who sees something?" I ask

"What?" she asks with a laugh like this is funny.

"He says he's keeping me because of it," I blurt out, dead serious.

"What? What do you mean by *keeping* you?"

I half laugh, half cry. "Stay with him or die."

She pushes back from me and looks me in the eye. *"Wolfe* told you he's keeping you?"

I nod, swiping a tear from my face.

All the humor leaves Layla's eyes, and she looks down in concentration, like she's running things through her mind.

"I don't want to know what you saw," she says, her eyes returning to mine. "I don't want you to tell me what it was, I'd rather not know. But can you tell me on a scale of one to ten how bad it was?"

"Twenty-five,"

"Fuck," Layla hisses. "Wolfe doesn't keep people for... anything," she whispers, probably trying to make sense of it all.

"Lucky me. I'm an experiment. I get to live at the clubhouse with my captor."

"Listen to me, Brin," Layla pleads. "Whatever you saw, I can't imagine. But you *have* to do what he says. You have to go along with him for now. This is... very out of character for Wolfe... and if I had to wager a guess, he's trying to keep from hurting you because you're my friend. He does have a heart in there somewhere. That has to be it."

"I don't believe you," I scoff.

The bathroom door swings open, Layla and I both straighten as two women come in. Layla knows them and they start to talk.

I take the time to fix myself up as they chatter. I wash my hands and smooth my hair.

"I might be his first of the weekend," a pretty brunette says. I watch her over my shoulder. "I haven't seen anyone in that lap. In fact, I've barely seen him at all." Her voice is husky and she seems older than me by a few years.

"Good luck. He doesn't believe in repeat offenders," another brunette, shorter with wild curly hair says as she applies her lipstick.

"The weekend is almost over," Layla says to them. "He *is* a man, you guys, he's not just a dick, Jesus. And besides, the guys have had a lot of work this weekend," she adds, looking at me.

I instantly know these women are talking about Gabriel and for some reason I don't like it. I wonder why a man with such a reputation for sex with women, anywhere and anytime, hasn't tried to have sex with me. He's had plenty of chances.

I pull my own gloss out of my purse.

"There are utility closets around. I'm going to go see if I can get lost in one with him before we leave," the older brunette says.

"You're so bad!" Her friend laughs.

I don't wait to hear the end of this conversation, I push past them and head back out to the dining hall, accidentally brushing into one of them on my way by—the taller one with the long straight hair.

"Excuse you, bitch," she says to me.

I turn back over my shoulder. "Sorry," I say as she laughs.

"Don't do it again, little Sandra Dee," she calls out.

I hold back tears as I move through the bathroom hallway and back into the dining room. I'm so out of my element with these people. Sandra Dee? From Grease? Is that how they all see me? Like a little goody-type girl with the bow in her hair?

When I reach the main room, Gabriel is at my table. He's clean now. No remnants of last night linger. He wears black jeans and a white t-shirt under his cut with his standard motorcycle boots on his feet. His still wet and wavy hair is tucked behind his ears.

I look around and wonder if he's been with every single woman in this room.

Everyone but me. The voice in my head reminds me.

I make my way to the table and notice he's right beside my spot, eating from a heaping plate. Another plate is in my setting with steaming eggs, bacon, fruit and toast. His clean scent consumes me before I even sit.

"Eat," he says as I take my place.

I can feel the eyes of the table on me as I sit and push away his offering.

"I'm good," I say in response.

Kai and Chantel's mouths actually fall open.

How dare I?

I look over at Gabriel just as he pops a thick piece of bacon between his perfect straight white teeth, biting into it, his eyes meet mine.

"Don't make me tell you twice," he says so low that no one else can hear as he pushes my plate back in front of me.

I decide to pick my battles, reminding myself that the only power I have here is the power of my choice, and the fruit does look good. I pick up a melon ball with my fork and look right at him, bringing it to my lips, I part them and place the ball halfway in, wrapping my lips around it slowly.

"Mmm." I make a moaning sound. "So good," I say.

Someone—Kai, I think—drops a fork, and I see that storm start to churn in Gabriel's slate eyes.

I chew and keep my eyes on him as I slide the fork out of my mouth, way more slowly than warranted.

"There you are." The husky voice from the bathroom sounds.

I get a better look at her. She's no older than thirty. Her hair is thick and she smells like fruity perfume. She wears a cropped white t-shirt and a high-waisted skirt. A short one, but you can still see the sliver of skin at her navel. An inked snake that peeks out of her sleeve must travel her whole body because it's visible at her waist and pokes out from beneath her skirt. The table is back to full chatter now.

"Got a few minutes to sneak away?" she asks Gabriel.

I don't look up. I look *anywhere* else. If he's going to go off with her like she's so sure he will, I don't want him to know I care in the slightest. I take another bite of melon and wait with bated breath for his answer. Layla sits down beside me with her own plate, having been removed from her previous spot by Gabriel.

"Why don't you ask Brinley how she feels about that?" Gabriel says smugly to the woman.

She angles her head over her shoulder and looks at me. Humiliation and anger bubbles up in me. I might snap.

"Sure, Sandra." She winks. I want to smack her. "You can come too. Don't bore me to tears," she says with a grin.

Wow. These women.

Fuck him and fuck her. I've had enough of people thinking they can walk all over me. I scoff with a bit of a laugh. "He can't be *that* good," I say to her.

"*Excuse* me?" she says, turning to face me fully like she might hit me.

I just pop another piece of melon in and smile and chew. I've never felt so free. Some small compartment of my brain tells me Gabriel won't let this woman hurt me, so right now I just feel strong enough to mess with them *both*.

"Oh, I'm sorry." I speak to her like she's a child. "Did I stutter? Let me speak more slowly for you. His dick"—I nod to Gabriel—"is it magic?" I cock my head to the side and someone snickers. I should probably stop but I don't. "Because you were just calling me a bitch not five minutes ago in the ladies' room but now you want to make out with me?" I ask.

The table goes dead silent.

"*Brin,*" Lay says, squeezing my thigh beside me.

"Cassidy, is it?" Gabriel says to her, keeping his eyes firmly planted on me.

"Chelsea," she corrects him,

"I didn't mean Brinley would come with us, I meant..." He turns his face up to hers and she melts beneath his gaze. I roll my eyes. "Ask her how she feels about me taking you into the closest bathroom and fucking you until you scream," Gabriel says, his eyes turning to firmly lock on mine.

"Have at it." I shrug back, calling his bluff. I look up at Chelsea "I'm not his keeper," I add.

Out of the corner of my eye, I swear I see Gabriel smirk.

"Am I missing something here?" Chelsea asks. I take a big sip of my juice and look back up at her.

"Nope." I pop my lips. "He's all yours, honey. Just might want to wrap that shit up, never know where it's been."

"Who the fuck do you think—" she starts, but Gabriel reaches out and grabs her arm. Hard. She stops talking immediately.

"Yeah, I'm gonna... go. I just wanted to see if you were up for a good time. I don't want to be in the middle of whatever this is," Chelsea says, gesturing between us.

"Good idea, Cassidy," Gabriel says without looking at her. "I wouldn't have fucked you anyway."

Chelsea takes off muttering something no one can under-stand about me, and Gabriel looks away from my eyes and goes back to eating as if nothing happened. I watch Chelsea go and try my best not to be happy that Gabriel turned her down. He doesn't say a word, only continues eating in silence, but I saw it, a sort of pride in his eyes when I stood up for myself.

That wasn't all Gabriel wanted. I know he was trying to make me admit my want, trying to make me submit to him like every other woman in here. Well, I won't, he's the one who wanted a wicked girl.

"What has gotten into you?" Layla asks, her eyes wide in surprise.

"I have no idea," I whisper honestly.

My short answer? Gabriel Wolfe makes me crazy. He makes me lose control in every way possible.

I ignore him while I eat but Gabriel stands up to leave part way through breakfast with Ax, Flipp, and Robby. He doesn't tell me where he's going, or when I'll see him again. He only gives me my marching orders with a squeeze to my shoulder. Ride home with Layla and the girls, and then start packing my things. I have no choice but to go with them in Chantel's SUV.

The whole way home I wonder when he'll come for me next. Layla complains that her honeymoon to California is being postponed because Sean 'has to work.' I don't say much. I just want to get home, have a hot shower, lock all my doors, and bury myself in bed.

I shoot up in my seat when we round the corner of Spruce because my house is a flurry of activity. Two vans are parked in front, and I instantly worry that a pipe burst or something until we get closer. There are stacks of cedar wood laying on my front lawn, a dumpster in my driveway and there must be ten men in various places, pulling down my old rotting porch.

CHAPTER 28

Gabriel

"I don't think they're taking it so well," Jake says when we're all seated in chapel later that day. I look to the clock on the wall behind him, then to the massive metal art piece underneath it that houses our club insignia. The deadly looking wolf skull that reminds me every day why I sit here.

"With the addiction services opening a month ago in the Chestnut area, they're really starting to clean up the streets. I think their Blue game is suffering," he adds, using the street name around Savannah for Fentanyl.

"Well, that's good news at least," I say.

We've just returned from meeting with our supplier out of Canada. Methadone is abundant up there and easy to get over the border if you have the right connections. We've just secured enough to supply two more clinics in the Savannah area for the foreseeable future. With the donations from the profits going back into the community under one of our dummy corps, we're able to pay the salary of two more counselors. We may sell drugs illegally, but not in the way most people would expect. I've made it my life's mission to make weaning drugs like methadone that help clean junkies up and services to help them recover more readily available. Some would say trafficking this sort of drug is illegal; I say it's cutting the red tape. It's also very profitable. So win, win.

Of course, Disciples of Sin—the suppliers of Blue and the H, whatever they're bringing in from El Paso—don't like it when we come in and open clinics, helping clean up the streets where they try to sell. It's bad for business for these junkies to have other options and resources.

"Where are we with the delivery of our message?" I ask.

"DOS's prospect checked into Peachwood Hospital in Savannah this morning, dropped off by a silver van. Max said no one went in, so I'd say the message is loud and clear," Flipp says, mentioning one of our newest members we sent out to watch the arrivals at the hospital.

"It'll be a while, if ever, that he says anything. Hard to talk with no tongue and write with no fingers." Kai grins. "Guess he won't be shooting a gun or blowing anything up anytime soon."

I shake my head.

"He got caught, he *should* be dead. It doesn't make sense," I say scrubbing my hand over my jaw. "They're keeping him alive for something."

"Probably gonna try to figure out how to pull more info from him," Kai retorts as he lights a smoke.

"I wouldn't worry about it," Jake adds. "Speaking of *should be dead*..." His eyes turn to me. "We're all trying to figure out what the hell is goin' on with you."

"The fuck do you mean?" I retort. I don't like being questioned.

"You know exactly what I mean. The girl. She knows too much... i.e. she should be dead. I didn't push you last night, but this club belongs to *all* of us. We want to know how you're gonna make sure she doesn't fuck us."

I clench my fist under the table to keep myself calm.

"The girl is *my* problem," I say.

Around the table, each one of them looks at me like they don't know what to think.

"I know this is unorthodox." I'm not going to show them an ounce of weakness. The way I want this woman is unexplainable and none of their goddamn business. "She's going to prove useful," I say just to shut them all up. "You have to trust me. Don't ask me again."

Jake sets his jaw.

I turn to Ax. "When you moved Layla into your house after two weeks, no one questioned you."

"Layla's my wife now," Ax answers.

"Wife. What even is that? A piece of paper? She wasn't then. You're all only questioning it because it's me," I say.

"Yeah," and "exactly," every single one of them says in some form.

"It's unlike you, boss, you know it is. We just want to make sure you're thinking rationally. With this face, I won't survive in Henderson," Kai says, mentioning the local penitentiary.

"The girl is my problem," I reiterate. "Do any of you doubt my decisions? My leadership?" My fist hits the table.

"Not at all, boss," Kai speaks first, everyone else either shakes their head no or speaks up with him.

"We all trust you... just... wanna make sure she isn't a distraction," Jake says.

"She's not," I tell them.

"Why her?" Kai asks, genuinely curious.

I look at all of them.

"When I fucking figure that out I'll let you know. Until then, she's my problem and I'm *not* distracted."

With that, I snap the gavel down, which tells them all to shut the fuck up.

I make it to the corner of Netherwood and Spruce just as the sun starts to set. The crew is hard at work just like they were told to be.

The wide old porch on her massive century home is almost completely torn down already and it's only been a day. New cedar sits on pallets in the driveway and Chantel's SUV is long gone but the bike in the driveway and my prospect sitting in a lawn chair under a tree tells me Brinley is here. I told her I had business and that she should ride home with Layla and the other girls, and pack her belongings, anything she wants to bring with her.

I see the drape inside her kitchen snap as I shut my bike off. I find myself wondering how I'll find her. What will she be wearing when I go in? Did she listen and get packed up and ready to leave or will she give me that feisty look and put up a fight? Will she be grateful I got a crew here to fix her porch or will she be pissed I took over?

"Thanks, bro," I say to Austin, our newest prospect, over the sounds of demo saws and construction chatter. I pat him on the shoulder. "You guys can finish up and head out, keep the neighbors happy, it's getting late."

"Cool, you just said as fast as possible, so we didn't want to stop until you said we could."

I nod. Good man.

"The boys or Shell got some barbeque going tonight?" he asks.

"Maybe, feel free to head over and find out," I tell him as he fastens his helmet.

I turn around and nod to the porch crew: two other club prospects, and an older member who barely rides anymore and his grandson who is a licensed carpenter.

"Good work, boys," I tell them as I move to head in.

"We'll have the rest of the old porch down by tomorrow and be starting on the new one."

"Take the scrap wood to Millers Farm, tell them to bill me," I say and nod for them to take off.

I push through the screen and make my way into the dim house as the sound of tools hitting a job box and trucks and bikes firing up fills the air.

I look up at the two-storey foyer. This house is large, much too big for one person. It's neat though, and it smells like a blend of stale air and lemon or citrus, but all the furniture is clean and uncovered and the walls are all pale gray.

"You're wasting your time here. I hope you realize there's not a chance in hell I'm going with you to live at the clubhouse."

I turn to face the defiant voice echoing from behind me. Brinley stands in her bare feet, little linen shorts with a black cropped tank top and her hair wild around her shoulders. Her nipples are hard underneath her tank and her arms are folded under her tits, forming a little shelf for them. Her face sits in a pretty, defiant little scowl, letting me know she'll be putting up a fight.

Fuck me, she's stunning when she's angry.

My eyes take hold of hers from across the room.

She's right about one thing. I am wasting my time, but not in the way she thinks.

I'm never going to be able to overcome my want for her.

There's no saving her.

Her breath shallows and her tongue darts out to wet her bottom lip. Outside, she's all strength and heat simmers in her pale blue eyes. When they meet mine, I see the tiniest hint of fear.

That split second is all my body needs for that basic, primal instinct to take over. My instinct to hunt her, my instinct to completely own her.

The last thread of my control snaps like a twig under the weight of my boot, and I know there's no going back.

CHAPTER 29
Brinley

I'm frozen, afraid to move, or breathe. In the short time I've known Gabriel, I've seen him angry, amused, terrifying, focused, godlike.

But I've never seen him like this. This look he's wearing I can't place.

He doesn't respond to me.

His eyes are primed and focused, they seem to touch every hair on my head, every stretch of skin. Like they're learning the planes of my body. I'm afraid to speak again or even breathe.

I wait like a fly caught in a spider's web.

The second Gabriel moves, I flinch. He smirks and calmly pulls his cut from his body, tossing it over the back of a chair in the side parlor. He turns and silently stalks back to the front door. Placing his hand in the centre, he leans into it and drops his head, pausing for a moment, almost as if he's collecting himself. I can see the rise and fall of his shoulders as he inhales and then releases a single deep breath. His other hand comes up, resting on the handle for a moment and then slowly locks the door with an audible *click* that seems to echo throughout the entire house. I can sense the danger, but I'm rooted to my spot, too afraid to go anywhere. Gabriel slowly turns away from the door and stares at his cut on the chair. A second passes. Then two, before he brings his dark gaze back to mine.

"*Run*," he growls.

I flinch again with the deep timbre of his voice in the quiet space.

"W-wha—?"

"It seems"—he starts to move toward me and I brace myself for flight—"we're at an impasse. So, I'll give you one minute as a head start."

It's in this instant I realize I am useless in the face of terror because I still don't move. I just watch in slow motion as my hunter stalks toward me, grips both my arms and pulls me to him roughly, our bodies flush and his sweet scent washes over me, drawing me in deeper.

"If I find you before that sun is set, I fuck you, and from this point on you *will* remember that I own you."

His lips hover over mine, both his large hands move up through my hair and I feel him, already hard and pressing into my abdomen.

"You may fuck me, but you'll never own me" I test him.

Gabriel grips my hair in one large handful at the roots and tips my face back sharply for better access.

"Fucking little brat." His deep voice makes a shiver echo up my spine.

His mouth comes down and hovers over mine, I wait, already panting because I can't move. The way he's wound his hands in my hair, he'd rip it from my scalp if I tried. I can only run when he releases me, and he knows it. His minty, bourbon-laced breath bleeds into me as he slides his tongue across my bottom lip. He sucks it into his mouth and then bites it hard enough to draw blood. My brain tells me it's pain, but my body ignites, my pussy instantly throbs, and I moan into his mouth.

"What are you *doing* to me?" he asks, his voice ragged and almost as breathless as mine.

I look into his eyes and test him further, remembering Layla's words. It's *my* body he wants, it's *me* that *he* is aching for. I find my power and arm myself with it. I look down, then back up at him.

"Please..." I whimper like I can't wait for him to devour me.

He growls into me, and I feel it, the moment he gives in and his control completely snaps, falling along with every inhibition I have to the floor below.

"Fuck it—"

He barely gets the words out before his lips come crashing down on mine, the same way they did in the woods but this time, he doesn't stop. Gabriel slides his hands out from under my hair to either side of my jaw in one fluid, intentional moment, tilting my face for better access, his tongue slinks inside and moves in a languid pace with mine to taste every corner of my mouth. This kiss is full of a passion I can't explain. It's lips, tongues, and teeth. With it he claims me, kissing me like there's no such thing as time. And I realize, I've never really been kissed before.

No other man should count.

I wrap my arms around his shoulders, feeling the muscles ripple under his shirt, and I long to feel his skin, his naked body pressed to mine. I slide my hands up and fist them in the hair at the nape of his neck. I pull tight, and he groans into my mouth. I can't get close enough, I desperately grasp and pull at him, forcing him closer. I sink right into him like his body was made to house mine, but there's no place I can burrow that gives me what I need. Gabriel kisses me so deeply that I don't know how long it's been since my last breath, and I don't care. Let me die

196

like this in his arms. Let this high last forever. Hands slide back into my hair—seconds later? Minutes? I have no idea.

He tips his forehead to mine.

"Hide well, little hummingbird. When I find you, I'm going to fucking ruin you."

Gabriel's breaths come as quickly as mine and my more sadistic side that I'm just discovering loves that I make him as uncontrolled as he makes me. A deep rumble courses through his chest, and he lets go of me abruptly, leaving me barely able to stand. His hands fall at his sides. I see his fists clench and his jaw tense.

"*Run,*" Gabriel commands once more, and then I'm flying.

I take off through the house as fast as my feet will carry me, almost tripping up the stairs as I go, my heart pounding in my chest. I think of every space I could hide as I run, listening to hear if he's broken his word, all the while I count. *Twenty-four, twenty-five...* knowing my time is limited. I push open every door as wide as they can go, so he won't know which room I've entered, and then make my way to the last bedroom at the end of the hall., It's small, unassuming, and quiet. *Thirty-eight... thirty-nine...*

I slide a rocking chair away from the wall just enough to get behind it and twist the handle I know is hiding in the wall paneling, opening the secret entrance to the old storage room in the attic. I carefully close the door behind me with shaky hands. *Forty-six... forty-seven...* My heart feels like it might beat out of my chest as I move like flames are chasing me, climbing up the stairs, knowing exactly where to go. I'm utterly terrified but somehow want him to find me all at the same time. *Fifty-one... fifty-two...*

I reach the top of the attic stairs, pausing to catch my breath as I quickly scan the room where my nana kept all her old belongings. I glance around, trying to determine the most inconspicuous spot. I slide over the top of my nana's cedar chest and crouch down behind it in the darkest part of the attic. *Fifty-six... fifty-seven...* I'm lightheaded and alive with need and desire. The thrill of waiting consumes me as I count the final seconds until my wolf comes to hunt me... *Fifty-eight... fifty-nine...*

Sixty.

CHAPTER 30

Gabriel

I watch her form disappear up the stairs in the dark house and I suddenly find myself at war with my own nature, fighting to give her the head start I promised. The beast in me pushes back against its chains, wanting to take her flesh between its teeth, tear into her heat and claim all of her. I've never been so hard. I've never been so desperate for any single thing in my entire life as I am right now, at this moment, for Brinley Rose Beaumont. The entire world could go up in flames around us, and I'd still find her and fuck her without pause until we both burned to cinders.

I glance out the back window of her house, watching the sun slowly dip below the fields on the horizon. The sixty seconds I gave her pass agonizingly slow as the patter of her feet sound from above me. The noise quiets, then disappears, and suddenly I'm bolting up the stairs behind her, positive this woman is making me lose my mind. I launch myself up them three at a time, following the trace of her jasmine scent that still lingers in the hall. I look to my left. The hallway lined with bedrooms is too easy, and the sun is disappearing quickly as I make the snap decision to run to the other end of the hall. I enter a bedroom there and pause, listening before exiting and continuing my search. There's no sound, my little humming-bird has found her hiding spot. Wherever she is now, she's not going to be there long.

I move through the space, my training taking over and I become light on my heavy feet. When I get to the last door at the end of the hall, it's open—the same as all the others. My gut tells me she's there and I never doubt my gut. I make my way in and stop to listen for the sound of her breath, a rustling of fabric, anything, but again I hear nothing. I look around the room as the last hint of the sun slips below the horizon. I start to leave, but something gives me pause and that's when I see it, a small handle in the panelling. A secret door, perhaps?

I make my way there and open it, a stairway leads up to the attic and I instantly know she is up there. It isn't lost on me that she hid where the only way out is through me.

I take those stairs just as quickly as the last, I'm not quiet about it, she has nowhere to go. She sucks in a sharp breath when I reach the top.

"Your scent calls to me, Brinley, there's not a space in this house you could hide." I smirk, knowing she's unleashed some-thing in me that can't be contained now.

I get to Brinley in less then three steps under the stairs behind an old cedar chest. I wrap my hand in her hair and drag her out by it. She comes easily and I press her face first against the wood wall, she reaches behind and begins to claw at me, slap me, anything she can. I press my cock into her ass, letting her know I'm about to violate her. It's the only warning I give. I crush her with my weight, taking over her space.

She's grunting, kicking, trying hard to reach any part of me. It only makes me harder.

"Found you, little bird," I say gruffly into her ear with a

tone of finality. I breathe her in, turning my face into her neck, placing my open mouth over the furious thrum of her pulse. She stops flailing and I feel the sting from where her nails gnashed into the skin of my forearms.

I pull my knife from its sheath and trail the back side of the blade up the back of her thigh. She whimpers when she feels it. The mix of pleasure and pain in her little noises makes my cock throb against my jeans.

I slide the knife under Brinley's flimsy linen shorts and with a sharp flick of my wrist, I slice upward until I tear through every last inch of them, they fall to the floor as I replace my knife in its sheath, pressing my chest into her back to hold her in place against the wall.

Brinley moans as I slide my hand over the soft globe of her ass and squeeze, hard. My hand comes down, laying a tight slap to her cheek and she yelps when she feels it. She calms as I smooth my palm over the sting and slide my other hand up into her hair. I can barely make out my handprint in the dimly lit attic but fuck, what I can see, makes me feral.

I spin her around and press her back into the wood, biting her lower lip and sucking it into my mouth, licking and tugging on it. My tongue slips inside and strokes hers, playing with her, knowing now that I've really kissed her, there will never be a day where I don't.

She melts into me almost instantly, her lips become pliant against mine as she lets me take her mouth. My cock twitches and strains further with every swipe of her tongue. She moans and whimpers as I slide my hands over her body, kneading every inch of skin I can, bringing her closer in every way possible. Brinley inches her needy pussy into my cock, her tense muscles loosen as she starts slowly molding into me. She picks up the pace, her tongue meeting mine and challenging me to keep up. She lets me claim her mouth as I kiss her, bite her, and then lick over the pain, all the while she trembles beneath my hold.

I pull her tank over her head and her hair tumbles around her shoulders. She looks up at me almost naked. Only one tiny slip of cotton remains between her thighs, keeping me from what I want, what I need.

Brinley sucks in a sharp breath when my fingers find her nipples, pinching them, bringing them to my mouth, sucking in the sweet little buds. Her honey flavor filling my mouth makes me feel crazed.

She moans and rocks her pussy into me harder.

"You act so innocent, little hummingbird, but inside that pretty little head you're just as fucked up as I am. I *want* it," I tell her as I slide my free hands down between her thighs, over the lace of her thong. "I want it all."

She moans into my lips.

"Inside, you've always craved this, haven't you?" I ask, knowing it's true. If it wasn't, she'd be crying, fighting me, not pushing her desperate pussy into my cock like it will bring her the reward she seeks.

I slide her thong aside and just as I suspect she's fucking soaked.

"Mmm," I confirm. "So wet for my cock, the prim and proper debutant is really just a dirty little slut begging for me to tear this pussy apart."

Brinley can lie, but her pussy can't. She's dripping. I grip her hair with my other hand and pull her head back from her roots. The soft, black waves trail down my forearm, her eyes are open and burning with lust.

"Am not prim and proper..." she half moans, and I chuckle at her, cursing as I slide the pad of my middle finger between her lips and over her clit.

"Yeah? Show me," I tell her as I keep her eye contact and

tease her clit in rough circles until she's bucking, arching, reaching forward, searching for more from me. Her eyes start to close, but I pull her hair again, so they snap open. I shake my head, a warning for her to keep them on mine. Time stands still as I trade between fucking my fingers into her tight cunt and sweeping my thumb over her clit, just before she's about to come all over my hand, I pull it away.

Brinley whimpers and pouts with the loss of contact and I know that pout will be my downfall.

"Not yet. I want that cum dripping down my cock, little bird."

I take her lip between my teeth, then release, watching as it pops back into place while I keep her hair in my hand as I unbuckle my jeans with the other. I free my hardened, leaking cock, and kiss her again.

Fuck. I could survive without food or water, but now that I've had them, I couldn't survive without these fucking lips.

I slide my hands down Brinley's thighs and lift her against the wall. She wraps her legs around my waist and slides my cock up and down against her dripping pussy. Her lips hug each of the barbells that run my length, her breathing accelerates with every single one. The sound drives me to the brink of insanity.

Never in my life have I gone bare with a woman, never in my life have I even thought about it. But with Brinley? I wouldn't dream of putting anything between us. Something about burying my seed deep inside her cunt electrifies me.

"Condom..." she mutters as I continue to slide against her.

"No condom," I say low. Her only response is a tiny whimper.

"You're too big," she says in a whisper

I smirk against her lips, just the feel of her against me like this... that feeling alone almost makes me come.

"Yes, I am... but you will fucking love it."

I guide my cock to Brinley's center, sliding through her slit to ready her as she moans and grips my shoulders. Her eyes meet mine as she moves her hips up. Just my tip slips into her, and we both suck in a breath as we stare at each other. For a few frozen seconds, our breathing syncs. I use my middle finger to circle her clit, begging her to accommodate me.

She moans, and all my willpower leaves me. I sheath myself in her tight, wet heat with one go, her walls practically strangling my cock, and she cries out as I fill her like she's never been filled.

"Breathe," I order, running my hands up her thighs, trying to calm her.

She does what I ask. I hear her inhale, her head falling against the wall as her legs quiver around me.

I force myself to breathe as I pull out and sink back into her perfect pussy. She's so wet there's no friction as her tight cunt swallows every barbell, every inch of me. I don't fill her without immense effort. We both suck in a breath as I push myself deeper, bottoming out in her and I stay there.

"Fucking Christ, Brinley... *Fuck,*" I mutter into her hair as her tight, wet heat seizes my cock like a vice. She pulses around me as she adjusts to my size, panting, and pushing her perfect tits against my t-shirt. The unexpected urge to feel her naked skin on mine overwhelms me.

Dopamine flows through my veins as the high of *her* spreads like wildfire through my blood.

The beast in me bares its teeth, knowing without question that it's finally about to be satisfied.

CHAPTER 31
Brinley

I feel everything in my body, every cell, every nerve ending. I feel his movements like an echo surrounding me. The warmth of his breath, the bite of his teeth on my neck, the pleasure and pain of Gabriel filling me, the reaction of my body to his.

It's all right here, so close, yet I can't quite grasp it. I'm floating.

This is ecstasy.

Gabriel holds my body up against the wall, keeping himself rooted as deep as he possibly can inside of me, bare. I have no idea if he's clean, but something in me says he most certainly would be. The odd thing that resonates with me is that he didn't ask if I was on the pill, which I am. But those are the least of my worries, because right now, I've never felt anything like him, and I swear he's going to split me in two.

My body fights to both hold him and push him out as the rough attic wall bites into my shoulder blades. Gabriel moves his hands down my thighs to my calves, where he unlocks my ankles from around his waist. He slides each of his large hands up my thighs, cupping them from underneath as he spreads me wide against the wall, holding me up with just the strength of his arms. Gabriel's thumbs press into my inner thighs with a bruising grip as he pulls out of me and brutally fucks back in. I inch up the wall a little further with every bottomless thrust. His hooded gaze bounces between where we connect and my expression, as if he's memorizing how every touch affects me. I feel every single wrung of the ladder along his shaft as my pussy swallows them one by one. I've never felt anything like him as he spreads my thighs even further apart.

"This tight little cunt... sucking my cock in so deep..." Gabriel growls as he watches himself fuck me slowly. "You're taking me so well, little hummingbird... Mmm... So fucking tight. So fucking wet. So fucking perfect. You're *ruining* me." His words are low and finish with groans that tell me they're true.

He drives into me again and again, all the while the wood eats at my shoulders. Somehow, it enhances the pleasure.

Gabriel doesn't take it easy; he doesn't let me fully adjust, he's on a mission for taking, claiming, his own pleasure at the forefront.

I want this. I never realized how much until his body connected with mine, but I want it. The brutality fuels me. I don't want his mercy or his ease. I *want* him to own me. I want him to need me so badly that it's a violent, uncontrollable want, a raging fire that can't be stopped.

Gabriel slams into me, pulling all the way out to his tip, then driving back into me again, my breathing becomes so shallow I may faint. But then, just when I think I can't take anymore, my core begins to tighten, and my body begs for more of the harsh way he fucks me.

I give in, I wrap my arms tighter around his strong shoulders and grip his hair, it's all I have for leverage. I start to move with him, my nipples graze his chest and harden further. My entire body begins to heat.

"That's it. You want to watch me fuck you? You want to see how your body begs for my cum now?" He nods to where we connect.

"I—I can't take it..." I trail off, watching us move together. There are no words as the pain blends into pleasure until there's no line between the two.

"Yes, you fucking can," he growls, showing me that he craves my submission as much as I crave the beast in him.

He's just as lost as I am.

We're lost together.

His hands tighten to a bruising hold around my thighs.

I spiral, electricity flows through every cell as my orgasm seeks my core. I whimper as Gabriel drives into me without relent, I've given up on trying to even breathe properly. He slows his pace but doesn't slow the depth he punishes me with.

"The things I want to do to you." *Thrust.*

"I want to break you." *Thrust.*

"Bruise you." *Thrust.*

"Tear you apart and then piece you back together." *Thrust.*

"Gabriel, please," I cry out as the orgasm takes hold of every fiber of my being.

"Say my name, say it as you soak my cock."

"Gabriel..." I trail off because I have nothing left as I come all over his cock.

His groan is deep and unforgiving as his name lingers on my lips. My body tenses and I pull so tight to his hair I think I could pull it from his skull. It's the pain he craves.

Gabriel bites at my skin, then sucks to soothe it, all while thrusting into me like a man crazed. I feel him stiffen even more just before his warmth spreads through me. I don't have any fight left when he bites my bottom lip so hard the taste of copper fills my mouth.

"*Brin, Fuck,*" Gabriel groans as his cock jerks and pulses inside me. The slow trickle of blood drips down my chin but I'm gone.

Let me bleed.

My head falls back against the dusty attic wall, and I feel Gabriel's tongue slide up my throat and over my chin, collecting my blood. I tip my head forward to see the scarlet of me covering his lips.

It's an oddly erotic sight, he kisses me and the taste of my blood, mixed with him, fills my mouth. Pulling his cock from me, he lets me down gently. I moan at the empty feeling. He holds me up by the shoulders and I stand completely naked before him as he stands almost fully clothed. I stare up at him, his cum dripping from me.

He makes a tsk sound as he reaches between my legs and skims his hand up the inside of my thighs, bringing his cum back up, he shoves it into my pussy with his first two fingers and groans.

"Every last fucking drop."

Gabriel's chest rises and falls as he tucks his still semi-hard cock into his jeans and does up his buckle. It takes every ounce of strength I have to not collapse. I'm sure my back is bleeding. These walls are old, dusty, and full of nails.

Gabriel doesn't speak. He simply picks me up bridal style as though I weigh nothing and brushes my sweaty hair off my forehead. His hand cups my face and he leans down, his lips brush mine way too gently after what he just put me through.

"Let's get you cleaned up," is all he says. I reach up around his neck and nuzzle my face into his t-shirt. It's warm with sweat from the humid attic heat and us. His scent is amplified, and as I breathe it in, he cradles me closer.

"The bathroom is down the hall," I say when we reach the bottom of the attic stairs.

"Fourth door on the right," he says as he walks the short distance to it like he's been in my house a thousand times.

"Right, I forgot, military brain," I say with a little grin.

"Can't help it, force of habit to know my surroundings," Gabriel says with a small smirk of his own. He grabs a towel from the shelf and lays it across my wide bathroom counter before depositing me onto it. The contradiction that this beast of a man would care about my body feeling cold when it touches the marble warms me in a way I can't put into words.

He takes in the sight of my back in the mirror behind me and sets his jaw.

"It's bleeding, isn't it?" I ask. I know it is, I can feel it drying to my skin.

"It's going to need to be cleaned," he observes.

Gabriel's eyes are devoid of emotion as he moves to my large, tiled shower and pushes open the glass door. He messes with the water temperature for a few minutes, it takes the old pipes a while to heat in here. He turns to me and uses one hand to tug at the back of his collar, pulling his shirt off overhead.

My eyes widen as he continues, unbuckling his belt, toeing his boots off and losing the rest of his clothes until he stands naked before me. The only thing that remains are the dog tags around his neck and the mural of ink covering his muscled body. My skin tingles and my nipples pucker at the sight of him.

He's... jarringly beautiful.

My eyes move quickly as I take in everything I can, not knowing when or if I'll see him naked again. Everything about him is powerful. His shoulders are wide and strong, extending into heavy, muscular arms, rippled with veins and tendons. His chest is chiseled and thick and leads to a defined six pack.

Various scars line his skin, one under his ribs, one in both his right shoulder and his arm that look like bullet holes.

When he turns to make his way into the shower, I see it—his entire back is covered in a lifelike wolf's skull, a scar settles through it's one eye, but it's not part of the tattoo, it's an actual scar, jagged and startling. Ink stretches over every visible plane of his skin; he has no other piercings besides his ladder. I try to take it all in.

"Keep staring at me like that, little hummingbird, and you won't even make it into this shower." He doesn't even face me as he speaks, but it's like he knows I'm staring at him.

I force my mouth closed and I watch as droplets of water rush over every part of him.

"Have you never seen a naked man before?" he asks with a tone that says he knows I think he's incredible.

I climb off the counter and narrow my eyes at him, feeling somewhat normal again. I step into the steamy shower and he moves back, swiping water and his wet hair back.

"Not like you," I say honestly.

He gently grabs my waist, turning my body into the warm spray and I hiss when the water meets my scratched up back.

He growls as he uses his thumb to gently rub any dust or dirt from the wounds.

"I thought you wanted to mark me?" I ask with a joking tone. "I thought you'd be happy I'm bleeding. Why does it seem to bother you?"

I feel him lean down over my shoulder. His lips hover beside my ear, and water drips from his chin as his teeth suddenly clamp down on my shoulder, and then he sucks.

My breath hitches with the contact.

"*I* want to mark you. I don't want anything else to," Gabriel says as he grabs the soap. "This is going to sting. But it's necessary."

It stings but it's not so bad, the scratches aren't deep and he has me cleaned up in no time. He pumps shampoo into his hand and massages it into my hair. His hands are overwhelmingly big on my scalp. I close my eyes and fall into his rhythm, helpless beneath his magic fingers.

"You like this?" he asks as the shampoo swirls down the drain.

"Yes," I mutter, my eyes still closed as I feel the slick conditioner cover my hair. "I think this is the dream," I blurt out.

"What is it about this that's your dream, little bird?" he asks, genuine curiosity in his tone.

"The way you touch me...violent one moment, soft the next. Hard and unforgiving, then washing my hair. It's overwhelming."

Gabriel wrings the water from my hair.

"I understand why you're so popular with women now," I mutter.

Gabriel lets my hair fall against my back and spins me around. His gray eyes are light and lucid.

"I've never showered with a woman before," he admits, leaning down to kiss my lips. The hard heat of his chest presses against my breasts.

I shudder.

"Never washed their hair." Another kiss

"Never kissed them the way I kiss you." He ghosts a finger over my pebbled nipple and his lips meet my neck, my collarbone.

"Never wanted to touch them the way I want to touch you."

He pinches my nipple and a zap of pleasure races through my core.

"Never been inside *any* woman without a condom. *Ever*." His hot lips wrap around a nipple while his hands skim my waist, around to my lower back. "But I would fill *you* full every moment I fucking could and savor the sight of my cum dripping down your soft thighs."

"*Shit,*" I manage as his tongue works in ways I've never experienced.

"Only you, Brinley." He squeezes tight to my ass. "It's only you I've ever felt the need to possess, to claim for my own."

"Why?" I ask, simply because I can't understand it. I've seen the women who hang around the club house. They're beautiful and wild in a way I'm not.

"I told you, I don't ask why," he says simply. "My men think you're clouding my judgement. They think you're a distraction, dangerous for me."

"Am I?" I ask in a breathless moan. All thoughts have left my head because his one hand holds me tight around my hips and the other has slid between my thighs, coming dangerously close to my already throbbing core.

"Yes," Gabriel answers without hesitation. "In the worst way."

"How so?" One finger enters me as his eyes focus on mine.

"There isn't a thought in my head that doesn't start and end with you," he says honestly as another finger enters me and works effortlessly to torture me in the best way possible.

"Oh..." is all I can say as my core begins to tighten again.

He adds a third, and I mewl into his chest as the water runs over us both.

"Like, right now, all the beast inside me wants to do is taste this tight little cunt."

"So then," I moan. "Do it." *Please, please, do it,* I silently beg.

Gabriel growls in response, seating me on the shower bench. He drops to his knees as water sprays down on my chest and his fingers continue their assault on my clenching pussy.

"You're dangerous because the pain I crave, you crave it too." He takes small bites as he works his way up my thighs, taking the time to pay attention to both legs, and the closer he gets to my center the harder he bites and I want it. *I want it to hurt.* What is wrong with me?

"I'm never not thinking of burying some part of me inside you," Gabriel growls, pushing my legs wide. "This pussy calls to me. It begs for me." He licks a firm trail up my slit.

My back arches so fast I nearly fall off the bench but he's there, wrapping his arms under my thighs and pulling me to him so only his face is my seat, and then he's making a meal of me, trading between suctioning his lips around my clit and fucking me with an expert tongue.

"*Mmm,*" he groans into me. My whole body quivers with the vibration of his mouth on me.

"You're my favorite fucking flavor, Brinley Rose." Gabriel makes it his mission to prove his words.

I don't stand a chance. He pulls me even closer, and I give in. He spreads my thighs wide and loses himself to me, sucking my clit into his mouth, like a man starved.

I look down at this intimidating viking of a man between my thighs and my insides churn with raw desire at the sight. Every part of me feels like it's on sensory overdrive. Gabriel works his tongue with perfect pace and pressure. He lifts my legs up over his shoulders and strokes my thigh with one hand as he adds two fingers to my needy pussy. Only moments pass before I feel myself starting to lose control.

"Fuck, Brin, you taste so fucking good. Open your eyes and look at me while I make you come."

I do as he says, tipping my head up and forcing my eyes to his. My legs shake, my cries grow louder but he never stops and before I realize what's happening I'm coming over his face shamelessly. Calling his name out, rocking my hips into him, taking what I need, whatever feels good without thought. Something I've rarely done with any man.

The thing is, Gabriel doesn't make me feel self-conscious, he makes me feel beautiful, encouraging me to let go, encouraging me to be me, whoever that is.

"Yes," I cry. I begin to mumble incoherent things as he doesn't let up on my still so sensitive clit and it wrenches a second orgasm from me in mere moments.

I think I'm yelling *"more, please, Gabriel, please"* as he holds me tight, taking over my being, making the choice for me. All I can think is, *God, if I remember any one feeling for the rest of my life, please, let it be this, falling apart with Gabriel Wolfe between my thighs.*

CHAPTER 32

Gabriel

I shut the water off as she comes down from the high of her orgasm and the water runs cold over my back. Cracking the shower door, I slip a thick towel around Brinley's shoulders then wrap one around my own waist.

Brinley's room is dark and quiet when we enter. She shivers as she sits down on the bed. Picking up my t-shirt, she tosses it over her head and reaches into a drawer, pulling out a pair of panties that look like little shorts. They cover only about a third of her perfect ass, and unbelievably I'm already thinking of taking her again.

"You look dangerous in my shirt."

"It's warm and I want to study the ink on your skin without one."

I raise an eyebrow. "If you're going to study me, I'm gonna need a drink."

"All I have is my father's old bourbon collection. It's still locked in the cabinet in the den. Two rooms down."

I nod. I noticed the space earlier but there's no need to

remind her I memorized every step of this place during my search for her.

"He saved it in that dark room for a special occasion and never even opened it," she says as I make my way out of the room.

"Sad, if you ask me. Waste of a good scotch," I tell her.

"Agreed," she says, following.

The den is dark when I enter. I flick on a lamp that sits under a big picture window. It's an old library of sorts with black out drapes. I pull them back, the moonlight and her vast property fills my sight. There's an old desk on one wall, it looks antique and expensive, and a wall-to-wall liquor cabinet. Chalked full.

"Key's in the second drawer." Brinley enters behind me.

I fish the key out and unlock the cabinet, pulling out a forty-year-old Boralini scotch that must be worth ten thousand dollars.

"I don't believe in special occasions," I tell her as I pop the cork and swirl the bottle.

Brinley shoots me a smirk. I don't think she intends to be sexy, but she is. She has this whole freshly fucked glow about her. Her hair is still damp and her face is free of any makeup. She's the most beautiful thing I've ever laid eyes on, and she doesn't even realize it.

"Neither do I, so... bottoms up?" she asks, making her way to an open shelf and grabbing two crystal glasses down.

I tip it back, drinking it straight from the bottle in a twelve-ounce curl.

"My dad is probably rolling over in his grave." She giggles as she watches me swallow.

Fuck me, that's good.

"What happened to them?" I sit in a leather chair in front

of an old stone fireplace, genuinely curious and still surprised I care. She sits in the one across from mine and we face each other at arm's length.

"My dad died when I was eighteen, I'd just left for college. He went to work that morning—he was a lawyer," she tells me. "Although, you probably know that."

I shake my head. "Never went further than their names and that they're no longer alive," I tell her honestly. "Once I knew they were dead, there was no reason for me to keep learning about them."

She nods and leans forward to take the bottle. "That makes sense," she says.

I toy with her for a beat just to see the spark in her eyes. I hold the bottle tight and don't let her have it for a few seconds. The look of determination I'm starting to crave comes out and I let her have the scotch as a reward.

"He was in the middle of his second meeting of the day and he just died. Massive heart attack. He was only forty-eight," she says. "I hadn't seen him in a month, and oddly enough, I didn't really know him, even though I spent my whole life with him. My mother died two years ago from a short battle with cancer."

I listen as she speaks because I want to drink in her every expression. The way the light reflects off her silky skin, the wave that takes hold of her hair as it dries. Her lips moving as she talks—every single part of her is perfection.

"He always wanted me to be something he wasn't able to be growing up. He sent me to the best schools, I sang with the worship team at our church." She grins "That's where I met Lay."

I grab the bottle back from her and take another big swig.

"And now look at you, here with me, and she's married to my Sgt at Arms."

"But where did that wholesome life get either of my parents?" Brinley asks as she pulls the bottle from me. "Both dead before they were fifty-five? A boring marriage. I never even saw them have a single affectionate moment. They had their dinner parties and school events and social status. Their country club, church life. They had all this"—she waves a hand around the stately room—"but they had nothing. I didn't know them, and they didn't know me. They thought they knew who I was and vice versa, but I learned more about them going through their things when they died than I ever did while they were living," she says, handing me the bottle back.

I reach out to pull it from her but wrap my hand around hers at the same time pulling her forward, she comes with it into my lap. I slide a hand up her thigh and it wakes my cock where she rests against me. I struggle as I watch her, fighting the urge to get used to her when I know where my club life could lead her.

I've always heard of an instant connection, the immediate, unspeakable draw to someone. Fucking Ax talks about it all the time. I just never in a million years thought I'd experience it.

I take a sip as Brinley trails a finger down my bare chest over the ink, her eyes focus taking it in. The lyrics and quotes mixed with vines and the club insignia, a reaper in chains, numbers, and phrases that remind me of my time overseas, my mother, men I've known that have died. It's an eclectic blend. When you're covering most of your skin, you have room to be creative.

"Are these bullet holes?" she asks as her finger runs over the raised skin.

"Yes." I take another drink.

"From your time as a marine?"

"One of them, yes," I answer.

She nods but doesn't question the other and takes the bottle from me and I wonder what it takes for her to get good and drunk. This scotch is potent—my guess is not much.

"Were you afraid when you went overseas?"

I keep my gaze on her while I take my sip.

"Mason said you went three times," Brinley admits with a shrug while she fluffs her long hair around her shoulders.

"No, I wasn't scared," I answer.

"Not at all?"

"No. There's no point in being afraid. It doesn't change the outcome," I say simply. "Everything dies."

"That's not true," she says, a coy little smile lining her face.

I study her for a beat.

"Everything dies," I reiterate.

"Love doesn't," she says with a wistful little grin.

I make a *pfft* kind of sound and run a hand through my hair.

"This is real life, not the writings of Fitzgerald." My brow knots as I watch the way her blue eyes hold the lamplight.

"You read those classics?"

"Yes."

"But you don't believe in love? Fate?"

"They aren't real. I've studied how the mind works for a long time." I twist a piece of Brinley's hair between my fingers, and she moves against me, her ass taunting my cock to go again. "They're what we use to give ourselves false hope that true happiness actually exists. As long as you understand it isn't reality, you can still enjoy them."

Brinley smiles. "Do you not have faith in anything at all? That someone is watching over you?" she asks, running a finger around the scar I earned on my ribs when a fence ripped me open in Iraq.

I look up at her and run a hand through my hair.

"I have no faith in anything but myself," I say.

"That's a grim existence," she comments, her words starting to string together a little. She shifts her weight in my lap and her ass offers my cock a hit of friction. Having her in my lap is so foreign to me. I've fucked a lot of women, so many that I've lost count, but human connection is something that feels new. Brinley continues to run her finger over the swirls in the vines on my skin, I don't hate it.

"When I was thick in the middle of my second tour, I got trapped in a cave filled to my waist with water. There were ten of us. We were heading to capture an operative for an ISIS leader," I tell her, watching her fingers skim my skin. "It was a trap and there were landmines under the water. Six of my men died. I thought I was dead. I carried a nineteen-year-old boy out on my shoulder. We left part of his legs in the cave. I still hear his screams every fucking day. I watched small children scream in horror as they watched their parents die, I stopped countless women from being raped—by both fucked up American soldiers and their own people. I watched a five-year-old girl have her arm and leg blown off at the hands of a car bomber. Yet pedophiles and murderers rot in jail cells until they're ninety when there are many more fitting ways they could be made to suffer. There is no God. There is no reason for anything. People die every day and life just goes on."

Brinley looks at me with a scrutiny I don't understand, it's not a judging glance but the look of a woman trying to understand who I am.

"Is that why your cut says Solider of Bedlam? It's the military men that wear that?" she asks.

"No, you earn that a different way," I tell her, not offering any more explanation.

She must sense I'm not willing to talk about it because she changes the subject.

"You must have faith in your country if you fought for it."

I take another drink; this conversation is getting a little too heavy.

"I don't have faith in my country, I care greatly about it, there's a difference."

"One isn't the other?" Brinley asks, taking another sip.

"Not even close," I tell her

"Everyone has faith in something." She says nothing else as I watch a rosy glow creep over her cheeks.

"Enough liquor, you'll be sick," I tell her. "It's old, it'll hit you all at once."

Miraculously, she listens and hands me back the now half empty bottle.

"You were saying you have no faith..." She smirks.

"So many died. So many fought. Gave this government their all. Only to come home to nothing. No help, permanently damaged—either mentally or physically, most of the time, both. Their government was nowhere to be found. They turned to drugs." I hesitate then add, "It's why we do what we do."

"Which is?" she asks and for some reason I'll never understand, I tell her.

"We help the addicts. The forgotten people. People don't realize the government helps cartels bring the drugs into this country, they create the addicts. They don't make it easy for people to get sober. They actually provide help for them to stay addicts. We fund clinics, and we help bring in the medications they need to help people get clean. Cheaper drugs for them means they can help more people get clean."

"Black market drugs?" Brinley asks. Smart girl. I remind myself, as crazy as it seems, I've only known this woman a week and a half. I look at her, still hesitant.

"I watched you murder a man," she scoffs. "I know where he's buried. I'm dead either way if I say anything, so what difference does it make if you tell me?" she asks with a cocky little tipsy grin.

I take my final swig. I lift her warm body off me and set her in the other chair then re-cork the bottle before I place it back in the cabinet and lock it.

"Yes, black market drugs. Methadone mostly, we supply it at a heavily discount price, it makes it more affordable for the clinics. The more they can get, the more people they can help. We also help bring in more addiction services counselors. We've helped fund and open four clinics in Atlanta this year alone, in the hardest hit neighborhoods. DOS doesn't like our business. Less addicts on the street, more watchful eyes on their corners equals less profits for them." I look out the window at the nothingness of her yard.

"There are a lot of soldiers turned addicts, chasing away the demons they adopted through the shit they were forced to endure." I shrug. "It's the only way I feel like I can help."

"I've never thought about doing something illegal for the greater good. Growing up, things were always black and white. Wrong was wrong and right was right." Brinley watches me, tucking her hair behind her ear.

"And now, how do you feel?" I ask, genuinely interested in her vision of me.

She rises and comes toward me, wrapping her arms around my waist, she reaches up on her tip toes and kisses the scruff of my jaw.

"Humbled. Mistaken." she answers honestly, and a weird twisting feeling settles in my chest.

"Then you understand why I do what I do?" I ask, wondering why the fuck I care what she thinks.

Brinley nods. "I think so. You're kind of like a scarier version of Robin Hood?" she asks with a little smirk.

I detach her arms from my waist and head to her bedroom. She follows silently on bare feet behind me.

"I have very selfish interests in this business. It pays really fuckin' well, but if I can help people that need it, I will," I say simply as I push her door open and turn on the lamp beside her bed.

"Does it ever bother you? Doing what you do illegally?" she asks.

"No. There's no better way." I grin. "And I may care about my country, but I fucking hate the government. I sleep just fine at night, little hummingbird, if that's what you're asking."

Brinley yawns and crawls up into her bed. I stare down, watching her tuck herself in as she pulls off my shirt and looks at me, assuming I'll follow her almost naked body into bed. The weight of both her beauty and her expectation of whatever this is, hits me and I'm not prepared for it. It settles like a rock in my chest.

I freeze at the side of her bed as the vision of the last woman I thought I could protect floods my mind. The way she looked while the life drained from her eyes.

I sober right the fuck up. I *don't* care about people for a reason. My world isn't the type that supports whatever is happening between us. I don't know what it is, but I know I'm not Ax, I'm not some lovesick fucking goon, and I've just told a woman I don't really know way too much about my business. Just like I warn my men, I'm letting pussy cloud my judgement.

I pick my shirt up off her bed and toss it on over my head and see the look in her eye, the one that questions if I'm just going to leave her here. If I was a good man I wouldn't, but I'm not.

"Remember to be smart, little bird. Remember whether I'm with you every second or not, I still own you," is the only warning I offer her before turning to head down the stairs.

I pull the front door shut and step out into the night. I press the lock button on the keypad and don't look back.

Right now, I need the clarity that only an intense session with my heavy bag and some target practice can offer me.

CHAPTER 33
Brinley

I don't hear from Gabriel for the entire week and I'm extra sappy about it because I've got my period. So essentially, I've been fluctuating between polishing off pints of Ben & Jerry's and talking to myself in an aggressive tone, practicing what I'm going to say when I do see him. The closest I come to hearing from him is getting a call from Mike telling me my truck will be another week or two while he waits for parts.

Life feels strangely back to normal. I should be glad. But now that he's been inside me... both my body *and* my head... now that I've seen that little piece of him, I can admit to myself that I'm both equally fascinated and angry that Gabriel just left me in my underwear in the middle of my bed.

What I didn't expect was to understand his business—to be proven wrong. My parents taught me that there was a line, a fork in the path of good and bad. You either walked down one or the other. Gabriel seems to be teaching me that there's a way to walk that line and you can do it with grace—for reasons that actually make sense. I didn't expect him to be doing illegal things for the *right* reasons, and it creates a very gray area of criminal activity I never thought I'd question. Now that I've had a few days to think, I realize I *wanted* to struggle with understanding it because it means that maybe what I've always believed isn't necessarily better, it's just different.

That being said, my boring life is probably for the best. If he really is done with me, I remind myself that not dealing with trucks blowing up and people getting murdered with no remorse is actually a good thing.

I talk to Layla every day and go to work, eat my dinner and do the same thing the next day. I sink myself into work. I've smiled and tried to pretend like I'm not changed by this man's invasive entrance into my life.

By Friday as I'm leaving for work, the construction workers and club members I've been bringing treats to all week from the town bakery, tell me they should have my porch finished today. It's so beautiful but I still have the matter of settling that bill. There's not a chance I'm letting my one-night stand turned captor turned the man who vanished pay for it.

I'm heading in for an extra day at work, I was only supposed to go in on Monday and Wednesday but as Dell said during my orientation, my work would probably allow for more hours if I want them. I'm having lunch with Layla and then I plan to spend the weekend curled up in my pajamas with some take out. Maybe work on my garden. I stop at the coffee shop for my usual latte before heading in.

"Got you one already," Dell says with a cheery smile when I enter the office. "I texted you."

I pull my phone out. "So you did." I smile

"Oh well, now I have two, I could use them today anyway." It's true, I haven't been sleeping the best. I have dreams that I'm not alone in my room at night. I tell myself it's just my spooky old house because whenever I fully wake up, there's no one there, of course.

"I pulled the marble samples for your client's backsplash, they'll be here at ten. I think the ones you chose will go so well with the kitchen counter," he says, and so goes the rest of our morning. We work well together even if I can't get his unconventional side hobbies out of my head after Gabriel's comment about him.

When I finish up and see my clients out at noon, I check my phone. Layla's running late so I just watch for her silver SUV out the front window. We're lunching at the bistro on the next block, and we planned to walk. I peek out the window for her ten minutes later. She's still not here but I can't help noticing a black Harley parked out front across the street. I've seen it every day around this time when I've been in this week. The custom red flames painted on the fender and the front panels make it stick out like a sore thumb. It looks expensive but it's the rider who has no qualms about making his presence known. He's tall and solid, and just like most of the guys I've seen in the HOH, he's covered in tattoos, with a wide jaw, unkempt wavy hair, and a gruff beard. He wears riding gloves and a leather jacket covered in patches as he leans against his bike casually smoking. I've never seen him close up, but my first assumption is that he's a warning. A friend of the club and Gabriel, letting me know he's watching me, warning me not to go to the cops. By the second day, I decided I was right, having received their message loud and clear. It has to be them. It's not usual for any outsiders to hang around like this.

Layla finally pulls up ten minutes later, and I make my way outside to meet her, noticing that my keeper is gone. We casually chat as we walk to the Two Spoons bistro and all through lunch.

"Still radio silence?" she asks as she shoves a bite of her club sandwich into her mouth.

"Yep," I answer, adding salsa to my fajita.

"Told you he'd just move on."

"Yeah, you did, but I have to worry. Going from the whole 'you have to stay with me' to absolutely nothing? Is he plotting my demise?"

Layla laughs, still unaware of what I saw. She's adamant she doesn't want to know.

"Sean knows the club can trust you, I'm sure he's told Wolfe that. My guess? They're keeping an eye on you to make sure you're trustworthy."

The rider across from my work flashes through my mind and it makes sense. That's what I thought too.

"They're not in the habit of holding people prisoner," Layla says, dotting her mouth with her napkin.

I nod.

"Can I be straight with you?" she asks.

I sip my iced tea. "Of course."

"You seem like you *want* to see him. You know, Mr. Not-my-type," Layla says in her best impression of me.

I scoff, my mind drifting back to my attic less than a week ago. I shut it out, locking it away. "I didn't expect to understand him or like him. But I could tell, that night in my house, the way he looked at me before he left, he doesn't want me to understand him. I could tell he regretted telling me as much as he did."

I look out the picture window behind her. "Doesn't matter anyway. He's probably had ten other women by now. It's been five days."

"Sean says he's barely seen him. He's working on two bikes right now, one for some NBA star and the other for a Kentucky fire chief."

"I'm going to the club tomorrow night. Come with me. If there is anything between you two, you'll know the first moment you see him."

I shrug as my phone lights up on the table. "I don't know."

DELL

The siding guy is here early for your meeting.

I'm done anyway. Want anything?

"Is that my brother?" Layla asks as she scarfs down her last bite.

"Yes, he's been great at showing me the ropes."

She giggles. "I think he always had a crush on you."

I smile back. "Not a chance."

"It's true, he used to ask me every day after school, 'is *Brinley coming over tonight?*'" Layla laughs. "I swear, he was a little lovesick teenager our senior year of high school," she adds, taking her last drink and finishing it with a little slurping sound.

DELL

Nah I'm good, but thanks for thinking of me. Take your time, I've got you covered.

Layla reads it from my lock screen and laughs "He's got you covered." She winks

"Shut up," I say, tossing my napkin at her.

When we round the corner on Main, the bike with the red flames is back right across the street from my work.

Layla spots him at the same time as I do and stops dead in her tracks.

I stop too because I'm instantly on high alert with her. "What?"

She pulls her phone out and presses one button on it, then starts walking again. "Don't look at him, just keep walking. Whatever I say, go along with it."

"Who? What are you talking about?" I ask, even though I already know because my gaze follows hers.

I watch the rider who's been parked in front of my work for the last week turn around and crush his cigarette butt under the heel of his boot. I can see it, even from a hundred feet away... The grim reaper on the back of a red Harley. The red banner above is glaringly obvious, and I already know enough to understand that this is bad news.

Disciples of Sin. My keeper isn't a friend of the club, he's the enemy.

CHAPTER 34

Gabriel

I put my phone back in my pocket. The AirTag I stuck under Brinley's car tells me she's still at work. I've run thirty-two miles in the last five days, tore my fists up on the bag and blew through almost a thousand rounds of ammo. Yet none of it is working.

I can't get my fucking head right and I've resorted to tracking her every move. I told myself on Monday it was because I had to make sure she wasn't gonna talk, but it became clear she has no intentions of going to the cops. Most of the time, from what I can tell, she seems skittish, like she's waiting for the other shoe to drop.

The other shoe being me.

I've fallen into this primal need that I have to see her again. I watch her in the night, in the hours when her sleep is the deepest. During the day, I use my truck to follow her on the way into the office, to make sure she gets in safe, then return again to follow her home at night. I can't shake her. I can't get the way her body molded to mine out of my head. I tell myself it'll pass but then one day blends into the next and still...

"Boss," Jake calls as I stare out the window. "Chapel."

I nod.

"Steele Street Clinic was ransacked in the middle of the night," Jake says as we all assemble. "Their entire methadone supply was wiped out."

"How did that happen? We have eyes on them," I say. We have multiple cameras in every location.

Jake shakes his head. "I dunno, man, it's like they knew the blind spots."

I look around the table at all my men. None of this makes sense. The faces I see here I've known most of my life. They're my brothers. To not trust them seems impossible.

"That's not all, there are more rumors everywhere. DOS members are talking. Word on the street is they're planning something," Jake adds.

"Glen Eden rally, maybe?" Kai asks.

"Not sure they'd wait that long," Flipp says as he lights a smoke. "That's not till next month and there'll be a ton of crews there, why involve them in our bullshit?"

I shrug. "It's what I would do. Easier to blend in with the masses."

The rally they're talking about, Glen Eden, is annual and massive. The biggest in the south, it attracts thousands, from every major player in the one percenters, all the way down to the smaller recreational clubs. It's a place for us to make connections with other crews and to bullshit and let loose a little. It's only forty-five minutes south of here in the hamlet of Benson, Georgia. The town is completely taken over, even the main roads. The acreage on the outskirts is owned by one of our sister clubs, Titans MC, and there are cabins and places for people to camp. It's an all-out party. New people, new women. One I normally look forward to, but this year the only woman I want is one who belongs nowhere near my world.

"Send a crew to Atlanta, help the clinic get cleaned up. The cops'll be all over it. Contact the PD there and find out what they know," I tell Robby.

He nods.

"Take a prospect and Flipp."

The Atlanta PD is a friend of the club, they walk a fine line between looking the other way and accepting our help. If there's anything they think will help us stop this from happening again, they'll tell us.

"On it." Robby nods.

"All right, next we need to talk about—"

The sound of glass shattering stops Jake from finishing his sentence as the main window in the chapel shatters. I catalogue every single thing around me all at once. It's not a gun that causes the window to shatter, something was thrown through it. I scan the room to make sure it isn't an explosive. I don't move as I start to count. If another hit is coming, statistically it will happen in the next twenty seconds.

My gaze lands on a brick with something tied to it on the other side of the room. Paper? The window on the east wall quickly follows, exploding inward as we all cover our heads. None of us have our phones in here, so we sit and wait for gunfire or another attack for the last ten seconds before I'm on the move, crawling out of the room with Jake and Ax behind me. I reach the main hall where the people hanging around the clubhouse are all on the floor. Broken glass is everywhere out here too—two windows are shattered and women are cursing, one is cut up and bleeding.

I nod to Flipp to see to her, and make my way to the door, pulling my gun as I approach but the assailants are long gone. Tires spewing rocks and leaving a cloud of dust that makes it impossible to see who it really was. I already know it was DOS but a visual of the vehicle would've been nice.

Nodding at the cameras, I look at Kai across the room and yell over the noise, "Check 'em." Then I head outside with Ax close behind me.

We secure the perimeter and notice the busted fencing in the distance.

"That has to be fixed by end of day. Call Stevens Metalworx and have them out here this afternoon," I tell Ax.

He nods.

When we're satisfied with the exterior, we head back in where things have calmed down a little.

"It was a superficial cut," Flipp tells me about the woman as I breeze by him to get my phone.

The rest of the guys follow and do the same. Someone is already sweeping up and I hear Kai on the phone with the window replacement company. This isn't new to us. Attacks happen more often than we care to admit, and we need to be prepared after what we did to Gator. The thing that makes no sense is that people don't just come onto our property like this and it's the second time in two weeks. How would anyone know exactly when we'd be in Chapel? Everything in me screams that something is wrong, but I can't put my finger on what.

I pick up a brick off the floor. Pulling the paper attached to it free, I inspect carefully. It's printed photos of Ax and Layla unloading his bike in their driveway after the wedding. Of Robby and his ol' lady Margo through their kitchen window eating. Flipp and his teenage daughter at her soccer game.

"Fuck, boss." Ax mutters, holding a brick and photos of his own. I take them from him, they're much the same—my men in various stages of their lives, at their homes. A note is buried inside Ax's, ransom style, that says, *"No one is safe."*

I move to the chapel, leaving Ax in the main hall as his phone starts to ring. Picking up another brick off the floor, I rip the photos free of the elastic holding them. There's five of them and they're all of me. But not just me, of Brinley too. One through the second story window of her den, I'm shirtless and holding her dad's bottle of scotch.

One of her heading out the door of the design studio midday with Dell. Me leaving her house the night I was with her and there's a note inside that says, "*In war, avoid what is strong and instead, always strike at what is weak. Have we found the president's weakness?*"

The last paper in the stack slips out from behind the others and a fury I've never felt—a deep, dark wrath—rises from a place inside me that I haven't allowed to see the light of day in a long fucking time. It's Brinley walking out of the local coffee shop by herself, only this time someone has scratched her face out with a red sharpie and scrawled the words "*dead bitch*" across the bottom of it.

"Boss!! We gotta fucking go, now!" Ax yells from the next room. He peers into the chapel, gripping both sides of the door.

I'm already moving toward him. The look he's wearing confirms everything I already know.

Brinley is in trouble, and I was naive enough to think this wouldn't touch her, even if I stayed away from her.

Of course it fucking would, carnage follows on the heels of every single thing I do.

CHAPTER 35
Brinley

Layla holds her phone close as we walk. I glance down and take notice that it's dialed a phone number and the call has been answered. She never pulls it up to her ear and it's not on speaker.

"That's Aiden Foxx, he's the DOS vice president. His half brother runs their club. He's really, *really* bad news. Don't make eye contact, act like you don't know anything about anything. We'll be back to Crimson in a minute," she says way louder than warranted then hangs up the phone as we close in on him. I realize she was letting Ax know what was going on without letting this man know she was on the phone.

Aiden doesn't take his eyes off us the entire time we walk to the office building, closer to him. He appraises us with the same commanding glare I'd expect from Gabriel.

"A word, ladies?" he says in a deep timbre as we cross the final stretch of sidewalk to my office doors.

I look at the door, so close yet so far, then back at him. His green eyes pierce through me. Layla reaches in front of me, her arm stops me from moving any closer.

"You have something to say, you can say it from there. And this is my friend, she doesn't need to be here, she just met me for lunch."

Layla faces me. "See ya, thanks for the visit," she says, clearly thinking he's here for her. But what I see in his eyes when he smirks in my direction tells me everything I need to know.

He's here for me.

The second his eyes flit from hers to mine, like she's not interesting him in the slightest, I know I'm right.

"Nah, she knows why I'd wanna talk to her, don't you, Brinley?"

Layla's breath hitches and her arm drops from me.

"We've been watching the Hounds of Hell for years, same as they watch us." He pulls a pack of cigarettes out of his pocket as he speaks and then tips his head down as he pulls one out with his teeth and lights it up, drawing the smoke in with a deep breath before he continues.

"Never seen your Pres with a woman. So, you see, Brinley, you've piqued our interest."

"She was a one-night stand," Layla says, and I wince.

I know she's trying to help but it strikes something, nonetheless.

Aiden takes another drag and leans back on his bike, folding his arms over his chest.

"It's true. Just one night," I say, wondering if he can tell I'm shaking like a leaf.

"I don't think so," he says, turning his eyes to mine. "Didn't your mama teach you before she died that men like us are bad news?"

My mouth falls open as I register what he knows about me. Personal things. Like how my mother is dead.

"There a problem out here?" Dell's voice sounds from the door.

I turn to face him. Bless his heart he's trying so hard not to look scared shitless of the torrid biker staring him down from the edge of the sidewalk.

Aiden grins and flicks his cigarette; it lands at Dell's feet.

"Be seeing you, Brinley," Aiden says as he swings his leg over the large bike and fires it up with a deep rumble.

Goosebumps break out over my flesh with his words as Layla and I make our way inside Crimson. By the time we get inside, I'm shaking.

"Are you okay? What did he want?" Dell asks. "This is the kind of shit you said your husband wouldn't bring around you?" he says to Layla.

"He has nothing to do with HOH and thanks for coming out, but... give us a minute now."

Dell looks at me and sets his jaw, understanding I'm somehow involved with Layla's world for the first time. He says nothing as he shakes his head and turns to head back to his office.

"You okay?" Layla asks when he's out of earshot, rubbing her hands up and down my arms. She pulls me in for a quick hug.

"Sean will be on his way here. My guess is Wolfe will be with him. They think DOS threw warning bricks through the clubhouse windows. It's unheard of for a DOS member, let alone their VP, to be in downtown Harmony like that. Sean says we'll be on lockdown until they can figure this out."

I nod, still shaken.

My phone buzzes in my pocket.

W

Don't fucking leave the office.

As scared as I am, I'm instantly annoyed that he hasn't contacted me at all and then, when he finally does, he thinks he's just going to boss me around.

"I thought you said it was one night?" Layla asks, as if I must be hiding something. Thing is, I'm not.

"It was. I haven't heard from Gabriel in a week."

Her mouth falls open. "Gabriel?"

I look up at her. "What?" I ask, "it's his name,"

"Nothing, just have never heard anyone refer to him by his first name. He really let you call him that?" she asks, her eyes scrutinizing.

I blink. "Yeah?"

"Hmm. From what Sean says, only his mother called him by his first name."

Layla pulls her phone out and tries to dial a number while I turn away, unsure what to do with the idea that no one calls him by his first name but he let *me,* because it's clear he's done with me.

I take a deep breath, trying to calm myself but it doesn't work. Does he know where I live? What could he want with me? I need to upgrade my security system.

The sound of Harleys coming in hot through the down-town core is impossible to miss. Before I knew Gabriel it would've made me uneasy. Now, it brings me a sort of comfort I can't explain. They're loud, even from inside the office building.

Layla and I both spin around to see them. Of course, her phone call brought Sean here and she's right, Gabriel is in front of him. Days without seeing him has made him even more disturbingly beautiful and daunting. My breathing speeds up as he pulls up and takes his helmet off, just as Dell comes out of the back office to the sound of the bikes.

"What the hell is going on?" he asks as Gabriel and Ax make their way into the building.

Gabriel is to me in three seconds flat, scanning me for injuries or anything that would alert him that I'm not okay. He touches my face, my shoulders, to see if I'm marked, but I back away.

"We're fine," I say, averting my eyes.

He sets his jaw. "You're done for the day. Let's go."

I turn my eyes back to his. "I'm here until three."

"It's your day off. And you're done."

The way he says it sinks into me and tells me not to argue, but I'm furious. I consider going with him just to give him a piece of my mind for not calling me all week.

"Got a prospect coming for your car. He'll meet us at your place." Gabriel doesn't say another word, he simply nods toward the exit and turns to leave the building.

I watch as he takes a seat on his bike, no doubt in his mind that I'll listen to him. I glance between him and Dell. The look of disappointment Dell wears is similar to the one I'd imagine my parents wearing in this scenario.

He lifts his hand in motion to the door. Silently telling me to go if I want.

Layla moves toward Dell and hugs him. "It's nothing. We're fine, this is a precaution. That other club is dangerous. Tell him," she says to Ax, backhanding him in the cut.

"Of course," Ax answers immediately. "Sorry, bro, guess we gotta do a better job of keeping that scum outta here."

"Seems so," Dell says, trying to sound authoritative but fails.

Layla makes her way over to me and looks out the window at Gabriel.

"I don't know what this is with you two but you're safe with him. Let him take you home," she whispers as she hugs me.

She follows Ax out the door with a "text you in a bit" and I turn to face Dell one last time.

"You sure, Brinley?" he asks, and I don't miss the double meaning of his question. Whether or not I'm okay and whether I feel safe to go with Gabriel.

I look between Dell, standing in front of me, and Gabriel through the window. One represents the life I had before—predictable, safe, boring. The other, although maddening, represents the unknown. Oddly enough, it isn't even a choice. I grab my purse.

"See you Tuesday," I say to Dell.

With one last glance to Layla and Ax standing by his bike I'm out the door, climbing onto the back of Gabriel's. He hands me my helmet over his shoulder. I put it on and the anger I feel mixes with something else, something deeply satisfying as I wrap my arms around his waist and breathe him in for the first time in five days. He brings a hand down over mine and squeezes.

I'm still angry but the odd thing is I've never felt safer.

CHAPTER 36
Brinley

The moment we pull into my driveway I'm mentally making notes for myself. I get off the bike without a word.

Number one, call a security company and have them here in the morning.

Two, maybe get a dog? Yes, that's what I'll do—a Doberman.

I unlock the front door with the keypad as a prospect pulls my car into the driveway followed by another member in a pickup truck. I head straight inside, slam the door, lock it behind me and lean my back against it.

I hear Gabriel's voice through the open window talking to the prospect. I close my eyes and pray he just leaves. I don't need him banging down my door. I need to save myself a little bit of dignity here. The weekend we spent together was... there are no words, but when he just stood at the edge of my bed and looked at me like he was done with me, that feeling is still way too fresh. Stupidly, for a split second while we were together, I thought maybe—just maybe—Gabriel felt the same way I did, like there was nothing on Earth that could ever feel as good as he could. Like our bodies were made for each other. Stupidly being the operative word.

I make my way through my house into my kitchen and fill a glass with water. As I'm about to take a sip, I hear the access to my keypad beep, followed by the horrifying sound of my front door unlocking.

He has my code? How?

Gabriel makes his way into my kitchen and tosses the key to his bike onto the counter. He says nothing, standing on the other side of the island. Knowing he can enter and exit my house any time he wants makes him seem even bigger, more intimidating.

His eyes drink me in like it's been almost painful to be away from me. I push the smoldering feeling of his gaze from my mind. He's been hurt, blood spots are visible through his white t-shirt on his shoulders, and I realize glass from the windows breaking must have cut him.

I fold my arms over my chest and do my best to appear as frustrated as I feel. The moment his eyes meet mine, I struggle because he melts me with that gaze.

"You can go," I tell him. "And I guess I need to change my code."

"No." He shakes his head. "Go pack some things; you're coming with me for a while until I can make sure you're safe. I thought I could keep you safer if I stayed away from you. I was wrong."

I put my hands on my hips. I still really don't like being told what to do. Someone has been doing that my whole life.

"The only way to show that Foxx guy I'm not of any interest to him is for you to leave and not come back. I told him you were just a one-night stand. I'm pretty sure he believed me," I lie.

Gabriel moves faster than I have time to prepare for and

both his arms cage me in against the counter as he towers over me.

"Pack your shit or don't pack your shit, either way you're coming with me. This isn't a discussion," he says, looking down at me. His body is so close to mine that it instantly ignites my own muscle memory, like he's a phantom limb I've been missing. I look away from his eyes and fight with everything in me not to feel the pull that tethers us together. Gabriel's hand comes up and tilts my face with a finger under my chin.

I push his hand away and watch as his jaw sets.

"You left a week ago and I haven't heard one word from you. I don't see you out at your other conquests' houses making sure they're safe, why me?"

Gabriel's hand is instantly at my throat. "This isn't a fucking game," he seethes.

I reach up and pull at his hand around my throat, he's never held it so tight, and I can't breathe at all. The fury I see in his eyes tells me I pushed him too far. I scratch, I fight with both my hands but he doesn't even flinch.

His lips come down to mine and hover as I silently beg for air.

"I didn't leave. I've been here every single night, hummingbird, watching you sleep. I've been with you everywhere you've gone—every time, every day since I left this house. But it wasn't enough. They know I was here and they *got* to you."

Gabriel releases my throat and I inhale in a gasp, reaching for my throbbing throat, choking back my breath. The realization that he's been watching me, been in my house when I was sleeping, has pulled the air from my lungs just as completely as his hand to my throat.

But fuck me, it also made me feel comforted. I sigh.

"Now, I won't tell you again, understand? Get. Your. Shit." Gabriel practically whispers but it's a warning. If I don't do what he says, something tells me I'll be leaving anyway with just the clothes on my back.

"Gabriel!" I croak out, still dizzy. "Please... where are you taking me? I don't want to live at the clubhouse," I spit the words out desperately.

He can't just pick me up and put me down whenever he wants. I have to have more dignity than that. I will not be his groupie, living in the club waiting for my nightly fucks.

He smirks at me, like he knows something I don't as his lips unexpectedly come down, almost enough to meet mine. I suck in a desperate breath with how close he is. Gabriel doesn't kiss me, though; he just holds his mouth over mine, nothing more than a whisper of air between us, sending my senses into overdrive. I pant against his lips, fighting the urge to kiss him. He pulls my bottom lip between his teeth and into his mouth, sucking so hard I can feel the blood rush to the spot he's claimed. I swear I feel the inner battle holding him back from kissing me and I realize I'll never understand what goes through his tormented mind. He releases my lip. It throbs as he pulls back and admires the mark I'm sure he's left there.

"Please. This is my home," I say, looking into his eyes.

Gabriel shakes his head slowly and reaches down, grabbing hold of my hand. He brings it up to his chest and slides it under his cut, placing it above his heart. As we stand here staring at each other, momentarily transfixed, I can feel the slow, steady beat of his heart through his thin t-shirt. His breath is deep and even as he pulls my palm out and brings it up to his lips, kissing it just once.

"No, little bird. *I* am your home."

He lets my hand fall to my side as I stand here just dumbfounded by his words before he adds, "And I'm not taking you to the clubhouse."

CHAPTER 37

Gabriel

I'm not making the same mistake twice. I thought I could just walk away and watch Brinley from a distance, get this obsession out of my head. I never go back on a decision but there's a first time for everything and fuck it, there's no stopping this now.

Aiden Foxx is definitely the lesser of two evils when it comes to the Foxx family, but the thought of him anywhere near Brinley makes me want to reach into his chest and rip his fucking heart out with my bare hands, then stuff it down his fucking throat. I saw those photos in my chapel, and it took me less than a second to know I was wrong in leaving her. I will burn the DOS clubhouse and everyone in it to the motherfucking ground. Then, and only then, will she be safe.

The July sun is sinking over the horizon, serving as a background in the Georgia countryside as we fill the open road with the sound of my bike. Brinley's arms tighten around my waist and my eyes move between the road ahead and the road behind. I take the backroads part of the way, just to make sure no one is following us. I haven't kept this place hidden since I bought it two years ago just to slip up now.

I make my way onto the unmarked side road and pull down the drive, pressing the button in the inside pocket of my cut to open the electronic gate. The laurel oaks offer shade as I slowly steer my bike down the long, winding drive stopping in front of the house. I pop the kick down and take in Brinley's expression as she removes her helmet.

My house is my fortress. There are only two people who have ever been here—Jake and Ax—and now it'll be her home. A deer flees into the bush beside us, causing Brinley to jump.

"What is this place?" she asks, taking in her surroundings.

"Home," I tell her, unhooking her bag from the back of my bike. "Let's go." I sling it over my shoulder. Fucking thing is heavy like it's packed with books.

"I—I thought—"

I take Brinley's helmet from her and start walking toward my front steps.

"You thought wrong."

CHAPTER 38
Brinley

I'm not easily surprised by people. Most humans are the exact same, standard, run of the mill people you think they are. I've always thought I was a good judge of character, but it turns out, I'm not. At all. And Gabriel? I had no idea who he really was. Gabriel makes me realize I've probably been judging people my entire life based on what I was taught. And who am *I* to do that? He's teaching me that people can't be defined by their job or their upbringing, even their criminal activity might not necessarily make them a bad person.

Is it wrong to help people when the system fails and then profit from it? Is that any different than my father making the most of a shitty real estate deal gone bad? One is legal, one's not. Says who? A made-up group of people, bound to serve and protect when it suits them?

I look around at this place, really take it all in, and breathe out a sigh... Maybe Gabriel is the one who has it all figured out.

There are no words to describe the serenity of what I see now. It feels like I'm walking into a treehouse. The wide front steps seem never ending. Like I'll be going up two floors just to get to the front door. The entire cabin is deep, stained wood and glass. It's a large A frame and appears like it wasn't built into the hill it sits upon, but like it sprouted up from the earth. Spanish moss hangs low from the trees giving the entire space an eerie and peaceful feeling.

"Why build it so high up?"

Gabriel stops in front of his solid glass front door. Nodding in the direction of his gate. "So I can see anyone coming from three hundred yards away. Three hundred yards at their fastest speed still gives me twenty seconds to prepare." He knocks with the back of his first two knuckles on the glass. "Bullet-proof, all the glass in the house is."

Oh.

From my viewpoint looking in, I can see straight through the entire house before he even opens the front door. The house sits on a bluff and there's a large, open yard and a lake behind it. The only rooms we pass to get to the main living area are a small bathroom and an office. The interior doors in the house are all glass as well.

The sun is still sinking slowly down behind the water as we enter the living room and I realize this might be the most gorgeous view I've ever seen. It's easy to see when the entire back of the house is glass too. I notice as I look around that the inside isn't overly large, but what is here is well thought out and so neat and minimal.

Gabriel leads me into the open kitchen and living room. It's a sleek, modern style mixed with rustic wood walls and open wrought iron railings leading to the second floor and a basement below.

I'm shocked that this is Gabriel's home. I move closer to the window and peer out. The water shimmers below us and a set of wooden stairs leads down to it. There's a small outbuilding and what looks like targets set up outside on the flat expanse of yard, and there are multiple black and white markers spread over at least half of it and into the trees beyond.

He has his own shooting range? Should I be surprised?

Gabriel removes his cut and hangs it over the side of the dark leather sofa in his living room. There are two of them and they face a floor to ceiling stone fireplace that houses a massive barn board mantel. Then I notice that there isn't a TV in this room and I find that odd.

I spin around and face him.

"Why am I here? Why was that man at my work today? I'm not going to stay in the dark on this. I can't go home and I want to know why."

I watch as Gabriel ignores me, walking to the kitchen to pull a mason jar out of the cupboard and fills it with water.

"Gabriel," I say as I fold my arms over my chest. "I want to know—"

"They think you're my weakness. They've made the threat clear," he says, turning to set his glass down, removing his gun and knife, placing them in a basket on the center of the kitchen island.

It isn't lost on me that most people keep things like fruit there.

"And why are *you* so hell bent on keeping me safe?" I push him. I'm done letting fear guide me. Too much has happened over the last few weeks, and I'm almost positive that if Gabriel Wolfe was planning to hurt me, or worse, he would've already done it, so I might as well ask questions and speak my damn mind.

"I told you, I don't ask why. I just know I have to keep you safe."

I place a hand on my hip and hold my chin up as he lifts his glass and takes another long drink.

"That isn't good enough for me," I say, hoping to appear as confident as I just sounded.

"I need to know why you didn't kill me that first night in the woods and then let me go. And I need to know why you're coming to my rescue now."

He sets the glass down on the marble counter and without warning, Gabriel turns and moves toward me with a stealth and speed I'm not prepared for. I know when I fire back it frustrates him. Probably because nobody else does it. Instead, I'm met with his large hands circling my waist as he tugs me forward, so my body is flush with his.

"I don't need to explain any of it to you. You're alive because I can't fucking bear the thought of this pulse not beating for me, and that's the *only* reason I can give you," Gabriel growls as he dips his head down and brings his forehead to mine, pausing to take a deep breath, collecting himself as his hands grip my waist so tight it hurts.

My breath rises and falls tightly against him. Gabriel holds me so close, it's hard to breathe.

He pulls back and his eyes trace the lines of my face. My eyes, my lips, my jaw. I watch his tortured expression of concentration as he finds my throat, places his palm against it and breathes deep.

"You will hold no space to fear anything in this world except me. If anyone threatens you or tries to hurt you, they will be met with a suffering so deep that Lucifer himself will beg mercy for their souls. I'll tear the flesh from their bones one layer at a time and rejoice like the angel of bloodshed I was trained to be." Gabriel's hands slide up my back into my hair pulling my head taut to his, he angles my face.

"I own *all* your fear, little hummingbird. No one else can have it."

"And what if I don't want you to own those parts of me?" I ask boldly.

He smirks, his eyes showing me there's no room for me to argue.

"I don't ask permission to take what's already mine," Gabriel says slowly just before his lips come down on mine in a crushing kiss.

I move to struggle from his hold, his words fueling me to desperately hold onto some semblance of choice, but Gabriel only holds me tighter and kisses me deeper. My arms are buried between us and I use what leverage I can to scratch through his t-shirt.

He pulls back slightly and uses one arm to pull his shirt off by the back of the neck. I trace my finger over the fresh cuts on his shoulders. They aren't deep and are no longer bleeding.

With the setting sun streaming through the window behind him, casting him in an otherworldly glow, the irony isn't lost on me that in this moment, Gabriel looks exactly like his name-sake. A wolf. A hunter. His hair is loose and wavy, framing his face, and his beard is a little thicker than the last time I saw him.

God, he's fucking beautiful.

"If you're going to scratch me up, you better fucking do it right," he rasps with a smirk that tells me he wants any pain I can offer him, while his lips come down again, and I'd be lying if I said I wasn't desperate for him.

Buttons go flying across the hardwood floor as my blouse is torn from my body. Gabriel devours my skin as quickly as it's revealed to him with rough, open-mouthed kisses. I can't keep up with the way he feeds on me. It's a chaotic sort of mayhem. He bites down my arms, up my shoulders, everywhere his mouth can connect, and I know he's been as starved for me as I have for him. I can't make sense of it.

I rake my nails down his shoulders as hard as I can, opening up the tiny cuts that already exist there. I don't do it on purpose, but I realize as he starts to bleed that I'm seeking Gabriel's blood. He groans into my collarbone before biting into my flesh. I yelp and dig my nails in deeper. His lips meet mine again and force me to open. Every single perfectly timed swipe of his tongue stokes the fire in me that burns for him.

A quick flick of his thumb and forefinger has my jeans undone. He lifts me with one arm and pulls them from my body and in one fluid motion they hit the floor, not once breaking the kiss to my lips. I wrap my legs around him as he begins to move. Gabriel presses me against the glass of the picture window. I suck in a breath when the chill of it hits my skin.

One finger trails the valley between my heaving breasts, downward over my belly button then abruptly into the black cotton and lace of the panties I'm wearing that are soaked right through. Gabriel growls a sound from deep within his chest as he's met with my desire.

"Look at you. I knew this dripping cunt would be ready and begging for me..." I let my head fall back against the glass as he roughly slides two fingers into me. "So you don't want my protection, but you want my cock?" he muses.

"I don't know what I want," I gasp as his thumb presses into my clit with perfect pressure. "I—"

"You want the illusion of choice so badly... give it to me, Brinley. How should I make you come first? How should I prove this perfect pussy is mine whenever and however I want it?"

My moans fill the air as he brings me to the brink of orgasm and then stops.

A desperate little whimper escapes my lips when Gabriel

pulls his fingers from me and it makes him laugh, a deep dark delicious sound I would get down on my knees and pray for.

"You don't *have* a choice, little hummingbird. Just like I don't."

His inked skin is a stark contrast to mine unmarked. His arms are flexed with the weight of me in his hands, and my nails dig deep into his shoulders. But his eyes throw me off the ledge when they meet mine. He looks at me like *he* is the one begging.

"I don't care how you take me; I just want you. I want it all," I beg, lost because I finally let myself believe what I've been fighting.

Gabriel is right, my body does beg for his. I want every single part of him. The thing is, now I know his secret.

His body also begs for mine.

CHAPTER 39

Gabriel

Nothing has changed in the five days since I was last buried in her, but everything feels heavier, more ominous. Brinley's safety rests in my hands. Five days ago, the only person I was trying to save her from was me, from my world. Her black hair is wild and everywhere, her cheeks are flushed, nipples pebbled, that perfect fucking cunt glistening. Mine for the taking.

The fire she doesn't know how to use yet creeps into her blue eyes, the embers burning. I want to stoke those embers within her, bring out her fire. Something about her being such a good girl makes me want to dig deep inside her soul and pull out every dark and depraved desire I can find.

"I don't care... how you take me. I just want you... I want it all," she says in the most honest little whimper, and her submission affects me in the most visceral way without even trying.

Brinley yelps as I lift her supple body up and toss her easily over my shoulder. She's about to learn what it means to have that little smirk fucked right off her face.

I hit the switch to turn on my bedroom lamp as I make my

way through the door. My boots are heavy on the wood floor. I flip Brinley back over and set her down on my bed. Her full tits bounce as she lands back against my duvet and her raven hair fans out behind her, framing her like some dark goddess. I watch her hungrily as her chest heaves. I lose the rest of my clothes in record time and stalk toward her, stroking my cock in slow purposeful drags as I move towards the bed. Little trickles of blood slide down my arms and she licks her lips as she watches. I'm beyond fucking hard. I swipe the pre-cum that leaks from the tip for her and she looks up at me, desperate, still always a little afraid.

I climb on top of her, sweeping her hair from her face before my arms cage her in and I hover over her for a beat, blood drips from one of my shoulders onto her and I use a finger to swipe it across her neck. Another drop, another swipe.

Fuck. This small amount of my blood on her skin makes me want to slice myself open so I can bathe her in it. Claim her in it.

The look in her eyes is pure terror now as she realizes I like the look of my blood on her.

"Scared?" I ask her

"Always."

I grin as I notch my cock against her slick center.

"Good, your sweet pussy is a desperate little slut for the fear I offer." The words are barely out of my mouth before I'm digging my hands into the curvy sides of her outer thighs. I drag her down below me further, lift her leg up and thrust inside her.

Her body spasms as I pull out and fuck back into her deeper.

"*Fuck*," we both groan, almost in unison. It's only been a week, but she feels brand new.

There's no stopping the rhythm I need to satiate myself

with her now.

It's brutal. It triggers the primal part of me, and I fuck Brinley like she's the air I need to breathe, like I worship the very ground she walks on.

I fuck her like I won't survive if I stop.

"You've fucking ruined me, Brinley," I growl as she clings to me, her breaths come in short pants.

I'm filling her completely.

"So full," she moans as I bite her neck, her breasts, her earlobe, anywhere my teeth can find. The more I bite, the more she moans, and the more her pussy tightens.

I lay my claim to her. My statement that she's *mine,* and she'll have the marks on her skin to prove it.

"Deeper," she moans. "More."

I lose myself with every thrust. The droplets of blood have grown as she digs into me deeper and the way she looks right now is too much.

"Beg me, Brinley," I tell her. "Beg me to feed this pussy."

"Please," she whines without hesitation.

"Attagirl," I growl. "You take my cock so fucking well," I tell her, so pleased.

"Say more," she whispers shyly.

My beast thrives.

I grip her hair and angle her chin up so I can take her earlobe into my mouth. My cock throbs with her black tresses pressing against my arms.

The fire in her eyes burns hotter and shows me that she's not only up to the task of offering me what I need. She thrives on it just as much as I do.

"Use me, Gabriel. Fill me up," she breathes out in a moan.

"You want me to fuck you hard. You need me the way I need you; and you don't know why any more than I do," I tell her.

I feel her hesitation to use words she isn't used to, but I want it and I'm not stopping until she gives it to me.

"Ask me, wicked girl, ask me to fuck you the way you need."

Brinley moans and squeezes her legs around me. "Please," she whimpers. "Fuck me," she adds so quietly and so politely, I can't take it.

I'm hers.

I groan, chasing my own high as I pulse inside her.

I move down to lick my own fresh droplets of blood from her chest, then move back up to her lips kissing her deeply, mixing the taste of us and my blood together.

It's a kind of high no drug could offer.

I'm fucking flying.

My hand slides to her throat as I kiss her, using it as leverage to fuck her harder. My balls tighten and churn as my release licks up my spine, my hips, centering so slowly I can hardly bear it.

"It's too much... I'm going to..." she cries.

"I know," I tell her. "I can feel your pussy begging me to paint your insides white, take me with you. Take all of me."

"Force me to... God, please force me to... I like it." She ends her words in a whisper as she lifts her lips up to mine.

"That's right, I am your god," I tell her.

"You are," she whispers.

Brinley's taunting words, the way she looks with my blood on her skin pushes me over the edge and fucking Christ, I'm coming, and I don't stop, gripping her throat and holding her tight, spilling into her just as she comes all over my cock. She squeezes me so tightly; I feel every single drop leave my body and enter hers. Right where it belongs.

Every single fucking day... I will *live* inside this pussy.

CHAPTER 40
Brinley

"I can't always be with you. I have to work. I have club business," Gabriel says as he sits down beside me on the balcony that extends off his bedroom. He's entering Kai, Mason, and a few of his men's phone numbers into my phone. He wears only black sweatpants and I wear his t-shirt.

The muscles in his arm flex as he passes me a glass with a tawny liquor. I take a sip and it burns down my throat but I need it to withstand the chaos that is Gabriel Wolfe.

"I have to work too," I say as I stare out at the shimmering lake beyond.

"No. You'll stay here until we figure out what DOS's plan of attack really is."

"I most certainly will not stay hidden in this house while you come and go as you please."

Gabriel takes a sip of his whiskey and swallows. I watch his throat work as he focuses on the lake.

"Fine. You can go to work. I'll have a prospect sit outside."

I start to laugh. "You're going to make a poor guy sit there all day long?"

"Yes," he says instantly.

"You're crazy."

"Also yes," he says, no hint of a smirk.

Watching the bloodlust build in his eyes as it dripped onto my skin tells me he absolutely is, and yet here I sit, already wishing he was inside me again.

I take another sip.

"Aside from work, you're here. I'm going to train you. You need to learn some self-defense. More importantly, you need to learn to shoot a gun." He stands. "Walk with me... I'll show you around."

I swallow my bourbon and stand, curious to see the rest of the house.

We move through the bedroom. It's stark and modern like the rest of what I've seen so far. His bed is iron and is even bigger than the bed at the clubhouse. I take in my surroundings as I move down the hall, finding what looks like one other bedroom on the second floor and a bathroom. I know there's also one that connects to Gabriel's room.

He leads me to the main floor I've already seen and keeps moving toward the stairs that lead below.

The basement isn't really a basement. The same wrought iron railings lead down to a huge space. It's wide open and French doors lead out to a covered patio overlooking the lake.

The entire floor is rubber matted. Mirrors line all of the back wall. It's not so much the space as what's in it. A large sparring area surrounded by workout equipment, weights, kettlebells, racks holding even more weights, a state of the art treadmill, a variety of punching bags in different sizes.

"Wow," I breathe out. "This is... something. No wonder you look like... that," I blurt out, and I don't miss the side eyed smirk he gives me.

"You saw the shooting range outside?"

I nod. "Yes."

"You're going to learn to use that too."

"I've never shot a gun. I have no intention of—"

"Of course you haven't shot a gun, but this is the place you're going to learn how to fight, little hummingbird. I meant what I said. I never want you to be afraid again, if you can fight me, you can fight anyone."

I gulp and look around, feeling the daunting weight of what I know he's going to put me through.

"Every minute you aren't at work and I'm free, we're here. You're mine to mold. Get ready."

"Awesome," I bite out.

Gabriel walks by and smacks my panty clad ass and I try not to think about the way him molding me excites me.

"Let's sleep. Training starts tomorrow."

CHAPTER 41

Gabriel

I look up from dropping my bag on the concrete floor. Last one. My ride report for service comes in eight hours. Another tour. The last one was eighteen months. They told me to prepare, to get myself ready.

I told them all to go fuck themselves. Heading to Kuwait doesn't scare me. If I die, I die. There's only one person I care about. Only one woman whose feelings and worry matter to me. The only reason I don't want to go is because I won't be here to protect her.

I look across the room at my father, sitting under the window smoking his breakfast weed. I'm surprised he's even alive after last night's fuck up. My uncle Ray had to go pick him up at the Cardinal Motel on 17. Fucking coked out rage caused him to nearly beat some twenty-year-old girl to death after he fucked her stupid.

My uncle has dealt with this shit before. This is the norm with him, and I'm surprised he hasn't taken care of my father himself yet. The only reason I can guess that he doesn't is because my uncle has his own shit to deal with. He hasn't been well and right now it takes most of his strength just to get out of bed in the morning. But it would be doing the club a favor, because at this point, Dad causes more shit than he's worth and we all fucking know it.

Especially when we found out the woman he hurt last night is the daughter of a rival club vice president. The Huesos Rosas MC, a major player in Atlanta and Columbus. We'll be trying to make that right for a long fucking time.

"Better go find your mother. She's been crying all fucking morning," he says in between puffs.

I flex my fists. The only reason I don't hit him is because my uncle told me I couldn't. It takes everything in me most days.

"We can ride together?" Jake says, patting me on the back, saving me from answering my piece of shit sperm donor.

"Yeah," I answer.

"She's at the garden center," my father adds before standing and stumbling out of the room.

I shake my head. At least I won't have to see him for the next year. Maybe when I come back, he'll be dead.

The drive to the garden center my mother volunteers at on Main takes Jake and I less than ten minutes. She sees me and starts waving before I even stop the bike. She's happier these days. My father doesn't pay her much attention now that he knows he's risking death at my hand by going near her. He knows she's under my protection and my uncle has made sure he won't touch her physically, at least while I'm gone. The promise of losing his hands seemed to do the trick.

She smiles at me but I see the sadness in her eyes as I approach.

"Gabe. My warrior," she greets me with a hug when I come to her. Her long dark hair is pinned back for work and the lines around her eyes remind me she's getting older. I hope to find her this at peace and healthy when I come home.

Jake heads off to talk to the blonde my mother works with, and she and I decide to go for lunch.

"A lot of these guys you're going with, this is their first tour?" my mother asks as we eat.

I nod and take a bite of my steak. "12th Expeditionary Unit, a lot of them are first tour."

"You watch out for them," she tells me.

I smirk, as if I wouldn't. My job is to work the fear out of them. Take that last final bit of hesitancy from them and stomp it out. They're there as a machine, not to feel. Then and only then are they ready to front line it.

"Don't worry about me. Shell and I have each other. As long as we know you and Sean are together, we'll feel better." Her voice breaks. I know this is hard for her.

"I'm not even going to be put in harm's way, Mom, and if I am... that's my fate."

"I just hate to see you leave. When you get back, you need to shed some of this anger you have for him and focus on your future. I know I'm not a good example. I've stayed with your father through everything." She reaches over and pats my hand, I know the speech that's coming. Theresa Wolfe doesn't let things go, not until she gets her own way. Even now, with no prospects for me, her brown eyes are full of hope. It makes the guilt surface tenfold because I know there'll never be a woman I settle down with or tie myself to, and that's what she wants.

"You aren't him. You need to let that go. Find a woman to be your queen. You'll be taking over this club one day. A life alone is a hollow one." She grins "Finding a woman to love is the beginning and end of everything."

I take a sip of my drink. "Thanks for the Ted Talk and The Great Gatsby quotes." I smirk, reaching over to put my hand over hers. "I have a woman to love—you. And Jakey will be taking over, not me."

She smiles and shakes her head. "Darlin', he barely makes it through the day without making a piss poor decision. He's more your father than you are. Ray won't have it. He's looking at you."

She smiles wide. "Once you're president, you find yourself an angel to be your queen. One who will be a safe haven for you in this bullshit way of life. One who will give you sons you can raise to be your legacy. Not his."

I'm not in the mood to talk with her about things that will never happen. Instead, I'll leave Mom with hope that it might.

"None of that matters now. If I make it back, I'll deal with that. Ray will be riding for another couple years at least, and I just don't see him passing up his own son. Jakey will straighten out."

"When *you* make it back," she says as I pull my hand away to go back to my food, savoring my last lunch with her before I leave.

I take another bite as four things happen simultaneously. Someone screams as a red El Camino screeches to a halt beside us. I feel a sharp pain in my shoulder before I see the gun and hear the invasive, unmistakable sound of gunfire fill the air.

I look at my shirt quickly soaking with blood, and I ready myself to dive on top of my mother who's sitting across from me, but I'm too late. The car tires squeal, spinning and smoking as it takes off, and my mother—the only woman I'll ever love—is already slumping out of her chair. What's left of her short life is seeping out of the bullet wound in her temple.

I didn't even have time to draw my weapon. I failed her.

I sit up in bed clutching my shoulder. The scar from the bullet I took when she died aches on nights like this. I'm drenched in a cold sweat. The shuffling of feet makes me act before my mind tells me not to. I grab my .45 from under my pillow and aim, watching as the flash of onyx hair darts behind the door with a scream.

Brinley. Not an intruder.

"Fuck." I lower my gun. She fell asleep on the couch in my living room and I just covered her and let her stay there.

"You *cannot* sneak up on me," I tell her, my tone angrier than I am.

She doesn't answer.

"You're safe," I say, forcing myself to sound less aggravated.

"Flashback?" she asks without coming back into my doorway, obviously terrified. I blow out a breath and run my hand through my hair.

"Come here," I tell her.

Normally, I sit in this haze, remembering how I found the fucker that killed my mother and slit his throat just an hour after she died. The memory of his life slowly draining from his eyes usually soothes me back to sleep, but as Brinley comes forward in just my t-shirt, the haze of that day starts to fade.

"From your time overseas?" she asks quietly in the dark.

I take a deep breath and lay back in my bed, allowing her to climb in beside me, pulling her close because fuck, I just want to.

She fits under the crook of my arm like the space in my body was carved out just for her. I breathe deeply, her jasmine scent blends with the scent of me in her hair, on her body and I can't decide which one I like the idea of better.

"My mother died in front of me. The day I left for my last tour in Kuwait. My father was a piece of shit. He beat her, fucked around on her. He was uncontrollable from the day she met him. The night before she died, he fucked and beat the wrong girl. She was the daughter of a rival Puerto Rican gang. *An eye for an eye*, they said. My father didn't have a daughter, so they killed her. *He* killed her."

"Jesus," Brinley breathes out, lightly tracing the ink on my chest. "Layla told me how much you loved her. She says Ax talks about her all the time."

"She was like his mother too."

"You didn't kill him after? Your father?"

I smirk with the knowledge that she knows me already. "I tried," I admit. *I really fucking tried.* "The thought of killing him is what got me through sixteen months of duty. Any second of free thought I had was spent plotting how I would kill him for her death."

"But you didn't."

"When I got home, my uncle was really sick—his illness was rare and came out of nowhere."

I set my jaw. Talking about this usually brings up the kind of anger I find hard to control. I let out a breath, instead of flexing my fists like I'd normally do, I run my calloused thumb over her soft cheek, down over her shoulder, back and forth up and down her arm as I talk. It settles me a little.

"He asked me not to kill him. Told me it was his final wish. He wanted me to keep the peace and said if I killed him, I was no better than he was."

"Your uncle was better to you than your father?" she asks softly.

"Yes, in a hundred different ways. He taught me to think clearly, be patient, be centered," I say honestly. "He said to kill my father would be the easy way out. He wanted my father to suffer until his last breath. And he did..."

"How?" she asks, turning her pretty face up to mine. I can't resist kissing her, I'm totally fucking obsessed with this woman.

"Before my uncle died, he pushed his nomination forward to have me take over his chair. I thought my cousin would be angry he wasn't chosen, but he was pretty fucked up during that time. He was in his experimenting era. He's settled down a lot since then."

"Was it a condition of you taking over to keep your father alive?" she asks, her warm body shifting against me already has my cock stirring.

"No, it was a request. You don't fight the request of a dying man. You respect it."

Brinley doesn't speak as I continue to stroke her hair and skin.

"A year after I got back, he'd missed two meetings. I decided I better see if he was alive. So, I went to his house. He'd been dead about eight days, give or take, when I got there, the coroner said. Went on a bender, they assumed, and choked on his own vomit. They had to cut out part of the floor where he'd started decomposing. He was alone. Not one fucking person in the world cared to check on him."

"Sorry you had to see him—" she says. I pinch her and she yelps.

"Don't waste the word sorry and *him* in the same breath. Shamus Wolfe was let off the hook too easy, as far as I'm concerned. My mother, she was incredible. She always kept her hope and positivity in any situation. She never complained and she did everything to shield me from him. It wasn't possible but she did her best. There was always a spark of life in her eyes, like she was always waiting for something great to appear around the next corner. My mother dying for no fucking reason is how I know there is no higher power watching over us. If there was, she would be the first person saved. People live and people die. It's all by chance. So I live how I want every fucking day, with the possibility of knowing death is always at my door."

"That's a realistic and pessimistic way to look at things,"

she says in a tired voice. "You don't believe in destiny at all either? Right place, right time?"

"No," I answer, almost still sure.

"I do," Brinley says, and I almost feel a bit of envy at how sure she is.

"Maybe your mother watched over you in the Middle East while you were gone. Maybe you were meant to run this club. Meant to do better than your father did. You already are."

"Or nothing is meant to be and I just make better choices."

Brinley yawns and snuggles in closer to me. "Possibly. It's like you don't want to let yourself feel, but I've watched you with your club. You do feel."

"Argh," I grunt, she's pressing out into the unchartered water of the things I don't discuss with people. "I don't have the liberty of being able to feel, doing what I do. Anyone I care about has death knocking at their door too."

"We all have angels watching over us, even you. Maybe you've just been riding faster than yours can fly. Maybe it's time to slow down a little." I feel her smirk against me. "Let them catch up."

My chest cracks wide open and I almost feel my heavy heart start to beat as I remember my mother's words... *Find yourself an angel to be your queen, a safe haven.*

I kiss her forehead, knowing I'm holding the closest thing to an angel in my arms right now.

My thoughts overwhelm me briefly.

Fucking Christ, it's like I don't even know myself anymore.

"All right, enough of that," I grumble. "I want the taste of your cunt on my tongue. Spread these thighs, now."

I flip her over and pull my shirt from her body as she gasps, and I show her until the sun starts to wake just how much I *feel* for her, with my cock buried as deep inside her.

CHAPTER 42

Gabriel

"Where are we at?" I ask at Chapel the next night.

"I think I have something," Jake says. "I've been thinking about it for a while."

I nod, letting him know he has the floor.

"At the Glen Eden rally, there will be a lot of HOH members there. We wanna patch DOS over, right? That's still the plan?"

I nod. "I don't want to kill them all, some of them will be useful. Only their piece of shit president and probably their VP, just because he'll be gunning for us if we don't take him out. It should be an easy patch over after that. We'll take a page from their books if we have to, but their kids are off limits." I turn to Kai.

"I think the rally will be the perfect place to talk to Otis about helping us," Jake says, mentioning the president of our sister club the Titans.

"I agree. You get everything on them?" I ask Kai. He understands I mean the DOS members.

'I'm working on it. But yeah."

"Good. I say we take out their clubhouse," I tell the table. "Can we get some ANFO?" I ask Jake. If anyone knows how we can get our hands on enough ammonium nitrate and fuel oil to take the building down, it's him. "I don't want C4. Don't want to risk any damage to any of the buildings around the club house. It's in a populated part of Savannah, we'll do it in the middle of the night, and we'll scope it for a few weeks to make sure there are no surprises."

He nods. "Easily. I know just the guy."

"Okay, we'll start scoping them. I wanna know everything these fuckers are going to do over the next month. We can't be too quick; they'll expect a fast retaliation. We have to be smart." I look at each one of my men. "Smarter than them, got it? Then we take their building down, take out their piece of shit president. Cut their Achilles heel."

They all nod.

"Good."

"What are you doin' with Brinley?" Ax asks me. "Lay wants to see her." He shrugs. "She's pissed that she's basically gonna be on house arrest until this shit is over."

I know Ax has told Layla she's only clear to go to the wellness center, where she works as a massage therapist, and home again if she has an escort or she's with him. All the girls will be in the same boat. We can't take any chances.

"Brinley's at my house," I tell him. Every eye in the room lands on me as I say it. I look back at all of them, one at a time.

"Your house?" Kai smirks.

"I know what you're all thinking. I'm keeping her there. I won't discuss it."

Jake chuckles, and the rest of the table nods.

"How do we all feel about Pres connecting with his human side?" Kai asks the table.

They all start hooting and pounding the table in response.

Ax pats me on the shoulder. "Welcome to the dark side, man."

"Fuck off," I grunt.

"We'll protect her like we do you, boss," Ax says seriously.

I nod and snap the gavel down, smirking back at them.

When I'm done with her, she'll be able to protect them.

"The first part of self-defense is always knowing more than your attacker," I tell Brinley two hours later.

We're in the gym after a difficult hour at the shooting range where Brinley effectively missed every single target. I expected that. It took me forty minutes to get her to even pull the goddamn trigger.

What I didn't expect was the darkness that lives in this woman runs deeper than I thought. When she finally did fire, all I could do was stand back and watch.

Brinley didn't stop until the fucking mag was empty. Then she turned to me, chest heaving, determination lining her face and demanded, "Again."

I'm not going to say it was easy for me to see her like that— hair back in a ponytail, hearing protection on, that concentrated look on her face, her plush lip between her teeth as she took her shots over and over. It took everything in me to remind myself we had a job to do.

I could fuck her later.

I keep reminding myself of that now, as Brinley stands before me, after a thirty-minute weight training session where she did surprisingly better than the gun range. She's already strong from daily yoga. Now she's only going to get stronger. I simply can't be with her every second, and knowing she can protect herself will give me the tiny semblance of peace that I never got with my mother.

"You won't see them coming. Time is never on your side, so you need to start focusing on being hyper aware in every situation," I tell Brinley as I push her shoulder, probably a little harder than I should. "Could be something as simple as someone shoving you."

Her mouth pops open in surprise as I push her again. "Nine times out of ten, your attacker will come at you from behind like this." I spin her around roughly and grab hold, reminding myself as I ease up a little that she *isn't* a soldier yet.

Her ass presses up against my cock, she shifts herself to try to break free and presses into me a little more. If it's on purpose I'm fucking proud of her because it would distract any man.

For the first time maybe ever, I have to force myself to focus as I wrap an arm around her neck tighter. She starts clawing at me.

"You can claw but it's not very effective," I tell her, knowing she's struggling to breathe, but I don't let go. She needs to know what it feels like so if it really happens, she isn't afraid.

"You need to be smarter than your attacker. Strategic, waiting that extra second to calculate could and will save your life."

I let go and she inhales deeply. Leaning down to rest her elbows on her thighs as her breath returns.

"You *son of a...*" She lunges at me, smacking at me for taking her breath. She's not helping me contain the urge to fuck her.

I grip her throat to calm her down and tsk at her. "The smart little mouth doesn't mean you're *thinking* smarter," I tell her.

"I couldn't breathe," she says, still a little out of breath.

"I know. And you better get used to it. I'll be choking you out every day until you can break my hold."

I pull a step stool from the wall into the center of the room, it will give her enough of a height advantage to wrap her arm around my neck. I grab a still scowling Brinley around the waist and hoist her up onto it before she can complain, then I turn so her front is to my back. I grab one of her arms and pull it around my neck, she grips tight and yanks on me, hard. I chuckle.

"Christ. Calm down," I tell her. "You'll get more chances to beat the shit outta me while you're learning."

"Well, there's that to look forward to," Brinley grunts out, still trying to keep her grip on me and failing. I grip her hand and pull it forward; she yelps with the pain.

This gets her attention.

"You're my attacker," I tell her as I wrap her arm back around my neck.

"The first thing I'm going to do is lower my chin. It's much harder to get in and to choke me if my chin is down." I tap her other arm.

"Now, lock your hands around my neck."

She does and gets a damn firm grip too, but not firm enough to actually do any damage.

We run through this a few times until she seems to get it.

I turn and face her. She's still on the stool, almost reaching my height. I kiss her lips once, and she scowls. I tilt her head, I can't help myself, and I run my tongue from her collarbone to her jaw, satiating myself until this training is done. She shudders as I lift her off the stool and place her before me, spinning her quickly so her back is to my front.

I wrap my arm firmly around her throat, explaining to her step by step how to break my hold. After a few tries, she does it.

"Attagirl... next, you're gonna step to the side and use your hand to swing backward. Aim for the groin."

Brinley does it, but I move in time for her to miss me.

We practice the motions thoroughly for a while until I'm satisfied with her progress and the sun has sunk in the sky outside. I take a few hard shots to the balls and Brinley seems to think it's funny as all hell. She's definitely getting punished for that later.

"I need water," Brinley pants.

I remind myself that she doesn't do this every day the way I do. I release the hold I have on her and send her for water, watching the way her chest heaves as she walks. Her blue yoga pants cling to her juicy fucking ass and somehow make it look even better than the perfection it always is. The little matching top might as well be a bra, one that's earning its money by holding those full tits up. A veil of sweat covers her and amplifies her sweet scent. Her hair is damp, her neck, her arms... every part of her glistens and fuck, all I want to do is lick every inch of her clean. I smirk as I watch her chug down half the bottle of water and then wipe her brow. I'm realizing there's a way to train her *and* get what I want. She turns to face me.

"What now? A hundred push ups? Some burpees?" Brinley asks, putting her hand on her hip, her chest still rising heavy.

She sets the water down, the look on my face must tell her that I'm about to challenge her.

Brinley doesn't move, just cocks her head to the side and stands there watching me, breathing deeply. I turn from her and move toward the patio door that faces my yard and the woods. I unlock it and swing it wide open.

Turning back to her, I stretch my hands out in front of me, fingers intertwined and pushing outward until they crack. Her eyes move over me trying to figure out what I'm doing, and I can almost sense her pussy getting wet from here.

I begin to stalk toward her slowly, reaching back to pull my shirt from my body as I go. When I reach the halfway point between us I stop and smirk at her.

I fucking love hunting her.

"Your attacker is coming, so move quickly, little hummingbird. *Run.*"

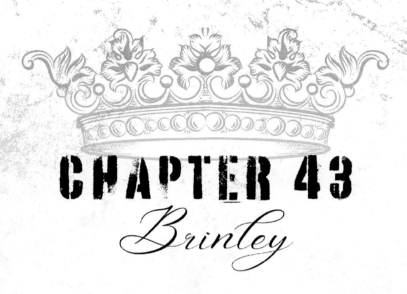

CHAPTER 43
Brinley

I don't hesitate or think, I just run as fast as my already screaming legs will carry me out the door and into the night. My pulse hammers away in my throat as I fly through the yard and head for the woods. I know there's a trail there, so I won't break an ankle. Gabriel tells me he runs it every morning.

I take to it, being as light on my feet as I can be. I know he's a runner so he'll catch me eventually and I know what he'll do to me if he does. That's the thrilling part. Because even if you're being chased by someone you trust implicitly, there's still a fear that ripples through you at the thought of being caught.

It isn't long before I hear the thud of Gabriel's heavy feet on the trail. He doesn't call out to me, he pauses and waits, so I dart behind a tree. The snapping of a twig under my Nike might as well be a goddamn bomb going off in the quiet forest. I hear his feet again and I sprint further into the woods knowing if I don't, I'm caught.

The trail ends and I stop, looking both left and right, trying to figure out where to go in the darkness. I go with my gut and turn right, darting behind a tree as I begin to move back toward the direction of the house, and then I hear him. The night is humid and everything is already sticking to me. I see Gabriel out of the corner of my eye and my adrenaline surges as he closes in on me. I turn to flee but don't even get to the tree line before he's gripping my hair at the roots and heaving me backwards toward him. My back slams into his chest so hard it knocks the wind out of me.

"Caught you, greedy girl. I bet that tight little cunt has been making a mess of these panties since the moment I told you to run," Gabriel whispers low against my ear, his arm coming around my neck and pulling tight.

"Let's see how much more of a mess we can make, hmm?"

I panic, forgetting everything I learned while training. Everything feels like it happens in slow motion as my breath is lost. I start clawing and hitting him, anything to get him to loosen his grip.

"No," Gabriel says into my ear, tapping my hip, a reminder to be calm. It works. I drop my chin and wiggle it under his arm as I simultaneously step out and fist him in the groin. He lets go of me and moves before my fist can make contact with him. I fall onto my hands and knees in front of him, breathless, dizzy, cut up, and filthy. He drops to his knees behind me and pulls my ass up, shoving my body into the dirt, and I take it because I have nothing left to fight him with.

His hands slide down my ass and he groans, pulling me back against his hardened cock. I whimper as the familiar deep desire spreads.

It's instant.

All Gabriel has to do is touch me and my body prays to him.

"My wicked girl, ready and on your knees for me. Now spread these thighs and show me you deserve my cock," Gabriel growls as his fingers slide down the center of my pants. He lifts the thin material and tears it outward from the seam, exposing my entire ass to the air, discovering I'm not wearing any panties underneath.

"*Fuck* yes," he says as he buries his face into my already dripping pussy, his hands squeezing my outer thighs under what's left of my pants as he fucks his tongue in and out of me.

I'm still face down in the dirt but I'm pushing back into him, crying out as I do because whatever he's doing is going to make me come apart on his tongue in what feels like mere seconds. His hands reach around and pull me closer by my hips.

I steady myself in a rhythm that I never want to end.

His hands move, kneading and gripping every part of my flesh they reach.

They slide upward and pull my athletic top down. My aching breasts bounce free as his fingers find my hardened nipples. He pinches each one and I cry out, tipping my head back. I push myself up on my elbows to get better leverage so I can ride his face.

"Fuck, I've been dreaming about tasting you for hours. Drown me, Brinley."

"Yes," I cry as I desperately grasp at the earth, rocking slowly into his face, I come in record time, feeling my pussy spasm around his tongue. Gabriel doesn't relent, he continues to fuck me with his mouth until I'm a begging mess before him. He raises up my hips even more and spreads me wide before driving his cock into my pussy viciously with a deep groan.

"*Fuuuuck,* this cunt. So fucking perfect." Gabriel spreads me even wider, and I cry as he pushes in that last inch. "Look at this soaking fucking pussy begging for my cock. Taking every inch, showing me you were fucking made for me."

"Please," I beg, which only makes him take me harder, deeper.

This.

This moment where he's wild and unhinged, this is what I crave every single day. It's what I've always wanted and never knew how to find. It's in Gabriel's unrelenting passion that he shows me what he's truly feeling. By the way he fucks me I'd say he needs me like he needs air in his lungs. That thought makes me feel like the most powerful version of myself.

My elbows slide ahead while rocks and twigs gnash at my skin as I'm pushed forward by him brutally fucking me. My pants hang in scraps around my thighs and I start to push back against him, rolling my hips to tease him as he slides into me. The power in me grows stronger as I realize I am absolutely the one he wants. The one he craves. How much more will he want me if I tease him the way he teases me?

I find my bravery easily with him. It pushes me to be bold, motivates me to be the woman I've always wanted to be.

"Give me every inch. Make me scream like you want the entire forest to know who owns me," I purr, finally feeling open and free, tossing my hair over my shoulder and looking back at him. He fists it and winds it in his hand pulling my head up.

"*Fuck,* Brin..." Gabriel pauses like he's studying me, and I know my dirty words have taken him by surprise.

He pulls my head up, bringing my back to his front. Another slow tug of my hair, a deeper twist of his hand turns my face to the side and his lips come down on mine, all the while he never loses his rhythm.

"Fuck the forest. By the time I'm done with you, there won't be a creature roaming this Earth that doesn't know who you fucking belong to," he growls, and I smirk into his lips.

"Make me come then, Pres," I whisper.

"*Fuck.*" Gabriel's lips come crashing down on mine again and a hand slides to my clit. He pinches it roughly between his thumb and finger, never letting up as he fucks me and I'm freefalling.

I come, then come down and the wave rises again. All the while he never stops, fucking me like he's bringing himself to the edge then holding back. Fucking me like the slow torture of not coming is one he not only wants but craves.

He slows his pace and I feel everything, every inch of him sliding in and out of me. It brings me back to life, stoking the fire still burning in my belly.

"Spit," he says, holding his palm under my lips. I'm so far gone, I do as he says and spit onto his first three fingers. They come down and slide over my clit as he groans.

"You can give me one more, Brin. Come on, baby, come all over my cock, *one more*," Gabriel orders.

The simple, gentle word *baby* rolling off his tongue is all it takes and I'm coming again, my legs quiver as I see stars for the second time in minutes. His hands grip me in a bruising hold at my hips as I feel him stiffen and pulse. His warmth spreads through me with my name on his lips as they move over my neck, and my shoulders. I'm exhausted, cut, bruised, and bleeding. I'm always partly afraid, and yet I still ask myself how I ever lived without him.

PB

How are things at the Wolfe den?

Isolated AF.

PB

It doesn't surprise me that the moment Wolfe claims a woman he keeps her hidden from the world. Can you not just have more sex?

Impossible.

I just need to get out of here for more than work.

PB

I would suggest we escape for a girls' night but he more than likely tracks your car.

HAHA very funny. He better not be.

PB

Sean says only a few more weeks and life can go back to normal.

I grimace at my phone. It sort of pisses me off that Layla knows a timeline but Gabriel hasn't told me anything yet. I bring my lip between my teeth and bite down.

I've been in this house for two days and haven't fully snooped through it yet. I begin to walk toward the bedroom. Gabriel is gone and I have no idea where. *Club business*, he said.

I pull his drawers open one by one, everything is neat, organized. Black boxers upon black boxers. Same with his t-shirts and jeans.

It's all perfect. Too perfect.

I push open his closet door and run my fingers along the soft flannels that hang there. Carhartt. In blacks and grays, you would think he had shares in the company. As I get to the back a small wooden box with an oval inlay catches my eye.

By the time I pick it up I'm convinced that it's probably knives or something demented but when I open it, I see different compartments. I pull each one out. The top one is full of medals and articles pulled from some sort of magazine. It's about a mission the E-12 Marines carried out to neutralize a warlord, but during the attack the enemy bombed their own village. I look away when I flip the page over. There are photos on it. One is a village with people everywhere. Dead people. Another just like it, a car blown to bits. No wonder he has no belief in God or the Devil. No wonder his faith in people is nonexistent. How can one see this sort of carnage and come out the other side with faith?

I pull the next two compartments out and they're filled with photos. Old ones. I instantly recognize him in the sea of kids. Big and strong even when he was young. He seems to be about ten, standing with his mother. Her beauty overwhelms me. Long dark hair, pretty features, and a beautiful smile— Gabriel's smile. There are other photos with the club, I see the man who must be his uncle with the president patch, him and another kid on bikes. Maybe Sean?

There's another of Gabriel in his teen years, arms folded across his chest. What hits me the most is it's the first picture I've found where his eyes have the same hollow and emotion-less look as they do now. I glance back at the first photos, the ones where his eyes have a mischievous light. I run my finger across them and smile. That's the Gabriel I wish I could've seen, before life jaded him.

I pull another compartment out and squint. I don't know what these are. I pick one up. It's small, the size of a quarter and it has the Apple logo on it. I flip it over and read the back. AirTag. *Can be tracked miles away, or even in a different country, provided it is within Bluetooth range of an Apple device on the Find My network.*

Is he *actually* tracking my car? I pick one up and put it in my pocket, tidying up this mess as best I can.

I make my way down the stairs and out the front door.

Pulling the device out, I look at it again and decide he'd probably put it inside. I open my door and begin my search, feeling down the cracks and crevices in between seats, under the dash, but it isn't until I get on my hands and knees that I see it, stuck to the underside of the driver's seat.

Motherfucker.

He makes me stay here every minute of every day while he comes and goes as he pleases? I make a promise here and now, no more. From now on, I'll be making him tell me *everything*. And this little tracker?

Well, two can play at that game.

CHAPTER 44
Brinley

Over Three Weeks Later

"Fuck you!" I spit out obscenities I wouldn't even have been comfortable with two months ago but now the sound of my voice echoes through the space.

All my clothing sticks to me with sweat. We're on hour two of this little routine we've got going. We've been at it every day and I'm about to go crazy. Always an hour at the shooting range, then hours in the gym. I've learned over the last few weeks that every plane of Gabriel's body is an integral part of the weapon he is. He's all rippling muscle, hard lines and simmering just below the surface is all his power and rage. It never ceases to both piss me off and turn me the fuck on to watch him hardly break a sweat in training with me.

"I *can't* do it... you're too goddamn heavy," I bite out. "And we're both already bleeding."

He could go on like this for weeks and I'm panting after the first forty-five minutes. At least this last week I've made it forty-five before panting, so I guess that's progress.

"Yes, you can, just get fucking angrier." Gabriel chuckles as I struggle to get out of his hold. I'm pinned below him; we've been working on this particular move for days. My lip is still bleeding from ten minutes ago when I tried to push him off of me from my stomach and he forced me back down. My teeth met the nice plush middle of my bottom lip, which in turn made me claw at his neck deep enough to draw blood.

"You're never more alive than when you're bleeding," Gabriel grunts as he holds me, trading between looking like he's either going to tighten his hold on me or kiss me, or both.

"If I gave up when I saw my blood in that cave I wouldn't be here. Every drop I bled meant I was still living."

I stare up at him as a new piece of his sadistic mind is revealed to me.

Gabriel leans down even closer, that cruel light in his eye glints as he holds me. "And I like the look of my blood on you, hummingbird," he says, his voice low and even. "It's when I feel the most alive. Now, secure your position and fucking *fight me!*"

I do my best to remember the steps while his forearm is currently cutting off my air supply.

"Come on!" he snarls. "Knee to my stomach, foot on my hip."

I try, but he weighs so much.

"Shit," I grit out but I somehow manage to find the will, simultaneously lifting and twisting his weight with my foot and my knee, using it against him.

"Attagirl," he growls as I pull my hand away while pushing up with my leg to escape his hold entirely. I fall onto my back on the mat, my arms in an outstretched U.

I feel like I might die. Every muscle in my body screams at me and I look like I've been run over by a truck, while he looks like he just got back from a leisurely ten-minute walk. I let my eyes rake over him, sweat glistening slightly on his chest. As frustrating as he is, that is a *really* nice half naked body to stare at while I die.

"Stop eye fucking your attacker." Gabriel smirks as he throws his t-shirt on over his head and makes his way past me, heading for the stairs.

I breathe out a sigh, surprised we're done for the day, but at the same time? Thank fucking God.

"I want to come with you to the Glen Eden rally this weekend. Layla is going, there are vendors and so many people. I *need* people. It's one day," I plead, taking a seat at his kitchen island. I'm showered and feeling slightly more human after that work-out, while he makes us a version of the same meal I've eaten every day for the last four weeks. Some form of protein, quinoa or jasmine rice, and veggies. I'm not going to lie and say the effects on my body haven't been startling. In just under a month I'm more sculpted, I've grown physically stronger, I'm lifting much heavier weights and I'm faster. Physically, I've never been healthier.

Mentally, I'm going insane.

Gabriel eyes me up, still shirtless, as he stirs chicken with some sort of homemade marinade, in a cast iron pan. As it simmers, my stomach growls but it's not the food that makes my mouth water. It's the sight of him.

There hasn't been a single day he hasn't been inside me every night before we spend hours lying in bed and talking. It's mostly him asking me questions about every single part of my life—what my favorite foods are, my other childhood friends, who has ever been mean to me.

He's making a list, says he'll save it for a rainy day when he feels like hunting. But through all of it, I have been able to get to know him a little better. Or as well as Gabriel allows anyone to know him. I know what makes him tick, like his morning runs, the passion he has for his work in creating beautiful bikes people fall in love with, how he never embellishes a story. He says it exactly like it is. The way when he tells me when he'll be home, he is—on time, every single time. He's also been honest with me whenever I've asked him a direct question. I realized it wasn't because he was keeping things from me, but because he's simply not used to having someone ask. Gabriel openly tells me whatever I'd like to know, except that he's tracking my car, but that's okay because I'm tracking him too.

When he was in the shower, I lifted up the thick insole in his boot and slipped the little AirTag in, super gluing it back down. At first, I felt bad for doing it without his knowledge but then I realized that's just my conscience, and if Gabriel himself has taught me anything, it's that I don't always have to listen to it if it's for the right reason. I've never even checked it, but I feel like if he's going to know where I am, I can know where he is. It's like I'm letting him track me by choice.

I breathe out a sigh. After that intense workout I'm sore, I'm exhausted yet keyed up, and I'm ready to lose my mind if he doesn't let me out of here for something other than work.

"It's not safe," Gabriel says without looking up from cooking.

"I'm not Rapunzel," I retort, bracing myself for an argument with him. "If I'm going to go anywhere, it's the safest place I could go. Layla told me nothing but good things ever happen at these rallies. She said it's an unspoken rule to keep the peace at them. There will be hundreds of people there, you said it yourself... and I'd be with *you*, plus"—I raise an eyebrow —"you could always give me my own gun if you're that worried about it."

Gabriel chuckles that deep laugh that I love. "Take it easy G.I Jane, hitting a few targets—"

"Seven out of ten, three times in a row yesterday," I remind him, smiling smugly.

"Seven out of ten," he repeats. "Doesn't make you an expert. You've never fired at anything *real*."

I sit back in the chair, looking down at my braised knuckles, swollen from hitting his heavy bag with him. This isn't going the way I hoped.

"So what? I need to hunt an animal or something before I can have my own gun?" I ask, my voice rising at the end. That doesn't sound like something I could do, but maybe that's his point.

Gabriel pours me half a glass of straight tequila; this isn't something I'd ever drink so I look up at him in question.

"For your muscles." He smirks. "And you won't be hunting a wild animal but... something like that."

"I want to go to the rally," I say firmly, lifting my chin.

Gabriel is neither fazed nor amused by my persistence, it's like something more is weighing on his mind. I remind myself it's probably how he's planning to execute the Disciples of Sin president and take over their club. The idea of what's in front of him settles deep within me as he fills our plates, working carefully.

I was right, chicken layered with brightly colored peppers, and quinoa. He looks like some sort of ominous *Food Network* chef as he licks his thumb and swipes sauce off the side of his own plate, keeping it as neat as mine. I'm absolutely starving after a grueling day of work and training.

The office at *Crimson Homes* is busy with two clients going simultaneously, both at different build stages. The air isn't easy going anymore but it is still relaxed. Dell doesn't push me and he's friendly enough, but I feel the looks he gives me every time he glances out the office window and sees a prospect waiting to escort me home after my shift. I know he wonders what the hell I'm wrapped up in, the same way I worried about Layla when I got here. But the discernment and silent judgement irritates me more often than not. He doesn't even know Gabriel.

I won't be able to keep this job for long if I have HOH members hanging around the building, but so far they're happy with my work and seem to need me.

It's a means to an end. Gabriel won't take a penny, nor would I offer him one anyway when I have a perfectly good home that I could live in on the other side of town. So I'm saving everything I have, holding on to a sliver of hope that I could maybe open my own interior design studio at some point when this is all over. One with local artisans' pieces and rustic Georgian vibes.

"*Eat,*" Gabriel says, breaking into the silence and causing me to flinch.

I muster the energy to fight back the tears and rage at the thought of him just dismissing my request.

I push my plate aside. I know I'm acting childish, using my rejection of this beautiful meal he's made, but I need him to listen. I need his attention. Hole a woman up in a house for almost a month and see how childish she can become.

"I'm not hungry, thank you," I say politely, shrugging my shoulders.

He stands over me for a few seconds, watching. I can feel his eyes roaming over me as I check my nails as if they're of the utmost importance. He moves to the other side of the table and sits.

"You're acting like a little brat, Brinley, and you'll eat what

I took the time to prepare you."

A simmering fury takes over and I raise my eyes to him. He meets them and we sit, dead locked while he waits for my response. I feel the tears in my eyes, the anger of this entire situation brimming to the surface.

"And if I tell you I *am* going to the rally? I have my own car. What will you do? Send me to my room? Ground me? *Oh, wait*"—I let out a haughty laugh—"I'm already grounded. *Permanently.*"

Gabriel's fist hits the table with a thud and I jump.

"Enough," he says as he picks up a forkful of food and eats. As threatening as he looks right now shirtless at the table, I stay as strong as I can, if for no other reason than to get my point across. He can keep me, but he can't own me unless I let him.

Leaning back in my chair, I fold my hands in my lap and wait. My stomach growls and I hope he doesn't hear it.

"Say you'll take me with you and I'll eat every bite," I demand, trying my best to sound bold.

He pops another bite between his plush lips. I eye him as he does. Those lips might be my demise. So full and perfect looking against the square, strong angles of his jaw, he's too gorgeous. I don't know how I didn't see the depth of his beauty the first time I laid eyes on him.

"You won't get very far with blackmailing me, little hummingbird."

"We'll see," I say curtly, like I would've before I met him.

Gabriel isn't used to people standing up to him and that's fine, but I want this. After being around him, I want to know *more* of him. More of his life. What drives him, which is why I'm so adamant about going to this rally. I need it and I won't let him push me around on it.

Gabriel takes another bite, chewing slowly and analyzing me. The longer I wait for him to finish eating, the more nervous

I get. It's like I can feel him calculating how he's going to handle me or *punish me.*

I feel his eyes on me as I start to lose confidence, fidgeting with the hem on my tank. I clear my throat and straighten up, resting my palms in my lap.

He doesn't speak, just continues eating, watching my posture, watching my nerves build under his stare. By the time his plate is clean my hands are sweaty, not knowing what he'll do. Gabriel's eyes never leave mine as he takes a long drink of his own tequila.

Finally, when I'm just about to crumble under the weight of his stare he stands and makes his way over to the kitchen. He pulls a roll of heavy twine out of the drawer. My heart rate instantly starts to increase as he starts to unravel a hefty length and cuts it.

He calmly puts the roll back in the drawer and begins to stalk toward me.

"When I was young, I fought for every morsel of healthy food I could put into my body," Gabriel says as he gets closer.

"My mother tried to prepare good meals, but it was always hard to do when my father drank, snorted or shot up every penny we had."

I breathe in a slow shallow pant as Gabriel moves directly behind my chair, sets the twine in front of me and swipes my hair off my neck, bending down to kiss my shoulder—once, then twice. He breathes in my freshly showered scent, his nose pressing into my skin, then slides his hands down both my arms, unclasping my sweaty palms from my lap and lacing his fingers through, forcing them to relax.

Just as I feel the need to clench my thighs together, he grips both my wrists hard and pulls them tight behind my back with no concern about hurting me. I jolt forward with the pain trying to fight him but there's no use.

"What are you doing?" I ask, my voice higher pitched than normal.

He holds my wrists securely behind the chair as he reaches for the twine.

"When I was old enough to work, I started buying my own food and cooking for myself and my mother with money he couldn't touch."

I feel the twine wrap around my wrists, and he pulls it taut. So tight it hurts as it digs into my skin.

"And I promised myself that good food would never go to waste. See, when you have to fight for something as simple as nourishment, you tend to appreciate it more. Something you wouldn't have ever had to learn during all those princess-like etiquette classes."

"What do you think you're going to do? Force feed me?" I spit out in question.

Gabriel moves in front of me without answering.

"Stop trying to fight it, it's a Klemheist knot, the more you pull the tighter it'll get."

He picks up my fork and loads it up with a scoop of quinoa.

"Now, I said *eat*." One strong hand holds my head still as he uses his thumb to press against a joint near my lower jaw. *Fucking hell.*

My mouth pops open instantly and he shoves the fork in, swiping it out and holding my mouth closed.

"I told you this once—you won't win." Gabriel bends down to look in my eyes before removing his hand. "Now do as you're fucking told."

Fury rises in me like I've never felt. I shouldn't fight back. I know I've pushed him far enough but the wicked side of me, that he does his damnedest to pull out every day, is the side that's hurt by his insinuation that I'm being a princess. Without thought, I spit the food out on the floor. I don't even raise my head back up before the knot at my wrists is pulled tighter by his hand. I cry out in pain and push the chair back, kicking at Gabriel. He easily places both his feet over mine to stop me and grabs my hair at the roots, tipping my head up to face him. He leans down and plants a line of gentle kisses up my jaw until he reaches the spot under my ear that he loves. His lips and tongue trail slowly along my pulse just before he bites my flesh. I whimper and ask myself why being tied here like this, completely at his mercy is doing it for me.

"You want to fight me? Once again you find yourself faced with a choice," he growls.

"You leave me no choice but to fight. I'm not just your captive. I'm your—"

Gabriel silences me with a kiss to my lips. His knuckles graze my cheekbone with his free hand, and I fight with tears in my eyes to not let him pull me under as his other hand stays rooted in my hair. He pulls back from my lips, and I watch as his eyes focus on my mouth. His jaw flexes, he swallows and I know he's just as strung out as I am right now. The thought of his hardened cock so close to me threatens to overtake every sliver of my anger.

"You're my little hummingbird." A sadistic smirk takes over his face. "And it's time to feed, little bird."

He picks up my half full glass of tequila and pulls my hair tighter. I watch his eyes as they focus, swirling it around in the glass before knocking half of it back in one shot and setting the glass on the table. Before I can register his movements, he's pressing that spot along my jaw that forces my mouth open. He leans down and spits the tequila into my mouth. I choke on it and swallow what I can as it burns my windpipe.

Gabriel uses his thumb to spread tequila over my lips before leaning down again and kissing me deeply. As he does, I confirm what I assumed, he's rock hard pressing against my arm. Warm and ready and tearing down my defenses with every swipe of his tongue. He still holds my feet down so clenching my thighs isn't an option.

"If you continue to fight, I'll have to find an equally creative way to feed you your dinner. The choice is yours."

My breath is heavy as I realize I'm fighting a losing battle. I want to make him hard for me. I want to have him force me. Those dark parts of me crave it.

I simply choose to give in, looking him dead in the eyes, I pop my mouth open and stick out my tongue.

He holds my hair and stands in still silence for all of five seconds before a low growl leaves him. Gabriel reaches down and gathers a bite for me on the fork. He brings it to my lips, I feel my chest rise and fall, and I lean forward. Keeping my eyes on his, I wrap my lips around the fork and suck the food clean off. His cock presses into my arm and I shimmy just a little to torture him with some friction.

As I chew, a drawn out, seductive groan escapes me that I couldn't prevent, even if I tried.

Fuck, it's so good, I really am so hungry.

I swallow and open my mouth, sticking out my tongue again to show him I've swallowed.

"More?" I ask sweetly looking up at him through my lashes, taunting him. It's the only power I have, and I realize it's the way I can breakthrough. The thread of control he holds is unraveling by the second as he gathers me another bite and I swipe it off, taking even longer this time to pull my lips from the fork.

"*So* good," I moan as I chew. I move a little more against his cock and I hear him mutter "*fuck*" under his breath. I'm testing him but he doesn't stop me.

"Feed me more," I tell him, but it comes out like a breathy whimper.

As my next bite is gathered, I see a wet spot through his light gray sweatpants where pre-cum seeps through, all for me.

I swallow that bite and smirk.

"More tequila now, please," I ask.

Gabriel picks my glass up and mouths what's left in it, looking down at me he uses his thumb to slowly pull my chin down. He doesn't have to try hard. I pop it open and stick my tongue out for him. He bends down and lets the tequila trickle out of his mouth into mine, slowly. I lap at it, my tongue skimming his lips, savoring him and breaking him. One more swipe of my tongue over his bottom lip and then he's kissing me, his thread finally snapping as the warm tequila floods my mouth and my pussy throbs almost worse than my wrists.

Gabriel pulls back and stares down at me, as if he's in shock that I've turned his punishment around on him.

I pant in a shallow rhythm as I let my gaze trail over his body—slowly, the way he would normally do to me. The way that used to make me nervous but now only makes me want him. Over his abs to the deep V of his waist and then down to his cock my gaze settles. I hold it then look up at him.

"Feed me?" I ask as I open my mouth for him looking back down to his cock. Not one second passes before he's wrenching himself free of his clothes and thrusting his cock into my mouth. I open wider and take him eagerly, gagging and sputtering around him as he hits the back of my throat. His other hand moves to my hair too and he loses it there, using his thumbs to slide down my cheeks and tug my jaw open wider. I moan against him. He thrusts deeper, holding his cock steady at the back of my throat. My eyes water as I look up at him through my lashes.

"That's it, little bird. Suck. Make me your meal like a good little cockwhore."

He pulls back and then slams into my mouth again and I can't resist. I let my teeth graze him.

"Fuck," he growls as I smirk around his cock, then gently lick over any pain I may have caused him, swirling my tongue against the ladder on the underside of his shaft.

"Use your teeth again and I'll be taking your virgin ass right here on the kitchen table."

I watch him above me. The dark beauty of Gabriel as he violently fucks my throat. It doesn't take long like this, and I can tell he's about to come. The thought of me tied up and at his will must do something to him too.

I moan around Gabriel as he forces his cock deep, drool runs down my chin as he hits the back of my throat over and over. He pulls out almost all the way, using his thumb to hold my chin down as my tongue lingers on him, he pushes back in, inch by inch as slow as he can allow himself. I swipe my tongue over every barbell as he groans, and I do everything in my power to make him feel all of it. My throat opening for him, my tongue against him. I moan, I'm so on fire for him I think I might combust. I'm desperate to be able to move, my hands are numb and heavy, still tied behind my back so tightly. I feel him harden even further against my tongue.

"Taste how out of control you make me, wicked girl," he grunts as he fills my mouth without warning. I gag around him and choke on his cum as it hits my throat with force. Gabriel steadies himself inside me for a beat and breathes, his chest heaving like he had no control over what just happened. I fucking love it.

Gabriel looks down and pulls his cock from my lips, swiping his cum back into my mouth.

"Fuck, you're stunning, all tied up, mouth full of my cock, my cum dripping from these pretty lips." He runs a thumb over my mouth. "Beautiful."

The deranged part of me blossoms under his praise.

He says nothing as he tucks his cock back into his pants and moves toward the bathroom. I wait, the pain in my hands takes over as the adrenaline of what he just did begins to fade.

Gabriel is back in less than a minute with a warm washcloth. He kneels down to my level and without looking, uses one hand to untie my wrists while he washes away my tears, my drool, his cum from my face with the other. I immediately pull my hands to my front when they're free and sets the cloth down. I watch as he begins massaging them back to life for me.

"You're the only person on this fucking planet that can make me lose control, Brinley. And me out of control is a dangerous thing to witness." Gabriel's eyes meet mine as he continues to rub and the pins and needles feeling in my palms begins to fade.

He sets the cloth down and lifts my plate. I watch as he heads back into the kitchen and puts it in the microwave to warm the rest back up for me. I could get up, but I don't.

Gabriel returns moments later and sets my plate in front of me. He lifts me up and sits in my chair, pulling me into his lap. His hand comes up to brush my sweaty hair from my forehead. He kisses me there. I could try to run or fight him, but I don't. I simply open my mouth again for my food.

"You can come to the rally on Saturday, but we'll have some work to do first."

He lifts the fork and begins to feed me the rest of my dinner. We sit like this, in silence, as I internally let out a scream of victory.

I hold my aching hands in my lap as Gabriel feeds me bite after bite. I take everything he offers.

To anyone on the outside, it would appear like maybe he serves me... like maybe I own him, not the other way around.

CHAPTER 45

Gabriel

"You want me to what?" Brinley asks as I take my shirt off. Fuck, it's hot. We just ran the equivalent of three miles and walked one through the trails that surround my acreage. I watch as her throat works to swallow her electrolytes. Fuck she's incredible.

Her little spandex shorts cling to her in all the right places, the loose t-shirt she wears over one of those little spandex bras is like a teaser and her dark hair is piled high on her head. She's growing stronger by the day and is being transformed into an unassuming little weapon under my command. She's still keeping the curviness of her form though, and I can't get enough of it, that full pert ass and grippable hips are what fucking dreams are made of.

I add a fresh mag to the Glock 43 she's been training with and hand it over.

"You wanna carry your own gun, you can prove to me that you can handle it. It's not something you toy with. I need to know you aren't afraid to shoot and that you can shoot *accurately* under pressure." I walk away from Brinley towards a tree thirty feet away. Her accuracy would never need to be more than that in a threatening situation and I'm hoping she's as precise as she has been over the last week. I take my place, beside a standing target with a fresh sheet on it. Its bullseye is less than a foot from me. I plant myself there and look into her eyes.

"No, uh-uh, you're absolutely crazy," she says in horror.

I smirk. "You're just figuring this out now?"

"Gabriel," she says in the way that makes my cock twitch every fucking time. "I can't."

I swear, I could bury myself inside some part of this woman all hours of the day and never tire of her. Something about her drives me to the absolute brink of insanity and settles me all at once.

"You can. You aren't the Brinley Rose they made. Be you, be strong. Be *my* girl," I tell her firmly.

Her pretty blue eyes narrow at me and she looks down at the gun then back to me.

I watch with fascination as she comes to terms with the idea that she could kill me right now. It's not the way fear lines her eyes but that spark of electricity when she understands... she holds all the power that drives me.

"You don't want to put a bulletproof vest on?"

"Not a chance," I answer. "That's why the target is on my right." I grin. "Better chance of survival if you hit this side of my body."

Brinley doesn't speak. She just tilts her hips the way I've shown her as the late July cicadas fill the air.

Am I scared right now? Not really. The only regret I'd have is not having more time with her. And if I have to go out, going by Brinley's hand, while staring at her beautiful face, is the way I'd want. She moves her left leg forward and the right leg behind a little, and lifts the gun, holding it with both hands.

"Your shoulder," I tell her, reminding her to lean it a little forward to help with the recoil.

She nods, determination in her eyes and every single feature.

Ten long seconds of silence fill the air and then Brinley's eyes meet mine once before she zeros in on her target and fires.

CHAPTER 46
Brinley

I watch in horror as the bullet hits Gabriel, and he recoils backward a few inches.

"Fuck," he hisses, and I scream, dropping the gun.

I run toward him.

"Oh my god, I *shot* you," I cry out, feeling like I'm going into shock. The bullet landed in the tree behind him and the skin of his bicep is torn open in a sickening way. It's already bleeding profusely.

"What have I told you? Never drop your gun. Holster it or set it down!" he growls.

That's what he's worried about right now?

Gabriel inspects the wound, his jaw set before turning back to me. I wait as he reaches down and calmly tears a clean strip off the bottom of my t-shirt, wrapping it around his arm expertly as he secures it before looking at me. His breathing is calm and even, like he doesn't even care I could've just killed him. I do a little dance of wanting to cover his wound with my hands and not touching it. I finally just drop them to my sides, willing my breathing to calm down.

"Does it hurt? I knew I shouldn't have tried that. I don't need a gun. I could've killed you. Oh my god," I cry, tears filling my eyes.

Gabriel looks down at me, gripping both sides of my face, the only expression of pain he shows is a slight jaw tick as he raises his wounded arm to hold me.

"While I'm happy to see how much you care about me, little bird, calm down. It barely grazed me. I've had way worse," he adds, kissing me. "Now, go back over there and this time, hit the fucking target."

"*What?*" I squeal. "No way, not a goddamn chance."

Gabriel reaches up with his left hand and brings it down to my ass cheek. Hard. *Did he just fucking spank me?*

He's never done that when we weren't in the middle of or about to have sex, and I'm not sure if it pisses me off or turns me on. Probably both.

"Take a fucking breath," he growls. "Don't make me tell you twice, Brinley. You have to rise above that fear. Focus."

And then his lips are on mine, forcing my mouth open his tongue slips inside and chases my own. The adrenaline from turning over this power to me mingles with my fear. I melt into him and I can't control the tears welling up in my eyes. Somewhere over the last six weeks, I've grown attached to him, more attached to him than I've admitted even to myself. Gabriel nips and sucks my tongue into his mouth, searching every part as if this is the last kiss he'll ever give me, and hell, maybe it is, because I know I have no choice.

Gabriel won't let me chicken out here. He pulls back from me, his eyes alive and vibrant from our kiss.

"Don't let that be the last time I taste those fucking lips," he says with that sadistic glimmer before he taps me on the ass. "Get going."

It's uncontrollable, the emotion flowing through me right

now mixed with the adrenaline of shooting him. I throw myself into his arms and do something I've never done. I hug him. Under the dappled sun filtering down through the canopy of the live oaks in his yard, I hold onto Gabriel for dear life. He stands as still as a statue for all of five seconds before his strong arms wrap around me and he hugs me back. I don't know how long we stay like this, but I know I need it. We both need it.

Finally, I back away and look up at him. I nod and walk back to my shooting position. I pick up the gun and take my stance. Looking at this man who has scared the living hell out of me, torn me to pieces, and built me back up into a stronger version of myself, a man who has kept me here day in and day out, a man who doesn't have faith in anyone has just put all his faith in me. He put this gun in my hand without hesitation and with the utmost trust. It hits me that I could end him right now if I choose, but I know without a doubt it's the last thing I'd want to do.

I push everything out of my mind and focus as hard as I can on the X in the center of the target. I block Gabriel out. I adjust my grip, forcing the shake from my hands.

"Don't think, Brin. Just *shoot*," Gabriel says.

I breathe in. I think of all his words. He will not die by my hands today. I've got this. I'm strong. *I'm his girl.*

I breathe out as I pull the trigger.

"Fuck yes, baby." I hear just before his body slams into mine. Gabriel picks me up and spins me around. I focus on the target that I hit just to the left of the X.

"A fucking bad ass," he says as he kisses every part of my sweaty neck, my shoulders, my lips. "*My* wicked girl... the things I'm going to do to you." He smirks. "But first"—he kisses my lips—"looks like you're also about to learn how to stitch a man up."

Oh joy.

This day just keeps getting better and better.

"You don't have anything to freeze it? Shouldn't we call Rick?" I ask as Gabriel places the sterile needle in my hand.

He ignores my obvious stress. "It's two stitches, you can do it. I'm sure you took sewing classes at some point?"

I make a face at him. "I did... with fabric not human skin,"

"There's no difference if you don't really think about it. This is the sterile side of the counter." He points to an area he's cleaned thoroughly. "This is the nonsterile side; you sit here, in the middle." He hoists me up with one arm as I hold my freshly washed hands up like I'm going into surgery. This man is nuts I'm pretty sure, and yet here I am listening to him so I'm not sure what that makes me.

He grabs a pair of small forceps and places a needle between its teeth then grabs a lighter, holding the flame to the end, curving it slightly. I feel green thinking about piercing his skin with it.

I watch in awe as he lays everything out, cleaning a glass tumbler and then pouring some gin inside.

"Antiseptic." He smirks, taking a sip. "In case your sewing skills are a little rusty."

"Careful," I warn him, trying to make light of what's before me. "I'm the one with the needle."

"Only because it's my right arm, hummingbird," he says, his brow furrowed. I know it takes a lot for him to trust anyone, to let me take control.

Gabriel pours iodine onto his arm and uses an alcohol-soaked cloth to wipe it clean, the flesh is loose and open and that's where I come in.

"Two stitches max. Simple interrupted stitch," he orders, approximating the edges of his wound.

I nod, because that I understand. He takes his latex glove off and places the needle in my hand from his sterile area.

"Fix me up, hummingbird, it's all you." With that, he turns and sits in front of me, placing his arm between my thighs, I start to feel my breath increase the same way it does when he chases me, but this time it's for totally different reasons.

"Come on," he coaxes. "Get out of your head, if I bleed out because you don't stitch me it'll be considered murder." He grins, and I laugh because I'm pretty sure that was just a joke, something I never thought I'd hear from him.

I take a deep breath and focus, bringing my face down in concentration as I poke the needle through his skin, his jaw ticks but he says nothing as I eye him in horror.

What am I doing? I ask myself for the thousandth time since I met him.

He nods and I continue, poking it through the top of his wound this time but not without great effort.

"You have thick skin," I tell him as he sits watching my every move, making me even more nervous. I use the small forceps to pull the needle all the way through fully, tying a square knot., Then repeat the process a second time.

"Don't pull it too tight," Gabriel says as I work.

"I think it needs three," I tell him as I eye it up. He inspects the wound and nods, turning slightly to allow me better access to the top of his arm for my last stitch. His free hand begins to graze the inside of my thigh, I flinch.

"You're distracting the seamstress," I tell him with a smirk, not looking away from my task.

"Let's see how well you work under pressure," he says in

his deep timbre, so close to me it gives me goosebumps. "I need a distraction, you fucking shot me," he adds, and I smirk as I focus, loving this side of him I never see—he seems light, play-ful... *almost.*

I push the needle through Gabriel's skin for the last stitch as his fingers skim over my clit through my spandex shorts, I'm already on fire for him as he plays with me through the fabric. I moan as I tie my last stitch. I set my tools down and look at him, no worse for the wear, his dark eyes say he wants me, and I feel the energy shift in the room as the golden sun peers through the back wall of windows.

Gabriel's hand moves to the valley of my heaving breasts, and downward over my belly button as I give his wound a final clean, becoming frantic to let him in. He turns his body when he sees I'm done, then abruptly lifts my ass off the counter and pulls my shorts and panties from me. I'm sweat-slicked and panting from the adrenaline of stitching him but I'm soaked just from his touch and proximity. Gabriel growls a deep sound from his chest as he's met with my desire.

"I forgive you for shooting me..." he says, kissing up the inside of my naked thighs. "And I'll reward you for hitting your target and for stitching me up. You've learned something new, one more thing that makes you stronger, little hummingbird," he says as his tongue traces up my center.

I let my head fall back, finished with my work and relieved it's over, I breathe out a moan as my hands move to his hair on instinct. Both of his powerful arms work now to pull me forward onto his face, gunshot wound forgotten.

"Your sweet pussy consumes me," Gabriel says. "I've never wanted anything as much as I want this dripping cunt on my tongue."

I whimper at his words and remember his powerful body ready and willing for me to take aim. The fucked up thing is it spurs me on, and the way he looks right now, between my thighs, ominous and wounded, his words and his tongue have both desire and adrenaline racing through my blood.

My heart quickens in my chest as he feasts on my pussy with the fervor of a man who could've just died. It's like it makes him even more hungry for me as he trades between pulling my clit into his mouth and lapping up every drop I offer him.

Gabriel pulls me to the brink of coming and then adds two fingers to my pussy, working them in and out of me in time with my bucking hips. I rock forward to the edge of the counter, slapping my hands backward onto it for stability, knocking some of our tools to the floor as he moves the flat of his tongue over me with perfect pace and pressure. I start to lose control. My legs shake and I shudder as a tight coil of lust rolls through me.

"Give me *my* reward now," he says as he moves his fingers, hitting the spot inside me that offers me no choice but to fall apart within seconds of his command.

"Come on my tongue with my name on your lips, give me every last fucking drop," he growls as I do just what he says.

"Gabe..." I cry, shortening his name, his response is to suck my clit into his mouth so hard I feel lightheaded.

"Again," he says in a low rumble. *He likes it.*

"Gabe..." I repeat, his praise pushes me over the edge once more. He tosses my legs over his shoulders, I'm unable to hold them myself. I come hard on his tongue, just as he wanted, trying not to tear the stitches out that I just put in.

My orgasm continues as Gabriel doesn't let up. I grip his hair so tightly I know it must hurt, but he doesn't seem to care or even notice.

My high crests and I open my eyes, loosening my grip on his hair, staring up at the wood beams of his ceiling while my breath returns to normal. I look down at him, still sitting between my legs, a beautiful god all of my own. My gaze moves from him to the floor where our needle and forceps lie, and as he kisses the inside of my thigh, a tiny smirk plays on my lips.

"Think this area is still sterile?"

CHAPTER 47
Brinley

The Glen Eden rally is something I really can't describe.

I take in the sights, the sounds, the smells and I can't believe what a world this is—the bikers world. I simply had no idea the way it encompasses people.

It's not just a hobby, it's who they are.

It's not just a vibe. It's a culture.

As we pull into the otherwise quiet hamlet of Benson, Georgia, and stop at the light in a sea of bikes, I feel like I belong as Gabriel's large hands settle against my jean clad calves. He strokes them gingerly as we wait for the light to change and a warm feeling of peace washes over me. For being such a heartless, cold blooded biker president on the outside, his inside is surprisingly thoughtful, protective, and downright fucking addicting.

After living with him for a month I know Gabriel can't help it. He simply oozes masculinity and power in everything he does. He's the provider, the caretaker, and the king of this world. When he touches me like this as I'm nestled behind him, while he's front and center leading his club, I feel like his queen.

I'm almost sad when the light finally changes, and he releases my legs to move his hands back to the handlebars. The further into town we go, the more incredible and over the top things become. There are vendors everywhere, women everywhere, some in fishnet shirts with nothing underneath, some in no shirts, and almost everyone wears leather like it was a prerequisite to get into the town. There are apparel tents, bike part tents, bikes themselves, Harley Davison is here, Indian Motorcycle, even BMW has a bike viewing area set up. There are beer tents and food trucks. It's full of chaos and laughter and feels like a party all amidst more club colors than I've ever seen. Clubs from all over, every part of the country, all different nationalities, even clubs from Canada joining in.

All to celebrate their love of riding. It's truly exhilarating to be a part of.

We ride through the whole town before hitting the outskirts where the party continues, as we're pulling into a campground of sorts, but it's on the property of someone Gabriel knows. The music is already going, and people have tents put up every-where between the trees. There are portable bathrooms and people barbecuing. It's like the owner has thought of everything.

"Pres," a gray-haired giant with a beard to match, who Gabriel calls Jack, says. Jack's smile is wide as we approach him, standing in front of a row of about fifteen yurt style cabins.

I look around as he talks to the man and a few others that have joined as the HOH files in and gets off their bikes. There's shade everywhere throughout the trees and a massive building in the center of the property. It reminds me of a mess hall of sorts from a summer camp I went to when I was young.

"I'm in Orlando for two weeks after this, so it's like a send off of sorts for me," Jack tells him.

"Heading down to see Skylar?" Gabriel asks him as Layla approaches and hugs me from behind.

I squeeze her back. "We're gonna have so much fun," she whispers so she doesn't interrupt the two men talking.

"Yep, grandson number two born yesterday. They're just a blessing those grandbabies," Jack continues.

"Congrats, bro," Gabriel says, and the other members offer their congratulations as well.

"Who's this beauty?" the man asks as I turn my full attention back to him.

Gabriel reaches between us and grabs my waist possessively. "This is Brinley," he says, pulling me closer, under the crook of his arm. I breathe in his leather and spice scent. His hand drifts down to my hip and he squeezes tight in front of everyone in the open space.

The gray-haired giant stands stunned for a few seconds and then chuckles, a deep sound that reverberates from his chest.

"Well, Brinley, this is a turn of events I wasn't prepared for. I'm Jack Walker," he says extending a mitt sized weathered hand.

"Brinley Beaumont," I respond.

"Never expected this guy to bring a plus one," he says to me.

"Neither did he." I grin.

Jack chuckles and scrubs his jaw, then turns to Gabriel but speaks to me. "You know, his mother always said he always chased the path he would suffer the most on and he wouldn't settle down until he was satisfied with his own suffrage."

"I could see that." I smirk up at Gabriel who squeezes me closer.

"Yeah, I bet you can," Jack grins at me.

"Fine woman, that Theresa," Jack says as if he's remembering a past life. It makes me wonder how well he knew her.

"She also used to say that the right person would only show up once you thought you'd suffered enough to deserve her." Jack claps Gabriel on the shoulder.

Gabriel looks down at me and uses his first two fingers to tuck my hair behind my ear.

He kisses my forehead. "You think I've suffered enough, little hummingbird?" he whispers in my ear.

I smile up at him. "Never," I whisper back.

"*Fuck.*" Jack cackles. "Let's go, Romeo, I'll show you to your cabin."

We settle into our surprisingly sturdy tent-like cabin, right beside Layla and Sean. There's a spot at the back of each cabin for the guys' bikes, it's clearly been designed to house an event like this.

I quickly change into a rather revealing black tank top Layla gave me, that has tiny little rips and holes in both the front and back. Then I slip on a short, distressed jean skirt that makes my legs and ass look amazing, and add a pair of black fringe ankle boots with a chunky heel. I give myself a little half turn and admire the way all this training has shaped me without taking away from my curves. If anything, all those weighted squats he's had me doing have made me more shapely and I love how feminine—yet strong—I feel.

This skirt is not something I would ever normally wear. Normally, I live in yoga pants or jeans, casual tees, and my chucks, but here I want to feel sexy.

I curl my hair and fluff it up around my shoulders, and give myself some cherry lipstick, a hefty dose of eyeliner, a few chains, and some hoop earrings before exiting the cabin. Sean and Layla, the entire HOH crew, Jack Walker, and Gabriel are all waiting and talking at the bottom of the cabin steps. The only one missing is Jake. Gabriel said he had a deal to work out in order to replace the methadone that was lost in another Atlanta clinic break in, so he won't be here until later tonight.

Everyone stops talking the moment my feet hit the steps. It's like a scene from one of the rom coms I watch, when the heroine gets a makeover. Layla lets out a low whistle.

"Fuck yes! Naughty little schoolteacher vibes, I'd do you!" She giggles as I feel my cheeks heat under the attention.

I'm too nervous to make eye contact with Gabriel until I hear everyone's chatter start to resume, but when I do, I can't help but notice the hunger I see in his eyes. I attempt to walk by him and give Layla a side hug. His hand darts out to wrap his first finger around my pinky and tug me close.

"This..." he whispers into my ear in a gruff timbre. "This is going to have me plucking out the eyes of every man here tonight one by one. I can fucking feel it."

I reach up and pat him on the chest under his cut before kissing him.

"No need, it's all for you."

I swear Gabriel growls in response. He takes hold of my hand under his cut, pulling it down and holding my palm up. I watch as he reaches into his inside pocket and pulls out a knife, smaller than the knife he wears everyday, the one that was inside me, but with the same kind of smooth bone handle and a leather sheath to match. It's small enough to fit into my hand and still conceal it which makes me smile.

"What's this?" I ask.

"The handle of my knife is made from wolf bone, hunted by my grandfather, as is yours now. I had this made from his knife. It's strong, sturdy and the perfect size to fit your hand. I trust you'll only use it if you absolutely need to."

I look down at it, understanding what it means. I'm strong enough. He's trusting me to protect myself. I take it from him and bend down to slide it into my boot, reaching up to kiss his lips.

"I'm a warrior now too, just like you?" I ask.

Gabriel pulls back and looks down at me as awe and admiration bathe his face. A flicker of light returns to his steely gray eyes, one like I saw in those photos from his younger years just before he bends to kiss my lips, people around us continuing to move and pay us no attention.

"You were always a warrior, little hummingbird, you just never knew it."

Gabriel takes my hand and leads me into a large crowd of people near the main mess hall building and settles in around a large stone fire pit with drinks in hand. It's unseasonably cool for late July so I'm glad for the fire as I sip my drink, spending the rest of the afternoon watching people from clubs all over America approach Gabriel and the rest of his crew.

I'm on my third or fourth butterscotch flavored shot when Gabriel whispers in my ear. "Slow down, you need to stay alert, and men tend to get handsy with women when they're drunk. I really don't want to have to kill anyone tonight."

"I'm plenty alert," I say back, but truthfully I'm a little tipsy. Layla giggles beside me.

I'm like a college kid having freedom for the first time, what does he expect?

Gabriel grabs my current shot from me and tosses it back just to prove a point. The face he makes when he tastes the sweet liquid makes me laugh.

"I wanted that," I tell him, with narrowed eyes.

He grimaces at the flavor, pulling his bottle of water up, he takes a sip. I haven't even seen him have a whiskey tonight. Probably for the exact reason he's telling me to slow down. He has to be alert.

Gabriel will be watching me I know, but I'm not worried

here. I'm on a stress-free vacation. Vacation from the four walls of his house, someone hunting me just to hurt him, the insanely surreal direction my life has taken in the less than two months since I've been home, all of it.

I let him win and don't search for another drink, knowing someone will bring another round soon enough.

The rest of the girls in our crew have arrived too and are catching up with us when I hear the distant sounds of church choir music. It fades when our music kicks up again then returns when the song ends.

"Is someone holding a church service here?" I ask Layla beside me.

She looks to the field behind our cabins. "Neighboring farm. They hold massive outdoor church services, conveniently every year around the time we all roll in. It will go on for a few hours every night. They're praying over us, praying we turn our lives around."

I look over my shoulder in the direction I hear a crowd singing "How Great Thou Art" only to have it disappear again when Van Halen starts to play through the DJ's sound system.

I pull my bottom lip between my teeth. I used to be in the crowd praying. Now, I'm being prayed for. Something about that feels unsettling as I try to push the hymns of my youth from my mind. I don't want those two worlds to collide.

"Boss." Sean motions to Gabriel, nodding to a group of men waiting in the crowd of people. I look up at them as best I can without fully turning toward them. They all wear jeans and cuts, I have no idea who they're with and won't until they turn around.

"They can talk now. Otis has to go soon," Sean adds.

Gabriel looks down at me, then across to Amber, Chantel, and Layla.

"Don't worry, Pres, we'll keep her safe." Chantel smiles at him.

Gabriel rolls his eyes at her and turns to Chris. He points beside me.

"This is where you live until I get back, yeah?" he says patting Chris on the chest once.

"Sure thing, Pres."

I have no idea what he's worried about, this place is such a fun—

Seriously???

I internally groan as I watch her approach.

Apparently, it was only a matter of time before someone brought another round. And here she comes, carrying in my next drink on a tray with twenty others. Dark hair loose and wild, leather shorts and a tight red tank top. Chelsea, the brazen woman who hit on Gabriel in front of our whole table at Layla's wedding.

Just when I'm starting to have fun, this buzzkill has to arrive?

CHAPTER 48

Gabriel

"We're not against the idea, Foxx Sr. is out of control." I stare across the table to Otis Malone, leader of one of our sister clubs, Titans MC.

"They won't come easily," I say back as Otis sparks up a joint.

"I think they'll come easier than you think," he retorts, inhaling. "I've known Aiden since I was nine. He won't say it outright, but Foxx Sr. has gone off the rails. He's making side deals; I know that from my own contacts." He puts the joint to his lips and inhales deeply again. "Club isn't happy."

"Where are you guys at with handling the problem?" his VP, Tyler, asks. Problem meaning the DOS president.

"We've got a plan. A solid one. He threatened our families, he won't be breathing much longer," Kai answers him.

I nod in agreement.

"Who's gonna take over that Blue train once this happens?" Otis stubs out his joint and leans forward in his seat, getting right to the point, knowing we'd never sell Fentanyl, it's not our game. In the name of good business, I won't insult him by saying it out loud, but the shit is fucking poison.

"Since you don't want to take it, we'd be happy to." He grins.

I look at the rest of my men, we've already talked about this.

"When Marco goes down, so will his deal with the K6's." I mention another well-known Atlanta street gang he shares his area with. "They won't deal with anyone but him. They own the west side, you can take that over, but only if you keep an eye on our clinics and help protect them. There will be backlash. It's the best we can offer you."

Otis leans back in his seat and thinks for a minute. "We'd expect their backlash but they're small time, they won't fuck with us." He thinks. "Give us a few minutes," he says to me.

I look at the rest of my men, we nod and stand.

"We'll be outside," I tell him, knocking once on the table.

I know Otis is going to want to talk this over with them. Unlike Foxx Sr., he wouldn't do a deal without the support of his club.

We make our way out of the hall and lean up against the cabin walls.

I blow out a breath. "I hate doing business like this before the plan has been executed."

Flipp claps me on the back. "We know, but we're gonna need their help in convincing DOS to patch over once we take down Foxx Sr."

I nod just as the door opens and Otis comes out.

He extends a hand. "You got a deal. We'll take their share, and we'll help you smooth this over with the rest of DOS once you do your part."

"Appreciate your help with this, we owe you one," I tell him, shaking his hand and clapping him on the shoulder.

Otis looks around to the rest of his men. "We take this to our graves, Pres."

I nod.

"*Fuck my life*," Ax mutters under his breath. I turn to face him, he's putting his phone back in his pocket and he just looks at me and throws his hands in the air "We gotta go, boss."

My adrenaline instantly kicks in.

"Who hurt her?" I ask as I start moving, ready to kill someone before he's even answered me.

Fuck. I knew I should've put a property cut on her, but I didn't want to draw any extra attention to her until after we'd handled the DOS threat. I couldn't risk her safety and now someone has—

"More like who is *she* about to hurt."

I stop and turn to face him, letting his words register.

"*What?*"

He keeps moving, I catch up.

"Apparently, Chris needs us to help him stop *our* ladies from knocking out some chick you dipped once and her friends. Chelsea?"

I can't cover the hundred feet I am from her fast enough.

The irony isn't lost on me. I worried the whole fucking time I was gone that someone was gonna try to hurt her, and instead, she's the loose cannon—the loose cannon I just gave a knife to.

CHAPTER 49
Brinley

I've never been the jealous type. Evan worked with tons of women. I was always pleasant when I saw them, baked them cookies at Christmas and remembered their birthdays. I never once worried that he thought about women other than me.

Gabriel has been in my life for less than two months and watching Chelsea make her way around the small group of us sitting at the fire pit, passing shots out one by one, flirting with the men, and kissing the women on the cheek, makes me want to smack that showy little smirk right off her face.

Chelsea is the type of woman you just know is the life of the party all the time. She's obnoxious and wants every ounce of attention on her. She's the type of woman I would've expected someone like Gabriel to be with—unafraid and confident. Her wild brunette hair falls over her shoulders and her tits are so perfect in her cherry red tank that they'd make the Playmate of the Year drool. She instantly commands the attention of every man here and seeing her this time feels different.

Last time I had to face her, I hadn't had Gabriel inside me. I didn't know him. Our connection, although strong, was nowhere near what it is now. I didn't have a real claim on him.

Now? I hate that he slept with this woman.

"Breathe, babe." Layla grins beside me. "Don't ever let them see you sweat. They circle in like vultures over a corpse. Trust me."

I nod and vow to hold my tongue.

Chelsea stops dead in front of us. "Wow... Sandra Dee. Hot makeover. Definitely an improvement." She winks with a coy little grin that I want to wipe off of her perfectly made-up face.

She puts a hand on her hip and thrusts the shots forward. I shake my head no with a fake smile. I want one but I wouldn't take it from her. Chelsea laughs, takes two of her own and sets the tray down on the table behind us. I silently hope that's the end of her but of course, she goes ahead and plops herself down between Layla and Chantel. I look around to see where Amber went and why she had to leave that damn seat open.

"God, there are not enough available men here. Since when do all these rough and tumble bikers bring their ol' ladies to these things?" she asks Chantel.

Chantel laughs. "Gotta start going for the younger ones, I guess. All the older ones decide it's time to settle down or something once they hit their mid-thirties," Chantel says, sipping her own shot.

Chelsea pulls a pencil case type bag out of her purse and opens it, removing rolling papers and a little baggy of what I assume is weed. I have no real idea because I've never smoked it. Chelsea is clearly an expert. She flattens her rolling paper out and adds the perfect amount of weed, rolling it and licking the side to seal it. She makes short work of firing it up and inhaling deeply. She holds her inhale for a few moments, letting the smoke settle in her lungs before she turns to me, exhaling it in my direction, then passing it to Chantel who happily takes it.

I wrinkle my nose. I smell it on Gabriel sometimes when he comes home from being in the clubhouse.

Layla chatters away to me as Chantel takes a few puffs and passes it back to Chelsea, who offers it to me. I shake my head no.

She laughs. "It's easy to dress the part isn't it, Sandra?"

My nails bite into my palm.

"Don't," Layla says in my ear.

I clench tight. I have no idea what it is about this woman that gets under my skin so much.

"I just prefer to keep my teeth white and my skin looking young is all." I smile sweetly.

"For a newbie sweetbutt, you sure are a mouthy one, darlin', it's kind of refreshing." She laughs like I'm the butt of her joke.

"So glad I can refresh you," I say as I pick up one of Chris's shots from the table between us.

Chris chuckles. "Calm down, tiger," he whispers to his side.

I nod.

Chelsea distracts herself when she sees another woman she knows and gets up to hug her.

I take the moment of peace to force myself to turn back and engage in conversation with Layla. I will not let this woman ruin my mini vacation.

I will not.

"Hold up, settle this," Chelsea calls to our group not five minutes later, rearing her ugly head. "When was the first year we rallied in Harmony?" she asks.

"Three years ago?" Chantel offers. I pretend I don't hear them.

Chelsea knocks back another shot. I watch a beautiful smile

take over her face in my periphery. "That's right. The night we had the party at St. Henry's old resort... I missed half of it because that's the night Wolfe took me into the shed and we... well, you know. I think we're due for another rally out there, aren't we?" She smirks right at me.

"Chels," Chantel warns.

I know she's trying to goad me. I know all about girls like her, I was bullied when I was younger by girls like her. My mother always told me they were jealous and maybe she was right because there should be no other reason for her to goad me. Chelsea knew the first day I met her that there was something between Gabriel and me, and she's trying to show me who the true veteran is here and who doesn't belong.

"What?" Chelsea is a little more loose now after a few shots. "Fucking Sandra Dee comes in and we can't reminisce?" She turns to me and guffaws a real hearty sound. "I have news for you, sweetheart. If you're going to flinch because Wolfe and I hooked up, you might as well not even look around because"— she leans in—"I'm pretty sure he's hit every chick here."

That's it. I go to move but Chris sticks his arm out in front of me and stops me dead. I look at him and he just shakes his head no.

"You're gonna get my ass kicked if you get in a fight. She's not worth it." He looks right up at Chelsea. "You have him. You win," he says loud enough for her to hear.

Bless him for defending me.

"*She* has him?" She laughs. "Tonight maybe, tomorrow he's a free agent again."

"She's with him," Chris says, trying to take the heat off me.

She shakes her head "Uh-uh. Y'all are fucking with me, right? Wolfe doesn't have an ol' lady. Especially not *her*. He'd fall asleep before his jizz hit the condom."

I look up at her and something in me snaps. Suddenly, she

is every single person who has ever tried to knock me down, told me to take a seat, act like a lady, fold my hands, or keep my mouth shut. She's the epitome of them, right here in front of me.

"I'm not an *old* anything but you will respect me, and my name is Brinley, you bitch," I seethe as I stand.

Layla rises too, and I swear I hear Chris mutter *"fuck me"* under his breath.

"You can't be twenty-years-old, and I know that pussy would bore him to fucking tears. What are you, someone's kid he's trying to do a deal with?"

"Chelsea, if this is true, Wolfe will have your head for talking to her like this," her friend warns her.

"She's right, he will," Layla chimes in.

I look at her friend but speak directly to Chelsea. "Your friend is smart enough to keep her mouth shut, but you don't seem to be. So, I'll tell you this only once." I close the distance between us in two steps with Chris on my heels. "*Gabriel* is mine, if you want to keep that face pretty, I suggest you keep those eyes focused on the grass and your well-used mouth shut when he's around."

"Or what?" she spits out, pushing me backward. "You won't invite me to your next slumber party, *Sandra?*"

I see red. I lunge at her. Maybe it's because Gabriel's been training me so frequently that hitting her just seems like second nature, or maybe it's because she's been grating on my nerves since the moment we met. Or maybe, I don't even care what the reason is. I instinctively bring my hands up and throw a right hook, making sure I follow through with my entire body. I hit her square in the face and it's a good one. Chelsea falls backward, landing right on her ass in the muddy grass. Blood starts pouring from her nose. Before I can hit her again, or even get near her, Chris has my body in his arms, pulling me back.

"Bitch!" Chelsea yells, clutching her nose.

Someone grabs a hold of her and presses a bandana or a rag against her face to help stop the bleeding.

"Hang around for a hot minute and you're a bad bitch, are you?" she yells as I struggle from Chris's hold.

"That's right, and don't fucking forget it!" I call out, doing my best to angle my chin the way Gabriel showed me to break free of Chris's hold.

There's no need because Chris spins me around and lets go of me. I stop dead in my tracks when I come face to face with Gabriel and Sean. My chest is heaving and I'm sure my eyes are wild.

Gabriel keeps his eyes on me, I can't tell if he's angry as he walks right past me. Chelsea's friend holds onto her arm as he approaches her. He towers over her and I see the fear in her eyes as he contemplates his words.

She looks from him to me as he finally speaks. I flex my aching hand.

"I don't even remember your fucking name," he spits out at her. "But if you even look in Brinley's direction again"—he smirks—"I'll *really* let her at you, and I won't stop her until your face is as battered as your used up cunt."

Chelsea's mouth falls open as he spits at her feet.

He turns and motions to Sean. "Get her outta here."

"On it." Sean grins.

I expect Gabriel to be pissed off but instead I swear I see a hint of a smirk as he scoops me up and tosses me over his shoulder.

"Christ, Brinley. I've been gone *thirty fucking* minutes."

CHAPTER 50
Brinley

"Put me down, I can walk." I hit his muscled back, humiliated that Chelsea saw Gabriel haul me out of there like some child ready to be punished. All the blood is rushing to my head and I'm molded to his hard shoulder.

"Why is the door locked?" he asks when we've reached the top of our cabin steps.

"The key is in my bag that you didn't let me grab before you tossed me onto your back like a caveman."

"You looked like you could use some reassuring that the only woman I ever want to touch is you," Gabriel bites out, squeezing my ass hard. "And I *am* a fucking caveman when it comes to you."

I try to take in where we're going from this viewpoint. Gabriel shifts me in his arms and his hand comes up behind my head, laying me onto his bike. My head rests between the handlebars and my legs straddle each side as my skirt gives way for my ass to rest against the warm leather. I realize we're around the back of the cabin.

"Their eyes met, and they stared together at each other,

surrounded by many, but alone in space," Gabriel says in a gruff voice that doesn't match the gentle words as his lips dance up my inner thigh.

I smirk, my eyes fluttering closed at the feel of his mouth on my skin.

"Odd time for embellished *Gatsby* quotes," I mutter, my breathing increasing.

Woods stretch out behind us and the music from camp is quieter here, the sound of the church service through a sound system is prevalent.

The hymn music has stopped and there's a pastor speaking into a microphone.

"What I'm telling you is there are many women here I've been with and I can't change that." Gabriel's slides his hand under my tank, over my rib cage to the base of my lacy black bra. "I don't want them. In a crowd of ten thousand, you're the only one I see," he says, ghosting his thumb over the lace, my nipples instantly peak with the anticipation of him anywhere near me. I pant.

"We can't," I watch as goosebumps follow his touch as his other hand roams up my thigh.

Gabriel chuckles like I must be crazy. "No one will come back here. And if they do, I'll give them less than a second before I shoot them."

"No...I have my period," I manage.

"There is no greater pleasure than to serve your community." The speaker's voice sounds in our silence.

Gabriel isn't fazed by my admission. He continues his slow ascent up my thighs with both hands now, his fingers wrapping around either side of my panties.

He pulls them from me, then gently pulls the tampon from my body. He folds it into my panties, places both in his cut pocket and then slides it off his shoulders, setting it behind me.

He yanks his t-shirt off over his head and tosses it to the side. I watch as his beautiful, strong arms work to unbuckle his jeans and zipper just enough for his thick, hard cock to easily jut out pointing straight at me. The gunshot wound on his arm is still wrapped in gauze from where I stitched it and the bandage strains against his muscles as he grips his cock.

"I spent a collective thirty-five months in this nation's longest war." His fingers slide down my body and into my pussy without hesitation. "Your blood doesn't scare me, little hummingbird. Besides, you've had your hands in mine more than once. It's only fair," he says as his mouth comes down on mine in a deep delicious kiss. One holds me firm, the other moves in and out of me as he pulls me closer, so we're flush, facing each other on his bike. We're really doing this, out here in the open, with a church service preaching to us in the distance?

"I don't think you understand," I pant as his mouth moves down to find one nipple then moves to the other. Tiny moans escape me as I do my best to be as quiet as possible in the open air.

"If it helps, I'll only have it for another day or two. You might want to wait." I suck in a breath when his teeth nip at the side of my breast. "This bike will look like a massacre took place when we're done," I plead in a whisper.

Gabriel chuckles, using my blood that coats his fingers as lube, wrapping his hand around his cock and stroking it. I look down at him and it does me in. I want him inside me, I don't care where we are, I don't care that I'm bleeding.

"Oh yeah?" Gabriel asks with a smirk, unfazed by the sight —in fact, I think he likes it. My eyes flutter closed with the way his tongue swirls against my nipple.

"Yeah, uh, ever seen *Kill Bill*? You know that scene? Show-down at the Blue Leaves?" I warn.

"One of my favorite movies," Gabriel whispers in a chuckle as his fingers slide back down between my thighs. I decide the moment his middle finger makes its way into my pussy that I'm done warning him. If he wants me despite the fact I'm bleeding, whatever happens is on him. Not to mention, I'm thoroughly turned on now and the idea of him inside me seems oddly soothing.

"We must show those who don't know the way to live." The mystery speaker's voice from the field behind us sounds as another finger slides into me.

"Fuuck," Gabriel groans as he looks down to his blood-soaked fingers. "The sight of your blood breathes life into me. I want every single drop of you," he says as he pulls them from me and paints the blood and my arousal across his chest.

"It belongs to me now, just like the rest of you." He looks down. "So fucking beautiful, Brin," he says as I whimper.

His large hands wrap around my waist as he lifts me up, while still keeping us and his bike stable. Gabriel pulls me onto him so I'm straddling his lap. He pulls his cut over my shoulders, to stop anyone from seeing me half naked, I assume. His hands squeeze into my ass under my hiked-up skirt. In one swift movement, his hard cock begins to sink into me. My pussy tightens around him and I clench him even more than normal as he begins to slide into my wetness.

"Be brave in guiding those around us who may dabble in darkness... criminal activity..."

The words that were made just for this event sound through the trees as my pussy eagerly takes the depth of Gabriel's cock and they don't bother me like I would assume they should.

I open my eyes and look at him marked by my blood.

A ritual is happening between us. I know he feels it too as he pushes in slowly, inch by inch,

"So fucking ready for me, this cunt... *fuck*," he grunts out, his brow furrowed. The only friction comes from the barbells lining his cock as my pussy welcomes him. He's an even tighter fit than normal. He rocks me forward until his lips find mine. "Bleed for me, Brinley," he commands into my mouth as he holds me at my waist.

My hands slide up his arms to his shoulders and my head lolls back.

We don't speak as he continues to push into me, rocking me down onto him until he's fully seated inside me. We both breathe out ragged moans as I meet his full depth. He gives me no time to adjust to his size, lifting me up and then driving into me again from below. My breath is a shallow pant as his hands move to my back, eagerly trailing my spine.

They slide to my breasts and Gabriel groans, squeezing them together as he takes my nipple back into his mouth and sucks in the peak.

"That's it, wicked girl. Ride me. Fuck me until your blood and cum drip down my cock. Make a mess of me *and* my bike."

His words do me in. I begin to move my hips slowly, we both moan. He fills me so full that I know I'm ruined for all other men.

"Only with the goodness we seek can you live a happy, full, balanced life..."

The speaker bellows in the background as I ride Gabriel harder. His hands squeeze my hips under my skirt as I do.

"That's my girl. Taking every fucking inch of me... this perfect, messy little cunt."

"Yes..." I chant.

"You want me to fill you up until I'm dripping down your thighs?"

"Yes..."

"Your blood and my cum will be there waiting for me when I take you again,"

"Yes..." It's all I have.

Gabriel rocks forward and leans me back, holding his bike steady by the handlebars as he fucks into me. I move with him in perfect sync, my head resting on the fuel tank as my hands come up above me to meet his, bracing myself against his forceful thrusts as my hips roll against him and the speaker's words become our soundtrack.

"Even the darkest hearts have light somewhere—"

Gabriel growls as he thrusts into me as deep as he can, it pinches, then an unstoppable pleasure washes through me.

"Take all of my cock the way your greedy pussy begs to, Brinley. Come while you listen to them tell you all the ways their God can save you."

"Yes," I cry, out biting into my bottom lip so hard I taste copper.

"But let me be clear, little hummingbird. The only one who can save you is me. And the only one who can breathe life into my dark soul is you. We save each other."

It's too much, his words, where we are, the depth at which Gabriel fucks me while I wear his cut. Our bodies moving together on the back of his bike to the holy sounds of the service beyond.

I crumble. I crumble like a pillar of salt in the wind beneath his strong hands.

I moan his name as he takes over, fucking into me like a man crazed. My hips quiver forward as the orgasm rips through me and robs me of my breath.

"I'm re-born in *your* name, Brinley Rose. And you in mine. Take every single fucking drop from me." Gabriel reaches down and grabs my ass so tight; I know I'll be bruised tomorrow but I don't care, I pray he squeezes me harder.

"Go and find those who need your help and do your duty... share your light, help them to be good like us."

The speaker finishes his sermon to a round of applause.

Gabriel squeezes my hips harder and groans into my lips, I cry out his name amidst the applause and cheers as I fully unravel.

"This tight, bloody little cunt taking all of me," Gabriel says as he pulls me up slightly and takes in the sight of my blood on his cock.

"*Fuck*, I love it," Gabriel growls, his eyes dark and full of lust when his gaze moves back to mine. One hand comes off my hip and moves to my throat, his lips hover over mine, a raw intensity lines his tone.

"*Now*, give me another one, Brin, and when you do, let every fucking person here know you're mine. Let them know who your king is."

Gabriel squeezes my throat even tighter, making it difficult to breathe as he takes total control, moving me the way he wants, just enough to keep perfect pressure on my clit, his cock buried so deep inside me. My muscles tighten and my pussy clenches around him as I do exactly what he wants.

I start to come again. My nails sink into his warm back and the way I'm crying out has to be noticeable to whoever is in earshot but I'm the furthest thing from caring.

"*Yours...*" I cry as my eyes flutter closed and my body goes limp under his hold. "I'm yours, Gabe."

"Fucking right, you are... *mine,*" Gabriel growls as he comes undone, spilling into me, uttering my name and words I can't quite make out, his face buried between my breasts.

"*Mine,*" he repeats.

His warmth consumes me. I feel him everywhere yet still I want more.

Gabriel and I melt into each other, our chests heaving, and

I know that any piece of the old Brinley is dead and gone. I've been born again right here on the back of his bike to this beast of a man who wants every dark and wicked part of me.

The man I know I'm falling desperately in love with.

Should I be scared to tie myself to him? To tie myself to his world? Maybe, but I'm not. The only thing that scares me is what will happen to me if I ever lose him.

CHAPTER 51

Gabriel

JAKE

All set brother. 9pm, St. Henry.

> Good man.

> Meet me at 8 at the club then we'll head out together. I'm taking Brin home first.

JAKE

You got it.

The St. Henry's cabin is the perfect spot to meet up with some shady guy Jake knows to buy ANFO. It has nothing on site, so if the guy is a crook he can't steal from us and it's registered to a numbered company making it totally untraceable back to the club. We've owned it for almost fifty years and usually only keep an overflow of bike parts there.

I toss my phone on the bed and glance down at Brinley beside me, still naked and asleep in our cabin at the rally. I run my finger through her hair and down the smooth slope of her spine. I can't sleep and the sun hasn't even come up yet.

The feeling I have when I look at her overwhelms me. The woman whose body first became my obsession is now the woman I can't live without. The woman who snuck up on me when I least expected it and took me out at the fucking knees.

We never even made it back to the festivities last night. Instead, we made it inside where we showered and ate barbeque from the grill outside the cabin, watching the fireworks show Jack put on for everyone from our deck. I listened as she talked about leaving Crimson, starting her own design studio, starting fresh after I put down the threat. And that's when it hit me how much Brinley trusts me to keep her safe. She doesn't think for one second this thing we're planning can go badly and that makes me feel something for the first time in twelve years.

Fear. But not fear of what could happen to me. Fear of someday losing her. It fuels me and pushes me to get this job done faster, more efficiently. I've been awake for hours, triple checking Kai's notes to ensure every single possible scenario has been thought of.

I kiss her shoulder through her hair. I try not to wake her as I stand and head for the shower. I have to meet with the guys this morning before this rowdy place wakes up. I stand and realize I'm still covered in her blood but it doesn't fucking bother me in the slightest. I want every single part of her laced with me.

I turn the shower on and let the hot water cover me.

Today.

Today is the first step in ending the Disciples of Sin and all their years of bullshit with us.

I'm desperate to put it behind me and move forward. I know now, after less than two months, that I want Brinley with me. But I don't want to hide her away, I want her everywhere I can take her. I want her to thrive in my world with me and come home to her every night. I want to sink into that perfect pussy every day until my last dying breath. I want to do things I've never fathomed, like add on to my home and create space for as many sons as she can give me.

Somehow, the thought of her body changing and growing, her carrying my child, fucking exhilarates me. And to watch her become a mother? To give a child everything I never had— with her it doesn't seem pointless or impossible. It seems inevitable. It seems like everything my mother wanted for me that I never thought she'd see.

I shut the water off and grab a towel from the shelf.

Today, Jake and I will meet his contact for our ANFO explosives. Then tomorrow, we make our move on the DOS clubhouse. We've had one of our newest prospects on watch, their entire local club is here somewhere in Benson for another two nights, minus their president who's apparently in Savannah to meet with K6.

When we take their clubhouse, we'll take them over. We want to remind every single one of them, every day, that they will serve us. They're going to help us clean up the Atlanta and Savannah streets instead of infecting them. Without their leader, we're confident we can bring them under our wing.

But before any of that can happen, Marco Foxx has to die and I'm bloodthirsty with the thought.

We've spent months planning this. We'll pull it off and come out the other side.

When I dry off and get dressed, I start to silently pack up the room as Brinley breathes softly in our bed. I watch her as she sleeps, and the warm feeling I get when I look at her that's been plaguing me for a while now, spreads through my chest.

Shit is just uncontrollable. Ax tells me I love her, but I

know better. This isn't love. Love is just a word—this is something more. This is an unadulterated need. I need this woman more than I need air.

When this is done, I'm gonna tell her just that, but until then my only mission is to keep her safe.

"Where are you going tonight?"

I look into the beautiful blue eyes, that are the means for my entire existence, on the other side of the kitchen island when we get home later that afternoon.

"I want to stay here, Gabriel. With you. Permanently. I don't want to leave. I want to sell my parents' old home. What's happening between us, how I feel, it's…"

I look up at her from adding balsamic dressing to a large salad for us, surprised by her honest and confident words.

"Unexplainable?" I ask.

"Yes," Brinley says with the cutest little smirk, her cheeks start to pinken and it goes straight to my cock.

"Did you think I was gonna let you leave?" I ask her in a teasing tone, but not joking in the slightest. There isn't a fucking chance on Earth she'll ever be sleeping in a bed other than mine again.

Brinley gets up and makes her way over to me, her warm body presses against my back as she wraps her arms around my naked torso. She stays like this for a beat before she speaks while I finish making our dinner.

"I want to know it all or I won't stay," she says simply then kisses my back. "And I don't mean physically, because I know if you want to keep me here, you will." She kisses me again. "I mean this, us, how we've become, how we've grown. If I don't know it all, I won't trust you and if I don't trust you, we won't be us."

I turn and face her, wrapping my arms around her, I kiss her sweet lips, her jasmine scent filling my senses.

I sigh. "There are things I'm programmed to keep from you, to protect you."

"I don't need protection. I *know* both versions of you. I know the man you *are* and I know the man you *have* to be. I want every part... the same way you do," Brinley says with a true boldness I haven't seen in her before. She's embraced her place beside me in this life. Not only has she embraced it, she seems like she will take it with pride and flourish in it.

"Tonight, Jake and I are getting the tools we need to take out the DOS clubhouse. Explosives."

"Why are you doing that?"

"It's a matter of principle. It's where Gator had his way with Mason's sister, it's personal to him to get rid of it, plus it's a total shit hole." She looks up expectantly, knowing I'm not telling her everything. "And then we're gonna take out their president, Marco Foxx."

Brinley looks into my eyes. "For threatening me?" she asks.

"Yes, but also for threatening all of us. And for letting Gator assault who knows how many other young girls there. He's poisonous. The building is poisonous. Once it's done, we'll patch over the rest of the club. DOS doesn't have chapters like we do—they're small time, relatively speaking. Their closest chapter is in Texas. They aren't coming all the way down here to fight if we patch over twenty members, they'll probably be glad we took them off their hands."

"When will you be back?"

"We meet the explosives dealer at nine, I'll be back here long before midnight."

"Is it that simple?"

"Normally, not really. But this time, we've planned this right. Jake and I are going alone. We'll be fast, we'll get it done."

Brinley thinks for a minute.

"Just you and Jake alone? That doesn't worry you?" she asks, pulling her plush bottom lip between her teeth.

I chuckle. "It's the way we do things. It's Jake's contact, but we take the risk together. Taking anymore guys would draw too much unwanted attention."

"Okay... and then after all this, things will settle down?"

I kiss her lips and push her dark hair from her forehead, tucking it behind her ear. "Yeah, I hope so."

Brinley nods like I just told her about a business acquisition. Like I didn't just tell her my plan to destroy property and kill someone, while making her dinner.

"Once it's done, I'm looking for my own design space. I want something of my own. I don't have any illusions about you or this life. This is who you are, and I won't try to change that. If I sell the house, I'll have my own money to play with to find a spot. I know downtown has some vacancies."

"I may know of some," I say, thinking of the buildings the club owns.

"I don't need you to handle this for me," she says then grins.

I kiss her.

"I've never... cared for anyone other than myself," I tell her truthfully. "This is foreign to me, but I want to keep club life and my private life separate. As separate as I can."

Brinley nods. "I respect that, but you *will* tell me what I want to know," she adds with a matter of fact tone.

I can't believe this woman has this kind of power over me. I'd tell her anything if it kept her here, warm against me every night.

"Now, you have business to handle, Mr. President," she says with a commanding sassy look on her face. "But first, where's my dinner?"

I grin. "Demanding, aren't you?" I smack her ass and she yelps.

The sound is downright fucking irresistible.

I check my phone to see that nothing has changed with Jake and then I start to plate my queen's dinner with an actual smile on my face.

Holy fuck, is this what it's like to feel happy?

"Do you know how fucking sexy you look like this?" I groan into Brinley's ear an hour later. It's almost time to go meet Jake but I couldn't resist when she got into the shower with me. Now that she's out, I can't resist her again, so she's pressed up against my bathroom counter, her wet hair dripping down her back, her perfect tits bouncing while I fuck into her from behind for the second time in less than thirty minutes.

"You're every man's fucking dream right now, and you're *mine,*" I whisper over her shoulder.

This pussy day in and day out, I'll never tire of her.

I used to think I wanted to die on the back of my bike, now I know I want to die buried to the hilt inside Brinley Beaumont with my name on her lips. Just like this.

"Look at us," I tell her, not taking my eyes off her. "Look at the way your body begs for mine." I reach around and play with her clit with one hand and a pink, pebbled nipple with the other, my finger and thumb rolling the bud between them. "These fucking tits, always so ready for my touch, just like every other part of you."

"Gabriel," she cries, and my cock pulses inside her.

"You want me to fill you up? A greedy, desperate little slut for my cock?" I ask. Brinley's eyes flutter open and she takes in the view of us in the still foggy mirror.

"Fuck yes," she whimpers, and the sight of her, pulling her lip between her teeth, her eyes hooded and glassy, does me in. I bite down on her shoulders in a frenzy as her sweet pussy clamps down around my cock like a vice.

"Harder," she cries out.

No, hummingbird, not quite yet.

Slowing my thrusts to an agonizing pace, I look down to where we connect then reach around and spread her lips wide, making slow intentional sweeps over her clit with the pad of my middle finger as her legs start to shake.

"Do you know why I love fucking you like this, little hummingbird?"

"Tease," Brinley accuses as her eyes turn to blue fire in the mirror, watching me take her deep and slow.

"Answer the question, greedy girl."

"Why?" she half moans as I increase the pace.

"Besides the obvious, that it's a fucking beautiful sight"— *thrust*—"I love watching you struggle. I love to see you fight to take in every single inch of me."

"*More,*" she says in a whisper as I increase my pace everywhere.

"There's nowhere else I want to be. I want to live inside you"—*thrust*—"Come now, Brinley," I tell her, grabbing her hand and replacing my fingers on her clit with her own.

She immediately takes over and it's the prettiest sight I've ever seen. I grip her curvy hips tight and fuck into her harder and harder while she plays with her pussy. I take in every part of her in the mirror, my balls churning as her eyes flutter closed and her mouth pops open. I reach around to her throat and pull her head level. Her eyes pop open.

"Keep them open, I want those eyes while you use me, use my cock, show me how well you can make yourself come."

I watch over Brinley's shoulder in the mirror as she works her fingers over her clit, her tits bounce. She speeds up, she slows down, her free hand grips the counter. She's not self conscious in any way and it's beautiful to see her lose every inhibition she has right here before me.

"I'm coming," she cries, and fuck, so am I. The vision of her falling apart is too much as my release consumes me, holding me hostage as I spill into her with some form of "*my perfect fucking cunt*" and her name.

Our chests rise and fall, and we come down as Brinley reaches a hand up behind her, to the back of my neck, leaning into me. I slide a hand possessively over her stomach and lean down to kiss her.

"Have you ever been in love?" she asks, catching my gaze in the mirror. I tip my head to hers and take in the stunning sight before me.

Us, together. Perfectly imperfect.

"No." I answer simply.

Her blue eyes turn to mine in the mirror. I bend down to kiss her shoulder and try to explain.

"What is love?" I ask.

She doesn't answer, she just keeps her eyes on mine so I continue.

"The day I met you was a rift in time. From that rift forward, there is only before I met you and all the days to follow. I just don't think the word *love* means enough to describe that."

Her lips turn up in a smile and she closes her eyes, satisfied with my answer. I kiss her neck. It's the most honest thing I've ever told another living soul.

The ride to the St. Henry's cabin is slow going with a thick fog ahead of a warm front. When we arrive, I'm ready to get this deal done and go home to the hot, naked body in my bed.

The cabin is used as one of our storage cabins for a reason. It's quiet, secluded and off the radar. It's also in the dead zone between Chatham and Liberty Counties that neither sheriff's jurisdiction ever wants to touch.

"Where is he?" I ask Jake, getting off my bike. It's 9:05 p.m., he's already late. I pull my helmet off and set it on the back of my bike, looking up at the sky. The fog is thick still but beyond that the night is clear and stars litter the sky.

> Here now. If this guy shows up on time, I'll be back within the hour. Be naked.

QUEEN
> I already am.

I smirk at her response, picturing all the ways I'm going to sink into her when I get home. I've never been more grateful to have such a secure property since she needed a safe place to be.

I flinch as the sound of a twig crunching under a boot startles me and it's a lot closer than Jake was when I turned around.

"The fuck?" I find Jake two feet from me, raising his hand

that grips some sort of pipe. It comes down in slow motion.I don't even have time to pull my gun before it connects with my skull.

"Sorry, bro—it's not personal, just business..." His voice echoes as everything goes dark.

CHAPTER 52
Brinley

My eyes flutter open to the sound of birds. I shoot up in bed. It's still dark but it's almost four. The last I remembered seeing the clock was after one, I fell asleep thinking Gabriel was just late for the first time ever, but now, a feeling of dread settles in my stomach.

Gabriel is never late. He always arrives on time or early.

I pick up my phone and hope to find a message telling me why he isn't here but there's nothing except a few pictures from Layla who's still at the rally with the girls. I text him but it's marked as undelivered. I call, straight to voicemail.

I feel my face contort. I know his phone is never off. He's always on high alert for any situation that may arise. I start to pace around the room, biting my nails as I do.

I try Jake and it also goes straight to voicemail.

I pour myself a stiff drink from the glass cantor on Gabriel's dresser. I knock it back and try to rationalize what is happening.

Fuck. I have no idea.

I pull my phone out and open the AirTag app. I haven't

even used it yet, but at least if I check where he is I'll be able to guess if he's safe before I decide to wake up half the club.

I scroll with shaky fingers to find Gabriel's location. I wait as it takes an eon to load. When it does, my heart drops into my stomach. He's at St Henry's cabin?

"The night we had the party at St Henry's old resort... I've had him once, I'll have him again."

I squeeze my eyes shut. No that's not it. He wouldn't. I instantly push that thought out of my mind. Chelsea was someone he bided his time with—nothing more, nothing less. He wouldn't touch her, that's not why he's there. I know it with everything in me. It must be where he met the seller, but something isn't right.

I pace for a few minutes and try to text him again, knowing in my gut that he and Jake must be in some sort of trouble. Maybe the sale was a set up by DOS?

Or someone found out they were meeting? Either way, he wouldn't be this long. I read his last text from me at 9:05. An hour. Even if the guy was later, he still would have been home hours ago.

I text Sean and Layla, but get no answer. I try to phone Sean, but he doesn't answer that either. I know they are staying at Glen Eden along with a lot of the club so I wouldn't be surprised if they drank too much.

I try to wrack my brain to remember who came back to Harmony and who stayed in Benson.

Flipp. Flipp came home.

I pull my phone out and thank my lucky stars Gabriel programmed his main men into my phone a couple weeks ago. As I wait for him to answer, I also let the inevitable sink in. Flipp is fifty years old. He isn't in the best shape so I'm not sure he could even help me.

He doesn't answer anyway so I continue my pace. I argue

with myself. I can't go there. If I do and he's involved with club business, he will be furious I showed up. If he's in trouble, am I ready at all to help him after only a month of training with him? I'm hitting my targets and I'm stronger but in a moment of real pressure would I help him or make it worse?

I remember his words from before he left and it solidifies my fate.

If I'm going to be late for any reason, I'll text you.

"*Shit, shit, shit!*" I yell into the quiet house because my decision is already made.

I'm already pulling on my jeans and my boots. If I get there and all is fine, I'll just turn around and come home. I go over my plan in my head as I tie up my Doc Martens. I can park on Hwy 6 and walk the last bit in. I'll take one look and if everything seems legit, I'll just sneak away. He'll be none the wiser and I'll beat him back home.

I grab my gun and check the mag, holstering it at my waist with shaky hands, then without giving it another thought, I'm charging through the front door and down the front steps of Gabriel's house before I lose my nerve, making sure to pull the damn AirTag out from under my front seat, tossing it into the grass before I enter the address of St Henry's into my nav.

In any other circumstance, I would've dwelled on this for the next hour, but I know with everything in me that something is wrong. For the first time in my life I don't think, I just do... and hope to God I've made the right choice.

As the dark highway passes by out my window, I realize I don't know what scares me more, finding out nothing is wrong or finding out that something is.

CHAPTER 53

Gabriel

I've been hit by shrapnel, I've been shot, I've seen a lot of men die. I've seen my own death at least a dozen times. The reason I always survive is because I anticipate the enemy's next move. But how do you anticipate an enemy's next move when you don't even know they fucking exist?

I'm in and out of consciousness, I don't know how much time has passed. Has it been an hour? Six? I have no idea. I woke up here after Jake hit me. I hang from the center of the room, my arms outstretched and aching. I can feel dried blood on my face and the throb in my head where Jake hit me with a fucking pipe. The tops of my feet graze the floor and they're zip-tied together, I think.

Jake. My brother, by all accounts.

Now, he stands in front of me with Marco fucking Foxx and I know for the first time in my life, my enemy has the better of me.

Subconsciously, I hear parts of the conversation like a fever dream. It brings me right back to the sounds of the almost dead men screaming. I can hear them so clearly. I'm back in that cave. I know I need to fight. I know I need to find my way out, to save anyone who can be saved but I can't do anything except listen in horror as I see her face in my mind's eye.

I let the darkness take me.

Icy water hits my face, and my eyes surge open, cloudy with the forced influx of water and my own blood. I shake my head and raise it. Yep, definitely bleeding. Pretty sure I'm bleeding from quite a few places, actually.

I have no idea how much time has passed since they dragged me in here, but it's enough that I've faded in and out like this at least three times. A few hours? Longer?

"We're gonna do this one more time."

I look up at Jake, my jaw set. At least that's not broken yet.

In my periphery, I see Marco snort two lines of coke off the table.

"I don't want to make this more painful than it needs to be, man. Fuck," Jake says, his eyes pleading.

Mistake number one: Never go weak with your victim.

"Just give me the accounts and this'll be quick." He holds a gun to my face for the fifth time tonight. I didn't give him my personal bank account info any of those other four times, so I have no idea why he'd think this time would be any different.

I'll sit through another hundred days of this before I ever let the fucker in the corner snort away the $1.3 million I've managed to personally save.

"Fuck!" Jake yells. "This is all your fault." He makes his way to the table and nervously carves out a bump of his own. I don't know how much powdered courage it takes to betray someone who's been like a brother to you, who's always been good to you, someone who's always given you way too much fucking grace.

I've been asleep for half of this, but my guess is a lot.

"It was supposed to be me. Not you. He always compared every fucking thing I did to *you*!" He bends down, keeping his gun on me and snuffs some more of that false courage up his nose.

Marco stands and smacks Jake in the back of the head. "Stop fucking rehashing history to a dead man."

He stalks toward me, and I know when I make it out of this, I'm going to separate every limb from his body and keep him alive long enough to watch me put them through the wood chipper out back.

A lead pipe comes down on my knee. I grunt out a strangled sound as my head falls back. That's feeling pretty fucking close to broken now.

"Did you know that you've been fucked from the start? Your VP here told us all about your meets, your latest clinics. He even let us onto your property so we could take that truck out as a warning." His grin pulls back over his yellowing teeth.

I think back to the night before the wedding when Jake disappeared. I thought he was hooking up. Motherfucker was letting that prospect in.

"You aren't letting the club do the right kind of business. We're fucking outlaws. Do you know how much money we could make if we mule in the real stuff?" Jake asks as he fidgets.

I instantly know he's already got deals set up in the event of my untimely demise. I don't wonder how long he's been planning this. I don't give a fuck. He's dead to me.

"You aren't getting out of here alive, so give us the fucking accounts," Marco snarls.

I spit blood at him. I force myself to grin and say nothing.

This time, the pipe hit comes down on my head and the darkness descends again.

"You should've said no when he nominated you. It was *my* place. I lived under his shadow my whole fucking life. Now I live under yours. No more. That gavel *is mine*."

I've been listening to Jake drone on since I came to again ten minutes ago, but my eyes are still closed as he paces back and forth in front of me. I have no idea where Marco is right now.

This little prick is whining, and I haven't been able to feel my arms for a fuck of a long time. I act as out of it as I can, groaning and moaning. But with as much clarity as possible, I search the room for my opportunity when he isn't looking. Right now, I don't see one, but I can wait. I will not die at the hands of this traitorous piece of shit.

"...You've limited our earning. Every opportunity we've had for big money, you turn down. You just focus on these fucking clinics. You know the big money is on the street. We could be earning three times as much."

I open my eyes and focus on him with a grin, deciding that without Marco here I may get him to fuck up.

Jake never knows when to stop talking. It's what's gotten him into shit his whole fucking life.

"But then we're just like every other piece of shit gang. We earn plenty from the clinics. Clearly, since you want everything I've earned. What I've worked for."

"Fuck you! You and your fucking honor. It's time this club started taking more, earning big money."

"You'll never get the others to agree."

"They'll agree when they start seeing dollars," Jake says, sniffing and brushing at his nose.

I raise my head enough to analyze him. He's spinning out, nervous, which is when he starts to panic. His plan is going to shit, and he knows by the look in my eye that I'll never give him what he wants. My money is protected if anything happens to me.

Because unlike him, I'm fucking smart.

"Your father wanted the club to earn and live outside the fucking ridiculous laws of this country without killing people needlessly. He never wanted it to be blood money. That's why he chose me."

"But you've fucked up! You've made it too easy. DOS was coming for you and you've been distracted by *her*. Someone has to take over, someone has to bring us into big money before DOS takes us out. I saw the opportunity. DOS is gonna work with us. You left me no choice."

I start to laugh, then spit the blood that's oozing in my mouth onto the floor.

"If I don't gut you, Mason will. He'll never work with DOS; you don't think things through. There's always a choice, you just never make the right one, and now you'll die because of it," I bite out to him.

"I've had enough of this shit," Marco says, coming through the door, he's obviously been outside listening to us. "Your plan of talking to him isn't working. He needs more motivation." Marco wanders to the table and puts on a glove, a cut resistant one, then picks up a two-foot-long piece of barbed wire off the table. He grins evilly as he moves toward me.

"Fuck! Fuck!" Jake grunts out as he paces more. "Just fucking tell us the fucking account information!" he yells.

"I'm gonna carve you up like dinner, son, and then I'm

gonna carve her up next. When you die tonight, picture her face on the end of my dick before I gut her like a fucking fish."

The deepest kind of rage seeps from my body as I struggle with everything I have against the chains holding me before the barbed wire is wrapped tightly around my chest and dragged downward.

I bite down on my lower lip as I feel my skin being ripped open. I hope the bloodcurdling roar that leaves me is loud enough to demand the pits of hell to open and swallow him whole.

I will not give in. I will not give up. I will get out of this, so no one hurts her.

CHAPTER 54
Brinley

The moment I pull over to the side of the road my phone rings. It's Ax calling me back. I pick it up and watch it ring for a moment before I answer.

"Brinley?" he says before I can speak. "What's wrong?"

I feel the fear creep up my throat when I realize I'm here and that I'm *really* alone.

"I think Gabriel is in trouble." I tell him the whole story as I fidget with my keys.

Ax tells me he can't get through to him or Jake either.

"I'm already on my way. When you called, I tried them both and they didn't answer, I have Kai with me. Gabriel will be just fine, don't worry, okay? I'm sure it's just a misunderstanding," he says in a reassuring voice that makes me see a side to him that Layla must see.

I hang up and put my phone on silent and then slip it in my pocket. One thing I forgot to tell him is that I'm already here. And I'm not leaving. They're too far behind me, even going faster than the speed limit, they'll need thirty minutes and Gabriel might not have that much time.

I stand beside the car parked on the side of the highway and pace as I chew my bottom lip. I pull my gun from its holster and check the mag again. I start to walk up the side of the gravel road that leads to the cabin, trying to keep to the sides as much as possible, my gun gripped in my hands and pointed to the ground, trigger finger extended down the side of the barrel like Gabriel taught me. I can see the cabin lights in the distance as my feet make crunching sounds on the tiny rocks underneath them.

A hundred yards out, I move to the grass to soften my arrival, and I listen. I take in the numbered plate at the edge of the street that confirms I'm in the right place. The driveway is so shrouded in shrubbery I can't see the full cabin from here. It's just dense and green. The thick sounds of crickets and tree frogs fill the humid air as I take in my surroundings. The cabin itself sits at the end of a deep drive. There are two massive outbuildings behind it that are bigger than the main house. The closer I get I realize he's still here, I see his bike and Jake's and another I've never seen before. I breathe out a sigh of relief when I see Jake pass by the window. I'm about to turn around and get the hell out of here when the most torture-filled, panic-inducing sound I've ever heard comes from the house. As long as I live I know I won't forget it.

Instead of running away like I should, I move faster, as quietly as I can, to the front of the house. I push down the nausea that fills my gut when I see *him* through the open door. I lean my head back against the wood siding and try to remember how to breathe before I can brave another glance back in.

My mind reels as I take in the scene before me. Gabriel is strung up by rope to the wooden beams in the ceiling. Crucifixion style. His face is bloodied and battered. It's difficult to see where the blood is coming from. His hair is soaked with blood and that makes me think his head has been wounded. Nothing is how it should be. His arms are a sick sort of colorless shade, except for the bruising that's already started where the ropes dig into the skin of his wrists. Blood covers him from head to toe and it's obvious he's been hanging here for a while. The blood has dripped down his body to form a pool of sorts under his feet, which barely touch the floor. He's been hit on almost every visible part of his skin, red welts blossom in so many places I can't keep track. There's bruising down his ribs, and he has numerous small gashes that drip blood down his chest.

And Jake isn't doing anything as another man scrapes a piece of barbed wire down his body, tearing his flesh open in the process. The man is older, skinny with a big, bushy gray beard. He's wearing a Disciples of Sin cut. Without the ropes, Gabriel would snap him in two. The more I watch in horror, the more I realize Jake is pacing like he's okay with this, or worse yet, in on it.

Oh my god. This is a betrayal.

I feel nauseous and lightheaded as I breathe in shallow pants, trying to remember every word Gabriel taught me, praying that the men inside don't hear me. Every part of our training flashes through my mind.

Pause, be smart, take in your surroundings before you attack, be aware of everyone's location, are there any other threats?

I pull my phone out and hit record before leaning it against the ledge of the window that sits adjacent to the door, hidden from plain sight as the men talk. Whatever happens, all I can hope is that the club finds it. I go over my plan in my mind— breathe, aim, and take the skinny one out. I don't want to shoot Jake, but I know I may have to, and if he's in on this then he's just another target.

I can hit them both and save Gabriel. I'm here for a reason, I tell myself over and over as I try to focus on their words.

"You're going to give me your account numbers now, before I slice up your other side," the stranger says.

"Wolfe, man, fuck. No amount of money is worth this. Just give us what we want, and I'll end it quickly for you. Marco, man, fuck... just wait, he'll talk," Jake adds.

Marco. *Marco Foxx.* It takes everything I have to not shoot Jake where he fucking stands. He's been working with the DOS president behind the club's back?

"I'll make sure Brinley is safe. I won't let anyone touch her," Jake adds before he and Marco argue for a few minutes about *my* fate. As they do, I keep an eye on the rest of the room that Gabriel's in, making sure there's no one else here.

There's a table with multiple tools and knives on it, drugs, drug paraphernalia, rope, everything they needed to get Gabriel into his current position. I run it all down and make sense of it all in my head. Jake must have lured him here and then stabbed him in the back.

"Time's up," Marco grunts as he moves to Gabriel's other side.

"Fuck, stubborn fucking—" Jake calls out.

"I'm about to shoot you *first,* you fucking pussy!" Marco bellows at Jake. "You obviously don't know your cousin here very well. You said he would talk if we threatened the girl."

"This is your own choice, just tell me and I'll save her," Jake pleads with Gabriel as Marco moves to put some sort of heavy-duty glove back on and pick up the piece of barbed wire. The marks on Gabriel's torso resemble the pattern on the wire, and I stifle down my vomit again as I stare at his torn flesh.

"I don't trust you," Gabriel says low, calm, his eyes are devoid of any emotion as another family member betrays his trust and lets him down.

I've seen enough.

I will fucking kill them and burn this house to the ground.

If I die, at least I'll die trying. Gabriel will not die before I've had the chance to tell him how strong and incredible he is. He may be an outlaw, but he's my outlaw and he is everything I could ever want. He's unforgiving and raw and the only truly honest person I've ever known, ever loved.

I take a deep breath and aim through the open door, I exhale just as Gabriel's eyes meet mine. No one else sees me but him. We anchor each other for a few seconds and he shakes his head no so slightly I would've missed it if I blinked. There's not a chance I'm not going to help him. I keep his gaze, nodding just once and then I aim and pull the trigger. Marco's body hits the floor with a grunt and a thud before my brain allows me to register that I hit him.

After that, I don't hesitate, I don't know if he's dead but I have to get to Jake before he gets to Gabriel or we're both done, and I didn't come all this way to let that happen.

I burst through the door without looking behind me to meet my fate.

CHAPTER 55

Gabriel

Brinley's eyes meet mine through the window screen and I wonder if I'm already dead. If I'm seeing those beautiful blues, I must be. But something in them isn't right. If I'm dead, her eyes should be happy, full of the light and fire I crave, not angry and afraid.

It's when she raises the gun that I know I'm alive and there's a good chance she's about to get herself killed trying to save me.

I shake my head *no* as carefully as I can so Jake doesn't take notice but she nods yes before taking her shot.

Fucking little brat to her core.

I watch in the same sort of slow motion I feel when I'm in combat as the bullet whizzes by me and hits Marco somewhere in the chest. He grunts and whimpers and falls to the ground, dropping the barbed wire behind me. His gun is on the table. I watch as Brinley kicks through the door in her fucking Doc Martens. She's got her hair in a ponytail and wears black jeans and a black tank top.

I realize this is a life-or-death situation, but fucking Christ, I've never been more desperate to fuck her, ever.

"Don't even think about it or I'll shoot!" she calls in a shaky voice as Jake spins around and then looks at his gun, also resting on the table beside me.

Mistake number two: Never ever put down your fucking piece.

He sneers at her.

"Lucky fucking shot. You're about to die, little girl." Tough words for a guy who moves like a complete fucking pussy behind me, using me as a shield.

He looks down at Marco, and I grin. My little hummingbird hit him square in the chest. He's gasping and gurgling and bleeding out on the floor. She's gonna be rewarded for an excellent shot the first chance I get.

"Maybe." Brinley grips the gun tighter, lifts her chin and actually fucking smiles at him. "Or maybe, I've spent the better part of everyday learning exactly how to hit my target, isn't that right, baby?" she asks me without looking at me, one eyebrow raised.

I'll admit, I've never known what love is, but this is the closest thing I've ever felt to it. Brinley looks like my fucking walking wet dream. I'm gutted and broken but I actually feel my cock swelling with just the sight of her.

"True story," I tell Jake, wearing a mangled grin of my own on my battered face.

"It definitely doesn't make me a perfect shot, but it might make me good enough to hit you," she adds sweetly.

"You're gonna go to jail for murder, you know that, right?" Jake grasps at straws, knowing he's fucked. "You're gonna spend the *rest* of your life in jail for killing two men, for what? A man you just met two months ago?"

Brinley cocks her head to the side and speaks to Jake as if

he's a small child, the polite tone of her life before me, mixed with the wickedness I've helped her uncover. What a fucking combo.

"Oh, I don't think so. I know how good my man here is at hiding bodies, and I'm sure he would do an extra good job of placing you so deep in the dirt no one would fucking find you."

"Sure would," I add with a smirk. I could fucking watch her like this all day long.

"Fuck!" he calls out, he's spiraling.

"This," I say to him. "This is why you could never be president of this club, and it's why your dad chose me," I tell him calmly as Brinley stands firm in front of us. "Because you aren't good under pressure, and you never, ever fucking think things through."

I watch her eyes, they nervously move between me and Jake. She's waiting for her chance, which won't be easy because Jake is firmly planted behind me.

She knows if she advances, he'll have an opportunity to get his gun, and she won't want to shoot him when there's a chance she could hit me.

"Fuck you both!" Jake pathetically yells as he sucker-punches me in the kidney.

I don't even make a sound. I can't even feel the pain. Adrenaline courses through my blood with the need to get free and keep Brinley safe.

"You can't stand behind me all night," I coax Jake to move. I'm ready to get this fucking over with.

"The gauze on my arm," I tell him. "She's already shot me once. And you see... my girl thinks I'm a little crazy, but I bet she'd do whatever I tell her to in this situation."

"What the fuck are you talking about?" Jake asks.

"Sure would, baby." Brinley doesn't miss a beat as she readjusts her sweaty grip.

"I'll gladly take another bullet if it makes its way through me to get to you," I tell him.

I make eye contact with her. I know him, he's going to make his move.I nod at her and mouth the words she needs...

"*Just shoot.*"

Just like I knew he would, Jake makes the wrong choice. He moves from my shadow, his arm reaches out for his piece on the table. The second he does, Brinley takes a shot. It may have been meant for his hand but it hits him in his forearm and instead of picking it up, he actually knocks his gun to the floor. He continues to reach but she shoots again, this time hitting him in the shoulder. He drops to the floor beside me, and stares up at me, poised to talk, probably beg, as Brinley moves toward him, probably for a better shot to take him out completely. She's fast but not fast enough.

Jake reaches out and grabs her ankle, pulling her feet out from under her, she lands on her back. She turns over to get up but Jake dives onto her and locks his good arm around her shoulders, sliding it up to her throat in a chokehold. Her gun is still in her hand, but Jake's knee is on her arm and when he pulls her body up, she drops it. He makes it to his knees, holding her back to his front. He's stronger than her and he tightens his hold on her neck, but he can't grab her gun from the floor anymore than she can. His free hand is useless, blood pouring out of the shots she landed. I see the panic begin in her eyes. He's choking her. I will fucking gut him if she doesn't do it first. My eyes meet hers trying to calm her and remind her.

"Be *stronger*," I tell her through gritted teeth struggling furiously at the binds that hold me.

She instantly seems to calm down and from there she doesn't hesitate for one fucking second as she dips her chin down, wiggling it under his forearm, then she finds the strength from somewhere to reach her hand backward and plunge her thumb into the bullet hole in his forearm. He howls as she spins out of his hold, picking up her gun and without any hesitation she shoots, hitting him in the stomach.

I expect her to stop but she doesn't. She shoots again, hitting him in the knee. He falls and slumps back against the wall, crying out in pain. Tears fill her eyes but she just keeps going, emptying the mag into him, one to the throat, where blood begins to leak in quick spurts, he covers the wound with his hand but it does nothing to stop the flow. She takes another shot that hits him in the chest. He hits the floor with a thud and blood spurts from his mouth. When she fires again and realizes it's empty, her arm falls limp at her side as if the weight of the gun suddenly just became too heavy. Two big tears spill onto her cheeks, but she knows she's done her job.

I look down at Jake, this man I thought I could trust, and I feel absolutely fucking nothing as the life drains from him. I grin with the satisfaction of knowing my face will be the last thing he ever sees.

Mistake number three: Underestimating my fucking queen.

CHAPTER 56
Brinley

On the short list of things I never, ever thought I'd do, killing a man is probably number one. Killing two men? Unheard of. Yet here I am, Brinley Rose Beaumont—a killer.

And I've never been more grateful to watch the life drain from someone's eyes as I am in this moment.

I stand in a fog as I realize I hit Jake exactly where I needed to and didn't give it any thought before I pulled the trigger. I start to shake violently as my body starts to go into shock. Gabriel's voice pulls me back from the haze. My eyes meet his and he holds them.

"Come here, baby," he says, guiding me. "Don't stop looking at me. Eyes on me."

I set my gun on the table and step over Marco's lifeless body, pressing myself against Gabriel, kissing any place my lips can connect. His swollen battered lips meet my head and his deep whisper tells me I'm okay, how good I did, how strong I am, that I saved his life.

It settles me and pulls me out of the shock.

"You did so good, but you're not done yet, baby. I need you to get the step stool from the closet in the kitchen and my knife from the table. You're going to have to cut me down." He nods in the direction he means.

I do as he says and cut him down quickly even with my shaking hands. He drops to the floor between Jake and Marco, his legs probably numb after hanging there for who knows how long. I scramble to his side and lean down to kiss him, his blood fills my mouth and I bring it in, I want it all.

"That was so fucking dangerous." He's angry but still kissing me.

He's alive, he's okay, and my gut was right.

"If I didn't come, you would've died," I whimper as he shushes my cries.

A few minutes pass as the feeling comes back into his arms and they encircle me, they stroke my face, wipe away my tears. His tongue sweeps into my mouth in a way that tells me even now, in the midst of all the wreckage and how angry he is that I put myself at risk, he's hungry for me. *Always hungry for me.*

"How did you find me?" Gabriel asks, his eyes are blood-shot and the skin around them is already bruised.

"You AirTagged my car," I admit what I know in a shrug. "I snooped."

Gabriel eyes me up in thought but doesn't say anything.

"It was weeks ago, and I was curious about you. I found more of them with your photo box. So I AirTagged your boot."

"There's a reason I did that—it was to keep you safe," he says with a smirk, amused that I was keeping tabs on him.

"I did it because I *could,*" I say in a cocky tone, kissing his chin.

Gabriel laughs, it's the oddest sensation amidst the carnage we lie in but it's so fucking beautiful.

"I think"—he kisses me—"you're even crazier than I am, little bird, but I want all your crazy. Every last bit."

"It's all yours," I tell him.

I've never felt like I fit in anywhere in my life before. I've always gone through the motions, doing what everyone else told me to do, doing what I thought was right, but here in Gabriel's arms, I belong. Being with him is as easy as bringing air to my lungs.

In his eyes, I'm always strong. I'm always capable. I'm simply and beautifully me.

I feel the tears come and I can't stop the words.

"In case it isn't obvious Gabriel, I love you," I tell him as I lean down to kiss him. "I love you so much."

His strong bloodied hands hold my face as he hovers over my lips.

"The way I feel about you, Brinley, a word as simple as love isn't enough. You're the blood in my veins."

I whimper into his lips with his words.

"You're the one I would sacrifice everything for." His lips meet my temple. "*You're* my need to survive." He smirks into my lips. "*And they slipped briskly into an intimacy from which they never recovered...*" Another kiss.

I giggle through my tears.

"Quoting Fitzgerald as we lie between two dead bodies?" I say as Gabriel's lips never once stop their path over my cheeks, my jaw, the corner of my mouth.

"Just working on being romantic," Gabriel says with a grin and a deep chuckle, before both his hands grip the sides of my face, focusing his stormy gray eyes on mine, as he falls serious.

"I love you, Brinley Rose." His deep timbre fills my senses, butterflies flood my chest and the carnage around us fades.

"*What the fuck!?*" I hear Sean yell in horror as we both look up at him from our place on the floor when he and Kai come through the door.

Gabriel doesn't move me, he just lets his head fall back against the floor in relief and says, "You're late. Call Rick, and I hope you fuckers brought shovels."

CHAPTER 57
Gabriel

"They're buried behind St Henry's. Myself, Ax, and Kai put them in the ground."

I look at my men, every one of them aside from Ax and Kai is fucking shell-shocked that Jake tried to do me in. Including me.

There was a good solid minute of silence when I played them the recording from Brinley's phone. Smart little hummingbird. But I wouldn't have needed it. My men would've believed me anyway. It took two hours for Rick to clean my cuts and stitch me up while the men worked to put the two traitors in the ground after we lit both their cuts on fire.

"Jake was like my brother. He let greed and envy cloud his judgement. From this point on it will be like he never existed," I tell them.

"Amen, brother." Kai knocks on the table.

I nod. "My only mistake was trusting him. I didn't see it until it was too late and that's my cross to bear."

"We all trusted Jake," Robby says.

No one is happy, aside from this choice Jake made, he's

been everyone's brother for thirty years, but once this meeting is over, we'll never talk about him again. He betrayed us and he got what he deserved. You don't turn on your brothers.

"I have a meet set with Aiden Foxx." I wait for the room to calm down with my announcement. "I plan to talk to him about patching over and I want to do it fast. While all this is still fresh."

Their chatter ensues for a few seconds before I speak again.

"I'm only bringing two of you. The rooftop of Savannah Meadows. It's crowded below, less chance of him trying to kill me," I tell them.

I look around the room. "Ax, I need you to be my VP now if you're ready to step up."

"Of course," he says, no hesitation.

"All in favor?" I ask.

I wait for the yay's. When they come, it's unanimous.

"And Kai, are you with me?" I ask, everyone understanding I want him to be my next Sgt at Arms.

"Hell yeah, brother, I've always got you," Kai answers with a grin.

"Kai to change?" I ask, and they all say yay in agreement.

"Shelly will swap your patches. Mason, you can move to Enforcer."

Once again everyone agrees.

I snap the gavel down and blow out a breath, glad rehashing that fucked up story is done.

"Now, outside of all that, there's one more thing. I know this is new, me having an ol' lady."

"We love the little assassin," Flipp says from his end and grins.

"Yeah, Brin is the one for you." Mason says, his face expressionless but sure.

"You seem fuck, I'm just gonna say it kinda happy," Kai says.

I blow out a breath and nod. "Yeah, she's the one," I agree, clearing my throat.

"All right. Fuck, boys," I say, changing the deeper subject I'm still not used to talking about. "It's been a day. Everyone grab a drink, a double. We've got a full house until this is settled. Ax, Kai, meet me in a half hour and we'll leave. Everyone else—eat, drink, see Shell if you or anyone in your family needs anything."

I make my way out of the room amidst the chatter, remembering as I pulled Jake's cut from his bloody body this morning and cut his VP patch off before burning it in the outdoor fire pit at St. Henry's. I know these boys will spend the night thinking about Jake and that's okay. They know not to talk about it in front of anyone. All the families will know is that he's a traitor, except my queen, because she was there and even if she wasn't I'd tell her anyway.

The main hall is full of club members' families. We had them all come here on lockdown for the next few nights until we can either patch over or kill every DOS member in Harmony.

Even through the crowd, I can spot her leaning against the bar talking to Layla, painted on jeans, tank top, her hair loose and wild, not a mark on her after what she endured this morning. Thank fuck.

I lean against the door frame of the Chapel for a minute and just watch her. I'll never tire of looking at her. I remain there, just because I want to see her reaction and pull my phone out of the basket we dropped them in before chapel.

It's time.

I watch as she pulls her phone out of her back pocket and reads my message.

QUEEN

Already?

Unless you want me to hurt you more than I need to?

Brinley rolls her eyes across the room and turns to face me just as Shelly pops up beside me. Instantly quelling my already thickening cock.

"You're gonna marry that one, aren't ya?" she asks, nudging me with her frail elbow.

"Me? Marriage?" I ask, wrapping an arm around her shoulder. "Come on, Shell, you know me," I add.

"Yeah, I do." She winks. "Got what you asked for." Shelly hands me the cut I had made last week from *Racine Leather Co.* the finest shop in Savannah, and I hold it up and smile. The buttery black leather with the Hounds of Hell insignia in the center and the *Property of Wolfe* scroll under it is exactly what I wanted for her. On the front over her heart is her very own patch *Wolfe's Queen,* and under it, a smaller patch that says *Soldier of Bedlam.* A patch she earned when she killed Jake and Marco, saving my life.

It's perfect and it's going to look hot as fuck on her.

"I also know you don't look at women like that. Ever. I just want fair warning so I have plenty of time to help plan another wedding is all." Shelly pats my back. "Both of you are down a mama," she adds.

I pull her tighter into the side hug. Shelly is, in fact, the closest thing I have to a mother.

I kiss the top of her head then let her go. "Promise I'll give you lots of time."

"Lots of time for what?" Brinley asks, approaching us,

"To torment me with those fucking jeans," I say, grabbing her around the waist and kissing her.

Shelly scampers off muttering something about us getting a room.

"What's this?" Brinley asks when I back up, looking down to the fresh leather in my hand.

I hold it out, Brinley raises an eyebrow and motions to take it, but I don't let it go just yet.

"It's an announcement to everyone who looks your way that you're mine, and if you put it on right now, you don't take it off," I tell her quietly so no one else can hear me. "And you wear it while I make *every* part of you mine."

Brinley doesn't even hesitate, she bites her bottom lip in a grin and reaches out to take it, then holds it up. I watch her, taking in the detail of the embroidery and the patches on the front.

Her eyes flick to mine in question as her finger runs over the *Soldier* patch.

"You took lives for the good of the club. You earned it," I tell her. "And if I do my job right, you won't have to do that ever again."

She nods. I can see the question in her eyes before she asks, "You wear it as pride for who you've killed?"

I shake my head no. "We don't wear that patch to boast, we wear it to remind ourselves that we're bonded, that there's nothing we wouldn't do for each other. Nothing comes before this brotherhood. This family." I watch as she takes what I say at face value and doesn't question it, slinking one arm in and then the other. Her eyes stay on mine the whole time. It's a perfect fit, and when she fluffs her hair and turns to look at me over one shoulder, I know this woman was meant for me.

"How do I look?" she asks, knowing full well I'm about to

bend her over the table she's standing in front of. Brinley Rose Beaumont looks like a future I didn't know I was missing, and as my body begs to touch her, I feel the warmth only she can bring spread through me, filling me with the truth.

I grab Brinley by her hips and pull her to me, wanting her to understand as I whisper in her ear, "Like everything I never knew I wanted. Like you're *mine*."

"Just relax," I tell Brinley ten minutes later as I spread her ass cheeks wide, willing my cock to stand down. I have to leave, I'm already almost late but my cock doesn't understand that at the moment with her bent over in front of me wearing her cut.

I run my hand along the small of her back and I've never been so fucking desperate to take her.

"Never thought this was how I'd deal with a traumatic day. But what can I say, you keep things interesting," she says over her shoulder.

I reach between her legs and play with her clit a little, sweeping my middle finger over it in slow circles as I use my other hand to pull out the medium-sized plug I put in her ass before we came to the clubhouse. She lets out a breathy moan as I do. I grab the largest sized plug next, coating it in lube and adding a little more over her ass for good measure.

"That one looks huge," she observes with her eyes wide.

"Maybe," I say, focused on how fucking good she looks like this, bent over my bathroom sink in my suite at the club.

"Wait until it's my cock." I smirk as I push the largest plug in a little, waiting for her body to adjust. I pull it out and recoat it in lube from her ass then push it back in,

"Breathe," I remind her. She does as I finish slipping it in. The little pink jeweled heart is the only thing that hasn't disappeared inside her and fuck, that's a sight.

"It's going to hurt," Brinley says, turning toward me and taking her bottom lip between her teeth.

I adjust my solid cock as my phone dings in my pocket.

"Fuck, unless you want me to take your ass right here and now, you better stop looking at me like that," I tell her.

She smirks. *Little brat.*

"Looking at you like what?" she asks, running a finger under the cleavage of her tank. "I'm sorry but the pressure, it feels kind of, um, good."

My phone dings again and my cock throbs even more. Three more hours. Three more hours until I own every hole this woman possesses.

CHAPTER 58

Gabriel

I stand on the rooftop of the Savannah Meadows hospital an hour later with Kai and Ax as Aiden Foxx and two of his men arrive.

"Fucker has a nice bike... I'll give him that." Kai leans in as they approach.

I grunt in response, eyeing up his custom Softail. "It's alright." I give.

The two men with him are ones I know. Damon Keller and Grayson Hunt.

Damon is another one who was apparently sick of Marco's bullshit, according to Otis.

"Gentleman," Aiden says as he stops in front of me. He's about my height and a big grizzly fucker. He's cool, reserved. He's nothing like his half brother.

I get right down to it.

"This morning, I buried your cocksucker brother in the woods with my cousin," I say as the two men behind Aiden draw their weapons.

Both Ax and Kai immediately draw theirs.

Aiden doesn't even flinch. He turns his head and gives him the hand signal to drop them. They do.

"Why?" he asks calmly.

"They were conspiring to take over my club. I didn't like that."

"Can't say I blame you," Aiden says and raises his hands in truce, then pulls a pack of cigarettes out of his pocket and offers me one. I shake my head. He lights it.

"My half brother had a fairly big drug problem. He's been out of control for years."

"Starting with allowing one of your members to rape my Enforcer's sister when she was sixteen."

Aiden inhales. "I understand why you had your panties in a twist over that, but you killed him so that's dealt with then, yeah?"

I nod. "Yep."

"And the way I see it, each of us lost someone today, so what's fair is fair."

"Agreed."

"I've heard through the grapevine you were planning on patching us over?" Aiden asks, sucking in another round of smoke.

"I was."

"And now?"

"Depends," I say, folding my arms over my chest. I turn to Kai and Ax. "Give us a minute."

Aiden turns and waves off his men until we're left standing alone.

"All due respect, you're lucky I didn't come and rip your fucking throat out for scaring my ol' lady. And your former leader was a fucking train wreck. I assume this means you're taking over, but I don't know how this works?"

"Well, we agree on one thing at least," Aiden says as he

stubs out his smoke. "And yes, I will take over. Marco was our president; we had our differences, but I have the support of all my men. And yeah, I came to... understand who your ol' lady was. I didn't know what Marco had gotten us into, I had to protect the rest of my men and our club. I had to understand how to stop you and your club from attacking us further. But it was nothing personal. It was business. Marco and I have been at odds for over a year. He was making bad choices, side deals, his drug problem was out of fucking hand. It's not what his father left him when he stepped down."

"Sounds like he got into bed with my cousin because they were a lot alike then."

"Mm-hmm," Aiden grunts. "Greedy and not the brightest?"

I smirk back. "Yeah."

"What do you want?" he asks.

"I want your club to give up their attacks on my clinics. There are plenty of junkies out there for you, our business is in recovery and it's *ours*."

Aiden nods.

"As a show of good faith, you can sit down with my sister club, Titans. Your ex-pres never would. They have a short deal with El Coas." I mention the crew that supplies the Blue to most of Atlanta. "They were going to take the share my club wouldn't when your brother was killed. I know the K6's won't work with you without him, but if you want to work with the Titans, it could be really lucrative for you," I offer. "Their buyers are very interested in increasing supply, they want to double it, if you can handle that. You'd split it down the middle with them taking over the old K6 territory."

He thinks for a minute, running his thumb and forefinger over the scruff of his jaw.

"So, this is a 'you stay out of my lane and I'll stay out of yours' kinda deal?" he asks, pointing between us with a smirk.

"Precisely, it would be a nice fucking change," I answer. "But if one of your club members touches another little girl and I hear about it, I'll cut his nuts off again. But this time, I'll mail them to you and then I'll take your fucking head for letting it happen."

Aiden pauses then chuckles a rich sound, and I wonder if we're really as alike as it seems.

"If one of my men touched an underage girl I'd cut their balls off myself. You have no worries there."

"It's settled," I say, extending a hand. He takes it. His ink is like mine, covering his hand.

"This will be a club vote but they'll agree, so set the meeting. My men just want some stability after the last two years."

"And we just want some peace. Get back to riding, with a side of fucking over the government." I smirk.

"Hear, hear." Aiden grins. "They say wolves and foxes are natural enemies, yet here we are playin' nice," he adds as he backs away, signaling to his men.

"We'll be in touch," I say and turn to meet my own.

Fuck, a sliver of hope settles in my gut. Maybe for once with the Disciples of Sin, we can just get some fucking peace.

I grin as I straddle my bike. Now, back to the club to pick up my girl for the best part of my day.

CHAPTER 59
Brinley

I can feel his eyes on me, that man of mine, from the other side of the room. My ruthless king who won't bend for anyone but will quote Fitzgerald while washing my hair.

Just the sight of him is making a mess of my panties with this goddamn taunting jewel in my ass. I'm hypersensitive, even though I just had him inside of me this morning in the shower when we got back from St. Henry's.

"You're gonna let me slip this inside you, Brinley. I almost lost you. I didn't think I'd ever see you again. Life is too short to not do what we want, and tonight I'll be taking every part of you and making it mine."

The clubhouse is buzzing with people. I do my best to make sure everyone is happy and serve food to our guests with Shelly and Layla.

"That man is burning a hole into you from over there." Layla giggles.

I look up at him and smile from across the room. *Yep.* He's definitely losing patience. I'm going to pay for that later.

"You okay?" she asks as we scoop mashed potatoes into serving bowls to take around to the tables.

"I am," I say to her. "I've got the realtor coming tomorrow to give me a price for my parents' place. I know this is fast"—I gesture to the new leather I'm wearing—"but—"

Layla starts to laugh, cutting me off. "You don't have to tell me anything. I knew Sean was it for me on our first date. I was wearing his cut after a month, even faster than the two of you. When you know, you know, babe." She smiles even wider. "Besides, I really love having you around."

"Same." I wipe the workspace down and shake my head. "Imagine those two little girls in the front row on Sunday morning now—"

"Ol' ladies." She laughs.

I swat at her. "Speak for yourself, I'm not an ol' anything."

"Hey, I'd rather be an ol' lady than some stick-up-the-ass-girlfriend. And by the way, that post you sent me"—she stifles a laugh—"it really does look like Evan's new girlfriend has a stick up her ass."

I laugh with her.

One of mine and Evan's mutual friends sent me a social media post this morning that told me Evan is dating the daughter of one of his New York bosses, and I sent it to Layla. When I looked at the two of them in that photo together I couldn't even believe that was the life I was living only a few months ago. His new love interest is a high society type, barely smiling with his arm around her. In the photo she looked exactly like someone I used to want to be.

"Me too." I nudge her. "Thank God I came home."

"Brin." Gabriel's voice sounds from behind me, inter-rupting Layla and me.

I smile up at him sweetly, clenching my thighs together. I

know how desperate he is right now and I use every ounce of will power to push through.

"You in a hurry?" I ask him as politely as I can. I see the tendons flex under the scruff of his jaw. His face is stitched and bruised but he's still so beautiful.

He grabs me roughly with his first two fingers in the belt loops of my jeans and tugs me toward him, kissing me once on the lips, gentle enough to almost do me in.

But it's when he leans down to say, "We're going to my garage," that I know I'm a goner. "You pushed me too far. You have less than one minute to follow me to my bike or I'm gonna take you on that fucking pool table."

I pull my face back from his.

"Why to your garage?" I ask.

Gabriel smirks as his minty breath comes down over my lips. His deep whisper is clear in the noisy room. "My house is too far and if it happens anywhere in this building, they're all gonna hear you scream."

"Oh..." I mutter, giving Layla one last glance over my shoulder.

She rolls her eyes but I don't even care.

I mean, really? Who am I kidding? I may be able to wear the mask of a good girl but I'm a total slut for Gabriel Wolfe and have been since the second I laid eyes on him in the middle of Main Street.

CHAPTER 60
Brinley

"That was a naughty little trick you played back there," Gabriel says as he flicks the overhead lights on less than ten minutes later when we enter his shop.

My body is primed after the rumble of his bike between my thighs and this jewel inside me.

"Does it have to be so bright? Holy hell," I mutter as his lips come down to my neck from behind.

"Fuck yes, I want to see every single thing as I make this virgin hole mine."

I moan as his hands come around roughly and squeeze my breasts, paying close attention to both my pebbled nipples through my tank.

"Gabriel..." I whisper as he presses his hardened cock into my ass against my jeans.

"Hmm?" he groans as I push back against him.

"Can we try something first?" I ask, trying my best to be bold as one of his hands comes down to pop my button and pull down my zipper.

It slides under my panties and the growl that comes from him makes my pussy throb.

"What is it this soaking pussy wants, little hummingbird?" Gabriel rasps into my ear as his tongue trails my neck.

"I want you to fuck me," I moan as he bites into my shoulder. "But leave the jewel in." Only with him can I voice these darker desires.

Gabriel spins me around and shoves two fingers into my pussy while he kisses me deeply. I whimper from the fullness.

"My dirty little queen wants it all tonight?" he asks, lifting me onto his workbench and freeing me completely of my jeans. He moves between my legs, fisting my cut. "This stays on," he growls into my ear as the pressure of the jewel in my ass is heightened with me sitting on the hard wood bench.

Gabriel spreads my legs wide, drops to his knees and pulls me close as he hooks his arms under my thighs. A slow, firm lick up the center of my slit sends me into a tailspin of sorts.

He murmurs my name into my pussy. "This fucking soaking little cunt, so ready to be filled," he says as he sucks my clit into his mouth.

My back bows and I cry out.

"That's right, baby, no one can hear you here. Scream as loud as you want."

I call out his name as he adds two fingers into my dripping pussy, then three, chasing them with his tongue but never quite letting me come until he's had his fill of tasting me and I'm panting for more.

Gabriel lifts me off the workbench and sets me on the ground, pressing my hips into it and pulling me back, my ass against his cock. I nearly start begging when I feel how hard he is against me.

I don't even realize Gabriel has unbuckled his jeans and

pulled his cock out until he's thrusting into my pussy with a deep groan of his own, my new cut still on my back.

"Oh, *fuck!*" I cry out as I'm filled to the hilt everywhere all at once. I feel his hand come down on my ass as he smacks it hard, the sting only heightens my pleasure.

"My messy little brat making me wait all fucking night for *my* cunt..." Gabriel grunts as he bottoms out inside me and we both try to catch our breath. So fucking full.

"When you push me too far, Brinley... you risk me losing control."

My head falls back against his chest as he thrusts into me again. "And then, you get fucked in every hole you have. *Hard.*"

Oh, please, yes, fucking do it, I silently beg as he makes good on his promise. I feel his finger adding pressure against the jewel as he fucks me.

"But you *won't* come, understand? Not yet," Gabriel says low into my ear as his finger works against my clit, threatening to throw me off the ledge I'm clinging to. The way he times his thrusts and the pressure in my ass is too much.

"The second I feel this tight pussy start to siphon my cock, I'm gonna take this ass," he says, and it's enough to give me the final push as I do just what he says. The heat coils in my core and starts to tighten. I white knuckle the workbench, and I'm about to come all over him. Just as I start to ascend, he pulls out of me, leaving me feeling empty.

I whimper and let out an almost painful cry which makes Gabriel chuckle.

"I want to feel the first one while I'm taking this ass." He grips my hips tight as he begins to position himself.

"Will I come? Will it hurt?" I mutter, half in a moan.

"At first maybe yes, but we've got you good and ready."

I nod, knowing that it's true. He's always playing with me

back there, getting me used to the idea. I've started to crave it as a result. Like he's training me for this the same way he trained me to fight, slowly and patiently.

Gabriel skims his hand over my dripping pussy, gathering my arousal on his hand and coating himself with it. I feel him spit just above my ass and I wait as he slides it over me. Warm pre-cum leaks from the tip, and I whimper with the contact.

He carefully starts to play with the jewel inside me, pulling it out then pushing it back in until I'm panting and *wanting* him to toy with me. He knows exactly what he's doing.

"That's it, little hummingbird, now you're ready for my cock. Beg for it."

I feel the jewel come out of me further and I push against him, searching to be filled again.

He chuckles.

"Please," I moan.

"Please what?"

"Fuck me..." I beg in a whisper.

He growls then leans down to speak low into my ear as he slides himself against me.

"Hearing you beg will be my undoing one day. There's nothing I wouldn't do for you when you beg," Gabriel says, the picture of calm as he lets just the tip of his cock presses against my back hole. He spits again directly onto his shaft.

"I promise this will feel good. You just have to breathe. There isn't a part of your body that won't accept me. You were fucking *made* for me, Brinley."

"Yes..." I whimper as Gabriel begins his intentional sink into me, each wrung of his ladder sliding in one at a time. The sensation is overwhelming. My back arches and I feel his large hands roam my spine, to my hips, to the globes of my ass as he spreads me wide.

"That's it... breathe, I'll do all the work for you." Gabriel sinks in another inch. Two fingers move into my pussy and he works them in and out of me.

"Fucking Christ." I hear him breathe as my ass takes in more of him. I rock slowly into his fingers which in turn, makes my body take more of his cock until it starts to feel... good. Really good.

"This ass... fucking swallowing my cock. So fucking mine already..."

I feel the pad of his finger pressing against my clit and my body opens right up for him. I lean back, pushing into him as he pushes forward.

Gabriel huffs out a breath as he roots himself that last inch and his fingers continue their gentle assault on my pussy.

My legs begin to shake. I'm in sensory overdrive. Gabriel pushes my cut up, his lips trail up my spine as he trades between biting my flesh and kissing me. I feel his hands everywhere, his body everywhere and then I'm being pulled up by my hair, his teeth graze my earlobe, begging me to come. He begins to move slowly at first, but then settles into a rhythm, he pulls himself almost all the way out, then moves back into me. Every part of me is slippery and ready for him, my body is done fighting him. I want it. I want *him*, and I will give myself to him however he wants to take me.

Moments pass as his pace increases and I meet him at every thrust until I can't hold on any longer.

"That's it, little bird, come with my cock in this beautiful ass and my fingers in your dripping cunt."

"Gabriel," I cry.

"Again."

"Gabriel..." A moan of pure pleasure leaves me as he wraps his hand tight around my throat, using it for leverage as he fucks unforgivingly into my ass.

"So soft. So fucking sweet, letting me stuff my cock into this tight little ass," Gabriel grunts as I come harder than I ever have, my cunt clenching and dripping around his fingers.

"Brinley... *my fucking queen*," he growls as I feel him stiffen inside me and fill me with warmth. "Every part of you is perfect," he groans, followed by only my name as he grips my hair tight before adding with his deep raspy tone. "I possess *all* of you."

My heart beats fast and erratic as I ride out my high with him, the leather of my cut sticking to my arms as a veil of sweat covers me.

I never want to come down. I'll never tire of him.

Gabriel falls into me, still gripping my hair in his hand, a layer of sweat covering his hard chest.

"And every single part of you is now mine," he breathes.

I smile as his lips meet my cheek, my neck.

"It always was..." I tell him.

And it always will be.

CHAPTER 61
Brinley

Two Weeks Later

"Oh my god, it's so beautiful," I tell Gabriel with tears in my eyes as I dismount from his bike in my driveway. My father's pickup truck sits perfectly restored, a beautiful robin's egg blue. "It looks brand new," I tell him, running my hand over the glimmering paint.

"It virtually is. Mike made it run like a dream too."

"I had no idea you were so close to finishing it, you said another... *wait*—" I turn and face him. "This is where you've been at night when you said you had club business this last week? In the shop with my truck?" I ask instantly, judging the look on his face.

He nods, looking way too serious for having just surprised me.

"And you aren't selling it. It's too pretty to sell," he says.

I look to the front lawn where the *for sale* sign already sits, my only connection to my parents.

"I won't need the money." I wager the idea of keeping it in my mind.

"Some mean, gruff biker did fix my porch for me and won't take a penny," I say as I eye the beautiful new cedar wrap around that will draw in any buyer, my realtor says. Layla and I have been decorating it up with Edison lights and furniture for the last week. I move toward my big strapping, secretly caring man and wrap my arms around his cut, the leather of my own pressed against his.

"I want you to keep it. It'll be the last piece you have of them after this house sells. No arguments," Gabriel says.

His thoughtfulness hits me as I turn to look at it. Not a soul outside this life would believe Gabriel has this side to him, I have no idea how I'm the lucky one who gets to have it all to myself.

"Besides, you'll look hot as fuck driving it."

"I will, will I?" I ask, reaching up on my tiptoes to kiss him, his words igniting me like they always do.

We wait for the realtor to come for the open house and chat for a few minutes. He's already had interested parties; he says he thinks it will sell in no time. As he sets up and we do a final sweep of the house, I feel a pang of grief wash over me for the first time. I was never really close with my parents but just letting this place go is a final, but necessary step in order to move toward my dreams.

"The realtor thinks I can get upwards of a million," I tell Gabriel as we stand in my childhood bedroom, now staged as a sitting room.

"Good enough for your store and to keep a good savings for anything else this beautiful brain can dream up," he says, wrapping his strong arms around my waist from behind me.

"Come on, there's one more thing I want to show you before we head home," Gabriel says.

Home. With him. Right where I know with every fiber of my being, I belong.

"Okay. Now I'm really stumped. Why am I *here?*" I ask as I watch Gabriel unlock the door beside the coffee shop twenty minutes later. It feels nice to travel around town with him and not worry about a thing. All has been quiet since the club settled and formed a truce of sorts with the Disciples of Sin. It's given Gabriel lots of time to catch up in the shop for a few of his high profile clients—and of course, now I know, work on my dad's truck.

It's not very often we make middle of the day trips to the downtown area on my day off, so I know something is up. Normally, we spend my days off in his bed, with no clothes or in his shower, the kitchen, the gym... anywhere we can be together.

So, the last place I thought I'd end up was here, across the street from the job I already go to three days a week.

"This is the building we bought the first day I saw you," he tells me with a smirk.

I look around. The street is still bustling with tourists in mid-August and people are hanging a banner over the town street, advertising a fall fair.

"Yes, but why am I here?" I laugh, looking up at him. His broad shoulders in his white t-shirt under his cut and his strong upper arms flexing. Goddamn, he is a fucking specimen of a man.

I stare up at him.

"Are you even going to take a look around or are you just

gonna push me into the corner the second we get in here?" Gabriel asks, swinging the door open.

I blink to stop my stare, he's smug as all hell.

I squint up at him in the afternoon sun. "Not sure yet." I shrug honestly, patting his cut on my way by.

He chuckles. "Get your pretty little ass in there before you tempt me too much and ruin my surprise."

When I step inside, my mouth falls open and I gasp. "Been working on it since you said you wanted your own space. Called in some favors to get the work done quickly," he explains. The space has been fully renovated. I can smell fresh paint and new wood. The floors are thick barn board and all the walls are covered in a white shiplap with inlaid shelving and basket weave lighting. The ceiling is vaulted and white with wide walnut wood beams extending from one side to the other. A cash bar lines the back wall and above it, smack in the center, is an intricate and stunningly beautiful pink neon hummingbird.

I look at him then back to the windows that flank either side, facing onto the courtyard between the buildings.

The whole front wall is windows facing onto Main Street. It's bright and airy and so beautiful, and I still have no idea what he's done.

"This space is yours, the club's numbered company owns the building but the lease is in your name, solely. Nothing to do with the club or me," he says proudly. "Welcome to *Humming-bird Design Inc.* Also registered solely in your name."

"How?" I ask in a gasp, my hands covering my mouth in shock.

Gabriel shrugs.

"Kai is really fucking good at what he does and the permit office was thrilled to have a new business take over. Not to mention, *Crimson Homes* is happy to refer their clients to you and they want you to freelance and still help them with their design build projects."

"What? I-I don't know what to say." Tears fill my eyes.

"You heard the realtor, he thinks we'll get an offer or two before the end of the weekend so I can pay you—" I start to panic when I think of how much this must have cost.

"No." He shakes his head "I don't want to hear it. This space is yours. For the first time in my life, I thought I might actually die in that cabin, and you saved me. I'm done living like a closed book, hoarding my money away. I want to *live. You* make me want to live."

I shake my head and blow out a breath, taking the space in again with fresh eyes, as mine.

"A legitimate business that's just for you. Your money can go into it from here on out. It will cost a lot to stock it, yeah?" he asks.

I look around still amazed. "Yeah..." I whisper.

All the ideas I have saved on my computer run through my mind as I think of the specialty shops I can order from and pieces I'm already in love with.

"I can see it all, samples along this wall..." I say excitedly with tears brimming over. "I bet I could reach out to Benjamin Moore and become a preferred seller." I touch everything as I make my way through.

"Maybe local artisans' pieces here to sell to clients who want unique decor."

I continue through the space and find the bathroom and private office in the back.

I'm full out crying when I'm done exploring this beautiful space that's all mine thanks to him. And through it all, Gabriel trails behind me with a look on his face I just can't place. Pride?

"I love you!" I cry, launching myself into his arms. He holds me tight and lifts me right off the ground. "I love you, I love you." I kiss his face, his lips.

He pulls his hands up and swipes the tears from my eyes.

"And I love you. But I'm gonna need you to prove it," he says.

I pull back to look at him as his mouth turns up into the smirk I love.

"Right here?" I ask as he hoists me up onto my new cash counter and loses his fingers under my blouse. They're warm on my skin and I instantly begin to heat. No blinds cover the windows, it's broad daylight outside. Gabriel reads my mind before I can say it.

"The windows are tinted; I'll keep you covered... don't worry and don't think about it, little hummingbird. Take what *you* want."

"Right," I convince myself. "Don't worry... take what I want," I tell myself as my head falls back with his lips on my neck.

Gabriel makes the choice for me as his hands squeeze my hips then slide up the back of my shirt, the feel of his lips on my skin taking me past the point of stopping. I ask myself how I got so lucky as to fall into the path of Gabriel Wolfe. The biker club king with the haunting gray eyes who managed to end the life of Brinley Rose Beaumont, the good girl who always did the right thing, but was never happy.

This ruthless man the world calls a criminal is the best man I've ever known. He's brought to life the woman I am now, and I silently vow from this moment forward to be his queen. To be the woman I was destined to be. The thought frees me.

I'll feel happy and alive, with my arms wrapped around my king, riding faster than our angels can fly.

EPILOGUE
Gabriel

Seventeen and a Half Years Later

"That's it, nice and slow," I tell my oldest son Sebastian. "Squeeze the trigger halfway, you don't want it to come out too quickly or you'll just make a mess and you'll have to start over."

His brow knots in concentration as he focuses on the fine lines he's mapped out on the gas tank of his own bike we've been refinishing. A bike he'll be able to ride anytime, anywhere, in just two short months when it's done and he turns seventeen. By then, he'll be able to get his full M class. He's already been riding with his permit for three months and he's a natural. It makes his brother chomp at the bit to get his permit, but he has to wait another two years.

"Fuck," he bites out when he moves outside the lines with the paint he's airbrushing.

"Eh," I tell him gruffly. "Not in front of your mother."

Behind me, my gorgeous bride of fifteen years scoffs, her attitude has only grown stronger as has her beauty. At forty-one, she looks better than any twenty-five-year-old could, she says it's thanks to always being sexually satisfied. Tells me it's the fountain of youth and she must be right because I don't feel anywhere near my almost forty-nine years.

"Sorry," Seb mutters.

"Same thing I say every time, Seb, you gotta slow down, take your time. You think your dad got this good by rushing?" Brinley asks. "And by the way, if you two think I don't know how you talk when I'm not around, you're fucking crazy." She winks. "Be cleaned up in an hour, I don't want grease monkeys at my daughter's graduation," she says, moving in to kiss my lips.

Her signature jasmine scent is like heaven in my shop.

I pull her close and linger there a little longer.

"Disgusting," Micah, our almost fifteen-year-old son, says as he comes into the shop. He's already too big for the suit he's wearing, and we just bought it last year for his own middle school graduation. Both my boys are almost as big as I am, much larger than I even was at their age and they'll be a team to reckon with one day.

"Agreed, can't you two cut that shit out," Seb says without looking up.

"Be happy we love each other," Brinley says, cuffing Seb on the back of his head.

"Mom, now I have to start that whole line over."

"Guess that'll teach you to mind your manners then, won't it?" she asks him with an eyebrow raised.

"Come on, let's let the hem out of those," she says to Micah when she eyes up his pants. She's wearing a little sundress, and it isn't without great effort that I don't kick both my boys out and take her right on my workbench. *Later,* I tell myself.

Seventeen years with this woman, three kids, two businesses, and club life, and the only thing that's constant is the way I want her. Everything changes around us daily. Kids grow up, people live, people die, people move away, our businesses have changed.

My detail shop has moved to our property. After Seb started preschool, we expanded here so Kai and I could work and still take the kids to school while Brinley grew *Hummingbird Designs* to become one of Savannah's most sought-after interior design companies.

The club has changed, we've patched in new members, seen members pass, and members retire. We've had times of peace and times of worry but through it all, I've never stopped wanting her, and I've always tried to make Brinley and our family my focus. It's been the greatest joy of my life to raise our kids with her and have my club family by our side.

I watch as Seb starts over, he's got the passion I had at his age. He's big like me but handsome so the girls are already coming around more often than not. He's eager to learn and eager to follow in my footsteps, a thought that fills me with pride and worries me all the same.

"Fuck yeah," he says as he masters his grid. The design is sick; I'll give him that. Even Kai is impressed with his skill.

"This bike is gonna get me every fucking girl in school," he says.

I chuckle and pull my mask off.

"It's gonna be hard to get *any* girl if your mother kills you for not being ready on time."

"Can we come back out tonight? When the party winds down?" he asks, looking both grown up and so young at the same time.

"Yeah, come on. If we don't hurry, both of them will be on us," I say.

Seb shudders. "Sounds like a nightmare." He laughs, knowing his baby sister is just as feisty as his mother.

I chuckle harder and pat his shoulder as we walk. It's

moments like this when the only regret I have is that my mother never got to see this life I'm living. Although, if I listen to my still faith-filled wife, my mother's been watching over us and guided me to my little hummingbird the day her long raven hair, shining in the sun, caught my attention. The day my life changed forever.

Brinley

Our backyard is bustling after a massive barbeque dinner with the entire Hounds of Hell MC, all the kids' friends and people celebrating our fourteen-year-old daughter Harlow's middle school graduation.

For nineteen full years, Gabriel has been the Hounds of Hell president, and the club has never been more lucrative or peaceful. Over the last sixteen years, he's had the club's help with founding an additional three clinics for a total of nine now in the Savannah and Atlanta areas and they're pushing into Florida clinics with recovery medications.

He's aligned himself with the right people for protection and is working for the greater good. He's also become an ear for any veterans who need help or need to talk, following their return home from active duty.

Is my husband unconventional? Yes. Does he do things that make me question his sanity? Also, yes. But he's a proud man who does so much more good than he does bad.

I stand close to the edge of the woods where long rows of tables have been set up with condiments and paper plates, watching our family and friends talk and laugh while music plays. Some of the kids dance and some swim in the pool that Gabriel installed ten years ago when he added onto the house to fit all our kids.

Our kids have grown up as club kids, but Harlow is the baby and every single person we love has fawned over her since the day she was born, and why wouldn't they?

I watch her now, in her pink graduation dress Gabriel thought was too short, holding Sean and Layla's three-year-old son Max on her hip as she talks to Shelly and some of the club elders. Harlow has been a joy since the day she was born—happy, always smiling, always willing to help. She's better than both Gabe and I are, that's for sure. And oddly enough, she has a heart for ministry. She works with the local Salvation Army and their community outreach programs in Savannah, and at only fourteen has more volunteer hours than most of her friends combined.

Gabriel thinks she's going to change the world someday and I don't disagree, but there's one thing about her that amuses me. She has her father's feisty I-don't-give-a-fuck attitude through and through. No one messes with her. On the outside, she's a sweet little thing. She looks a lot like I did when I was young, with her long black hair, but she's a thousand times more beautiful than I ever was. It's truly the bane of Gabriel's existence that soon enough she'll have boys calling on her.

I snort back laughter every time I think about it. Good luck with her brothers and Gabriel on standby. She'll be thirty before that poor girl gets a date.

"How is she that old?" My husband wraps his arms around me, the way he always has from behind and kisses my neck.

"Time flies when you're having fun, baby." I turn to face him, patting the intricate hummingbird tattoo that takes up some good real estate below his left ear over his pulse point. A reminder every time I look at him that even if he is a man of little words, his actions and acts of service are and always have been his love language. There hasn't been a moment since I've been with Gabriel where I haven't felt completely taken care of and loved without measure.

I look out to the lake where the sun sinks behind the horizon as our party wears on.

"I'm gonna head to the shop soon with Seb. I promised him we'd work on his bike tonight," he tells me.

I giggle.

"I'm pretty sure Seb is making out with Robby's grand-daughter in his room, they're in the same class next year. Apparently, they're bonding over that," I tell him. "He thinks I didn't notice them sneak off together."

Gabriel chuckles into my ear. "He's not as smooth as he thinks he is," he says gruffly.

"I was just like him at that age, all I thought about was girls. He won't take it too far; he knows the limit." He kisses me. "Guess that means we're waiting to work on the bike until tomorrow."

"Mm-hmm," I say. "I don't even want to think about it, that's your department but I'm not trying to be a forty-year-old grandmother. Hell, some women are just starting to have kids at my age."

"Mmm," Gabriel groans into me, setting my cells on fire. "Is that what you want, for me to put another baby in this womb?" he asks in that voice that still drives me wild. His large hand presses against my low belly possessively.

How this man can be almost forty-nine and still be in better shape than most men half his age never ceases to amaze me. Gabriel even still looks the same just with those threads of silver through his dark hair. In my opinion, he hasn't grown older, just better.

"I find it weird that I have to say this twice in one day but... disgusting," Micah says as he passes by us, shaking his head.

Gabriel and I both chuckle as he heads over and meets up with Sean and Layla's oldest son who's only a year younger than him.

"A toast," Shelly calls out to the group of more than a hundred as all the solar Edison lights throughout our yard flicker on with the setting sun. "To our baby, Harlow."

We all turn and face Harlow who's smiling her beautiful smile and is thoroughly embarrassed by all the attention.

"Nana!" she whines as Shelly waves her off.

"Stop, baby, you're getting a toast whether you want one or not."

Harlow sets Max down and moves over to join Shelly across the yard. I spot Dell and his wife of ten years and nod. He's still a joy to consult with and has finally stopped looking at me like I made the wrong choice when I chose Gabriel.

"To the sweetest soul we know, moving on to high school next year. Break some hearts, have some fun, and for God's sake, if you're thinking of bringing a boy around, don't bring him around here if you want him to live."

A chorus of *hear, hear*'s spark through the crowd from Sean, Kai, Robby, Mason, Flipp, and Gabriel followed by laughter from the crowd.

I look at my baby, she looks at me and rolls her eyes with the idea of all the overprotective men in her life acting like cavemen. The room toasts and the party continues with all the people we love surrounding us. We may not be perfect, but damn, we all love harder than any family I've ever known.

I laugh and give her dad a little backhand in his muscled chest.

Gabriel pinches my waist as the festivities continue. I use the back of my nails to grip and dig into his forearms behind me and he grabs me hard around my waist, pulling me into him where I feel his cock starting to swell already.

"You're in the mood to tussle, little hummingbird?" he asks, pulling me backward from the table with his lips on my neck. "Everyone is busy..."

"Mm-hmm... seems like it." I smirk as Gabriel pulls me into the treeline.

"Think you still have what it takes to catch me, Pres?" I turn my face up to him and his lips come down on mine only once before his gruff whisper takes over and I prepare for flight.

"I guess we'll see, wicked girl..."

"Run."

THE END

acknowledgments

What a wild ride Gabriel Wolfe took me on.

To my amazing husband for researching every single thing he could about club life with me, for taking a back seat to Gabriel as he always does with every MMC I write. For always taking care of me as I write endlessly, some days placing food in front of me when I'm in the 'zombie zone.'

To Tabitha for the incredible character development that comes so naturally to you. From finding Brinley's good girl personality to our joint Gabriel obsession, love of sculpted hands and early morning convos about ritualistic sex, I could not have made this book (or any books) what they are without you, your mind (which is my mind) and your sparkle.

To Jordan-Can you freaking believe that bonding over Sons of Anarchy was the seed that planted this *entire* story? From your insight into club life, your friendship and no holds barred comments that had me cackling with my morning coffee. I will say it one more time. You need to edit for a living!

To Rose, for being my unofficial assistant with all things Paisley. To my BETA's Rose, Katie, Bryanna and Ada for jumping on board this crazy journey with me. I love that we could talk about it all, no matter the time of day and the laughter kept me sane. For all the incredible suggestions, laughs and ah-ha moments that truly make my books the absolute best they can be. To Cathryn and Caroline, thank you for making my book into an actual beautiful, grammatically correct book and not just a really long, confusing word document.

To you, my ARC readers and all readers alike, thank you. I may not do it better than anyone else but I pour my whole soul into these stories and every comment, like, share, edit, mention is noticed and loved wholeheartedly.

Lastly: YES another book in the Hounds of Hell universe is coming. Stay tuned for Aiden Foxx in 2025

about the author

Paisley Hope is an avid lover of romance, a mother, a wife and a writer. Growing up in Canada, she wrote and dreamed of one day being able to create a place, a world where readers could immerse themselves, a place they wished was real, a place they saw themselves when they envisioned it. She loves her family time, gardening, baking, yoga and a good cab sav. For more information, you can follow her and/or reach out anytime.

@authorpaisleyhope – INSTAGRAM

authorpaisleyhope@gmail.com

Made in United States
North Haven, CT
18 September 2024

57569988R10248